Col

33

First Edition

Published by: Temple Rose Publications, Bristol, UK

www.templerosepublications.com
First published 2018

Author website www.petewheldon.com
Facebook: Pete Wheldon Author
Twitter: @idowse

Trade ordering information:
contact@templerosepublications.com

info@templerosepublications.com
ISBN: 978-1-9995879-1-8

Acknowledgements

First and foremost, my gratitude goes to Sarah Webster for her work in plot and character development and her mastery of writing. Without her encouragement, I may not have finished this book. Huge thanks go to Kim Brooke for her unflinching long-term support and proficient editing skills.

My thanks go out to Jonathan Sayers; whose creative and thoughtful awareness uncovered so much. The crucial transition from linear to 'circular energy' especially. Thank you, Claudia Ascott, for your open-minded support. My thanks forwarded to Paddy John, who first counted the numbers and whose patient counsel allowed me to assemble the pieces. For Helen Fothergill, always supportive, thank you for helping me expand my ideas. For Isabel Feuille, who taught me how to find 'tiki' stones. Big thank you to Tony Kennish, who got the sticks working.

'The lunatic is all idée fixe, and whatever he comes across confirms his lunacy. You can tell him by the liberties he takes with common sense, by his flashes of inspiration, and by the fact that sooner or later he brings up the Templars...There are lunatics who don't bring up the Templars, but those who do are the most insidious. At first, they seem normal, then all of a sudden...'

Umberto Eco, Foucault's Pendulum

Science is nothing but perception.

Plato

1 Affairs of the heart

'Bollocks!'

Nick slams the tankard down in frustration.

'Giving a dog acupuncture? Don't give me that! You'll be telling me next she's taking it to a bloody faith healer!'

Yet again, I realise that my sceptical friend is the worst choice of audience to hear my customer's recent veterinary success story.

'In fact, research has shown...' Simon, the rational member of our unlikely trio, interrupts, wafting the tip of a well-chewed pen.

'Research my arse!' booms Nick, currently two pints ahead, having been the first to arrive, and thirsty, for our regular Friday night meet-up.

'Turn it down over there – is that Nick again?' Chris, our landlord, calls over an audience of bobbing heads. 'They don't need to hear you on the other side of the M32, thanks mate.'

I study Nick's crimson face in fascination. Veins reminiscent of blue cheese bulge at his temple, while beads of perspiration weave a jerky path towards his prominent jaw.

'Just another bloody pseudo-science air-head! If she, if she…'

Nick's rant stops short as he gasps for air, his familiar face contorting in pain. Bewildered eyes momentarily fix on mine as if trying to convey a mute question, and he falls forward, hands clenched to his chest. I lurch across the bench and with a good grip on his arm, pull him towards me. An unfamiliar gurgle alerts me, and as I stare at the back of Nick's head, a stream of vomit bursts across my lap. Its sudden heat jerks me upright, dropping my hold and pulling back in shock. Nick continues to slump to the floor, legs curling between table legs like a middle-aged foetus.

'Right, that's it, I've had enough. Out of here right now!' calls an irritated Chris, his customary patience exhausted.

But Nick isn't going anywhere.

Simon, on my right, jumps up, hand to mouth, as more glasses crash to the floor, spilling their contents across the legs of my jeans. He is retching as he stumbles to the pub door, an arm elbowing the startled audience and pursued by the pervasive smell of pickled egg.

Unconsciously, I move the table aside and fall on my knees next to my old friend.

'Nick. Nick, jeez, c'mon man, get up will you, c'mon...' I shake him ineffectually as if all that's wrong is a loose wire. 'What the fuck!' I feel panic rising and look up to see a bemused audience of pub regulars.

A none-too-happy Chris is calling over their heads as he makes his way from the bar, but before he can arrive, a young man appears, one hand gripping my shoulder, firmly guiding me away from Nick's now inert body. He kneels, taking Nick's wrist before loosening his tie and collar and turning back briefly to flash me a glance of reassurance. I catch my breath at the first sight of his radiant silver-grey eyes.

'It's OK, Sam', he says.

The stranger arranges Nick's unresponsive body impressively, like a well-rehearsed extra in a crime drama. In a daze, I start to stand up, absently wiping vomit down the side of my jeans, trying to understand the increasingly surreal scene. As I do, this stranger with close-cropped hair and milky-brown skin, effortlessly pulls a phone from the pocket of his black ski jacket, and within moments, is talking into it. A hushed audience of 20 or more listen in. His soft, articulate Caribbean lilt fills the room...

'Male, mid-forties, suspected heart attack, require cardiopulmonary resuscitation unit, urgent. Location King's Head Public House, St Johns Avenue, Bristol.' Our miracle-worker turns towards me, continuing to nod into the phone. 'What's his name please?'

'Ah, yes...um,' I stumble, my mind blank. 'It's Nick, yes, Nick Quinton Robbins,' I reply, at some level surprised to be reciting his full title. The stranger repeats the details before continuing. 'Ya. Billy Wells, Hughenden Road, Bristol. Ya, will do t'ing. Ya, I'm a Cardiac Nurse with Dr Rolling's Team. Ya that's right, at the Heart Institute.'

I shudder in fear.

My best, my oldest friend. The classmate who took a detention rather than split on the guilty party, the pal who would cheerfully turn up brandishing jump leads on Christmas morning, is hanging onto life in front of me.

I'm soon startled by the familiar voice of Rangi, Nick's wife, arriving from her Yoga class. The silent crowd parts to let her through.

'Sam? Sam, what's going on? Don't you know that Simon's outside, white as a sheet standing next to a pool of sick and you lot are all standing around...oh my God, Nicky! What's happened to you?'

Rangi catches her breath, staring in shock at the sight of her husband's prostrate body. Her gloved hand covers her mouth as I reach out to hold her arm, preventing her from interrupting the lifesaving efforts of this 'Billy Wells.'

In moments it seems the pub is filled with fluorescent jackets, as Nick's inert body is expertly removed. Rangi climbs up into the back of the ambulance, her long delicate fingers holding Nick's limp hand. Even after 15 years of living with him, she is still very much in love, I reflect, as the doors shut. Then they are gone in a blaze of blue light.

I turn to Simon, who is now shivering next to me on this dark, damp December road.

'I only wrapped his Christmas present this morning, no, yesterday. I don't know, whatever. I got him those Squash shoes he likes – the colourful ones. You know?'

Simon glares at the vomit streaking the front of my trousers with no apparent interest, his normally bright face now ashen and subdued.

'Are you going home?' I ask.

'Yes Sam. I'm a...I'm leaving.' Simon's voice is hollow and submissive. 'She'll ring if there's any news - won't she?'

I meander home through the silent streets, dully contemplating the possibility of a future without my ebullient friend. 'He's only forty-two,' I call out into the mist.

Inside the house, my heart feels edgy as I grapple with the showerhead to sluice away the residue of vomit, but the task proves too much, and I feed my putrid jeans into the washing machine. They'll have to wait until the morning. In the meantime, I'll do the only thing that comes naturally in times of crisis: clutching a freshly-opened flagon of cider, I retreat to the sofa. Unable to provide any practical assistance as my best friend lies poised between life and death, I down its contents in a bid for my own oblivion.

The next morning, still in ignorance of Nick's fate, I clambered downstairs with a head full of morbid thoughts. The cider had done its work; its anesthetising effect producing a fitful sleep. Breakfast was overlooked and instead I found myself absent-mindedly sorting out the contents of the under-stairs cupboard. I distractedly moved on to mopping the kitchen floor, a task I had put off for months, or quite possibly, years. That done, I put the kettle on and sat down at the kitchen table, vaguely polishing a silver prize cup that had lurked in the recesses since moving-in day ten years ago. It had belonged to my long-departed father. I had, I reflected solemnly, no such cups of my own to polish.

Something else about last night's drama was dragging my thoughts back to the present. As if Nick's collapse hadn't been enough, *something* else had unnerved me, but I couldn't quite order my thoughts to remember what.

Then it came to me. It was that 'Billy' bloke. How come he'd said: 'It's OK - *Sam.*' Who had told him my name – and when? I'd never clapped eyes on him before and yet he'd swung into action bang on-cue, calmly taking control and acting like he'd known me for years.

Who was this guy?

And what about those piercing silver-grey eyes? The kind of luminous intensity that bored into you, with even the briefest of glances.

My hand trembled as I poured the breakfast tea.

I was still dwelling on this stranger when the metallic clap of the letter box announced the morning post. Right on top of the circulars and appeals was a white square envelope that caused my stomach to clench. The handwriting was unmistakable: that girly way she always wrote her 'S's with the childlike twist on the end. It was from Debbie, my ex.

It had been over a decade since there had been any direct contact between us. Ours had been a bitter break-up after seven years together. And though the ever-observant Rangi had since suggested that, towards the end, *'the writing was on the wall'*, to me, Debbie's curt dismissal came out of nowhere. Stunned, hurt and needing somewhere to lick my wounds, I'd taken my camper on a road trip across Europe, determined to put the English Channel between me and the sympathy of well-meaning friends.

The envelope contained a black-bordered card and a hand-written note. Debbie's father had died, and his funeral would take place the following week at the local cemetery.

Clutching its contents, I sat on the stairs, casting my mind back to the period I'd worked so hard to forget. Letting very little grass grow under her feet after our break-up, Debbie had met a bloke called Martin and moved to

London, quickly dropping off everyone's radar. Since then, the only thing I'd heard on the grapevine was that a child had followed soon afterwards. And now, a decade later, here I was being invited to her father's funeral. The note explained that I'd been one of his 'favourites'. That he had enjoyed our chats together and had made a point of requesting my attendance at his funeral because...amongst several other bequests, he'd left *me* his large astronomical telescope!

How about that - Good old Gordon! I remember him well. He'd been pretty high-up at the local water company, a real collar-and-tie man. Nice bloke though, and like me, he'd spent the last few years living a solitary existence. But back in the day, we'd sip dry sherries waiting for the Sunday lunch to cook as he entertained us with congenial stories. Now I come to think of it, that was one of my fondest routines with Debbie. He was always generous with the contents of his wine rack and we'd go back to my flat afterwards, comfortably nourished by his table and his good humour.

I felt disturbed and on-edge at the prospect of seeing Debbie again and traced my steps back to the kitchen, only to find last night's cider flagon empty. As I forlornly reflected on the turn of events, my thoughts were derailed by the arrival of my next-door neighbour.

'Good morning and good health Sammy! Are you about and indecent?'

Just what I needed at that moment: the larger-than-life retiree, Kate O'Mahoney. She had become a frequent visitor by way of my back gate and door; the key to which she'd acquired at some point and had never quite got around to returning. Her mind was as sharp as a twist of lemon.

'*Those* –' Kate blustered as she stepped into the door frame, an arm outstretched behind her, pointing accusingly back to the garden. '...dreadful grey underpants of yours! For the Saints' sake Sammy, use something longer than a 15-minute bloody wash cycle on that old tub of yours.'

'You shouldn't be staring at my underwear,' I faltered in reply.

'What's the matter? Hung over again - *are we?*' Kate scanned the kitchen for evidence.

'No, not entirely,' I replied gruffly. 'Just had a bit of a shock. Looks like Nick had a really bad heart attack in the pub last night - it's bloody terrible.'

'Oh, my dear, that's not good, not good at all.' Kate paused before adding, 'Is Nick the dark one, a bit on the flashy side?'

I nodded as she filled the kettle before taking up her customary place at the table. Her hand reached out, seeking mine. She looked sympathetic, though I knew this could just as quickly turn to admonishment. She often managed to make me feel like an adolescent, even at nine in the morning.

'I've also had some surprising news. I've just been invited to attend Debbie's father's funeral,' I said raising my eyes to catch her attention.

'What? Your old Debbie?'

I nodded.

'Oh – how intriguing. So, you'll be going, will you?' Kate asked, her attention shifting to peer suspiciously at the floor.

'I suppose I should. It's been quite a while,' I paused. 'Anyway, he left me an old telescope, so I'll have to really. One needs to pay one's respects.'

Kate continued her critical examination, ignoring my shambling response and addressing me from the feet upwards. 'Samuel. Do my eyes deceive me... have you *cleaned* this floor?'

3 Steam-driven

'Howizzit goin'?'

'Oh, hi! Its Billy, isn't it? How are you?'

He nodded, smiling broadly.

'I've just heard the great news ...that Nick's on the mend.'

I offered my hand to Billy and shook it vigorously, adding: 'Thanks for your help. You may have saved his life.' I surprised myself by reaching out with my left hand to briefly grasp his upper arm. Although we had only met a week ago, the dramatic scene in the pub made him seem like an old friend.

I had just finished a long day fitting a kitchen and was meandering through the newsagents, when *he* appeared, his perfect white teeth lighting up the middle aisle.

'You stopped your work today, Mr Sam?'

'Please just call me Sam, if I can call you Billy?' He glowed. 'Yes, another day over, thank God.' I paused. 'Do you live around here then?'

'Ya – not far away, I live with some of my ma's family.'

'Not your own place then?'

'Na, I only lived in this manna for a few months.'

'Next please.' Our meeting was interrupted by a glowering shop keeper.

'Sorry Billy, let me just pay for this stuff and we can carry on outside.'

It was dark and drizzly. Impulsively, I suggested we retreat to Bindi's Place, the nearest warm café. I would have suggested the King's Head, but Billy didn't seem the kind to spend a lot of time in the pub; he looked far too healthy for that habit. He ordered green tea while I had my usual builder's brew and we settled around one of the dark heavily-carved tables. The café had been going for years. Its previous owner had run some sort of import-export business out of Pakistan. Large containers would block the road, while their cargo of middle-class knick-knacks was unloaded. The business evidently proved profitable; it wasn't long before he retired and set up the café with the poorly-constructed furniture he couldn't shift after the arrival of Ikea. This gave the old Victorian corner shop the tawdry atmosphere of a Bollywood bazaar.

'Once again, I must thank you for what you did for Nick.'

Billy replied, tilting his head and offering an intimate smile. 'I visited him this morning in his ward. He is doing well; I think he'll recover fine. He's still young and quite fit.'

'That'll be the squash he's so keen on playing,' I replied.

We talked about the events of that awful night as I found myself becoming increasingly curious about my new acquaintance.

'What made you become a nurse, then Billy?'

'Ser' veese to ma broova's and se istas.' His reply took me by surprise. *'Service to his brothers and sisters?'* I creased my forehead.

'When I was a little boy on St Kitts, I use' to collect poorly creatures. I had little cages that I would keep them in. I must have been good at looking after them, for soon I had lots of people come. I liked nursing them better: chickens, dogs, cats and even goats. There was no vet nearby, and *countra folk have no dolla for sick animal.* People would give me what they could afford. Just enough to cova' the cost of the food and 'erbs I was givin' them. When I was sixteen these people helped me to learn at the medical school, where I trained to be a nurse. I was the only brova in that year.'

'This can't have been easy for you being the only man?'

'But you see Sam, it's the challenges that make you a bigga man.' Billy sat up puffing his broad chest.

'What brought you to Bristol then?'

'My ma was originally from here and my father has always lived in Bristol.' Billy's eyes gleamed as he spoke.

'So, are you staying with your Dad now?'

Billy smiled. 'No man, I stay with my aunt Patricia and my uncle. Up the hill, in Horfield.'

'A charity gave me money for education. I could have gone to America, but Bristol's for me. It's where my roots are - and the *heart* is here, this is my journey, my heart's journey.'

'What do you mean – *your heart's journey?'* I shifted back in surprise.

'We must all follow our passion, our own t'ing; our hearts have a bigger mind than our heads.'

Billy placed his right hand across his chest in emphasis. 'Trust what your heart says to ya and you cannot do no bad *t'ing.'*

Half an hour ago, my 'heart' had been full of Debbie and thoughts of good times now long gone. Billy seemed to be offering answers to questions I had not yet asked. He didn't say a lot, but what he did say seemed to come from somewhere else entirely.

'If you don't mind me saying, you look very fit. Were you one of the famous St Kitts athletes?

'Oh, no man. My friends were all big on running and all that track *t'ing*. I love the cricket man. It's in ma ancestor's blood...'

Billy paused, smiling, as he reached to pick up my recently purchased edition of *Model Railway News*. He studied the cover carefully. I felt my face flush.

'You like models?' he enquired graciously.

'Just trains - steam trains.' I replied, as my insides constricted in readiness for the familiar mockery.

'The old-school steam – *ire, very ire.*' Billy nodded in time. 'I use ta work on dem trains on my island when I was a boy, you used to be able to go right around the coast. It wa' the best way to go, it wa' as if *the island had a necklace t'ing.'*

He paused, looking directly into my eyes.

'My favourite was Number Five, it smoked and steamed in all the wrong places, but she was a sweet ride, not like them big diesels they have now. It was the last one, there were no more, and there was seven, the '*smoky seven'*. Trains from long ago.' Billy paused, reflecting before announcing with obvious pride, 'It was a *0-4-2*.'

I was astonished at his explicit knowledge.

'The t'ing waz built by *Kerr Stuart in 1916 - number 1314*.' Billy's face lit up in remembrance. 'My uncles, they pay me to polish the signs, especially the big nameplate.' Billy sat back contently. I glanced away noticing the café windows opaque with condensation. Ghostly figures drifted past in the January twilight.

'Don't look surprised man, St Kitts have the sugar train since a long time. My kin, they work the line for many, many years. Eustace, my great uncle, was the first black driver. It's for the tourist now. I used to collect the fares, but the boiler on Five now no good, she rusts. Someone should make her go again,' Billy said with a look of wistful innocence.

I was warming to this young man. Was Billy a kindred spirit? His mild manner made him seem almost serene. I felt a real connection with him, too, as if we'd known each other in another life.

'Hey man, don't look surprised, I even had ma own toy train. Do you have trains?' Billy asked as if still the child; flashing a disarming smile.

'...Err... yes,' I hesitated.

'I bet it's a big *t'ing*.' Billy swung his arms out playfully.

'Well yes, quite big actually. It runs along a shelf from my front room, high up on the wall, way above the sofa, through a hole I made in the wall and down to the kitchen.' I shuffled upright as I warmed to my pet subject. An enthusiasm that had often exposed me to ridicule. 'Would you like to come over and work the set sometime?' I asked tentatively.

'Cool man, that's so *cool.* Yes, I'll come in a couple of weeks when I've finished my current rota.'

'Maybe a Saturday afternoon?' I offered.

Billy smiled. 'Sure. I'll bring pictures to show ya. You will like them.'

I fumbled in my jacket, finding my little builder's notebook and handed Billy my address.

'Shall we say about two, then?' I said, as we wrestled with our coats.

What on Earth were you thinking of?

I slumped onto the kitchen chair, grasping the Marks & Spencer presentation box between outstretched hands, staring glumly at the dazzling white contents.

Underwear.

At the first sight of Debbie's handwriting, my heart had lurched alarmingly, and for a few days I was half panicked and half excited at the prospect of seeing her again. But what was I doing buying underwear the day before Gordon's funeral? Did I seriously imagine there was going to be a chance she might *actually* see them? Would that be before, during or after her father's dispatch to the afterlife? I kicked myself for allowing the sordid fantasy to take shape. 'Just go, pay your respects, mumble a few condolences and escape before the penalty shootout.' That's the pitch - quick in and out job. Gordon: I liked you, you were a cool dad from what I could see, one of the best; you deserve more respect.

The next morning, I faced breakfast with depressed indifference. The funeral was at 11 o'clock, giving me just enough time to get clobbered-up with the suit I'd hired for the occasion. My apprehension grew as I struggled into this unfamiliar uniform. What was I going to say to *her?* How weird it felt to imagine her with a child. And would *he* be there? Mr Excitement – Brummie Martin from Aston? *Aston Martin*? Would he be comforting her with a proprietary shoulder? Was there going to be a wake? I might have to cry off that bit. With a couple of brown ales inside me I'd stand a good chance of saying entirely the wrong thing in the wrong way at the wrong time.

As I started up the approach road to Greenbank's cemetery chapel, a familiar figure separated from the small gathering of mourners and walked towards me.

'Hello Sam. I've been so nervous about us meeting again.' Debbie lightly stamped her feet and rocked from side to side as she spoke.

'So now we're both orphans...' I returned her tentative smile, shivering slightly from nerves and the cold wind.

The chapel building, now disused and partly boarded-up, added significantly to the prevailing air of desolation. A vintage hearse was perched at the brow of the little hill, its rear door open to reveal a purple draped coffin. Small groups of late middle-aged men stood silently, hands clasped in dignified contemplation.

'I'm glad you asked me.' I turned to face her soft brown eyes.

'I wasn't sure you'd come,' she ventured, as we turned and slowly paced up the hill. Her long black dress fluttered as she pulled the tailored jacket closer, briefly exposing a delicate silver necklace. Her hair was shorter, just touching her shoulders, light brown rather than the vividly-remembered blonde. The same fine wisps of hair that had enticed me at Dave and Moira's party 17 years ago, still framed her elfin face.

'Why wouldn't I?' I replied, cautiously.

'Because of the way we parted.' Debbie looked down before raising her head to give me the full blast of her gaze. I felt an unwelcome pull of desire.

'Water under the bridge, definitely water under the bridge. It's been over ten years now. That's quite a long time you know...' My stomach felt hollow in pain as I recalled those days, weeks, months after our separation. A lot of time may have elapsed, but the strong emotions had lingered, lurking just beneath the surface. And now the shock of seeing her again, looking so vulnerable, was opening the floodgates.

'How have you been getting on, anyway?' I said, endeavouring to inject more confidence in my hesitant voice.

'Oh well. Up and down. It's been a challenging few years.' She lifted an arm and then dropped it slowly down again.

'I understand you've got a little, um…'

'Child? More of a monster really.' She grinned. 'Yes *Josh*. He's here. George, Dad's friend, remember him? He's keeping an eye on him. It's his first funeral so...' Her hand motioned a perilous sea crossing.

I was intrigued at the prospect of meeting her son. From time to time I had brooded about the chain of events before and after our split.

As we approached the waiting clusters, a gangly kid appeared from behind the hearse and strode purposefully towards us. He was kitted-out in a mini-me version of the surrounding dark suits. But his long blonde hair, at odds with their formality, fell haphazardly to his shoulders. Shuffling several yards behind was the dimly-remembered George.

'Josh - this is Sam, an old friend, He knew Grandad many years ago. Before you were born.'

'Grandboy!' Josh stamped a foot in protest, his voice strained. 'You know Grandboy always called himself that.'

I solemnly shook the politely-proffered hand. His young face curiously familiar: the eyes the same dark brown as his mum's, and indeed, my own. I offered a warm smile to allay his distress. George approached and breathlessly introduced himself.

'I believe they're ready to start the ceremony,' his voice quivered.

'Yes, of course. We can't keep Dad waiting.' Debbie's brave smile wobbled. I could see her eyes were now pink-rimmed. 'I'll miss him. He was such a lovely man. Always healthy and bright, right up to the end. He even died in his sleep you know. Typical of him really, he never liked to trouble anyone...' She nodded recognition to several of the mourners.

I cast my eye around for a sight of Aston Martin.

'He's not here.'

'Sorry?' I replied.

'Martin. He's not here. I don't have much contact with him now. His new wife is not keen, if you know what I mean. He picks Josh up from school. So other than the occasional practical matter I have little to do with him these days.' I studied Debbie's face. At 39, her delicate features were showing the first imprint of weariness.

The funeral service took place around an open grave, the mourners falling silent as the coffin was brought into view. I stepped back several paces to allow Debbie and Gordon's closest friends to take up their positions. It was a bright, late winter's day. I gazed out across the graves and down the hill, where the vista opened out in a city-wide panorama, then slowly cast my eyes around, recognising a few of the mourners and offering a nod in respect. Dava and his wife with their two children. Pakistanis by birth, they'd run the local shop for decades and undoubtedly supplied Gordon with countless copies of his morning Daily Telegraph. Two ancient sisters, Rose and Margaret, neighbours of Gordon, stood close by. They were rumoured to have been born in their house and had continued to live there as spinsters. The big, black lumbering frame of 'The Jamaican', Gordon's allotment friend, cast a shadow on the grave. As the pall bearers approached, the chaplain, a tall, thin, carefully-groomed man, stepped forward. His winter tan and even teeth conveyed middle-class affluence.

'Brethren and Friends: It has been a custom among the Fraternity of Free and Accepted Masons from time immemorial, at the request of a departed Brother or his family, to assemble in the character of Masons and, with the solemn formalities of the Craft, to offer up to his memory, before the world, the last tribute of our affection.'

He paused and with a hesitant smile, slowly scanned the 30 or so mourners. Six stout pall bearers braced the ropes to slowly lower the draped coffin.

'Soft and safe to thee, my brother, be thy resting place. Bright and glorious be thy rising from it. Fragrant be the acacia sprig that there shall flourish. May the earliest buds of spring unfold their beauties o'er thy resting place, and there may the sweetness of the summer's last rose linger longest. Though the winds of autumn may destroy the loveliness of their existence, yet the destruction is not final, and in the springtime, they shall surely bloom again. So, in the bright morning of the resurrection, thy spirit shall spring into newness of life and expand in immortal beauty, in realms beyond the skies, until then, dear brother, until then, farewell.'

As the chaplain's long dark cassock whipped-up in the bitter wind, I caught the unexpected glimpse of a pair of dainty purple slippers.

'The Lord blesses us and keeps us. The Lord makes His face to shine upon us and be gracious unto us. The Lord lifts upon us the light of His countenance and gives us peace. Amen.'

There followed a common utterance from the Brother mourners.

'So-mote it be!'

The aroma of stale beer and warm meat pie permeated the air.

Four weeks had passed since Nick's heart attack and it was another busy Friday at the King's Head, noisy enough to necessitate the raising of voices.

'*Soo* Nick, how you doin' with those stent things inside you?' I inquired; the pitch of my voice betraying concern for an old friend.

'Great, never better, got my energy back, and more,' he replied with a knowing wink.

'You're not thinking of messing around again, are you?' I said, with more than a passing memory about our misspent youth.

'Oh no, Sam. Rangi's more than enough for me. I'm well past all that business, not being a free agent like you. You're the only one likely to get up to any messing around these days.'

'What me? No, I don't think so,' I replied waving a dismissive hand.

'Always surprised me that you're still single the way you used to carry on. There was a constant stream of women in your life when we had that flat in Cotham. Often wondered why you didn't end up with someone a bit exotic - like Rangi. You used to come home with all shapes and colours...'

'Come on, there were only one or two, mate, I wasn't *that* lucky,' I replied, casting my mind back 20 years or more.

'Well, I've had a lucky break. Three stents fitted and a big warning.' Nick tapped his chest as he whispered with a strange sense of pride: 'Going to have to ease off the booze and, er ... especially the *Charlie* from now on. A big no-no, apparently.'

'That'll cheer Rangi up,' I said, raising my eyes.

'Yeah, her and my bank balance.' His smile creased into the expression of someone having a difficult bowel movement.

Nick had spent two weeks under the care of the Heart Institute and another two at home recovering, so this was the first chance for our regular Friday get together since his 'wake-up call.' The conversation continued around the finer details of Gordon's funeral.

'So, what happened next?' he leant conspiratorially over the small table.

'After the service, about 20 of us walked around the corner to Gordon's place. The house felt a little creepy. Not much had changed since my last visit ten years ago.'

'Did any of the Masons come back?' Simon looked serious as his eyes focused on me.

'Oh yeah,' I replied, 'They were a friendly bunch.'

Gordon and Irene had owned the detached house for 50 years. The front looked out over the same wooded graveyard where Gordon had now been laid to rest. You could probably spy his final abode from the upstairs windows, especially in the winter months.

'I felt sorry for Debbie. Apart from the two old girls who lived next door she was the only woman there. The old dears left after a quick sherry, leaving Debbie alone with me and all these dark-suited grey-hairs. I think she was only really on nodding acquaintance with most of them.'

'Did you recognise any of them?' Simon shifted to face me, a look of curiosity on his broad shiny face. As someone whose history degree had turned into a professorship and a comfortable career at Bristol University, local politics and history were of natural interest to him.

'Actually, I did. I didn't know any of them enough to talk to, but John Dunkley, who owns that posh antiques shop, was there, along with Harris the councillor.'

'Oh, now *I'm* getting interested.' Nick spluttered crisps.

'Weren't you approached by them once?' Simon inquired, shifting position to face him.

'Oh yeah. If you're still working for the Council after five years and you're a bloke, then you're likely as not to cop a tap on the shoulder. Dad was a Mason you see, I think that's why I was asked; his eldest son and all – a *Lewis* you know. I went along to a couple of their dinners. All very black tie and port, if you know what I mean.'

'So why didn't you join?' I asked.

'I was tempted, oh yes. I was quite keen for a while. It would have meant lots of useful contacts. What put me off was all that God-bothering they keep on about.' Nick spat the words through a shower of crisp shrapnel before raising his voice: 'You're supposed to believe in some sort of supreme being nonsense: '*The Great Architect of the Universe*', they call him.' He paused a moment, scanning our faces before raising his voice '*What – a – load – of – shit!*' He frothed and spluttered.

'I guess you're not a believer then?' Simon announced, leaning back and bracing himself for the inevitable explosion.

'No, No – *NO!*'

It's fair to say that Nick had very explicit views. Any transgression into something he judged to be a little too 'woo-woo', was always instantly and firmly dismissed. Anything that might threaten to fall off the edge of his world, was not up for debate. His interest in pushing the frontiers of knowledge had waned in recent years, as his energy was sapped 'fighting' for more funding or working on yet another 'insane' Health and Safety audit.

I had known Nick from school, but only really made friends with him when we both arrived at Bristol Uni. That's when we met Simon. It turned out that we all had an interest in sharing the same flat as *Michelle,* a stunningly attractive fellow student. Later, we consoled each other in the King's Head, which, funnily enough, has remained our favoured pub ever since. By the end of my first year studying Architecture, I was bored, and found myself yearning for more of a challenge. Leaving Nick and Simon to complete their degrees, I headed for the hotter reaches of Australia's Northern Territories, and the birth of my career in carpentry.

Although they had remained close friends, Nick and Simon went on to work in very different circles; Nick inhabiting the world of local politics and Simon pursuing his academic leanings. He had married young after meeting Inge, a Swedish palaeontologist, at the local history group. Highly elusive from the start, she seemed these days almost completely absent from his life, only occasionally surfacing from a dig on some remote South American peninsular. Enquiries as to her current whereabouts rarely resulted in anything more than a shrug.

'So anyway ... it was all very respectful. The Masons lined up to shake Debbie's hand. It hadn't occurred to me that Gordon was a Mason, let alone such an obviously important one, but what happened next was really interesting.'

The three of us crowded around our usual table. Rangi was busy with her yoga class, but due to arrive soon. Old Tom, a crinkly regular of indeterminate age who would often surreptitiously slide over, was slouched nearby, fast asleep. Even with such a small audience, I was beginning to savour my moment.

'Well, after about an hour of polite port-sipping, I found myself talking with Debbie. She had big concerns about emptying the family home and was keen to sell quickly. She hardly had any time to clear it. Teachers only get a few days' compassionate leave and that's it.' I paused, studying their avid faces. 'She was asking me about checking the roof and guttering when two of the mourners approached and introduced themselves as Daniel and 'Peachy'; fellow '*Brothers*' from the Lodge. What a pair - Daniel was tall with thin, shiny black hair and a fair dusting of dandruff. The other bloke was short and rotund, a little bit of a butterball with big red rosy cheeks.' I rubbed a finger in circles against my cheek in emphasis.

'Get on with it, Sam - *for fuck's sake!*' Nick hustled, seemingly now fully recovered from his heart attack.

'OK. Well the lanky one produced a little brass cabinet key from his waistcoat and asked about a briefcase belonging to the Lodge, that he reckoned had been in Gordon's possession. He explained that if the key unlocked the briefcase would she mind if they took the case back with them? Debbie looked a bit taken aback but admitted that she'd seen a black doctor's case upstairs and had wondered if it might contain important documents. It was locked, and she'd never found a key.'

'Go on', Simon said, his forehead furrowed in keen interest.

'She went upstairs and brought down a large black bag. It had a chunky, brass lock on the front. The tall bloke gave the key to the short one who unlocked it without any trouble.' I paused, looking directly at Nick's puckered face. 'We were both dead curious about what was in there.'

'Ahh... it be a skull and a collection of *old bones*.' Old Tom had awoken and observing our huddled manner, had sidled along the bench seat.

'Shut up Tom,' Nick snapped. 'Come on Sam ... what was in the bloody case?'

'Jewels, well, at least that's what *'Peachy'* described them as. The pair of them seemed quite happy for us to look at the contents, although, I'm not so sure that *my* interest was entirely welcome. The first thing out was a large heavily-embroidered sheepskin apron, just like the one the Masons use, only bigger and much, much fluffier.'

'Dad had one of those,' Nick interjected. He continued, staring absently into space: 'I took it out once and used it to polish the bike – but forgot to put it back. He was *not* a happy daddy.'

'Yes, yes, but not like this. This was much bigger than I've seen before, it was deeply embossed and looked *really* old. That was the biggest thing. Then there was this large white sash and at *least* two mayoral looking chains of office. One had a prominent square and dividers set in a circle with a capitol G inside.'

'G, that's for Geometry and God, that's what it means...' interrupted Tom.

'How do you know that?' I asked, raising my glass as if to support the question.

'I used to be a Mason, 'ere in Brizzle. I'd go to the Lodge up on Park Street regular like, but after a few years the misses said she didn't care for it, so I stopped going. The bar was nice and cheap, but the cider was bloody awful. Typical, really. Funny lot they were.' Old Tom gazed up at the drawn curtains, summoning-up memories of an earlier life.

'Well, you're full of surprises, Tom.' Simon raised a glass of cloudy cider, tipping it slightly in respect, towards the pensioner's gaunt frame.

I continued. 'There was also a pair of gauntlet-like white gloves with a similar deeply embossed pattern to the apron. While Debbie was asking the tall one about how old this stuff was, I got a closer look at the biggest and most elaborate jewel. It was suspended from a purple sash and very striking, quite beautiful. It was a cross containing loads of deep red jewels that looked as if it was made from four smaller crosses.'

'Like a Tau?' Simon suggested.

I took out my builder's note book and sketched the design.

'Across the middle - two swords. Over that, three triangles, forming a sort of nine-pointed star. It was all in gold, apart from the jewelled cross, and looked bloody expensive. Loads of dosh. You could see why they were so keen to have the bag back. Everyone was being very polite, but after that they took off pretty sharpish, leaving just Debbie and me.'

At that moment, Rangi arrived from her evening class; her dark curls pulled and folded into a large bun, revealing a freckled, but otherwise blemish-free face. After a few hellos and the unwinding of several brightly-coloured scarves, she turned towards me and with her lilting voice asked how I'd got on.

'I was just telling Nick and Simon how it was all very intriguing, what with all the Mason stuff going on.'

'Mason's stuff, what Mason stuff? Rangi paused, shivering as she removed another layer. 'I'm not interested in all that. How did you get on with Debbie?'

'Debbie? Oh, yes, Debbie, fine. It was just fine. We had a nice little chat. I met her son, Josh, for the first time.'

'Great.' Rangi nodded smiling. 'That must have been nice for you.' She continued to disrobe as she spoke. In 15 years, she had singularly failed to acclimatise to our Northern climate.

'Are you going to see her again then?'

'Yes... well, yes. I offered her the use of my van on Monday to clear her dad's place, there's quite a lot of stuff to sort out.'

'That's nice of you, Sam.' Rangi smiled and looked pleased as she sipped from a fresh glass of cider.

'It's OK,' I shrugged, 'I'm a bit stuck for work the early part of next week anyway. I can't finish that big extension job I've been on for ages.'

Rangi nodded, prompting me to go on.

'The plasterers need to do their job before I can finish-up. So, no trouble at all.' My face flushed with embarrassment.

'I'm sure she will be very grateful.' Rangi's dark eyes lingered on mine.

One day's work soon turned into several, as the enormity of the task became apparent. I could see that Debbie was struggling, having so little time, let alone the physical challenge of moving stuff around. How could I say no? Josh had been sent back to London, leaving us alone. Or so I thought. After my first outing to the city tip on Monday I returned to find Claire, Debbie's prim friend, in the front garden with a large dog.

'This is Norton, Sam.' Debbie waved the end of a lead before letting it go. A corpulent black Labrador wombled enthusiastically across the lawn towards me.

'He's very friendly,' I replied as a wet snout was thrust into my crutch, dripping something clear and sticky onto my work boots. Clearly age and weight had long since put pay to a more athletic expression of doggie joy.

'So, who's Newton then?' I asked.

'Norton. He's called Norton, not *Newton.*' Debbie untied the lead. A few moments later I found myself absently fondling his soft, black velvet ear.

'Dad must have been a secret motorcycle enthusiast,' I replied with a puzzled frown, having failed to visualise Gordon on any kind of bike, let alone a Norton.

'Hello Sam, it's nice to see you again. How's life been treating you?' Claire asked stiffly. She looked trim and efficient in her office clothes. Some years had passed since we'd last met, but her calculating gaze hadn't changed.

'Well, thanks. I'm living nearby these days, just down the hill. How about you?'

'I've been looking after Norton over the weekend. He's a real character, very sweet. He must have been a terrific companion for Gordon.' Claire offered a quick smile as she turned to leave. 'Must go, though. Work calls.'

After a brief breakfast, the dog shuffled over to what was obviously his favourite chair, huffed a few times and promptly fell asleep.

'Don't forget Dad's telescope, you should move that first,' Debbie called, as I made my way upstairs. 'It's all packed and there's a few books and instructions that go with it. Small back bedroom.'

Lunch was sandwiches at the kitchen table, surrounded by enormous, garish coloured plastic tubs and overstuffed refuse bags. Neither of us spoke much, respecting the solemnity that seemed to permeate the house. Debbie continued to stare at the floor, as if already in another world, her tired eyes lined and puffy.

'He's mournful. I can tell he's not his usual happy self.' She studied Norton's half-eaten breakfast before sitting down and tying her hair back. 'I could do with a bath. My hair is filthy.'

'Is it? It looks fine to me. Your hair always did look good to me.' Debbie turned to face me, letting her shoulders slowly drop and offered a weak smile.

'I'm sorry Sam, all this clearing out, there's too many memories. I never realised how difficult it was going to be. I know we have a bit of a routine going, with you calling '*Dump, charity or keep?*' But it's having to make all those awful decisions; one after another, after another. Do you realise, most of Mum and Dad's stuff will have to go to the tip?'

'Yes. I don't suppose you have any room in London?'

'God no! Two bedrooms, a poky living room, and that's it. Barely enough room for a premature adolescent. You're really welcome to take anything you want, you know.'

'Thanks. I'll keep that in mind.' I didn't tell her I already had a house overflowing with my own stuff.

'Oh Sam. The minutiae of it all, the countless bloody bits and pieces.' Debbie sounded desperate as she stood up, reaching out and gathering-up a box of expensive-looking photo frames.

'Every dress-up dinner and dance they went to, Mum insisted on having a silver frame for the group photo. Forty years' worth, and where are all those people now? What is the point of all this?'

The frames clattered as she shook the box and a short sniffle told me she was crying. I stood up and for the first time in 10 years, held her in my arms. She sobbed quietly, shifting her small frame so her weight was against me. Damn death, what a bummer it all is. Why do we have to lose our loved ones like this? How is it that when you are just getting the hang of this life thing, along comes extinction? I thought about my own experience with Mum and Dad; losing them both within a couple of years, over two decades ago.

'Come on, just pick one frame - your favourite. Take out the other photos and file them away or better still scan them into your laptop. That won't take too much room. I can drop the frames at a silver dealer I know. They might be worth something.'

We ploughed on and steadily the rooms emptied. Debbie washed and cleaned, while I continued with the task of distributing the contents of Gordon's home to various charity shops. I kept a bag of VHS tapes for Old Tom, a well-known enthusiast of vintage movies. At one point, I surprised Debbie with a little pile of canvases and a pot of brushes.

'I'd forgotten about those. I did them at art college.'

'Art college?'

'Oh, it wasn't that serious. I just went on Saturday mornings for a few terms.'

She held up a colourful abstract.

'Looks great to me. You must keep them. I didn't know about your arty side.'

'There's a lot you don't know, Sam...' Debbie's smile lingered.

We were both so emotionally and physically drained by Saturday, that our planned celebratory dinner never happened. The respective lures of a long hot bath and an early night proved too strong to ignore.

'Funny how different it looks.' Debbie's voice echoed off the bare wall. 'I'll get the agent over on Monday. It's almost done.' She stepped closer and wrapped her arms around my waist, resting her head against my chest and letting out a slow sigh before tightening her embrace. I carefully stroked her head, hardly daring to breathe.

'Thanks Sam. You've been amazing.'

'That's OK. Beats working.' Debbie chuckled, knowing that the last six twelve-hour days of sorting had far exceeded my normal schedule.

'I'm looking forward to my sofa. I'll drop you and Norton off at Claire's with those two bags. Pity you're leaving so soon. Maybe dinner next time, eh?' I said, turning the front door key.

After starting the clackety engine, I let it idle for a moment before switching off, surprising a tired Debbie. Something was nagging, *something* was not yet complete. What had we forgotten?

'Did you check the loft?' I asked.

'No, I thought you did that when you had your big ladder out.'

'We'd better check, just in case there's a box of banknotes up there.'

'That would be *very* handy,' Debbie smiled, patting my leg.

Armed with my largest torch, I prised up the hatch by the upstairs bathroom and watched as pockets of dust fluttered to the floor, a sure sign no one had recently been up there. The torchlight revealed it to be empty. Fair enough, I thought, it's time for that pint I'd promised myself. As I twisted at the top of the ladder to get the hatch to sit down correctly, a ray of torchlight reflected on something in the dark recess. Once again, I hoisted myself up and sat on the edge of the hatch, peering into the damp loft air. About four metres away was a large old-fashioned toolbox. I crawled over, carefully avoiding stepping on the old lath and plaster ceiling. The box was unlocked and inside was a collection of old tools, some wrapped in oil cloth. I sighed, recalling some of the 'donated' toolboxes I had accepted, all with lovely, but antiquated tools, long since made redundant by the lithium battery. I closed the lid and slid it across the boards to the open hatch.

I opened it up in the back of the van and Debbie joined me.

'That might even be my Grandad's old tool box,' she said, absently. 'You know, I can't ever remember seeing Dad using tools.'

'Do you want them?

I closed the lid carefully and pushed the box against the wall of the van, releasing a little sigh.

Debbie's smile lingered on my face. 'I wonder if Daddy had forgotten he even had this old box?'

Gordon was not the forgetting kind, I reflected, as I slowly drove home.

Gordon's old toolbox remained in the van, abandoned and covered with plaster bags, while I cleared the detritus from the house extension job I was finishing. Billy was due to visit on Saturday afternoon and getting the place organised, and more importantly the railway running sweetly, preoccupied my thoughts. On Thursday night, after watching Russel Crowe in 'Master and Commander', the lingering image of pirate treasure triggered the recollection of what I had left in the back of the van. Debbie had once said I looked a bit like Crowe, which had pleased me no end. Although it was late, and I was dressed only in a towelling bathrobe, I felt compelled to retrieve the box. And as I carried it into the house my mind went back to the strange circumstances of its discovery. Why was the loft empty except for the toolbox? As a builder, I'd been in any number of lofts and learned that the only time they are ever empty is either the day people move out or the day they move in. There's always, *always* stuff in people's lofts. If it's physically possible for the owners to get it up there, that's where it will end up.

Placing the box down in front of the sofa, I carefully opened the lid. Inside was the collection of a professional carpenter, probably pre-Second World War. I removed a large wrapped wood block plane and noticed for the first time that the tools were sitting on a removable tray.

What lay inside initially confused me. It had nothing to do with carpentry and everything to do with academia.

The first items were books. Biographies of people I recognised as being associated with Bristol: Edward Colston, William Draper and Isambard Kingdom Brunel. Thinking they might prove handy for future reference, I placed them on my book shelf. My eyes then focused on an un-boxed and seriously mouldy VHS tape, the title unfamiliar. It was pointless keeping it for Old Tom as the spores might infect his player, so I dropped it into the waste bin beside the sofa. Next out was a big fold-out map of Bristol, printed on the kind of cloth used for the early Ordnance Survey maps. This was no regular map, though; it bore the title *'Telluric and Geomagnetic Flow.'* Much of the detail, such as roads, street and building names seemed to be missing. Long blue and red lines criss-crossed the city. Next to the lines were groups of numbers and what looked like equations. I found the squiggles indecipherable for late-evening study and carefully refolded and returned the maps to the toolbox. Then came two other maps, rolled-up and bound by blue and red ribbons respectively. These were like the first two, except they featured circles, very large circles, that intersected each other and appeared to be about a mile or so across. One map bore the title '*Cabot Circus*' and the other, '*Temple Circus*'. Both were dated 1972. Then came seven more books, each carefully wrapped in a piece of white linen. One was titled 'The History of the Society of Merchant Venturers of Bristol City' and dated 1903. Three were marked 'Freemasonic Library' with a stamp in red ink, reading 'DO NOT REMOVE'. The other three had no markings on the sleeves or inside covers. No record of who the printer or publisher might be, but all of them had the number '33' in the centre of the second page, followed by an address: Golden Square, London. As I turned the pages, I found that many had images or diagrams that were protected by thin tissue paper. These books were obviously old and precious. One particular page jumped out at me: it had an illustration of the Earth with geometric lines forming a grid that covered the entire surface of the globe. The page was entitled '*The Five Platonic Solids*'. Other pages showed more geometric, multi-faceted ball shapes - like gemstones. What could all this stuff possibly mean?

Finally, I pulled out two box files containing reams of notes bound with blue and red cabinet ties. Each set bore the date 24th June 1972 and was titled in contrasting green ink: 'Colston Study Society.'

As I read and read, a Wikipedia of information flooded my brain. An array of strange images and incomprehensible texts flashed past as I skimmed each fascinating page. The last document, another fold-out map, was a big one. I got up, joints creaking, and cleared the kitchen table, before spreading the cloth map across it. Light was appearing through the curtains as I studied its curiously familiar landscape. The whole of Southern Britain was stretched out in front of me, from Birmingham to the South Coast. Two bold lines, running about an inch apart, had been drawn across the map, from Cardiff to London, as if bracketing the 'M4 Corridor'. The uppermost line was marked in blue: '*Physical Manifestation at 51.51 degrees*'; the bottom in red: '*Spirit Manifestation at 51.428571 degrees.*'

My eyes ached. I was now dizzy with fatigue, so I dragged myself off to bed. But instead succumbing to sleep, I found myself staring vacantly at the dark ceiling, my mind turning one extraordinary phrase over and over.

Spirit Manifestation. *Spirit* Manifestation?

What on earth had Gordon been up to?

Billy arrived looking oddly nervous, prowling along the hallway like a tom cat in a strange alley.

'How are you?' I asked, as we passed into the kitchen.

'Good, I'm very good. It's just a bit cold, this winter is sooo long.'

'After the heat and humidity of St Kitts, it must be a nightmare for you.'

'It's the darkness t'ing'; the Island is either bright and sunny, or it's night. Here it's kinda grey *ahl de time*.'

'Green Tea?' I'd remembered his preference from Bindi's Café and had made forays into the exotic teas section at the corner shop.

'Ya man, that be good.' Billy stood near the back door, a good spot as it turned out, to view my little performance. I picked up the remote control from the kitchen table and tapped out a familiar code. The unmistakable sound of a train whistle pierced the air.

'What's that?' Billy twisted in his shoes as he searched for the source.

'Look up,' I replied.

Billy's big, white teeth glowed as a huge smile spread over his tanned face. 'Hey man that's amazing, you would not know it was there, until you looked up.' He left the kitchen, following the train as it passed through the tunnel above the door. The train, a 2-6-4 Castle Class, whistled and chuffed, as I followed, brandishing the wireless remote.

'The buildings and t'ing, there be *ire*. The train. It's, it's so cool!'

'It's run with the use of computer chips, the sound, *everything*. Every train is fitted with one, and they respond to this.' I waived the remote and started up a second train that had been patiently waiting at a nearby station. The swooshing sound of steam filled the narrow hallway.

'Amazing. What a great thing to do, to run it along the wall. Train sets I've seen work on boards and t'ing, in the middle of a room. This way, along the shelf, it's like you go on the journey with the train from one room into the next. That's magic *ire*.'

'Thanks, Billy.' I gave him my best smile. 'It works kinda well doesn't it? I never liked the 'playing God' view of train sets. With this you get a sense of discovery as your eyes follow the train. I've just finished a big job, so I'm spending a bit more, with a branch line planned to go into the dining room – through there.' I pointed enthusiastically towards the back wall. 'I'm rather excited about it...'

'More tea, Billy?'

It was after five, and three hours of driving trains in and out of stations, running the Express or moving coal to and from the yard had passed in a blur.

'That was so chillin' man, I loved it. Thanks Mr Sam.' A warm, wide smile passed over his face as we bumped knuckles.

I switched it all off and returned to the kitchen. As Billy followed me in, he noticed Gordon's half-folded map.

'May I look Sam? I love dem maps and t'ings.'

Billy unfolded the entire map on the table as I cleared space. I watched as he slowly stretched his arms to grip the edges as if steadying himself in a storm. His lanky frame towered over the map and for the first time I noticed that he had a little dimpled chin. I made tea and emptied the contents of a packet of ginger biscuits onto a small plate. Billy continued to study the map in silence.

'Can I ask you Mr Sam, where did this map come from?' he asked, without looking up.

'Sure ... it's from a box of maps and papers that belonged to my friend's recently-departed father. By the look on your face, you might understand what it's about. Because I haven't a clue.'

'It's the science of *da spireet* world. It's sacred ideas, very ire man, very ire. It's what is *beyond our sight.*'

'Beyond? Beyond what exactly?'

'Beyond the physical world.' Billy stood very still. I could see he was composing his thoughts.

'The Earth is a conscious t'ing, just like us, man, every t'ing is conscious energy.' He tapped his head with his pen, studying me carefully. 'Do you know much about Plato? He was the man who said our whole world was built on geometry. Plato, he talked about the five perfect shapes that can all fit inside a circle. You must start by thinkin' of the Earth like that circle, or no - more like the skin of a football. With the five shapes inside it.'

Billy smiled as I nodded encouragingly. Something was tickling my memory... it was one of the books in Gordon's toolbox, the one with the diagrams of the Platonic Solids. I'd done plenty of geometry during my abortive attempt to become an architect and remembered the building blocks of all structures: the sphere, the cube, the pyramid, the octahedron, and the dodecahedron. My mind's eye could see what Billy was describing.

'So, imagine the Earth was that sphere, containing those shapes, all fittin' inside of each other with their points touchin' up against the skin of the planet. And if you had special glasses that allowed you to look through it like an X-Ray, what you would see would be a great big crystal sittin' in space. An' inside, a mass of energy flowing out and in and along the edges. What they called facets. An' when two flows of energy meet, the crossing places, where those edges come together, they form a spinning shape. A vortex. Jus' like the ocean when two strong currents meet and twist aroun' each other. These places pass energies to and from the centre of the Earth. Kind of like an invisible tornado that never moves much a t'ing.'

I took a deep breath. This whole spinning energy crystal business was beginning make me feel queasy and *ever* so slightly irritable.

'Yeah, well it's certainly an interesting theory, Billy, but where's the proof? You're talking about something that nobody can see, or even measure. It's a nice idea, but ...'

'Some people can see these energies, Sam. Ancient peoples were aware, some could see more than others. That is why they built on those special places. They were sacred sites and they understood the loving energy of Mother Earth and the Universe passed through those places. It's called the *'Grid'*.'

Doing my best to ignore the New Age 'loving energy' side of Billy's description, I steered him back to safer ground.

'So, you think, do you, that some of the ancient sites were deliberately built on these vortex places, thousands of years ago, when people had no technology to measure the Earth's surface?'

'Yes Sam. I'm sayin' exactly that. You heard of the Great Pyramid of Giza?'

'Of course. Is that one of them, then?'

'Ya man. It's in a very special place, it lies on the Prime Meridian.'

'Sorry Billy, did you say *Prime* Meridian?'

Billy went on to explain that if you drew great circles from the pyramids in Egypt going east, west, north and south, they would go over more land than ocean than any other position. The ancients measured the Earth from Egypt, not from London, and that was the starting point for other countries to build their shrines and monuments. As he warmed to the theme, he seemed to be sparkling with energy himself. My mind went back to a book I'd read, years earlier, about the Giza pyramid being a receptacle of ancient knowledge, all encoded in its dimensions. But how could the Egyptians have known how to do that stuff? It was 5,000 years ago.

As we both re-examined the map, I looked up, studying him with what I hoped was a kindly expression. I didn't want to rubbish his enthusiasm, but this was way out of my comfort zone. Just a bit too weird for my taste.

'Sorry Billy, but I'm having a hard time with all this. There's a lot of cranky stuff you can get on the internet. You've got to be more discerning you know, and not just believe everything you watch or read. My university friend Simon, you remember him from the pub?'

Billy nodded.

'Well, he's an academic and he'd be asking you for evidence. You just can't go around saying this stuff without any proof...'

Billy drew a large circle in silent response, thought for a while, then said: 'If you want evidence that we live in a world constructed using geometry, you have to make the effort to understand what the ancients knew. The Ancient Sumerians divided the Earth into 360 segments to reflect our movement around the sun; one degree a day. The number 360 has the advantage of being divisible by two, making it easier to calculate angles. But the numbers between one and nine contain one really strange result.'

To show willing I tried it on my calculator and read my results out loud.

'360 divided by 1 = 360: by 2 = 180, 3 = 120, 4 = 90, 5 = 72, 6 = 60, 7 = 51.428571, 8 = 45 and 9 = 40.'

'Wow! That's weird isn't it? What went wrong with seven?' I looked up to an expectant Billy.

'How come it's the only number that doesn't divide cleanly? And what a crazy number!'

He talked about seven being a magic number, the *key* sacred number, as in: seven days of the week, seven musical scales, the seven keys of heaven. A number that had been worshipped for all time. He reminded me that the line across England on Gordon's map, described as the 'Spirit Manifestation', was at 51.428571 digital degrees in the Northern Hemisphere. I let that sink in for a few minutes.

'What about Gordon's other line then, what's that about?' I wanted to know more, and Billy was keen to explain.

He talked about the Earth and the Moon having a harmonic, mathematical relationship. He said the ratio of their respective sizes was 3:11. He grabbed a pen and drew two circles - a small one touching the edge of the larger one. Then, he drew a horizontal line through the centre of the Earth, and two straight lines from the points where the line hit the edge of the Earth rising to meet in the centre of the small circle, the Moon. There was a very clear triangle and Billy said the base angles of that triangle were both 51.51degrees.

Time was getting on and my stomach was starting to gurgle. Billy carried on without even noticing. He pointed out that Gordon's two parallel lines were like a narrow band going all the way around the Earth. They weren't very far apart. The 'Spirit Manifestation' at 51.428571 degrees and the 'Physical Manifestation' at 51.51 degrees. Interestingly both these lines went through Bristol – and London.

He went on to reveal that the angle of 51.51 degrees was the pitch of the slope of the Great Giza pyramid, concluding that whoever designed that pyramid, built it to reflect the dimensions of the Earth and its relationship to the Moon. Billy was glowing, but I felt the need to draw the session to a close.

'Why would Gordon have drawn them on the map? What good is this knowledge?' I asked.

'It's a mysterious harmony all t'ru nature, as if de Earth, Moon and Sun had been designed by a... supreme architect!' Billy paused studying the map before turning to study me. He raised his eyebrows slightly and smiled.

'Another *um* - Ginger Nut, Billy?' I proffered the remaining biscuit, but he shook his head. I took it for myself and nibbled the edge thoughtfully. I was floundering in a sea of numbers.

I couldn't help feeling grateful that neither Nick or Simon were present to hear all this magic number business. Nick would be shouting and frothing by now. Simon? Silently nodding while vigorously tapping the table with the end of his chewed pen, offering that special look of detached pity he saves for the most deluded of our community.

'I must leave soon, my aunty is cookin'.' My stomach rumbled quietly at the mention of food. If you want to start, Mr Sam, go an' look. Look dis *t'ing* up.'

I watched Billy write. He spoke each instruction out loud.

'Open Google Earth: click on Tools, click on Options, set Show to Decimal Degrees. Ok? Oh, an' search for Avebury, Marlborough.' He put the pen down with an air of completion.

We had spent over four hours together, but it seemed like minutes. What a fascinating bloke, I thought, as I watched him putting on his black quilted jacket. He offered an elegant hand and I shook it firmly. Billy's broad grin warmed my heart. I closed the door behind him and before heading to the kitchen I made a detour to the front room. Pulling aside a curtain, I watched as he confidently made his way through the winter gloom. I pursed my lips in indecision - torn between affection for Billy and bafflement at his whacky mathematical theories.

9 Avebury

After a foraging trip to the corner shop with my head full of Billy and his mysterious manifestations, I decided to check out what he had told me on Google Earth. Under Tools, I clicked on Options and changed Show to read decimal degrees rather than hours, minutes and seconds, and zoomed to the centre of Avebury Stone Circle. What I discovered confused me, as if the results at the bottom of the screen had been superimposed by a prankster. Slowly though, the truth seeped into my obstinate mind. This was a world-famous stone circle, one of the largest in existence and a centre of major global, cultural and historical significance. And as I moved the mouse pointer, Billy's numbers appeared at the bottom of the screen. Sure enough. The centre of Avebury was precisely located at 51.428571 degrees latitude.

How could that possibly be?

It was late by the time I drifted from Avebury to another ancient enigma. The Giza Pyramid. Billy had implied that these two sacred sites were somehow numerically connected. Just how far away was Giza, and how could it have some sort of global relationship with a ring of stones and a large ditch in Southern England?

I played around with a few ideas before turning away from latitude to longitude. I calculated how far in degrees the Great Pyramid at Giza was from Avebury. The distance to Avebury's stone circle was 33 degrees, coincidently the same number that kept appearing in Gordon's mysterious books.

But what about 51.428571?

My focus kept returning to this number. There's more here, something else, I reflected. But what was it? I stared at it for a while, and idly started adding the respective digits together, each one plus the value of the next one and so on. 5+1+4+2+8+5 made 25 and 7 +1 equals...33. My heart thumped with excitement. That bloody number again!

How was it possible that thousands of years ago, our ancestors not only designed and built the Avebury monument, but appeared to locate it with such extraordinary precision? And why? Unless all this was just chance, a random event, as Nick and Simon would so readily claim.

'This is lovely Sam. It was nice of you to suggest we meet up again.' Debbie, who even managed to look elegant in a thick winter coat, smiled affectionately. We found space on one of the front rows of tables directly in front of the pub and close to the surprisingly busy road. Although it was out of season, we jostled for space with a dozen leather-clad bikers and a multi-national spattering of tourists.

'That's OK,' I replied. 'Josh and New'- *no,*' I corrected myself. 'Norton seem to be enjoying the day out. In fact, where are they? We could eat now if you're hungry. *Are you?*'

Debbie nodded approvingly as she cast her gaze around for Josh and the dog. 'Have you noticed the number of crows' nests there are? You can see them very clearly while the trees are still bare.' She sipped from a small china cup, the tea steaming in the cool, dry Spring air.

'Yes, they make quite a racket with their caw-cawing all the time.'

We took in the curious appearance of massive megalithic stones, jumbled together with road signs for Swindon and the A4361.

'Look, it's 51. 4-2-8-5-7-1 degrees,' I said, transfixed on the little screen.

Debbie frowned in response.

'You mean just around here. That number you're all excited about.'

'Yes Debbie, yes it's *exactly* that number. So exactly in fact, that it passes through these very tables.' I said, pointing at the weather-beaten top.

'Sorry...' Debbie paused, looking confused. 'What, this pub?' She glanced back to the front door, '...the Red Lion?'

'Yes look, this GPS thing, it tells you exactly where you are on the Earth's surface.' As I pointed at the screen, I could see the last digit of the eight numbers, changing as I moved around. 'It reads precisely 51.428571.' I repeated the numbers slowly. 'Do you see? If I step this way it goes down a digit, 51.428570, and over on this side of the table, it goes up a digit to 51.428572. This is what you get when you divide the number of degrees in a circle, 360, by seven. These same sequences of numbers just repeat over and over, 51428571; 51428571; into infinity. And here we both are this lovely Spring lunchtime, at exactly that latitude.'

'So, this line of latitude runs through the centre of Avebury stone circle?'

'Yes. Exactly through it!'

'So how do you think they managed that feat of precision?'

'I really, really don't know. They can't have done it from watching the sun rise or set; as you can see, Avebury sits near the bottom of a shallow valley, almost surrounded by hills. It would be very difficult to get a precise fix on sunrise.'

'What about sighting the stars, sort of triangulating, or something?' Debbie offered.

'They're not supposed to have had theodolites or even lenses four and half thousand years ago, I said and shrugged my shoulders.

'How about measuring the shadow that's cast? Isn't that how the ancient Egyptians knew where they were?'

'I've been pondering that, Debbie...'

'Sam, please call me Deb. It's been a while since anyone called me Debbie.'

'Oh yes, sorry, you've always been Debbie to me.' I smiled and thought about how much we had both grown up since we met at Dave and Moira's party all those years ago.

Josh appeared, dragging an exhausted-looking black labrador behind him.

'What have you been up to...?' Deb sounded strained.

'We've walked all the way around, along the top. You can see for miles.' Josh pointed at the chalk embankment, face flushed with the wind and sun, his long hair blown into a tangle.

'It's a long way, isn't it? I remember doing the same thing on my previous trip, maybe 20 years ago,' I said to an unimpressed Josh.

'Poor old Norton, he's getting on. Get him some water from the bar, Josh, and let him rest,' said Deb as she bent down to stroke the dog's collapsed frame with a look of concern.

'I can't see how they could have done it without very accurate optical equipment,' I continued. 'Quality lenses have only been around a few hundred years. It's a mystery and I can't find anything on the net, or even in the Avebury bookshop. I was checking before you arrived. Nothing. Not a word about it.'

Deb nodded in reply before scanning the hills to the south.

'It's nice here, I love the little tufts of trees on those mounds along the hills. Aren't they tombs or something?' Deb pointed at the smooth chalk ridge several kilometres away.

'Hello. Excuse me, do you mind if I sit here?' A small, balding man in his late fifties interrupted. He waved his laden tray towards us.

'Yes. Yes of course,' I said and shuffled along the bench. His thin frame looked lost in his brown Driza-Bone coat. His tanned face betrayed the weathered features of a farmer.

'Sorry, but there's so many tourists these days. The pub gets very busy.' He paused before adding, 'I think I might be partly to blame.' He looked at us in turn and smiled.

'How come?' I enquired of our new neighbour.

'I spend a lot of time at the Stones. I bring tourists with me, usually a minibus load. It's becoming more popular every year. Sorry, I should introduce myself - *Denis*.' I shook his warm hand as our eyes briefly meet.

'Very multicultural.' Denis raised an eyebrow and cocked his head backwards, smiling. 'I translated my website into Cantonese a few years ago and now it's all taken off. I escort a dozen or so at a time. This last lot are just leaving for Heathrow.' He nodded towards an obvious group loitering in the car park.

'You show them around Avebury, like a conducted tour?' I enquired.

'Yes, a bit of a tour. We start off near my home, at Glastonbury Tor. Then we do Stonehenge, before arriving here via Silbury Hill.' Denis grinned, flashing a mouth of well-maintained teeth.

'So, Denis you must know the history of Avebury pretty well,' I asked, reflecting on my good fortune. He might be just the person to provide some answers.

'I've been hooked ever since I came to the UK 30 years ago.'

'Don't tell me. That's an Aussie accent?' I smiled confidently.

'Yes and no, I was born near Auckland in New Zealand, but the family moved to Australia soon after.' Denis emphasised the New Zealand bit, which I acknowledged with an apologetic smile.

We let our new friend finish his lunch before making more enquiries. My curiosity was piqued by my recent discoveries and I was sure Denis could fill in some of the detail.

'Of course, as the stones didn't come with a dedication or a manual, no one knows for sure how it all came to be. The presence of Silbury Hill, Europe's largest man-made hill, 20 minutes' walk away just added to the enigma. You can see the mound clearly from the south side of the circle. Avebury, Stonehenge. These sites were much bigger than they appear now, in fact they were huge; massive complexes that were continuously added to for hundreds, maybe thousands of years. It's quite possible that here at Avebury, there was an effigy constructed of a serpent or dragon. Its length flowing right across the downs. Avebury is just one part of a substantial arena.'

Denis drew his arms across the horizon as if he was conducting it.

'But why? What's this all about?' I said mystified.

'Energy. Currents of geomagnetic and telluric energy that are mostly undetectable to modern man, but maybe not to our ancestors. They flow all around the site like ethereal streams.' Denis studied us both before shrugging and announcing defensively, 'This is only *my* own view of course.'

'Go on.' Deb leant forward in evident fascination.

'I'm a dowser. My dad taught me, when I was a kid growing up in Oz. Very useful to know how to find water. Especially where we lived. I use rods like these.'

He pulled out a pair of angled wire rods from an old leather rucksack and held them like a gunslinger from the Wild West.

'I use them to help me detect and map different paths of energy.'

I studied Denis with growing scepticism.

Our food arrived, so we let Denis finish his. Deb called Josh to join us at the table. We ate hungrily and in silence. When he finished, Denis made his excuses and set off to do a little 'mapping' with his rods, inviting us to join him later.

'I can dowse,' Deb said as she pushed her tray aside.

'You can do what?'

'Dowse. What's wrong with that?'

'Come on Deb, it's all a bit hocus pocus this dowsing malarkey, wobbling sticks an' all.'

'I bet you could if you tried it. Everyone can with a little bit of effort.'

'Where did all this come from?' I said with a hint of irritation.

'Dad. He taught me when I was a little girl. I preferred using a pendulum to the rods, though. He knew how to dowse because he was a water engineer. They were often taught to dowse. He told me it was quicker and more accurate than the equipment the engineers were given.'

She looked serious. I thought about the toolbox with the books and maps.

'Do you think those maps of Gordon's...?' I asked hesitantly.

'Ask Denis, not me. I've not watched a pendulum spin for decades.'

After lunch, we set off to explore as Josh bounded ahead, only held back by Norton's insistence on sniffing every stone and tree. There's a great sense of space at Avebury. The enormous sky reminded me of a scene from a Sixties' spaghetti western. It took a good hour to walk along the chalk bank surrounding the ditch. We could see Denis below us, some 50 metres away, among a group of four or five big, four-metre-high stones. He seemed busy, bending down to place a marker every few steps before making a brief note on a pad that swung from his neck.

We walked along the chalk path at the top of the mound surrounding the stones.

'Sam. How's Billy? Have you seen him recently?' Deb inquired.

'He's good. Such a nice guy and mature for his age. I doubt if he's much more than about 25, so I'm not sure where he gets all his knowledge from.'

'It sounds more like wisdom. I'd love to meet him,' replied Deb, lost in thought.

My heart fluttered in anticipation of a re-run of today's outing.

'We've not made any arrangements to meet again. I do have his address and phone number, though. I'll call him soon.'

We walked down to meet Denis.

'Have either of you ever dowsed?' he asked, as we approached.

'I have.' Deb raised her hand with the enthusiasm of a school girl. 'It was a long time ago. Dad worked for a water company. I watched him dowsing the neighbour's front garden as he worked out the course of a water pipe. I begged him to teach me. I was about eight or nine, I think.'

'Good. Well here's a smaller pair of rods for you.' Then Denis turned to me.

'Sam. Try these for size.'

Denis handed me two vinyl covered pieces of wire about 30 centimetres in length. The ends were bent at right angles, about 10 centimetres long, forming an 'L' shape.

'Now hold the rods as if you were holding a pistol.' Denis demonstrated with his own rods. 'Tip them forward slightly so they are pointing down a little bit. That's right. If you go too far, the rods will swing about, you need to keep them in balance and both pointing forward, in neutral so to speak. It's a good idea to walk about with them for a while, to get a feel for them in your hands. These are delicate instruments, so hold them lightly.'

'What are they made from?' I asked as I studied the familiar shape.

'They're made from the finest man-made coat hanger wire.' Denis grinned before adding in a conspiratorial whisper: *'They're very cheap to make, but quite expensive to buy...'*

'The first thing to understand is that there is a protocol or method that we need to follow if we are to get reliable results.' He spoke with well-rehearsed confidence. The three of us stood near the centre of the circle. Josh watched for a while before boredom set in. Clearly exhausting Norton with another walk would be a lot more fun. Denis told us about two 'energy leys' called the Michael and Mary Lines that crossed each other close by. He chose to measure the Michael line. By dowsing it, we would detect and measure its width at that point using the dowsing rods. He explained that a network of detectable energy paths covered the entire surface of the Earth. He added that it was important that we clear our mind and just let go. If we try too hard it might not work. The trick was to place the mind into neutral.

Obediently asking the question, '*Please show me the energy line,*' Deb and I moved forward purposefully, while Denis urged us to walk quicker and become more nonchalant in attitude.

'Stop trying so hard, Sam,' Denis said softly.

I heard a squeal of delight and turned to study Deb's frozen stance. Her rods had crossed over forming an X.

'I can still do it,' she announced excitedly.

I got nothing.

I must have spent half an hour crossing an invisible line that apparently swirled through Avebury. The rods bounced around but nothing noticeable happened. Deb's rods seemed to obey her every command. They were supposed to 'open up' or 'close in' as you crossed through the path of this invisible energy. I watched amazed as she chased the centre of the 'Michael Line', with the fervour of someone hanging onto an excited bloodhound. My rods refused to conform and swung up and down and sideways impotently. After about an hour we called a halt and walked together back to the car park. For the first time I had the opportunity to speak to Denis about my own discoveries.

'You know Sam, I think you have stumbled upon some interesting facts, something that will add to the whole debate about Avebury. I'd love the opportunity to help with your dowsing again. Why don't you come to Glastonbury? We could have a walk around the Abbey and practise with the rods a little bit more and I could introduce you to some friends. I just know they would be fascinated by those maps.' Denis puckered his lips and looked thoughtful. 'Those charts of yours... they may be a *lot* more interesting than you realise, Sam.'

By the following Friday and our regular meet-up at the King's Head, I had devoured several more books on Avebury and broached the enigma with Nick and Simon.

'That pub. The Red Lion you said? Used to sell damn good cider. What was it called, Simon?' Nick's forehead creased.

'There's a bit more to this than the quality of the cider, Nick.' I felt a twinge of irritation at them both for their lack of interest. How could they not be curious about its puzzling location?

'I imagine it's all just down to coincidence, Sam,' Simon responded with a dismissive shrug.

'Coincidence? I don't *think* so! This was an enormous effort by some group or other over generations, and if the anthropologists are to be believed, the average life span five thousand years ago was about twenty-seven. These massive structures were designed and constructed by little more than teenagers!' I said forcefully.

'Look Sam,' Simon placed his hand on my arm to calm my frustration, 'I have a Ph.D. in History. I know what I'm talking about. It's just a big calendar to predict the seasons so they knew when to plant stuff. There's no real mystery.'

'I don't think there's much mystery about it, Sam,' Nick joined in. 'You seem to be making a lot of fuss about it all. You've always been a bit of a dreamer, haven't you? I bet if you search 'Wikipedia' it'll tell you all you need to know.' He gave me his patient look before suddenly raising a hand in exclamation. '*Sheppey's!* That was it. I'll have a pint of Sheppey's please, Landlord.' He held his tankard aloft, expectantly.

I continued to prompt them. How a man called Heath worked out that the stones in the main circle and the two smaller inner circles, encoded accurate information about the movements of the Moon over long periods of time.

'It also turns out that the monument's latitude of 51.428571 is encoded into the shape of the outer circle and the positions of the obelisks at the centre of the two little circles inside. This structure was planned by some very, very clever people.'

'Yeah, yeah. It's your round.' Nick waved a smudgy glass.

I returned home, initially despondent and frustrated at the lack of support for my new-found discoveries. I wondered how Billy had known about this latitude thing, when even on the internet there appeared to be so little information. Maybe Billy was some sort of secret Caribbean Druid person?

As I calmed down, the resistance I'd met from Nick and Simon provoked me to delve further. Sod them! Maybe I could learn to dowse like Debbie. I wasn't going to be put off by their scepticism and I hardened my resolve to dig deeper into the mystery.

11 Crumbly's Café

A cold, early April shower smeared the windscreen as I emerged from the woods at the top of Bristol Hill, looking down to the cathedral city of Wells and the Somerset Levels beyond. To the south, Glastonbury Tor rose impressively out of the flat, marshy landscape.

After our meeting at Avebury, I had left it a couple of weeks before calling Denis. He seemed genuinely enthusiastic as we arranged an early morning dowsing lesson in the grounds of Glastonbury Abbey. The bait was tea and cake afterwards at one of the most celebrated cafés in town.

This time I found the dowsing easier. I was able to concentrate without the previous distractions, and it wasn't long before I was getting some sort of reaction. Denis explained that although many people learn quickly, they fall into the trap of self-creating '*psi lines*.' Our own thoughts can produce a field of energy of varying frequencies that surrounds the body. To a teacher like Denis, these thoughts are the first step, the first projection of our consciousness into a morphic field known as the ether. So, by *looking* for lines of energy, we are projecting them ourselves and effectively using the dowsing rods to chase our own tails.

My first experience of the Michael Ley line happened soon after we arrived at the Abbey. I followed Denis to a quiet spot in the grounds. We stood under a tree and stayed still, not speaking for several minutes. Then Denis, talking softly, coached me into expanding my sensitivity as I focused my thoughts on my fingers. I began to explore the world using just my fingertips. With my eyes closed, I moved a hand slowly forward, reaching out in hopes of connecting with the energy ley close by. After several gentle attempts, I became aware of a cool breeze passing across the tiny hairs right at the very tips of my fingers. As I focused on this sensation, it became clearer and stronger.

'Now pull your hand slowly back and forth, can you feel the edge of the Ley?' Denis's gentle Australian burr resonated against the bare walls of the ruined Abbey.

'Oh yes! Now I can. Wow!' I exclaimed as this new awareness seduced me. As I focused I found this tantalising breeze had a shape. There seemed a definite edge. It had ... *form*.

Denis said the Michael Ley was about three metres wide at this point. It varied in width as it emerged from the sea at St Michael's Mount in Cornwall, then onto Glastonbury, then Avebury, before disappearing into the ocean again at Hopton-On-Sea in East Anglia. I soon found the edge again and experienced a gorgeous, sublimely loving sensation. I moved my hand delicately backwards and forwards caressing the invisible ley.

'Wow, Denis!' I exclaimed. 'It feels like a, well, a sort of muscular *snake*!'

'The Chinese call it Dragon energy, or Lung Mei.' Denis gave me a discreet smile as we shared awareness of his secret world. 'It's subtle; very, very subtle, therefore we don't consciously experience it in our normal crowded, distracted existence. Our ancestors appear to have been much more aware of these paths of energy and maybe other frequencies too. Practise and meditate, that's my advice, it'll soon come to you without conscious thought.' Denis studied my face carefully before adding, '...and use this knowledge with discernment Sam, with *discernment*. Do you understand?' I nodded slowly in confirmation as my cheeks flushed from his surprising change of tone.

Crumbly's Cafe is well hidden behind Glastonbury's busy High Street. The unsuspecting visitor is lured along a narrow passage lined with cramped shops. A Somerset souk. As the passage opens out, it reveals a small whitewashed courtyard, six or seven metres across. At the further end sits a jumbled, heavily-restored, 400-year-old cottage; the home of the café.

It all looked very convivial in the spring sunshine. Denis sought out a small group sitting outside and introduced me, before establishing who wanted what. I felt anxious as I took a proffered seat and sat down. A largish woman raised her hand in welcome. She was swathed in a green velvet dress that easily reached the cobblestones. She introduced herself as Sophie before offering a brief biography for each of her friends. I nodded, smiled and shook hands and began to relax. My attention was repeatedly caught by Sophie's three elaborate necklaces, suggesting some strange ethnic and organic origin. But her booming voice had an unexpectantly northern intonation.

'...Ee, you look a little dazed Sam. It *is* Sam, isn't it?' She inquired. I nodded in reply.

'I feel it. I've been with Denis over at the Abbey.'

'Bin teaching you dowsin' has he?'

'Yes, I feel a bit blown away by it, this sense of discovery. I've always been dismissive of that stuff, though I realise now I made no effort to understand or actually learn.'

'I know what you mean, luv. Denis taught me, and half the people in this café.'

'It feels like quite a little community; very mixed.'

'Aye, it's mixed alright. Glastonbury's like two very different dimensions occupying the same space. There's the mostly straight-thinking farmers and their families, and *then there's this lot of jessies...*' Sophie waved her fleshy arm as if casting seed.

Denis returned, carrying a large tray laden with pots, cups and slices of sponge cake so large that their towering layers seemed to defy gravity.

'Sophie teaches Earth Spirit Awareness - part of the Witching Collective here in Glastonbury,' Denis announced blithely.

That made sense.

I had entered a different world. One where there appeared few conversational boundaries. I picked up snippets that would have made many of my old friends choke on their coffee. Someone was trying to write a book about the 11:11 phenomenon. Amazon-bought healing stones are 'crap' and, apparently, the new Chakra Polishing Centre is '*really* exorbitant.'

Denis asked if I had brought any of the maps I'd promised. Producing a cardboard tube from my rucksack, I spread the cloth map that Billy had been so interested in over the empty tea cups. It quickly drew a small crowd. Several evident experts appeared, exchanging ideas about the significance of the two latitudes.

'Definitely. It's high-level Mason stuff. Maybe even beyond the 33-degree level, I would say,' said John, a tall 60-year-old, sporting a compact pot belly and a tiny cowboy hat balanced on his naked head. A small tuft of hair had escaped the razor, just above the nape of his long neck. It was tied to form a little ponytail and jiggled distractingly whenever he spoke.

'Have you followed the line either side of Avebury, to see what else is aligned with that 51.428571 latitude?' Denis asked, as order was slowly resumed.

'Yes. I followed it using Google Earth across Wiltshire to Bristol. It goes through the middle of Bowood House, through the little domed tower in the middle of the main building, then on into the suburbs of South Bristol. It passes through the centre of Knowle housing estate,' I replied.

'...Which, rather interestingly, happens to be laid out as a hexagon. As is Clifton Cathedral,' said Colin, introduced to me as a former social worker and now refugee from Bristol City Council. 'I used to work a lot around Knowle.' He raised his eyebrows as if to signal a mutual secret.

'The great Architect of the Universe wanted the structure of his creation to be perfect, so he used the geometry of six to make it so...' Denis quoted.

'I've often wondered about that hexagonal layout up at the Cathedral. Of course, it relates to matter rather than life or spirit. Funny that they would design a cathedral around the geometry of the hexagon rather than the much more common Vesica Piscis.' Colin spoke with an air of studied authority.

'What's a Vesica Piscis?' I inquired, glancing around in embarrassment at my ignorance.

Half a dozen voices clamoured to explain the Latin name in a jumble of words and accents.

'...and that,' chimed Sophie, 'also happens to be the Yoni, the reproduction, the birth canal.'

'...and don't forget, were talking about the birth of all geometry. The measure of the physical world,' John responded, gesticulating with theatrical relish.

A glance at my watch reminded me that I needed to leave and get back to Bristol for a meeting. Declining the temptation of more cake, I left the group, thanking Denis and promising a return visit. I set off in a pensive mood and as I crossed the isolated landscape of the Mendips, I pondered on all the baffling explanations I'd heard at Crumbly's.

I was confident that a quick Google would give me a nice clear understanding of the 'Vesica Piscis', which, as far as I'd been able to gather, is some kind of sacred symbol. I was in for a big surprise. The first shock was that Wikipedia was hosting a full-scale slanging match between various contributors, involving eclipses of the moon and their relevance to the geometrical figure. Not only that, Vesica Piscis cropped up in several categories – including mathematics, masonic symbolism, astrology and... female genitalia.

The Latin name translates into 'fish bladder' – a crude description of the symbol's shape. But much more importantly, the design is a mathematical configuration. To create a Vesica Piscis, you draw two overlapping identical circles. But it's not any old overlap. They must be drawn in such a way that the centre of each circle touches the circumference of the other. So what you end up with are two thick crescents surrounding a pointed oval – and it's that central section that forms the almond, or fish shape.

The origin of the twin circles dates back as far as Pythagoras, at around 500 BC. He saw the left circle as 'limited', the right as 'unlimited', and both held together by the central 'potential'. Two hundred years later, Euclid – the Egyptian mathematician - was using it to construct an equilateral triangle. In fact, these two overlapping spheres provide the building blocks for every other polygon: squares, hexagons, rhombuses can all be created using the proportions of the Vesica Piscis. So, it's a perfect geometrical entity. Wikipedia went on to mention square roots and 'harmonic structures' but that's where my eyes began to glaze over.

At some point in history, the design passed into the realms of sacred symbolism. In fact, the phrase 'sacred geometry' was sprinkled liberally throughout every reference I found to the Vesica Piscis. In ancient mythology, God was depicted as a sphere: an eternal unbroken line suggesting perfection. And of course, the sphere is an obvious representation of our sun and moon. When the divine sphere extended itself to create a duplicate, the second sphere became the Goddess. The merging of the two deities as the Vesica Piscis created a third entity - their offspring – the central fish.

Early Christian artists jumped on this symbolism, seeing it as a device for presenting God, the Virgin Mary and Jesus. The stonemasons of the Middle Ages used it in the design and decoration of churches and abbeys. It appears as the underlying form behind a lot of Christian art and the geometrical system of measurement in architecture. Apparently, you can see sculptures of Christ enclosed within the almond frame, carved over doors of many Gothic churches. Even some of their floorplans are based on the Vesica Piscis' sacred geometry.

And then astrology seems to enter the mix. A lot of European Gothic cathedrals are littered with astrological symbolism, which seems odd when you think that astrology has pagan overtones to a lot of Christians. The Age of Pisces, a period of 2,160 years, began with the birth of Christ. The Virgin Mary is represented in the Zodiac as Virgo, and Christ, born of the Virgin Mary, as Pisces, the sign of the fish. Chartres Cathedral in France is a prime example of this mingling of the two belief systems. There are astrological references all over the place; one stained glass window contains the 12 signs of the zodiac and there's a giant astrological clock.

Before the Christians, the rules of sacred geometry were applied by the ancient Egyptians and then the Islamic architects, who were far more sophisticated builders than their Northern European counterparts. And even thousands of years later, the Vesica Piscis turns up as one of the most important emblems of Freemasonry. The Masons' view of God as 'The Great Architect of the Universe' is portrayed by the huge pair of compasses. The Rev Dr George Oliver, quoted as one of the most prolific authors on Freemasonry in the 19th Century, described the Vesica Piscis as constituting 'the great and enduring secret of our ancient brethren.'

As well as looking like a fish, the Vesica is believed to symbolise the vulva in female anatomy, the external female genitalia. It has been used throughout the ages to depict the 'divine wellspring', the source of eternal life, and has been strongly associated with many goddesses of fertility, including Aphrodite, the Greek goddess of love, and the pagan Great Mother Goddess. Over time, the symbol was also extended to represent the womb and the mother.

Who'd have guessed that two overlapping circles could provide a representation for the geometry of Life itself? In every respect, you could call it the Gateway to Heaven. But it also turns out that the Vesica Piscis is all around us, even today. Its design has been borrowed and adapted to produce the logos of countless corporations around the world, from Chanel to MasterCard.

This was a lot to take in, particularly since my interest wasn't born out of idle curiosity. What I hadn't shared with my new friends, for reasons I can't quite explain, was the fact that Gordon's other maps showed an enormous hand-drawn Vesica Piscis overlaying the very centre of the City of Bristol.

'Hello stranger!' Old Tom's eyes widened in surprise.

'I've brought you some tapes. They're all old movies, if you don't want them it's OK, I can take them to the tip.' I held up the black bag and jangled the contents.

'Come in, come in - you haven't been here for a while, have you, young Samuel?' Tom was unshaven, and his grey beard covered his face like a threadbare carpet. A dribble of egg yolk had meandered down his grey cardigan, bringing a splash of colour to his otherwise monochrome appearance.

'I hope I'm not disturbing you,' I said, as I followed him along the dark hallway to the kitchen. The bare varnished floorboards were intermittently covered in ragged strips of carpet. The walls a dark, purply-brown colour that hadn't been in fashion since the advent of flight. Tom opened the kitchen door and ushered me in with a strange sly grin on his face.

'Wow! I stepped back in shock, as four fluorescent citrus walls shrieked their presence. 'This new colour scheme ... it's a bit on the bright side for your taste, isn't it?'

'It's the Social.'

'The Social *what*? I stammered, confused.

'Had a visit by a pretty lass a couple of weeks ago. She said I ticked all the right boxes.' Tom flashed his pale gums and missing teeth. 'They're all as keen as mustard to come here and do stuff. Two lovely girlies painted this out. Took'em a week. Some sort of volunteer thing. They get points, you know.'

'But, painting it *orange* Tom. That's a bit strong isn't it?'

'I know, I know. It's very bright, quite the wrong colour, I'm going to complain about it. The *girlies* will just have to come back...' His lecherous grin and flickering eyes said it all. Devious old Tom. He could be very canny when he wanted to be.

'Staying for tea? Or maybe a drop of cider?' Tom raised a whiskery eyebrow. 'I've got a gallon of Hancock's 'Weak Knees' on the go.'

This was fresh cider drawn from the original oak storage casks on the farm. Dry and clear, this 'nectar' tasted exclusively of freshly squeezed apple juice. The most dangerous of ciders, its light, easy drinking hid the wildly varying amounts of alcohol a barrel might contain. It was a liquid lottery - *Somerset Roulette.* Sometimes six percent, sometimes more, much more. We sat at Old Tom's Formica-covered table and clinked glasses. It wasn't long before I was bringing him up to date with the story of Gordon's toolbox.

'...Thirty-three-degree knowledge did they say?' Tom casually looked through his new collection of VHS tapes as we chatted about my visit to Crumbly's. It seemed that Gordon had excellent taste.

'That's top of the pyramid stuff; it's an honorary degree.' Tom continued as his voice became matter of fact. 'Anyone with a little bit of money and some effort can work their way up the first 32 degrees, but 33 is different. *Very* different.'

'What's so different?'

'Don't know, didn't get there. You only learn what you need to learn to get through a degree. It's not mapped out, like you *know* what's about to be revealed. As any old Mason will tell you, Freemasonry is not a secret society, but it is a society of secrets, and you might have some big Mason secrets in that box of yours!'

The tone of Old Tom's voice had suddenly darkened. My face flushed as I felt my stomach churn in discomfort.

'There are some very powerful people in Masonry, the ones that use it as a ladder to gain control and influence. I wouldn't mess with them – *don't meddle in their stuff, Sam...'*

Tom's manner was abrupt as he pronounced each word. I was shocked, having never seen this side of him before. He continued to glare at me in silence until I slid my eyes to the floor. My mind raced through the imagery of that night. I recalled the expensive books with page after page of diagrams and strange symbols. One page contained nothing but drawings of Egyptian obelisks. And all those maps. Those bloody maps of ... ley lines.

This toolbox didn't belong to me, it belonged to the Masons. What had started out as innocent curiosity was becoming a frightening obsession. I felt the grip of paranoia emerging as my legs jiggled uselessly under the table.

'Tom. I think I'd better get back home. If I drink anymore I'll fall over.'

I left Old Tom's rather too hastily. As I retreated, I could hear him calling out to me about some job or other. Fitting shelves for Tom could bloody well wait, I thought, as I grappled with my keys.

Gordon's toolbox? What the *hell* am I going to do?

Take all those books and maps to the recycling centre and just throw them in? The council staff might discover the contents and trace them back to me with their CCTV cameras. No, that won't do. Perhaps I'll stuff it all up in the loft like Gordon did, and just forget about it. Except I wouldn't be able to stay away, I'd creep back, drawn by the very intrigue of it all. I would never, ever leave it alone. '*The mole's outa the hole on this one*', I called out.

'Fuck it...!'

I shut the door, turning the mortice key with a reassuring clunk, before hustling along the hall to the kitchen and sliding the big top bolt shut on the back door. Then, out of the kitchen and into the back room - and the wood burner. 'Coal not wood, it burns hotter' I told myself as I gathered up the scuttle.

Within 15 minutes, the embers had a threatening red glow.

I dragged the box towards the fire, still covered in my tell-tale fingerprints, as I nervously plotted the deed. The maps? Easy, but not the books. Every page would likely have to be torn out. Quite a job. I decided I needed the help of an old hand saw. Soon I was cutting the bigger books into manageable squares. After that I fed Gordon's notes, one scrunched-up A4 sheet at a time, through the open top lid of the now raging fire.

The whole operation took an hour.

I collapsed in dazed relief and watched through the viewing window as the final pieces were consumed.

Maybe fire was appropriate.

My home was now sterilised of all things strange and not knowable. 'Goodbye weird world shit,' I called drunkenly enough for Kate to hear. I slid onto my side on the empty toolbox, spilling the last of the cider before letting out a long shuddering sigh and slipping into oblivion.

Several hours later I came to; every sinew and muscle of my body aching. My hangover spiked by daggers of anxiety, I tentatively retraced last night's frenzied events. The pungent aroma of old bonfire burnt my nostrils as I painfully turned onto my side. I studied the new carpet of white powder covering the floor with languid distaste.

Was this dust all that remained of Gordon's profoundly disturbing legacy?

I gingerly sat upright and rubbed uselessly at the charcoal smears generously covering the front of my T-shirt. I needed water *so* badly. I shambled into the kitchen. Returning, glass in hand, I studied the pinkish glow from the woodburner. Melted to the hot plate lid was a thread of red ribbon that had bound one of the pages of notes. I pulled it away and added it to the remains still smouldering in the fire. But, as I did, I spotted next to my right foot, a singed fragment of paper. Crouching, I reached for the survivor and read out loud Gordon's last word.

Colston.

For builders, after the short days and bad weather of winter, the spring brings more adventurous work. I kept focused on the tasks ahead, ignoring what was now very much behind me. I had no reason to call Deb, other than to say hello, and so I didn't. My working week kept me busy and I was enjoying being back in my old routine. I didn't need any new complications in my life. The bonus was that Friday nights with the others would be far less fractious. Nobody even mentioned the Gordon stuff. We'd moved on to other less contentious topics.

But a few weeks later, in early May, something happened that set my pulse racing. It started with a call from a property management company, asking if I would repair some broken leaded lights at Trinity Church, just on the edge of Clifton Down.

It was a busy spot and, not wanting someone to drive into the ladder, I chose to do the work on a dry, sunny evening. It was a simple enough repair; two diamond panes of glass about 20 cm long had broken. Using a scalpel, I cut the lead bead and removed the broken glass before offering-up the new piece and cutting it to size. As I cleaned the newly inserted glass with a rag, my eye caught an obelisk reflected in the glass pane. I watched as it slowly moved with the setting sun. Something about that obelisk was nagging at my memory.

I made my way down the ladder and strolled across the road towards it. The five-metre column stood alone, surrounded by the green expanse of the Downs. It sat atop a two-metre-high square pedestal and on its side was a large rectangular grey slate panel.

'The entire Dedication

Composed by Sir WILLIAM DRAPER

In 1768

Is now

In accordance with his original intention

Inscribe on this monument

On its removal, hither

From the grounds of Manilla Hall

1883

JOSEPH D WESTON MAYOR'

'These two monuments were erected by Lieut. General Sir William Draper K.B. In the gardens of his house Manilla Hall on the site of which Manilla Road now stands. Born in Bristol in 1721 he was in 1744 elected a Fellow of Kings

College Cambridge but chose a military rather than an academic career. The Cenotaph commemorates the 79th of foot corps which he himself raised in 1757 for service in the East during the Seven Years War. This regiment was later disbanded.'

As I surveyed the obelisk, my eye was caught by another monument about 20 metres away and closer to the road. It was a large, rectangular cenotaph, complete with stone casket sitting on scrawled legs; on top, a metre-high marble urn with stylised flames. I walked towards it and soon realised that it was in direct alignment with a small domed roof on the far side of the road. After a cursory look at the urn, I crossed over and turned into Manilla Road to get a better look at the four-quarter dome at the top of 'Tower House'. On the collar of the dome was a continuous band of decorated tiles depicting the five-petal flower. The Templar rose petal? I recalled Gordon's books. Was I staring at a Knights Templar symbol? I turned and sighted back towards the obelisk. All three monuments appeared to have been clearly and deliberately aligned: obelisk, dome and flaming urn.

I loaded the ladder onto the van and headed for the nearest pub, my nerves jangling from the addictive thrill of discovery. The hunt was back on, I decided, as I supped an indifferent cider. I tried to remember back to that night studying Gordon's books. What did that page say...the one with the beautiful drawings of monuments, domes and vessels spouting out flames?

The text came back to me. 'Obelisks, domes and flaming urns - *we are man* (penis) *we are women* (womb) *we are enlightened* (the light of the flames).'

Enlightened? But to what?

And what had been said about the secret function of obelisks? Something or other, something... I couldn't remember.

Then I thought back to the three biographies that had escaped the wood burner.

Bristol's forgotten hero: Draper. He was one of them.

14 Norton comes to stay

A few days later Deb's friend Claire rang.

'Hello Sam. How are you?'

'I'm fine, quite busy really...' I said firmly, determined to turn down any job she might have in mind for me.

'Oh, OK, only I've got a bit of an urgent problem and wondered if you could help?'

'I'm really busy right now - lots of roof repairs to deal with, so...'

'No, no ... it's not building work, it's Norton. Could you look after him until the weekend?'

'I thought he was with Deb in London?'

'He was, but she's on a course in Harrogate till Friday and asked me to look after him for a week. I was in London, so I stopped by and collected him. I was going to drop him back next Sunday to her place...'

I heard a sigh.

'It's my sister Jane. She's left her husband – *again.*' Claire sounded like she was letting go of a heavy box.

'...and so?'

'She's frightened of dogs. Really frightened. She got attacked by an Alsatian in Eastville Park when she was a kid. She's a couple of hours away on the train from Hereford. She wouldn't even come into the house with Norton here.'

'Umm...' I drifted a moment, trying to imagine what it would be like to be savaged by dear old Norton.

'Please Sam, I've no one else to turn to. It's only a few days.'

'OK. Bring him over. You've got food and stuff?'

'Yes, yes, everything you'll need. Thank you - *thanks* Sam,' Claire said, blowing me a telephonic kiss. Quite a turnaround from her usual snooty manner.

Oh well, he's not much trouble. He'll love riding in the van and can sleep in the kitchen by the back door. I'll walk him around the little park nearby.

I'd only just finished dinner when Claire arrived. As I opened the door, Norton squeezed his way in and bundled down the hall. I helped unload the double-parked hatchback, discovering he had all the doggie accoutrements of a *grand dame* departing for the summer season.

A cursory peck on the cheek and Claire was gone.

I gathered-up the various bowls, toys and bits of smelly bedding and made my way to the kitchen. As I approached I could hear the plastic clatter of the rubbish bin.

'Norton! You, you… naughty dog.'

The detritus of my culinary efforts lay scattered across the vinyl floor. Norton grinned, expressing a canine innocence that contrasted wildly with the yellow bin lid firmly jammed around his neck. I threw down his belongings and wrestled with his newly-acquired collar, both hands encountering something very slimy. I watched in horror as strands of gloop trailed through my fingers.

'I've been had…' I cried out, lurching to the sink.

I made up Norton's bed in the kitchen with somewhat more effort than I do my own, while he cheerfully padded about the house. I proudly called out to him, to show him his new quarters. Getting no answer, I made my way along the hall, checking the dining room and its dog-friendly wood burner, before reaching the living room. He had discovered the sofa and was now resolutely refusing to shift. That first night was to become a battle of wills that I would eventually lose. 'Tomorrow,' I waived a finger at his comatose frame '…there'll be a tough new routine.'

I was interrupted by the rarely-heard ring of the land line.

'Hi Deb! Lovely to hear from you.' I tried to steady my breathing at the sound of her voice.

'I've just heard from Claire. Thank you so much for this! I'm really grateful that you offered to look after Norton.'

I pondered on the 'offered' bit.

'No problem. He's a lovely old boy and I'm looking forward to giving him a little holiday.'

'Great. Josh isn't home until Sunday evening, so I don't mind picking him up either Saturday or Sunday, whatever is convenient for you.' Her voice flowed like honey over a hot crumpet.

'That's a lot of driving in one day. Why don't you come over on Saturday and go back Sunday afternoon? There's room to stay if you want.'

'Oh, what a lovely idea. I hope it's not going to trouble you too much.'

'Not at all, come and stay.' I sounded cavalier.

After a few more pleasantries we said our goodbyes. I replaced the hand set and slumped back, preoccupied in thought.

Oh, Dear God - Oh, shit!

What have I just done?

In an hour I'd gone from anticipating a relaxed, inebriated weekend with a few mates, to the challenges of catering to the needs of a dog and its owner. Deb – *my Debbie* - in this house, a house she'd never even seen. I contemplated the enormity of my offer, with the dawning realisation that my 'casual' living arrangements wouldn't come close to Deb's *minimum* standard of interior décor.

I started to panic.

'Oh no! The toilet. The bloody toilet. What on earth am I going to do?'

In the end, that particular problem was easily fixed. I bought a new one, installing it in a fraction of the time it would have taken to sort out its predecessor. I made a secret pact not to deface it before her arrival.

I had, by now, decided it was better *not* to bring up the subject of my recent explorations. Eventually Deb was going to inquire after the contents of her dad's toolbox. I had to steer clear of the painful description of my tearing, sawing, and then burning a collection of, probably very rare, antique manuscripts, books and maps that her father had obviously very deliberately stored. Damning evidence, if ever she needed it, of my unchanged irresponsible behaviour. Oh, hell, it didn't look good. Norton raised a questioning head, sensing my anxiety. I fondled his ears, 'Don't let on, mate. Mum's the word.'

15 Draper points the way

On Deb's arrival, I gave her a quick tour, nervously explaining that she could sleep in my room while I would make use of the sofa. The back bedroom had become my modelling workshop with far too much to move and reorganise. She smiled throughout the tour in a manner reserved for reassuring single, sad, middle-aged males. I made tea and produced some posh biscuits, as we settled around the kitchen table. Norton soon appeared offering up his best 'poor starved animal' pose as he dribbled near my left leg.

'So, Sam, how are you getting on with Dad's old tool chest? I've become really intrigued with all this after our day out at Avebury...'

I stared into her soft, trusting eyes and contemplated feigning deafness, but realised I had no choice. Sighing and, with puckered lips, I hesitantly told her the truth about my long night with the wood burner.

'You've been getting paranoid on that pot again, haven't you?' she responded, glaring intensely.

'No - *no*, it was the cider, those last three pints were really, really strong.'

'Jeez...'

Deb turned away and looked out of the kitchen window. Her face expressed all I needed to know about disappointment.

We sat in silence.

I took the opportunity to study the pattern on my Grandmother's biscuit dish and reflected on how deeply attractive plate designs once were. Norton shuffled closer before laying his dripping jaw on my recently washed and ironed jeans. I didn't protest. Eventually, Deb turned back and faced me with a deep thoughtful frown.

'Well, did you at least get something out of those books and maps before you burnt them?'

'Oh, yes. Lots of stuff, really good stuff. I've even discovered an alignment in Bristol. It's an obelisk, a dome on a building and a flaming urn thingy, just as described in one of Gordon's books.' I talked quickly.

She tipped her head down, raising her eyebrows a fraction as she studied my guileless grin.

'Show me?'

We set off with Norton's large black body squeezed into the footwell of the Transit. Heavy Saturday traffic held us up. On arrival, I offered to walk him while Deb headed purposefully for the obelisk.

'Where is it pointing?' she enquired as I approached.

'The alignment? I don't know, haven't checked. Do you think it's pointing somewhere then?'

'Of course it is! The inscription says that it was Sir William Draper's intent to have the obelisk and cenotaph moved from their original positions in the grounds of Manilla Hall. It looks likely that the Hall was knocked down long ago. Then the obelisk was moved to its current location. It may have symbolic meaning of course as: *'We are men, we are woman, we are illuminated',* but there is more to it than that. I can sense it.' She spread her arms out like a scarecrow, pointing first at the dome on Tower House, then south west to the obelisk now almost equidistant from us. Turning to the obelisk, she continued: 'It's not pointing this way towards the west with the Gorge and woods beyond. There's not much out that way as I remember.' She ran her finger across her lip in momentary reflection. 'That's towards the city isn't it?' She pointed along the alignment and out, beyond the grey domed tower. I studied her in silence, before turning, trying to visualise its path. There *just* might be considerably more to this obelisk business, I thought, grinning broadly.

'We're going to need a bigger map...' I said, feeling a surge of excitement.

After a detour to Stanford's, the map shop, we returned home. I quickly cleared the kitchen table as the kettle boiled, before unfolding the map and examining the familiar streets with renewed enthusiasm.

Using an old spirit level as a straight edge, I drew a pencil line from the obelisk through the cenotaph and across the road to the domed roof, then extended it across to the centre of the city, about a mile away. At first, it seemed that the line was going to pass through the medieval centre. The crossroads of High Street, Wine Street and Corn Street, where the High Cross once stood. But instead, it passed just south and through the east end of the nave of All Saints Church, one of the oldest churches in the city.

'That's where Edward Colston and most of his relatives are buried,' Deb announced. 'That end of the church must be about where his monument is. I went there on a school trip years ago. It's no longer used as a church, though.' She looked up and smiled as our eyes met. My heart lurched.

I paused in thought, tapping with an extended finger the position of the obelisk on the map.

'Did you notice on the inscription, when Draper was born?' I asked.

She scrawled through a dozen pictures on her phone before adeptly zooming in.

'1721.'

'And when did Colston die?'

Deb continued to scroll, this time scanning the internet.

'Hang on a moment, let's see what Wiki has to say about him. Ah-ha – 1721. Same year! That's quite interesting isn't it?' She raised her eyebrows.

It's often puzzled me that Colston's name has been used so much in Bristol. If the Council can nail something in place long enough, they will invariably title it Colston something or other and it's been going on for 300 years. The centre, the St Augustine's Reach part of it anyway, is dominated by a 15-story concrete office block of Sixties design with COLSTON TOWER emblazoned in large red illuminated letters across the top. At night, the sign is on its own, no other signs come anywhere as close in size or effect. It dominates the centre and can be seen way across the city. Who is it that feels the need, in the 21st Century, to revere Colston so graphically and on such large scale? ...And why?

I retrieved my battered edition of the A to Z from the dashboard of the Transit and flipped through the index. I read part of it out loud.

'Did you know that there's a: Colston Avenue, Colston Centre, Colston Close, Colston Court, Colston Dale, Colston Fort,' – I caught my breath, 'Colston Hall, Colston Hill, Colston Mews, Colston Parade, Colston Place, Colston Road, Colston Street, Colston's Alms-houses and Colston Yard ... all listed in here?'

'Don't forget my old school: 'Colston's Girls.' Deb said. 'Oh, and Colston Weir, don't forget the weir. Our gang of girls used to go there at lunch time for a fag – and sometimes to meet boys.' She cocked her head coyly and grinned, her flushed cheeks revealing considerably more about those teenage meetings. After a short, thoughtful pause, she continued. 'You know it's only a silly coincidence about his death and Sir William's Draper's birth, we mustn't read too much into that, Sam.'

I wasn't listening.

I'd started to trace the line back to Clifton Downs from its probable terminus at All Saints Church. It passed over the Cenotaph, isolated by an acre of grey paving slabs, before crossing Colston Avenue. The line appeared to pass through the centre of the sombre monument. Interesting, but not as intriguing as its next stop.

'What's the name of that large Art Deco building on Colston Avenue? Where Claire works.'

'Er, it's called - *Colston*. I think...'

'Have you got Google Earth on that fancy phone of yours?'

'Yes darling, it comes with all the trimmings,' Deb flirted.

This was the first time she had called me *darling*. She'd been in a very different mood earlier, I reflected.

'Can you find Colston Avenue on Google Street View?'

'Is that what you're looking for?' She offered me the screen.

'Can you check it for me?' But by now I had already guessed the answer.

'It says...' Deb squinted at the image, '...it says COLSTON in large letters over the main entrance.'

'Good, what else?'

'Three horizontal lines and then the number 33.'

'I knew it – *33!* it's that bloody number again. This is no accident, Deb, there's something going on here - *in this city!'* I looked up and into her face as I repeatedly tapped the map in emphasis. 'Something's up. Someone or some group or other, seems to have sufficient power in Bristol, to move the pieces around - the buildings and stuff – as if it was some sort of board game...' I spluttered.

'You'll never guess what else?' Deb turned the handset towards me.

'There are two enormous flaming torches on the face of the building, on either side of the entrance sign. They must be three metres high.'

'So, there are! Twin flames. How very curious all this is becoming.' I rocked my head gently, deep in thought.

'Do you think we might be onto something?' She tilted her head and raised her eyes offering a coy smile. Our eyes met and lingered.

Deb's short but full-on visit left me feeling inspired by our shared interest in the unfolding 'coincidences' and I resolved to become more focused on research. I loitered at work, limiting myself to simple tasks, while my thoughts strayed down more esoteric avenues. I'd hurry home as soon as I could legitimately escape, to devour another intriguing book or watch a YouTube documentary. Six months ago, I had no idea about any of this. Now I wanted to become an expert.

After everything I'd discovered about Avebury, the Great Pyramid at Giza, and my dowsing experiences, I'd become fascinated about the whole Earth Energy business, but I still wanted to find a documented explanation. I was hankering for some kind of evidence, if only to provide ammunition against Nick and Simon's scepticism.

And to my shame, I had to admit that Billy's 'crystalline planet' theory no longer seemed quite so whacky. I'd discovered that there were periods - way, way back in time - when all the major continents were fused together in one great big territorial mass. And then, over time, they'd gradually pulled apart. It was the breaking away of these land masses that created mountains, valleys, volcanoes, and the great fault lines that cause the earthquakes. So far, so rational. In fact, documented and proven geology.

But I was beginning to see a link with Billy's crystal theory, because the breaking apart of the continents wasn't random. The pattern of tear-lines from these tectonic shifts formed the outline of a tetrahedron. And a tetrahedron is composed of four equilateral triangles – one of Plato's sacred solids being an equilateral triangle. The stress lines caused by the continental drift described the outline of a cube combined with an octahedron – two more of Plato's magic shapes.

Where it became interesting was that back in the 1960s, scientists in Russia set about plotting the locations on the Earth's surface where there were measurable electromagnetic energy disturbances – places like the Bermuda Triangle and the Devil's Sea off Japan. What emerged was another dual crystalline structure, an icosahedron and a dodecahedron (Plato's Fourth and Fifth Solids). This seemed to be straying remarkably close to Billy's theory. These scientists created a model of the combined crystalline structures inside a globe representing the Earth and marked the node points where the angles touched up against the Earth's 'skin'. What they discovered was amazing: natural phenomena, like volcanic activity, clusters of ore and oil were sited at these hot spots. Then they found correlations with the sites of ancient civilisations, the birth places of major religions, philosophies and sciences *and* sites of sacred monuments – including the Great Pyramid at Giza, the Stone Heads of Easter Island and Macchu Pichu. In fact, over 3,000 monuments fitted into a grid that they laid over the Earth's surface, which could be seen in their diagram as 12 pentagonal slabs.

These scientists published their research in the Russian journal of the Academy of Sciences. They talked about a 'matrix of cosmic energy' that was incorporated into the Earth while the land masses were forming.

I started to grasp this wider perception. My own research began to fit with what I'd heard from Billy – and Denis. Perhaps a new understanding was emerging.

The final piece in this bit of the jigsaw was provided, again, by Plato. He was quoted as saying that if you looked at the Earth from outer space it would look like a ball sown together with 12 pieces of cloth. Described in geometrical terms these would be the 12 pentagonal faces of a dodecahedron.

Another of my discoveries was that Geodesy – the science of the measurement of the Earth's surface, may have originated in Egypt. Eratosthenes of Alexandria was recorded as the first person to estimate the radius of the Earth. So, the ancient Egyptians knew how to divide the planet into 360 degrees. Not only that, they built a lot of their most important sites on geometrically-related latitudes.

I owed Billy an apology for doubting his crazy ideas. It turned out he was way ahead of me in the knowledge stakes. And I needed to pick his brain some more.

We'd talked about another session working the trains. Now, more than ever, I valued his insights, but I also missed his beaming face. So, I sent him a short text inviting him to come and visit. I didn't have to wait long for his reply: *Hiya Sam Steam, love another smoke-up, Sunday morning 11am?*

He arrived, beaming his biggest smile.

'Where's all ya stuff gone, Man?'

'Well, it all needed a clear-up and sort-out. I've been a bit too busy to get around to it until recently,' I said, trying to look nonchalant.

We worked the trains for a couple of hours, taking turns to be driver and signal man (or '*Operations Manager*' as I later promoted myself). I could see how much pleasure he got from it, though I could think of nothing less cool for a mid-twenties man to be seen doing. Pity really, because there is something quite exhilarating about a well-marshalled goods yard. We took a break and between sips of green tea Billy produced a collection of well-thumbed photographs from his rucksack. Most of them featured his younger self in St. Kitts, standing in front of various steam trains. He pointed out one - *Old Smoky.* Number 5. The images were sun-bleached, and every picture framed by tall, dangly banana trees. I studied the familiar face of Young Billy, all shiny and new. He looked athletic even then.

'If you're not up to much after lunch, I wonder if you'd fancy getting out into the park, or maybe the countryside for a walk,' I said cautiously.

'Ta will be cool.' After a moment's reflection, he asked if I had ever been to Paradise Valley at Leigh Court.

'Leigh Court?' I thought for a moment. 'No, not for years.'

'I cycle there when I get a chance. I like it – 'tis good for the soul. How about going there? It's very good, we would like it.'

The Manor of Leigh Court and its estate is at the east end of Leigh Woods as they spread south from Brunel's suspension bridge. Paradise Valley is in the public part of the estate, tucked away discretely at the end of half a mile of pot-holed lane.

Norton would be enjoying this, I mused, as we made our way along a slippery path that had the engaging sign: *'To the Grotto.'*

'There is good energy here. I can feel it around me.' Billy looked thoughtful before offering a gentle smile. 'Did you bring your dowsing rods?'

'Yes. Mind you, I've not used them much recently to discover energy leys. More for discovering hidden water pipes.'

The track narrowed as the side of the valley got steeper. Looking east, the Avon Gorge came into view through the trees. The Suspension Bridge was only just out of sight as the gorge wound its way towards the city. We were 20 or 25 meters above the river, with the path offering a stunning vista, when Billy signalled our arrival at the Grotto. It turned out to be a simple seat, wide enough for two to sit on, beneath an arched canopy. We sat together silently taking in the view. The Avon meandered in front of us as it flowed towards the vastness of the Severn estuary with its awe-inspiring tidal drop, considered one of the highest in the world.

After 15 minutes of contemplation I'd had enough.

'My arse is getting cold,' I announced.

Billy returned my smile as we stood to leave. I prompted him to pick up on our discussion about Leigh Court; a subject he appeared very familiar with.

'Dis grotto is placed very carefully, Mr Sam. Some of the energies from the river rising and falling comes through this place.' Billy turned and with a playful smile, lifted his forearm up and down mimicking the whistle of a steam train. 'It's a meditation station, *woo-woo!*' he called out excitedly to an audience of trees, as we picked our way along the muddy path.

'It's part of a device t'ing. It gathers up the electro-magnetic energies that flow with the river as it moves up, down and in an' out of the gorge. Spinning the currents around in a great circle near the river in the field below us. The railway curves along part of it. It's cool Sam. It's tapped into near where the grotto is and funnelled into the side of the Court. Like a great Catherine wheel with only one firework on it.'

'How big is this circle?'

'Over half a mile. You can see it on Google Earth, Mr Sam.' Billy turned to me with a gentle smile and an expression that suggested it really was *all so simple*.

He pointed out a gap in the hedge to the east of us. I produced my dowsing rods and set out to locate the promised flow. The path was narrow, more of an animal trail, as I fought my way through bramble until I came to a small clear strip of grass. There was now a good view east towards Avonmouth. Billy followed through and watched closely as I walked at a tangent to the envisaged line, just as Denis had taught me at the Abbey.

I soon found something interesting.

'Oh yes. Yes, here it is, but I can feel more than one flow. It seems, well, complicated.' The rods swung together, crossing before swinging back into the 'open' position. This action was repeated a few feet on. I glanced to my left and glimpsed the large Georgian sash windows glistening in the spring sunshine.

'The house is about 100 metres away I'd say.' I checked with Billy.

He smiled mysteriously. 'There's lots and lots of energies and t'ings here about. The men that did this, they placed it all very carefully. They know exactly how to work these unseen flows.'

'Which men, Billy? Who knows about all this?' I said with a sigh as my shoulders dropped.

'Not always the architect boss knows. Often, they just follow directions. This is the knowledge of the Elite, the *illuminated* ones. What we see here is the Elite's doing. Many of them do not want the rest of us to understand and benefit from this knowledge.'

'But... like who?' I repeated my question, conscious of a deep frown spreading across my brow.

'First it was the Templars, Mr Sam, – then others, many others.' Billy raised his arms and spread them like an Italian explaining a car accident. He looked coy, though. He knew a lot more than he was saying. It's as if there was some great secret that he *wasn't* going to answer until the right question had been asked.

'I've read that the Templars knew stuff, you know, discovered knowledge and great treasure underneath that Temple Mount in Jerusalem. At the time of the Crusades.'

'Yes, Sam. The records have long gone but the knowledge is still with us. It's here.' He pointed towards the Suspension Bridge and the city that lay beyond. 'It's still here to this day.'

'How do you know all this? Who told you about it? How did you even know what questions to ask?' I was frustrated with the enigma that was Billy.

'I just know, I've always known. I'm an old soul, Mr Sam...'

We walked in silence among the redwoods, larch and oak, down a slippery path that led to the ponds and sat down on a fallen trunk. It felt as if we were quite alone, our thoughts only interrupted by the chatter of birds and the flow of a small waterfall. The moist air carried a strong scent. The wood was teaming with life.

After a brief silence, heavy with unspoken thoughts I turned to Billy.

'I feel that I'm on a journey of some sort, one that I'm not in control of. As if I'm being led gently by the nose, spurred-on by the occasional jerk. I was well set-up a few months ago. Just trucking along, minding my own business. Money coming in. It was all nicely organised, you know. No worries, as the Aussies say. But recently, since Nick's heart attack I suppose, pieces of some sort of fantastic puzzle keep falling into my lap. Especially when I don't even want to trespass into - *all this*.' I gesticulated, trying to conjure the right metaphor. 'I'll tell you what it's like.' I turned back to face him. 'Imagine someone giving you a giant jigsaw, say 1000 pieces, minimum. Only halfway through, you get the feeling it may be a trick, and they've put three or four different jigsaws in the same box, because just when you think an image is coming together, something else crops up that shows you a whole new picture? And yet somehow, I get the impression that all these different pieces are linked in some way.

I paused briefly to catch some stray thoughts.

'I'm trying to fit it all together. But maybe I'm just wasting my time?

Billy listened intently, as he absently swung his feet.

'But I have got a few sections together. Not without considerable help from you, I might say. Oh, and Debbie – bless her. Little pictures are starting to develop.' I used my hands to pluck at the air. 'I can make out vague-looking outlines, but not the bigger picture. I just can't get high enough to get the perspective I need. I do have a gut feeling that it does, somehow, all hang together.' I paused and studied the ground.

'There's more - much, much more to Bristol. Isn't there Billy?'

'Ya, man.'

'Can you help?'

'I can shine a torch for you, Mr Sam.'

His look of confidence inspired my growing visionary curiosity. It felt exciting; empowering even.

'Bloody great, Billy.' I laughed, adding, 'Come on then, let's go. I'll buy you a cider at the local!'

As we drove to the pub, my mind strayed back to Billy's mention of the Templars. I tried to recall what I'd read about the medieval order. It was humbling to accept that the twenty-something native of a small Caribbean island seemed to know more about my home town than I did. Clearly, a bit of revision was called-for.

The Order of the Knights Templar was founded in France, sometime around the beginning of the 12th Century. A kind of hybrid between soldiers and monks, they were a small band of noblemen specially-selected to protect Christian pilgrims travelling the dangerous route to the Holy Land. They set-up headquarters in Jerusalem, on what was believed to be the original site of King Solomon's Temple.

Fairly early on, their leader visited England on a fundraising mission. As a result, the Templars were granted lands right across the country, including, of course, Bristol. Over the next two centuries they gained wealth and influence throughout Western Europe and the Middle East. In fact, they've been described as the earliest bankers, because one of their services was to provide safe houses for pilgrims' valuables. The pilgrims could journey on, supplied by a cover note from the Templars that allowed them to draw funds from other Templar bases on their travels.

But as they continued to amass property and power, it made them a bit too much of a threat – especially to the Pope, who officially disbanded the order in 1312. He had many of the Templars in France executed, but they got off much more lightly in England, where their persecution was delayed and short-lived. Even so, the organisation was stamped out from that point on – officially at least. Rumours continued that they still existed as an underground organisation. What has spawned all sorts of legends in the intervening years, is that while they were in the Middle East they were reputed to have been given unique knowledge by the Sufis – the Islamic mystics. And these 'secret' insights would presumably have been handed down through later generations of Templars.

There seem to have been several hotly-disputed legends linking those Templars who may have fled to Scotland in the 14Th Century, with the subsequent formation in the Sixteenth Century of the Scottish Freemasons. And there's a further element of confusion surrounding the Order, because the modern-day Freemasons include several 'Knights Templar' members. But these latter-day Templars only date back to the 19th Century and the formation of the Sovereign Military Order of the Temple of Jerusalem. This organisation claims to have no direct descendance from the original

Templars and was founded to carry out charitable works and promote humanitarian causes.

Billy supped from his half pint, while I downed a big sleever, quenching a serious a thirst. The sun had made an appearance and I was in a good mood as we lounged in the garden of a quiet pub near Clevedon. I was keen to talk.

'It's funny you should have mentioned the Templars, Billy. There's not much information around about what they got up to in Bristol. Some pamphlets from the local history group and that's about it – very little in the way of records left anymore. I was also thinking about what the Masons might understand about the world that's not common knowledge. You know, the secret stuff and where it may have originally come from. I found this book in the library – *The History of Freemasonry in Bristol.*' Billy looked-up at first surprised, then with a wry smile creeping across his tanned face. 'It's an awful read, you wouldn't want to be seen carrying it around, but it did get me thinking.'

'Such t'ings as?' Billy asked.

'The Masons in Bristol certainly seem to have been very interested in the Templars. They had their own special degrees - levels of attainment that they awarded themselves. The highest levels are actually called the Knights Templar degrees. Some claim they are directly descended as Brothers since *'time immemorial'*. It's all very heady stuff, with their own 'Bristol Degrees' and big links with America. Interestingly, after American Independence, their first overseas Consulate was here in Bristol, in Queen Square. But, aside from that, what did the Templars know about this '360 divided into seven' thing? The heptagram around the Earth. *God's Latitude*... Did they get into all this dowsing and Earth energies stuff?'

Billy nodded and smiled in confirmation.

I continued: '...and what about all this global geometry; the Earth as a faceted diamond. I'm guessing they knew *exactly* why Avebury had been built - didn't they Billy?'

'Yes. The knowledge has been around for a long time. The Greeks understood this. They knew the Earth was round and *they* got their understanding from the Egyptians and Babylonians, who had the most advanced knowledge of all. They studied the skies carefully and recorded the celestial movements.' Billy looked relaxed but thoughtful.

'Right. So, the Templars came to Bristol because of ... all this *secret* knowledge?' I asked.

Billy shrugged non-committedly and sipped his cider.

I continued, 'After their dissolution, they used Bristol as a staging post for their exploration of the North American continent - didn't they? That's why

Bristol Keep was constructed. A massive castle to store their wealth while it was steadily redistributed. The idea that the Templar fleet left La Rochelle, their base in France, for Scotland at the time of their arrests, doesn't make any sense. The trip, either through the Channel and the North Sea or by way of the Irish sea and over the top of Scotland, would have been perilous at *any* time, let alone with the French fleet on their tails.'

Billy studied me thoughtfully as I continued, 'If you had several ships packed to the gunnels with gold and stuff, would you risk it all in some of the world's roughest seas? Logically they'd have taken the shortest route, knowing they had somewhere secure to stash it all at the end. Having your wealth stolen on land is one thing, but losing it to the bottom of the Ocean is pretty final, especially in the 14th Century...'

I took several gulps of tangy cider and returned to the subject.

'If you can use dowsing to follow a path across land, you can do the same over water. I've not tried it yet, but I'm convinced you can dowse from the bow of a ship as easily as you can across a field. Easier, I reckon, because there's no obstructions. You could tack from side to side, zig-zagging along the 7th Latitude - 51.428571 degrees-following the same flow of energy that passes through the centre of Avebury, but this time, east from the River Severn, pursuing an invisible, but utterly reliable path.'

'What gets in the way?' Billy enquired as if he already knew the answer.

'Nothing, apart from a little peninsular in Wales. The energy line takes you from near Clevedon on the banks of the Severn, all the way across the Atlantic.'

'To where, man?' Billy grinned.

'Nova Scotia, top bit, and only a few miles from where John Cabot landed in 1497. They followed the unique frequency of *God's Latitude*. Like following a stream to its source.'

'So, Mr Sam. You are sayin' that the Templars knew about America years before Cabot? That they had their own secret way of navigating that they used to get there? All from here - from Bristol?'

'Yes,' I replied quickly, '...and it's been their secret ever since.'

Billy's eyes shone. I don't think I had told him anything he didn't already know.

17 Masonic plots

A few days later I called Deb and I told her about my day with Billy.

'When do I get to meet him?'

'Oh, soon. Yes, you must meet him. He works shifts at the hospital. Never quite sure when he's about, but I'll call him in the week.'

The new map proved to be fruitful in revealing a previously hidden aspect to Bristol. It became a permanent feature on my kitchen table, rapidly acquiring cup rings and imprints from rainbow-coloured rice. I decided to re-read the tedious 'History of Freemasonry in Bristol', suspecting that there was more to be gleaned beneath its proclamations of brotherly love and Masonic lore. Maybe the Masons had their own alignments of significant monuments or buildings in Bristol?

According to the book, the earliest recorded history of Freemasonry in the city was from the mid-18th Century. The various groups would meet in pubs, but by 1816 most of the dozen or so lodges were in premises on Bridge Street, before they consolidated in 1872 at 32 Park Street - the premises they still occupy. They took over the former museum and lecture theatres of the Bristol Institute for the Advancement of Science and Art. Press articles mentioned the museum's *'Temple-like decoration and useful meeting rooms'*. Back in 1820 it had cost £14,000, having been funded by public subscription, but by 1872 the Institute had accepted an offer to sell, and moved to a purpose-built museum at the top of Park Street. This was courtesy of the charitable donations of W.H. Wills, the Bristol tobacco magnate - and prominent Mason.

At a meeting held to discuss the vacated premises at 32 Park Street, the building described as a *'most desirable property'* and the Deputy Provincial Grand Master was empowered to negotiate the purchase. The deal was soon completed, but the sale price of £5,960 represented surprising depreciation of £8,000 in 50 years of the museum's tenure. At the time of the transaction, the Honourable Brother Mason, William Cowlin, an experienced local builder commented on the purchase:

'Fools build houses; wise men live in them.'

It seems that the Freemasons got public subscription to build the Institute to their own specifications and then cannily bided their time for 50 years before acquiring it at great commercial advantage.

I had drawn a line on the map, from Cabot Tower on the summit of Brandon Hill, to Freemasons Hall in Park Street and on to the circular footprint of the Knights Templar Church in Temple Fee. It's wasn't a vague alignment either, but one that took in the gravel ring remains of the original 12th Century Templar Church, proceeding diagonally through the main entrance of Freemasons Hall, before climbing Brandon Hill to pass through the 1897 constructed Tower.

John Cabot's first sight of Nova Scotia was recorded as being at sunrise on 24th June 1497. This is the feast day of St John the Baptist and the most significant day in the Templar ritualistic year. The date is still celebrated by Templar lodges and Freemasons throughout the world, as they acknowledge the role of St John in instructing Jesus into the hidden mysteries of the Universe. So, did this alignment offer a clue to the circumstances of North America's discovery? Brandon Hill was originally known as St Brendon's Hill, after the 6th Century saint. His claim to fame was a journey he made, which was recorded in the 9th Century manuscript 'The Voyage of St Brendon the Navigator'. This described how he, along with 60 followers, journeyed West from Ireland across a vast ocean. Writers have speculated that this may have taken them as far as Newfoundland and maybe Nova Scotia.

18 Collecting thoughts

Another Friday night, and the King's Head was typically busy.

I realised I was going to have to be a bit more strategic in discussing my research. Simon, as an historian, was very knowledgeable about Bristol and, if approached the right way, could be of great help. But the more esoteric stuff I'd save for the denizens of Crumbly's café.

'Yes of course,' said Simon. 'Temple Meads station was named after Temple Fee, the peninsular of land on the south side of the river. The land was granted to the Knights Templar by Robert de Berkeley, Earl of Gloucester in 1145. The classic shape of the round Templar Church was completed about two years later. It's considered one of the earliest communities, maybe even the first in Britain as Temple Church in London wasn't consecrated until 1185, 40 odd years later.' He was clearly in lecture mode.

'Why round?' I enquired.

'Very common with the Templars. They built them like that all over Europe. Modelled after the round temple that supposedly sat where the alter of Solomon's Temple was. There was a big dig in Bristol in '72.'

'Yes, in 1872,' I said quickly. I thought this nugget would impress.

'Oh no, it was 1972. My old professor was in on that. Quite a bit of useful work was done.'

'Well actually there was also one in 1872.'

'Really...? Simon studied me carefully with a deep frown. 'I have *no* idea about that one. Anyway, they found the remains of a big shed next to the church. There was evidence of tanneries and other outbuildings as well. I've been saying for years that Bristol was much more significant to the Templars than has been generally acknowledged. It seems they did a lot of business through Bristol, with at least two ships registered and berthed at their own dock.'

'What were they trading in?'

'Wool - a lot of wool. They had a big place at Templecombe, about 40 miles south of here, and brought wool up for processing. They shipped a lot to France, especially to their big base at La Rochelle, and brought back wines, olive oil, dried fruit.' Simon sipped at his cider between sentences.

'I read that there was a lot of development in Bristol during their time here.'

Simon nodded. 'Well, yes. By far the biggest was the diversion of the river Frome in the mid-13th Century. A huge job. Probably the biggest engineering project in Europe at the time. The St Augustine's Reach was a hand-dug trench, massive in length and width. It transformed the commercial and strategic viability of the city. Though by the beginning of the 20th Century, it was mostly filled-in, as business went to less tidal ports. Redcliffe Bank was also built, straightening the river bank and allowing ships to berth on the Temple Fee side of the Avon for the first time. Yes, Sam, I think you could say the city was effectively remodelled during that period.

'It seems to me that once the Templars were dissolved, Bristol went into relative decline.'

'You *have* been busy, Sam,' Simon scoffed.

I ignored the taunt and added, 'Not only were St Augustine's Reach and Redcliffe Bank completed, but the castle was entirely rebuilt. I've seen the sketches. It was massive, with a 20-metre-tall monster of a keep. All very, very secure. It must have completely dominated the small town, which at that time, was mostly huts and fields. Plus, the first substantial bridge over the Avon was built, connecting Temple Fee to the city.'

'Hmm, I suppose so,' Simon frowned into his empty glass, 'You're right, the bridge *was* built about the same time. The Avon was diverted along a new trench that became the moat of the gated defensive wall across Temple Fee. Part of it has recently been exposed. You can still imagine its path, just follow the course of Portwall Lane. The Templars were *definitely* involved with that. We even have the receipts for that job.'

Rangi arrived, smiling radiantly, her black curls cascading onto a hand-knitted multi-coloured jumper. She sat down close to Nick, playfully patting his thigh and exchanging hellos with everyone.

I was compelled to add my own idea.

'It seems to me, that they were almost certainly one of the wealthiest organisations in Europe. They had the resources to transform Bristol - *to mould it to their own needs*. Bristol had been a bit of a backwater before their arrival, wouldn't you say?' I said looking to Simon for approval.

'Why are you bothering with all this, Sam? Bristol's a long way from Jerusalem,' he retorted; his tone betraying that his interest had waned.

'How are you getting on with your dowsing?' Rangi interjected, sensing Simon's growing irritation.

'Oh fine. It's proving to be a very useful skill.' I returned her smile. It was characteristically thoughtful of her to show an interest.

'Bloody bollocks...'

I had been so drawn into my chat with Simon, that I hadn't noticed Nick's glowering expression.

'There's no harm in dowsing, Nicky.' She turned to face him. 'Sam's just opening his mind up a bit, taking an interest in the world – that's all.' Rangi turned back with a broad grin and a wink and reached over the table placing her delicate light brown hand on top of mine.

‘Sam, why don’t you come over on Tuesday evening? Nicky’s at his squash night. I’ll cook that lamb with coconut the way you like it. *I’m* interested in what you’re doing, even if he isn’t.’ Rangi flicked her head towards Nick, in mock despair.

‘I’d love to.’ I glanced at Nick’s scowling face.

‘And I’ve got some ancient Maori secrets you might be interested in...’ she added with an enigmatic look and a wide South Pacific smile.

19 Maori tales

I started to feel anxious as I approached the converted chapel that was Nick and Rangi's home. Nick had shown increasing signs of irritation towards me and, as a result, I was looking forward to having Rangi to myself. She was proving a faithful ally in fuelling my new-found interest. But ... earthy and bohemian with an infectious smile, she was well-aware of her disarming skills. It was probable that I'd reveal more about my inner life than I intended.

The bang of the gothic door knocker echoed throughout the house. Rangi threw the door open wide and surprised me with a traditional *hongi,* the Maori nose kiss.

'It must be a couple of years since you've been here, Sam. Now don't forget to take off your shoes; you're in a Maori house now.'

Her long mauve dress billowed out as her bare feet padded across the wooden floor. I followed her to the spacious kitchen. This was part of a dramatic open plan home that was living room, office and kitchen all in one. Ten metres long and seven wide, it stretched all the way up to a vaulted ceiling adorned with carefully-varnished beams.

'Way too long. I just love this place. It's so different.' I stood near the centre, scanning the galleried walk that gave access to the bedrooms.

'Yes, it reminds me of the *whare puni* living-hut-of my childhood.' Rangi smiled, waving her arms around the open room.

'You've decorated it beautifully. Nice mix between Kiwi and English I'd say.'

'*Maori* - and English,' She corrected.

I opened a bottle of sparkling cider, sharing its contents as she started to serve the meal.

'Paua fritters to start!' she called from the cooker, where she was shaking excess oil from her famous mussel fritters. 'These should be sea snails. Sorry it's not authentic, Sam, but you can't buy the real thing here.'

'You say that every time I come over, but I reckon they're just brilliant.' I'd been hoping these would be on the menu. The real deal or not, they always tasted good to me. 'It's so nice to be here again.'

'You're a good man, Sam,' Rangi reached over to touch my hand as she began to sit down, offering me a gentle, empathic smile before adding, '...well mostly anyway.' She leaned her head in emphasis.

Feeling a little chastised, I retreated to the small kitchen with the empty plates and collected the aromatic lamb stew. Several small dumplings bobbed in a large, ethnic bowl as I returned to the table. The meal was eagerly consumed.

'Rangi, you've done it again! Loved it. One day you must show me how to make this stew.'

'Can't do that. I'd be giving away too many special secrets.'

'Ah.' I raised a finger and two eyebrows. 'Talking of secrets Rangi – so what's this *Maori* knowledge you've promised to enlighten me with?'

'Give me time, Sam. We need to clear away and make space to talk properly.'

As I stacked plates into the dishwasher, she produced a bowl of fruit and placed it on the small table in front of the sofa. Time to relax. I allowed myself to become enveloped by an avalanche of scatter cushions.

'I know that Nick is a very special guy, but this is a long way from your home. It must be so different from your village life in New - *no* sorry, Ao-tea-roa.'

'As a matter of fact, I was conceived *here* - in Kent,' she announced.

'That's news to me,' I replied, bewildered.

'Yes. Although both my parents were New Zealanders, they met in London in the Sixties. Dad, a Maori of course, but my Mum was a *pakeha*, a white Kiwi. When she got pregnant with me, they returned to New Zealand. Mum died when I was very young, and Dad moved back to the village of his birth. So, I'm half *pakeha.*' She flashed her bright teeth.

'I spent a lot of time with my *whanu* - family, Dad's relatives, as he worked away a lot. I had a special upbringing. I missed not having a mum of course and Dad tried his best. It was Paora, my grandfather, who was a *tohunga*, a priest or spirit man, who brought me up. He'd take me on long walks looking for wood fairies! Reading the small tiki stones that line the paths which no *pakeha* ever sees. That's why I'm a healer. Paora taught me how to see and *feel.* How to look with my eyes *and* my heart. To trust my intuition. Anyway, Sam, enough about me. Come on, how is it with Debbie...?' Now curled up on the opposite sofa, she motioned me to speak with a cupped hand.

I told her about our recent meeting and subsequent discoveries and theories. She probed further.

'I thought she was lovely when you first met. You two just *looked* like a couple.' Rangi leant forward and waved a finger. 'Don't cock it up again...'

I flushed with guilt.

'I'll try. It's not easy,' I stammered.

'Yes, it is.' She leant forward. I braced myself. 'It's called commitment. You've allowed yourself to get sloppy and dull these last few years. Drifting from one cider session to the next.'

I felt chastened. Imprisoned amongst the cushions and immobilised by her glare.

'Do you think Deb is good for me then?'

She smiled. Her eyes softened to express loving despair.

'Oh yes. And lately you've changed. You've lost weight. Got a bit of a sparkle about you. Even so - maybe a little less to drink, eh? More of the right kind of food.' She pointed to my belly.

'Oh, I don't know, really I'm...'

She interrupted. 'No, no, there's something else going on here. You seem more focused than you were. Like you've found yourself - with that project of yours?' Rangi leant over to emphasise the point.

I sucked through my teeth, trying to summon the right words to convey what was going on in my head.

'The *jigsaw*, I call it. Lots of jumbled-up bits of stuff. Facts and ideas that just come to me. I'm struggling to fit it all together,' I flustered. 'I know there's a bigger picture. Something wonderful, something...' I grasped. 'I just *know* that something really special is hidden here. Right here in this city.'

She narrowed her eyes and studied me contemplatively.

'I don't doubt it at all, Sam. You spoke about the Templars having their 'ley lines', as you call them, to navigate across the Atlantic.'

'I know it sounds like a mad idea...' I replied with a shrug.

'No, you might actually be right about that one. It's a great secret of the Maori, known to the *tohunga,* - that they used the stars and other ways, including that same method, to navigate the Pacific, just as the Templars may have done in the Atlantic. The Maori called them the *'lines of light'*. Our navigators were super-sensitive and could feel with their hands, in the way that you dowse, and some may even have been able to see the energy. The *pakeha* have no idea what we secretly understood about the world. What they teach at university is often way off the mark. They think we would have devised some mechanical thing to make it across all those thousands of miles of open ocean. Sailing from one little dot of an island to the next one. We did not. Our navigators were the elite. They understood the secrets of the priests. This is what you're looking for Sam. Except in a funny sort of way you're trying to understand it backwards.'

'I am?'

'Well, you're looking around at these curious buildings, monuments, obelisks, what have you, and trying to find the link between them. But you are only just beginning to understand the true, higher *divine* knowledge, behind their construction and placement. This sacred knowledge is normally only accessible to those who have spent a great deal of time studying and growing in self-awareness.'

'Sounds like I'm trying to short-circuit this *awareness* as you call it.'

'Well yes, in a way you are.' She stood up and walked slowly to the large double doors at the back of the house and studied her small, well-attended garden. 'You see, these navigators were the supermen of our culture. They had to stay awake for days, while being acutely aware of their surroundings. It wasn't just about following a path of light. No; they had to observe every detail about the ocean, its colour, texture, and smell. Even the *thickness* of it. They had a far greater understanding about the ways of the sea than the *pakeha,* who really have no idea, no idea at all.' She let out a sigh. 'They certainly didn't need the white man's tools, like compasses, maps or even sextants.'

She continued to pace between the doors and the large sofa,

'You see, the planet is strongly effected by very subtle influences. Most of this lies just beyond our normal senses, so for a long-time western science has missed it. Our world is subtle, it's *so* subtle, Sam.' She clenched a fist and shook her head in emphasis.

'When I was ten my uncle challenged me to swim across the bay near our village. There was sand all the way around and hardly any rocks. He told me to stand at the edge of the water and focus all my energy onto the large Pohutukawa tree on the opposite shore. Then, he *blindfolded* me, telling me to continue looking straight ahead. Now I had to swim to the other shore, to swim directly towards the tree that I had been focusing on.'

'I dived through the waves, I was young and very fit. I powered my way towards the other shore. I'd swam across the bay many times, it's not too far and a lot quicker than walking. So, I had an idea how long it would take. But time started to drag, as I swam on and on with no sign of the bottom. I was becoming impatient to feel that familiar soft sand. Was some trick being played? I stopped and found myself still in deep water. I removed the blindfold and could immediately see Paora were I had left him. He waved and smiled and was some distance away. I turned to look for the Pohutukawa tree and found that I'd swum out to sea, 50 metres or more away from the shore. I had swum right past the peninsular and into open ocean. I was amazed, I had set my focus on that tree.'

She paused, offering me the bowl. I took a ripe kiwi fruit and a large napkin. She seemed to catch her thoughts for a moment, before continuing.

'You see Sam, what I had not been aware of was the subtle influence of the outgoing tide. Little by little with each stroke I was being pulled off course. Do you understand what I mean by *subtle* and how powerful it can be? Big changes can come from small effects.'

'What do you know about Earth energy, then? I asked.

'When the kumara crop was ready, we would store them in shallow dish-like pits on top of hills. Directly in the path of the energy lines that flowed along the top. My uncle's job was to create a vortex by drawing another line of energy through the big one, the Dragon Line we called it, and over the kumara pit. He focused his attention to change the flow.'

'I've managed that. Denis the dowser showed me. He called them psi lines,' I added.

She smiled and continued. 'This vortex of energies helps to preserve the crop's chi energy; its life force. That way the crop keeps much longer. It's the same when it comes to burying people.'

'Wow, Rangi, you do make New Zealand sound really intriguing.'

'You should go sometime – you'll love it,' she said, smiling even more.

My fantasies about faraway lands, were suddenly cut short by the metallic clunk of the door handle.

'Hi Nick, I've been enjoying Rangi's great cooking. It's been a while...' I started to stand, offering a hand.

He smiled briefly, but instead of shaking hands, walked directly across the room to the kitchen.

'Is there any left?' He looked flushed and unsteady.

'Yes, of course, Nicky dear. It's in the oven already for you,' Rangi replied.

'I think I'll have another shower. The walk up the hill has got me sweaty again.'

He glanced across the room, offering a short nod and a tight pursing of the lips, before climbing the open tread stairs and disappearing into the master bedroom.

I lowered my voice and leant towards Rangi. 'He's pissed off with me – isn't he?' She busied herself fiddling with a large greenstone earring.

'It's not what you think, Sam. He doesn't care about you being here. No, not all.'

'Then why is he being so offish with me? I sensed something was up on Friday night.'

'It's Billy – he's jealous of you and Billy. He thinks you've, sort of, hijacked him. He's not seen Billy in weeks. He's got this thing about him being some kind of angel. Crazy really.'

I was starting to feel uncomfortable. Perhaps it was time to leave. I called up to Nick, who soon appeared wrapped in a large white towel.

'Cheers, Sam. Look, I'll catch up with you on Friday. OK?' He relaxed enough to return my grin.

Rangi and I embraced with a long hug.

'You've given me a lot to think about - thank you,' I said holding both her hands and squeezing.

'Keep on the trail, old Sam. You'll get there, wherever 'there' may be...'

The door shut with a thud. I walked down several stone steps to the pavement before stopping to take a deep breath. My outbreath turned into a long sigh.

So much going on...

The early May sun was starting to set as I meandered unsteadily along Devon Road. I reached the old railway bridge and made my way down the steps to the cycle path. As I approached the bottom I unconsciously looked up. My eye caught a council road sign.

Colston Road. BS5.

'Another one for the list,' I muttered and sauntered the rest of the way home.

The balance of my invoice from the extension job was eventually paid and I found myself cheered by a flush bank account. I decided to take a couple of weeks' holiday and invest my time in delving further into the world of Bristol's mysterious 18th Century merchant.

At the termination of the alignment from Sir William Draper's obelisk on Clifton Down to All Saints Church, just over a mile away, lies the marble tomb of Edward Colston. A full-size sculpture of the man lies on a metre-high pedestal. He is framed by a large inscription recording his charities and the foundations he was involved with, from around 1691 until close to his death in his 85th year, on 10th October 1721. Hospitals, alms houses, schools and churches all benefitted from his philanthropy. At least £70,000 of a fortune, estimated to be £300,000, was given away and much of it in Bristol, the city of his birth. His fortune would be the equivalent of around £4.5 billion in today's money. By any measure, Edward Colston was seriously rich.

Even so, there's not a lot of documented information about his life. The definitive biography: '*Edward Colston His Life and Times*' was published in 1852. It's a laborious read; the author was evidently paid by the word. A whole host of tributes are paid to this 'great and pious man,' and at times, reading the litany feels like wading through treacle. Other than that tome, there are there are a couple of books from the early 20th Century, plus a handful of leaflets and the occasional local news article. But Colston is not a popular subject; his links to the slave trade inhibit all but the most daring of modern historians. And yet his life spanned one of the most eventful periods in British history and the uber-wealthy Colston would certainly have had his fingers in a lot of pies.

What I found so interesting was *why* didn't he show up more in the historical records? Other than those two or three biographies, court records and some occasional custom receipts, not much can be found about him. He may well have been the richest man in Britain at the turn of the 18th Century, but between 1636 and his death in 1721, his name was absent from almost all social and court announcements. There was very little in the way of newspaper articles or contemporary records. His financial might appears to have been barely acknowledged throughout the historically-dramatic period from the 1680s to 1720s.

What I gleaned was that Edward was the first of 11 children born to parents William and Sarah. He came into the world on 2nd November 1636 in the house of his maternal grandparents in Temple Fee. A few days later, he was baptised in the ancient font of the nearby Temple Church, the site of the original round Knights Templar church and encampment.

Members of the Colston family had held the highest civic offices in Bristol since their arrival in the city in the 14th Century. Edward's father, William, had been a member of that most exclusive of Bristol's commercial fraternities, The Merchant Venturers, since 1634.

The Society of Merchant Venturers goes right back to 1497, when it helped fund John Cabot's expedition to Newfoundland. Since then, prominent people – even outside of Bristol – have been affiliated to it. Current members include Prince Charles and George Cary; less recently: Margaret Thatcher and Winston Churchill.

William was also member of the Corporation of the City, a Sheriff, and Treasurer of the Queen Elizabeth's Hospital School in Bristol. A staunch Royalist, he was to become a marked man and ultimately stripped of his office by Cromwell in 1645. Having reacquired his status in the Restoration of 1661, he became an Alderman and then Deputy Lieutenant of the Corporation of Bristol shortly afterwards. He died in 1681 and like many other members of his family, was buried in All Saints Church. The building probably adjoined his ancestral home in Corn Street, now long-since replaced by St Nicholas Market.

Edward's birth in November resulted in his being sent out to be nursed in the healthier atmosphere of the family estate of Chaunters Place. This was in Hambrook, in the Parish of Winterbourne; a small hilltop village about 10 miles north of the City. The estate has long-since disappeared, but its location is signalled by the presence of a 'Colston Close' situated at the end of a country lane bearing the intriguing name of Green Dragon Way. Records are scant, but it looks likely that he was educated at Christ's Hospital School in London after his parents fled Bristol at the time of Cromwell's protectorate.

Colston's next appearance in the records is on 24th June 1654, when, at the age of 17 years and seven months, he was apprenticed to a Humphrey Aldington, Mercer of London. There's a gap in the records from 1662, when he was 26, until 1672, when London's Customs House shows him to have been trading as a merchant. By the following year he had been enrolled into the Society of London Mercers. This effectively gave him the licence to travel and trade freely aboard.

So, what was he doing during that missing decade? He could well have been absent from England altogether.

His ancestors had long-established trading links throughout the Atlantic coast of Europe, the Mediterranean and as far as the Caribbean. He would have had several successful and influential relatives and family friends to call upon. At that time, the freedom of individuals to travel was a right for only a minority. Colston would have met merchants of diverse nationalities and acquired a working knowledge of their languages and customs. What might he have come to understand about the world that was beyond accepted common knowledge, through these multi-cultural contacts?

Back in 1610, his grandfather had been Deputy Governor of one of England's earliest but short-lived settlements in North America - at Culper's Cove on the Avalon Peninsular of Newfoundland. Could Colston have travelled to the then-unexplored North American continent? Maybe renewing his family's earlier trading interest?

One morning, my research into Edward's sea-faring adventures was interrupted by a steady 'tap-tap' on the front door.

'Hello Billy, - what are you up to?'

'I'm goin' to work now, but I have invitat-*shon* from Joseph and Patricia, my uncle and aunt.'

'Oh yes?'

He handed me a small envelope containing a hand-written note:

We would love to meet you and thank you

for your kindness towards Billy.

Please come over on Tuesday or Wednesday

next week for a meal, about 8.00?

Regards Patricia.

PS. Do you like goat curry?

'I'd love to, Billy. How about Wednesday? And *no* problem on the curry front either.'

Billy smiled, looking embarrassed as he smoothed his fingers through close-cropped hair.

'Yah that's good man. You come next week.'

He turned and walked briskly down the hill. His polished shoes complemented his business-like demeanour. He was on his way to the hospital, possibly about to save another stranger's life.

Should I say something to Nick about this? 'Oh, by the way Nick, Billy's invited me to dinner with his aunt and uncle - are you coming as well?'

I didn't want to lose Nick's friendship over the time I was spending with Billy. After all, it was Billy's choice who he spent time with and he did appear to enjoy our sessions together. But what about this father of his, who was apparently living in Bristol? Billy never talked about him. Were they in contact? Had they fallen out for some reason? Was this why he stayed with his uncle and aunt?

My queries about Billy brought on a sombre mood as my thoughts speculated on Josh's parentage. Could Debbie's child be mine? It all seemed to happen so quickly, our break-up and the baby's subsequent arrival. Those same brown eyes? It was certainly possible. After ten years of idle speculation, I was beginning to feel the need for a clear answer.

21 Callaloo soup

My eager preparation for dinner with Billy and family was interrupted by the phone.

'Oh, hello Debbie – *sorry*, Deb - how are you?'

'Fine. Just thought I'd let you know, I'm coming down on Friday afternoon, seeing the solicitor to sort out some more paperwork.'

'Do you want to stay here?'

'No. No, that's OK – thanks for the offer but I'll have Josh and Norton with me, so I'll stay at Claire's.'

'Has her sister left then?' I checked my watch while continuing to polish my shoes.

'Yes, finally. You sound out of breath?'

'Sorry - I'm just on my way out. Dinner with Billy's aunt and uncle...'

'Wow! Sounds like you're already part of the family.' Deb's gentle mocking caught me off-guard.

'No, I'm not trying to be part of the family,' I replied abruptly, surprising myself. That didn't come out at all well. Why was I being so defensive? 'Sorry about that, Deb ... bit knackered and I'm running late.'

'Don't worry about it. How about meeting up on Saturday? Josh wants to visit the SS Great Britain. We could walk around the harbour.'

'Lovely idea. Call me first thing Saturday morning. I can be free all day.'

I set off to Billy's with a light step, reflecting on Deb's call and the opportunity to get to know Josh a bit better.

Joseph and Patricia's house was a bus ride away. It was nearly identical in layout to mine; a typical late Victorian terrace. They lived on a quiet side road, one of the few places in Bristol you can find children playing along the narrow street.

I was greeted at the door by a tall, portly black man with a disarmingly brilliant smile and big round spectacles. He extended a large welcoming hand.

We exchanged greetings as I was ushered in.

'I've brought some Dragon Stout and a bottle of White.' I held a shopping bag aloft and gently jangled my offering.

'Dragon Stout!' Joseph exclaimed, with the expression of someone who has a long, intimate acquaintance with its smooth dark bitterness. 'You're most welcome, Sam. Come in and meet Ma.'

Patricia wore her hair in a tight bun, showing her smooth black skin to its best. Like Joseph, she was greying at the temples. I guessed they were both in their late fifties or early sixties. Her trim figure reflected what looked like a busy life. She reminded me of my mother when I was very young, with her billowing patterned dress and an apparent lack of makeup. I offered my hand and she gently shook it, looking directly into my eyes. There was a hint of coyness in her smile.

'Billy's been telling me about your wonderful railway. I hope he's been no bother to you.'

'No, not at all Patricia, it's great the next generation can still enjoy a rather old-fashioned toy.'

'That's no toy man,' Billy said, as he entered the room. He smiled briefly at his aunt before shaking my hand.

'Please Sam, sit down - you'll make the room untidy,' Patricia said, motioning me to a high-backed dining chair. Billy sat opposite, dressed in a plain white T-shirt that contrasted with his coffee-coloured skin. The room would have originally been the back parlour with a step down into the kitchen. It had been modernised, with the original kitchen area extended from half to the full width of the house. At the far end of the room was a large Victorian sideboard festooned with photographs and memorabilia.

Joseph slumped into a leather arm chair and, with a beatific smile, studied the table and the recently-deposited bottles of stout.

'Have you lived here long? I asked politely.

'Forty years, almost to the day, is that not true Ma - *Patricia?*' Joseph lent to his side and called to the kitchen.

'Yes. Our church helped us to buy the house soon after we got married. Bless and praise them. Without their help, we would have struggled to get our own home. How the young manage today, I've no idea,' Patricia replied between the clatter of pans and plates.

'She is always busy in the garden,' Joseph announced, nodding through the double doors and out into the well-groomed garden, now in twilight. The large kitchen window played the frame to an immense display of brightly-coloured blooms.

'She likes to grow flowers for the church,' Billy added.

Patricia returned from the kitchen, carrying a large battered aluminium pot. Clouds of steam escaped as she placed it carefully onto the pine dining table. I caught the aromatic scent of the Caribbean.

'Do you like Callaloo soup, Sam? she asked, signalling to Billy to start distributing the small pile of cutlery and plates.

'Never had it Patricia. Will I like it?

'Try it. It's almost the national dish of the St Kittians. Billy won't eat meat, so there's plenty. There's prawns in it - try some.'

It was delicious, and so was what followed, a pungent goat curry. Food that was obviously cooked with love and some sensitivity. Billy dined on a zingy mixture of rice, peas and ackee, sharing an occasional ladle with me. The yellow fruit of the ackee reminded me of scrambled eggs with its fleshy, slimy texture.

I asked Patricia if they had children of their own.

'We've not been blessed by the Lord, so it's been especially delightful to have our nephew coming over to stay with us,' she smiled, glancing across to Billy.

'Mum never married, so I have no brothers or sisters.' Billy added.

'We have great hopes for him, we're very proud of what he is doing.' Joseph reached over and patted Billy affectionately.

'My younger sister was careless and often impulsive,' said Patricia, pursing her lips.

'Quite a handful when she was young,' Joseph interjected as he raised his big brown eyes, gently shaking his head in recollection. 'Ma and Pa were not at all happy when they discovered Mary was pregnant, and from a white man,' Joseph added.

'Is that why she moved to St Kitts?' I asked.

'Oh yes. Yes, it was,' Patricia replied a little hesitantly. She opened her mouth as if to continue, but then stopped - clearly deciding not to air the family's dirty linen in front of a stranger.

We fell into an uncomfortable silence.

'But our uncles were pleased to see her.' Patricia cheered up. 'The pair of them lived alone on the Estate; the owner never visited. There are plenty of rooms there and a big, big long kitchen.' She opened her arms wide in theatrical emphasis.

'My Ma, she sorted them all out, she was the *big boss*.' Billy chortled.

I turned to Billy.

'How are you settling into life in Bristol?' I asked.

'Tis good the sun is about. I like the warmth, *and the light*.'

'And how are the studies going, you must be getting close to completing?'

'Yes, I'm learning. Learning lots. The staff are all good. I like my new friends at the hospital. Thar from every place in de world.'

'Making new friends, that's good,' I said reassuringly.

'Oh yes, Mr Sam. Lamin - he is a good friend and we spend time together. He's from the Gambia. We work same shifts. He has many family and friends back home.'

Patricia questioned me about my family and home life. Although flattered by her interest, I felt the familiar twinge of isolation whenever I was reminded of my long-departed parents. I wondered if they would have been proud or plain disappointed in the life choices I'd made.

My ruminations were suddenly interrupted.

'Joseph! You know that you can't drink the stout anymore...!' Patricia managed to mix commanding with compassionate to great effect. We had just finished the meal and Joseph had taken that as his cue to open one of the bottles. It struck me now, that I hadn't been offered a drink, other than water. The wine bottle remained worryingly unopened.

'Sorry Sam, Joseph has the Diabetes, and is no longer allowed his stout.'

'...or my lovely ginger cake,' Joseph pleaded.

'Too much processed sugar,' Billy added. 'They give us lectures about food; what's good and bad for us. It's a big, big problem, and some doctors even call sugar the White Death. It makes me a little sad that I come from an island that was once covered in sugar plantations.'

'It's a terrible poison alright,' said Patricia. 'The Lord in his wisdom has given us temptation, so that we can learn to better control our desires while we are here on our blessed Earth.'

Joseph looked suitably admonished. His dark jowls and large round glasses brought me in mind of Mole pleading with Toad.

'Talking of sugar,' I continued, 'I've been reading about Edward Colston recently.' Billy turned looking directly at me with a sly smile.

'Yes, Bristol's great benefactor! Huh! Benefactor to *some*,' Joseph exclaimed, resuming his attachment to his favourite arm chair.

'He might have had plantations on St Kitts 300 years ago, he certainly owned a large share of a sugar mill in Bristol. It would have made sense to have owned the growing of it as well. At the end of the 17th Century sugar was big business,' I said.

'Not a good man. He bought and sold slaves. My ancestors,' Joseph sat up, studying me carefully.

'...and mine, don't forget my ancestors too,' Patricia added.

The atmosphere cooled. Oh dear, this was a bad move.

We sat quietly for a few moments until Patricia broke the silence.

'We must always forgive, because the past is there to teach us to do better in the future,' she proclaimed.

'Our people were just another commodity to that man.' As Joseph spoke he let out a sigh, frustrated by the whole debate.

'The truth is...' Billy began to speak.

'Ah, yes, the truth Billy. We all need to hear the truth.' Patricia's tone was abrupt. Billy quickly turned towards me, avoiding her gaze.

'The truth is that this was over 300 years ago, when the world was very different. Slaves of all races were traded.' Billy sounded almost apologetic.

'And even today, there are still people in slavery. God help them all,' Patricia interjected.

'Billy said the other day that if it hadn't been for slavery there wouldn't be a black American culture - you know, Michael Jackson and that,' Joseph added, looking directly at Billy.

'Or athletes,' replied Billy.

'What do you mean?' I asked.

'The truth is...' Billy looked up at Patricia defiantly, 'that only the ablest slaves survived. The fittest, the strongest. The gene pool was distilled if you like.' St Kitts is very proud of her athletes. World-class from such a small population.'

'But Billy, that's not exactly a good excuse for slavery,' I said.

'No, but it is what happened,' Billy continued. 'History might say that in producing so much sugar, Colston and all those other merchants, brought more damage to more people for far more years. Sugar is highly addictive and destructive to health. He as likely made his fortune from selling the sugar, not trading the slaves.'

'It was a pretty cheap labour force that helped build his fortune,' I replied.

Patricia turned to Billy. 'That's enough about Colston. Joseph will need his sleep. Have you said all you need to say Billy?' She said, firmly turning to a slightly shocked Billy.

'Yes, that's all I want to say - Aunty Patricia.'

I got the impression that there was a battle of wills going on. Maybe it would have been better had Nick been there as well. I returned home unusually sober and now increasingly puzzled.

The Brunel Buttery on the edge of the harbour, is an undocumented Bristol institution that has survived for decades. Dispensing tea, coffee and an excellent bacon sandwich, it has changed nothing but its customers since Debbie and I used to meet up there. The dining is strictly 'al fresco'- on one of the two rows of trestle tables. The only shelter is from two small trees, whose stunted appearance is the probable outcome of years of abuse by small boys and urinating dogs. As I waited patiently for Deb and Josh's arrival, I recalled her irritation in the old days when I routinely landed a dribble of bacon fat down my clean shirt. 'I'm not going shopping with you looking like that,' she'd hiss bossily, and, to my surprise, I'd feel a glow of pleasure.

'Hello Josh. How are you?' I asked, as he bounded up to the table. I could see that Deb was still some way along the harbour wall, swinging a small multi-coloured rucksack. She soon spotted me and responded with an enthusiastic wave.

'We're doing a project on sailing ships, and I'm doing the SS Great Britain,' he replied, ignoring my question.

'It's not really a sailing ship, Josh,' I corrected gently.

'It's got masts; six of them.' His blond mop bounced around as he climbed onto the bench seat. He looked bright and shiny like a new pound coin.

'Actually, it's more famous for its ground-breaking iron hull and screw-type propeller, than for any sailing it might have done,' I said with authority.

'He had a funny name. Didn't he?'

'What – Isambard Kingdom Brunel?'

Josh nodded.

'That's because he took his wife's maiden name, the name she was born with, as his double surname,' I continued. 'Did you know that Isambard, means iron giant in Germanic? That's an old German language that no one speaks anymore.' He appeared unimpressed by the curious relationship between Brunel's name and his subsequent engineering masterpiece.

'Hello Sam.'

I stood up and lightly embraced Deb, kissing both her smooth cheeks and picking up the subtle scent on her skin.

'Where's the bacon sandwich then? I thought you'd be tucking into your second one by now!' she said playfully.

'Well. Actually,' I said, sitting back down, 'I don't really fancy them so much these days. They're a bit greasy, aren't they? But I'll have another tea if you're going to the counter?' I waved my empty cup.

We sat and chatted, planning the afternoon. I felt relaxed and rather excited at the prospect of the three of us spending several hours together. Deb proposed that we visit the SS Great Britain first, then lunch, then back along the harbour to the M Shed, Bristol's recently reopened community museum. Poor old Norton would have to wait in the sheltered car between walks along the harbour. The grand finale of our day would be a trip on the harbour railway, a half hour with steam in open carriages along two miles of track.

I'd not visited the SS Great Britain in 30 years and as we approached I could clearly see the ship's array of towering wooden masts, festooned in flags, as if awaiting the start of a great celebration.

'It was nothing more than a rusty hull when I came here before. Looks like it's changed a bit,' I commented, as we stood in line at the ticket office.

'Have you not bothered in all these years? Time you caught up.'

'When you don't have a family you....'

Deb held her hand up dismissively. 'You should have been more curious. This is one of Bristol's greatest attractions. They went all the way to the Falkland Islands for it. Quite a job.'

Yes, I should have been more curious. Her frequent visits in twin roles of school teacher and mother, amply qualified her as a guide. We clambered up and down stairs, visiting cramped dormitories with diminutive box-shaped beds, in contrast to the grandeur of the first-class dining room; all polished glass and white linen. I was struck by the significant changes since my last visit. Countless volunteers and businesses had been busy since then, marshalled into what was obviously a huge effort to bring the SS Great Britain back to life – and that included the story of the ship's creator.

Isambard Kingdom Brunel, whose extraordinary vision resulted in the SS Great Britain, was born in 1806, the son of a French asylum seeker. He was 20, with a good education in both engineering and mathematics in France and England when he went to work for his father. Marc Brunel had done very well in his short career as an engineer and inventor, but by the time Isambard was 21, his father was burnt out. Brunel senior demonstrated great confidence in his son by handing over the day-to-day management of a prodigious project to construct a tunnel under the river bed of the Thames at Rotherhithe.

Brunel was now responsible for one of the most formidable civil engineering projects in the world. Shortly after taking charge he was involved in a serious accident when part of the roof collapsed, flooding the tunnel. His perceptive thinking and bravery saved many lives and his reputation among the working men grew. It wasn't long though before the tunnel caved in again, this time killing six workers. Brunel was feared drowned in the filthy water. He had been seriously injured and was unable to walk properly for months. Leaving London for Bristol to recuperate, he become involved in an ambitious plan for a bridge across the 150-metre-deep Bristol Gorge. The bridge was considered the wonder of its age, and a favourite project of Brunel, but was never completed during his lifetime. He proved his extraordinary skills and confounded the engineering competition, with a design of great elegance and confidence, right the way down to fashionable Egyptian decoration. But by the time the bridge was completed, the Sphinx and other appendages had long since been budgeted out of existence.

But Brunel's greatest achievement must be the design of the Great Western Railway. At the time, it was the country's most ambitious rail route, from Bristol directly east to London. This would lead to a revolution in commerce, dramatically reducing the journey between Britain's two premier ports. The epic construction of the Box Tunnel near Bath, still in use today, resulted in the death of at least a hundred men, with many more injured. By now Brunel had earned the reputation of a man who, obsessed with the fulfilment of his vision, was prepared to endanger the lives of his workers.

After leaving the SS Great Britain, we sat down close to the harbour's edge. While Deb set out a carefully-prepared lunch, I headed for the liquid delights of the pub and returned armed with a tray full of glasses.

'I was re-reading up on Brunel. Did you know that he built an alignment into the Box Tunnel? Deb spoke between bites of falafel.

'No? What do you mean?' I replied with a frown.

'His birthday is on 9th April. He's got the alignment of the tunnel, east to west, so that you could look through the tunnel and, on his birthday, see the sun rise at the far end – if you were mad enough to stand on the tracks, that is. Its within half a degree. That's pretty close, isn't it?'

What a cool thing to do. I suddenly recalled Gordon's unread Brunel biography. It was still languishing on my alcove book shelf after emptying the toolbox. The old boy had obviously been a fan.

We sat for a while, mesmerised by the glinting water. Josh had disappeared, no doubt exhausting Norton further along the harbour wall.

'By the way, I forgot to ask, how did it go with Billy the other night?' Deb ventured.

'Billy? I'm not sure. It was an odd evening. Billy, well, he seemed in good spirits, but I sensed some tension from his aunt, Patricia.'

'What do you mean?'

'I don't know.' I sighed. 'I ended up feeling as if I shouldn't have been there. Don't get me wrong, they were very nice, the meal was great. She's certainly a good cook, but there was a bit of an atmosphere. Like they'd been having a row before I arrived.'

'I get more intrigued by Billy, every time we talk of him. When *am* I going to get to meet him?'

'Oh soon.' I paused, recalling his visits. 'It's not easy though, he's a generation younger than us and has his own mates. I like him. He's a very charming and intelligent bloke. Knows stuff, lots and lots of stuff and he's very discreet about it, certainly doesn't shout it out. I get the feeling he could do any job he set his mind to. Why he's only a cardiac nurse and not a full-on heart surgeon, God only knows.'

Deb called to Josh, who let the ever-enthusiastic Norton bound up. He quickly discovered the cake I'd saved for my final treat. I glared at him as he wiped the icing sugar off his jowls with an enormous purple tongue.

'*Fuck*,' I whispered.

'Sorry Sam – did you say something?' Deb enquired.

'Time we set off to the museum, perhaps?' I said jumping up and checking my watch.

We slowly made our way around the boat yards. Deb seemed increasingly interested, not only in my own research, but in surprising me with her own knowledge.

'I've been reading up about Nicholas Hawkesmoor, the architect. Have you heard of him?' she asked.

'Wasn't he rumoured to have been a Mason before there were supposed to *be* any Masons? Along with Christopher Wren.'

'Yes, he could have been, certainly. Wren seems to have been very interested in the Esoteric. There's a lot more to the layout of St Paul's in London and the surrounding area than first meets the eye. A bit like what we found here in Bristol. There was quite a change in attitudes to the world around that period; a kind of renaissance in thought.' Deb paused as she gazed over at the multi-coloured hues of the houses across the harbour in Clifton Wood.

'When was that exactly?' I replied.

'Between the 1660s and early 1700s, *and* incidentally, that's when Colston was around.'

'This could be fruitful.' I mused.

'I got interested because Hawkesmoor was involved in building Castle Howard, near York, around 1700. Do you remember the early eighties' TV series, *Brideshead Revisited*? It was filmed there.'

I nodded and grinned in recollection of the flamboyant Antony Blanche.

'Yes. Loved it,' I replied. 'Especially the teddy bear.'

'Well, I've been doing a bit of research and just about the biggest obelisk in the country is there, along with fountains, temples, pyramids – *yes,* pyramids,' Deb nodded knowingly, 'and a stunning, beautiful mausoleum. I think we should go there.'

I caught my breath as I registered the implications of her suggestion.

'York? Sounds like a bit of a hike,' I replied cautiously.

'We could go for the weekend. I've got an aunt who lives nearby. Maybe stay overnight? Josh would be with his Dad...'

A weekend away. Just the two of us? I skipped through a variety of pleasing scenarios.

'What a lovely idea.' I smiled encouragingly.

'We can use Dad's old Volvo. I could collect you. I've got to be back in Bristol in a couple of weeks anyway.'

'That will be nice, back to Bristol. More paperwork?' I said.

'It will *not* be nice...' Deb said abruptly. We stopped, turning to face each other as her smile dropped.

'I'm taking Norton to the dogs' home...'

'Oh no!' I replied, wincing at the idea of the poor old boy behind bars,

'I'm afraid so. He's too old and too large for the flat. Josh likes the fun bits of dog ownership but not the maintenance, if you know what I mean?'

'Oh dear. No, Norton won't like that at all. He'll miss his armchair. Poor old chap.' I felt a pang of pity.

'I've tried everything else.'

'No, no, he can't go there. Not the Dog's home.' I confronted her face-on. 'What about Claire?'

Deb looked blankly at the ground.

'No - her sister. Remember last time?'

'Oh shit, yes.'

We walked in silence towards the large warehouse repurposed as the M Shed. It gave me time to think.

Oh, how could I *not* do it? I've got the room and it's not too far from the park. He wouldn't be that much trouble, surely?

'I'll take him, Deb. Until we can find him a new, proper home. At least he's been to my place. He knows his way around the rubbish bin part of it, anyway.'

'You don't have to do this Sam,' she replied quietly.

'I do, and I want to. I couldn't bear to think of him being in a cold concrete cage with only a blanket for comfort. Have you still got his favourite armchair?'

Deb leapt up, hugging my neck.

What the hell. The poor thing was getting on and had obviously given and received a lot of love back from Deb's Dad. And my offer would surely generate a bit of karmic payback for burning Gordon's precious books.

The ground floor of the M Shed reflects Bristol's enduring relationship with vehicles of one type or another. Usually the faster the better. The display is dominated by a dark green double-decker bus: the Bristol Lo Dekka. I made my way to the back seat, breathing in the aroma of leather, rubber and youth.

Josh bounded ahead through the exhibitions before racing up the spiral staircase to the first floor.

'This room is all about dead people,' he announced, as Deb and I approached.

The three of us meandered around the atmospherically-lit displays. Photographs of local celebrities were displayed in moody shots, along with a large section devoted to Bristol's predilection to riot.

'Sam, come here, look at this.' Deb beckoned from behind a display.

I couldn't catch what she was looking at, as the view was hidden by a castle-sized oak door and frame. As I approached and turned the corner to stand next to her, my attention was immediately caught by a familiar sight.

'It's the '*Some Who Have Made Bristol Famous*' painting!' I grinned with the familiarity of it. 'I remember this. It used to be in the Bristol Museum at the top of Park Street. Yes, I've seen this before, loads of times. There must be about 50 people in it.'

'Look who's there,' Deb said, pointing at the substantial Victorian canvas.

There, on the front row, was Edward Colston. One of the few to appear as a full-length figure. He was dressed in a long black curly wig, natty crimson waistcoat and black buckled shoes; his right hand holding his chin in deep contemplation. As with his tomb at All Saints Church, and his statue in Colston Avenue, he was staring at the ground.

'Look at his hand, Deb, do you see? The index finger on his left hand, it's clearly pointing downward. Straight down.'

'You're right. Do you know, there was a picture of him at my school? I looked at it so often. I swear he has an extended finger pointing at the ground in that one as well.' She seemed transfixed by the enormous canvas.

'Odd how this painting has been tucked away in a corner,' I said, casting an eye around the adjoining exhibits.

'Funny - I've not seen a single reference to Colston here. And yet if you look out the window you can't fail to notice that the Centre is dominated by a large red sign shouting COLSTON TOWER,' Deb observed.

'I'm reading his biography - the big, sort of official one. On the inside cover there's a portrait of him from the knees up, with his school depicted in the background. In that one his finger is *definitely* pointing down,' I replied, absorbed by the image.

'So, either he had an enduring shoe fetish, *or* – could it be a kind of secret sign, to those in the know?' She paused as she studied the canvas. 'But saying what? I wonder'

'Maybe it's a reference to the Creator,' I said, before quoting:

'Man's life consisteth not in the abundance of the things which he possesseth; and that he walked not in the smooth beaten path, - but in the rough, less-trodden road whose end is in happiness and glory.'

'Did Colston say that?'

'Yup.' I grinned, rocking on my feet.

Suddenly, my eye was caught by a figure at the extreme left of the canvas. Standing side-on to the viewer, in full 18th century dress uniform was a senior soldier, his hands resting on a sheathed gold-handled sword.

'Who is *that?* He's the only subject in the whole group not looking out at the audience? He's staring intently at Colston. Right into his eyes. Why is he doing that? Who is he Deb? - Deb?'

Deb silently passed me the guide map, each figure codified with an outline drawing and a number referenced by an index down the right-hand side of the sheet. She ran a finger smoothly down the index before stopping, tapping repeatedly. It read:

Sir William Draper.

23 The immortal Colston

It was beginning to feel like I was being stalked by Edward Colston's ghost. His hold on me prompted me to delve deeper into his story. Even when I tried to take a break from him, little nuggets of information would fall my way that would rekindle my curiosity. Repeatedly popping up, like some weird game of whack-the-mole, were the numbers 33 and 72.

Colston's will (33 pages) was a dense but quite revealing read, thanks to the insights it provided into the mind and character of the man shortly before his death. His testament was that of a serious, careful man, but with a twist of the mysterious.

I discovered that he lived for so long that by the time he died, he had no close surviving relatives. He never married and had outlived his immediate family. A major beneficiary was his grand-niece, Sarah Colston. But she would only receive his bounty *'if the man she marries would be of sufficiently amenable personality as to alter his surname within six months of marriage to that of Colston – immutably, so that all progeny would carry forward the name of their benefactor.'* This seemed not so much a will as a bid for immortality, from a man who possibly felt isolated at the end of an unusually long life.

The Trust that managed the major part of his immense wealth *'to the use of them and their Heirs for ever'* consisted of five individuals. Thomas Edwards, the Elder of Bristol, an old family friend and solicitor, and his son Thomas Edwards the Younger. This would have kept the legal management of his funds within one family for a long time. Then, Francis Colston, who is referred to as his kinsman, without specifying in what way they were related, and Robert Carr, a silk merchant from Ludgate Hill in London. This was probably the same Robert Carr who was a close confident of the then Duke of York, a very significant member of the Establishment. The final member of the Trust seemed to have been the recipient of the bulk of the money. Henry Hoare was a banker, whose father, Sir Richard, the former Lord Mayor of London, had founded one of the earliest private banks, C Hoare and Co, in 1672. I was surprised to discover it still exists, with just two surviving branches.

Henry was known as 'Good Henry' because of his philanthropy, funding several churches in London. He purchased the impressive Stourhead Estate in Wiltshire in 1717. This was also the same year as the 'official' foundation of English Freemasonry in London. The Estate certainly took on a very Masonic appearance. His son, Henry, inherited within a year of its purchase. He decorated the Estate with elaborate garden ornaments, lakes, temples and one *very* large obelisk. At some point, the original medieval Bristol High Cross, a seven-metre-high, heavily carved monument, ended up in the grounds. It had once stood within a few feet of Colston's tomb.

During his lifetime, Colston lent out considerable sums, acting as a banker to other merchants. And yet with all this wealth he chose to rent his home. In the Spring of 1689 he acquired the lease on a relatively modest three-story property in Mortlake, Surrey, and remained there until his death in 1721. The interior of the house was reputedly austere, and he lived modestly with just four servants: his carriage driver and gardener, Arthur and John; a housekeeper, Alice and a female simply listed as 'Black Mary.'

It would have been natural for Colston to have followed his father into membership of the exclusive 'Royal Africa Company'. The RAC had the licence to trade with the West Coast of Africa and this included its market in slaves. Colston became a member in 1680 and regularly attended meetings for the next ten years, but beyond 1692 there was no longer any mention of him in the minutes. During his active years, he rose to the position of Deputy Chair and was able to *'put William, Prince of Orange, on to a good thing,'* by gifting him £1,000 of stock in 1689. This would have poured quite a lot of cement between him and the Crown, and yet, interestingly, there were no records of any court visits that I could find. Had Colston been deliberately keeping a low profile?

The traffic in human beings was a staple revenue stream for Bristol merchants for centuries, and was declared by the Mayor, in 1713, *'to be one of the great supports of our people.'* By 1755 there were 155 Bristol merchants engaged in the trade. But the city couldn't seem to make its mind up about Edward Colston. There was no denying that amongst other ventures, he had been a successful slaver whose political and religious views verged on outright bigotry. Flip the coin and on the other side he was a major philanthropist who would pay off the debts of total strangers incarcerated in the debtor's prison. To this day, his name is writ large across the city and no visitor can escape his presence. A large statue of the man leaning on a walking stick or maybe a surveyor's rod, yet again looking down to the ground, is positioned on Colston Avenue, the busiest intersection in the city.

He probably earned a fortune but gave significant sums away. In 1709, during a period of intense food scarcity, when staples had risen to twice their usual price, Colston gave £20,000 to the London Committee for the relief of the poor. A vast sum at the time. He donated large amounts to both Christchurch and Bartholomew's Hospitals in London.

Then, in 1713, he contributed towards the cost of rebuilding, to his own design, the tower of All Saints Church in Bristol. The tower is one of the most unusual ecclesiastical motifs in the country. It rises in two steps to over 25 metres and is capped by a stone dome, possibly emulating the Dome of the Spirits in Jerusalem. This cap is surmounted by no less than eight flaming vessels, with a further four marking out the corners of the square tower four metres below.

Colston amassed a fleet of at least 40 ships, but during his career never once insured a vessel. Fortunately, he never lost one either. There is an astonishing account of one of his ships, which, punctured in the bow, had the hole plugged by a dolphin that had been drawn in by suction. As a result, the crew were saved. Another ship was lost at sea for three years and then amazingly, returned with crew and hold intact. Colston's response to this miraculous reappearance was to instruct both the ship and its contents to be sold for the exclusive benefit of retired seamen.

By 1708, at the age of *72,* he was *'inclined to retire from business'* becoming a recluse at his home in Mortlake. But maybe the most extraordinary aspect of Colston's life was discovered 122 years after his death and can be found in a footnote on the very last page of his biography '...the Life and Times.'

'In the year 1843, while the Churchwardens were making some improvements in All Saints Church, Francis Edward Colston, the then descendant and representative of the family, expressed an anxiety that they should avail themselves of the opportunity, and endeavour to ascertain the exact spot where the remains of his Philanthropic ancestor were deposited. This was done, and the lid of the coffin was removed, in the presence of the Treasurer, Vicar and Churchwardens, and Mr. Henry Penton, from whose Memorandum we quote, 'The immortal Colston himself, lying in all the apparent tranquillity of sleep. The features were so perfect, as to be readily recognised; so much so, that it is not improbable that a cast of his head was taken for the celebrated monument of him in the church, - sculptured by Rysbeck. The face was covered with a sheet, quite strong and perfect, and a diaper cap or napkin on his head; his cravat and shirt exactly of the make and form of those sewn on the same admirable monument in front of the vault. The whole was sacredly and immediately closed and replaced; a leaden plate being soldered on, inscribed – Edward Colston, 1721.'

After 122 years, Colston's mortal body should have been reduced to bone and dust, but instead, his features were *readily recognised.* Colston may have achieved the immortality he craved, not only through the extravagant use of his name throughout the city but at a corporeal level as well - through the immaculate preservation of his bodily remains.

The *immortal* Colston?

'How'd you sleep?' Deb gently inquired.

'Not so good...'

'Hmm, oh dear, I imagine it wasn't very comfortable?'

'Oh, I think there was much wrong with the sofa. Nice length and breadth and that gold trim was appealing. It was the clear plastic it was wrapped in that gave me the feeling of sleeping on an oversized condom.' I grinned wryly.

Deb gunned Gordon's old Volvo up a small incline as we passed the fields of 'God's Own Country,' East Yorkshire, on route to Castle Howard. The night before we had spent with Dillis, an aunt of Deb's of some distant variety, who obviously didn't care for anyone contaminating her pristine home and wasn't going to countenance any 'funny business,' under her roof.

'I'm really, really sorry, Sam.'

'That's OK. It must be difficult for her, and even for you, to think of yourself as 'single' with Josh and his Dad in the background. I wouldn't imagine you exactly feel footloose and fancy free.'

'You do understand - *don't you*?'

'Yes – *yes*, of course I do,' I lied.

'Anyway, she only had a single bed in her spare room; I just don't think she has that many visitors.' Deb pressed hard on the throttle and the heavy estate mustered another team of horses. I turned, looking out of the side window, apprehensively assessing the distance to the deep drainage ditch.

'Well, Norton didn't fare any better, I could hear him from my room, making terrible little whines every ten minutes. Glad I brought his basket and an extra blanket. Garages are such cold, drafty places - poor old thing. How could she make him sleep there?' Deb pursed her lips.

'She's a little, shall we say – *OCD*, isn't she?'

Deb rolled her eyes and nodded.

I warmed to the theme.

'Dinner was interesting.' I paused in reflection. 'Great pork pie. They certainly don't do pies like that darn-*sarf*. It was the radish-infested salad I struggled with though.'

'Oh God, oh my *God!* She is bonkers.' Deb laughed.

'...and the pickled onions,' I continued 'six each, for heaven's sake. One is enough. It was probably a good thing we didn't actually, you know - sleep together.'

Deb giggled like a teenager, her laughter infectious.

'A right proper Yorkshire salad that was,' I said, attempting the accent.

'She *was* sweet though.' I continued, 'That homemade wine, what was it - parsnip?'

'Not sure what it was. 'I had the most amazing dreams, though.' She tipped her head back, her honey-coloured hair laying with almost perfect symmetry across her shoulders.

'There we are.' Deb nodded towards a small hill in front of us.

'Stone me, what's *that* doing in the middle of Yorkshire?'

'This is the '*Monument*' Sam. It marks the beginning of the Stray, an arrow-straight road that runs for several miles across the valley to the edge of the Howardian Hills. I've printed a local map from Google Earth, you can see it quite clearly.' She leant behind me, pulling a blue display book from the seat back. Several A4 prints were carefully slipped inside. Her teaching skills coming to the fore. 'It must be 15 metres, maybe more.'

The top of the stone column flowered with large, flame-like ornamentation.

'Looks like '*the-shaft-of-illumination*' to me,' I bellowed and spread my hands in mimicry.

'It was. At one time, the flames coming out of the top were so bright, you could see them flicker from one end of the valley to the other. From York to Scarborough on the coast.'

'Bloody hell...'

'This is a *very* special place Sam, there's a lot more to see. I've done a bit of homework.' Deb gave me her serious look and I felt my heart swell against my ribs.

'Wow, this is a seriously impressive driveway,' I said, as we continued our progress along the undulating Stray.

'This first gate is the Carrmire Gate. See the castellated walls at each end with towers stretching out from either side of the road.' She pulled the car to the grass verge, allowing an impatient driver to pass.

'It's like something out of the Crusades, but weirder,' I said in awe. 'Look at the entrance with those obelisks surrounding it. They do look rather odd; castles and obelisks together.' I took a couple of photographs before we set off to our next, even more promising-looking gate, about half a mile along the Stray.

'It looks like there's a bloody pyramid sitting on top of that arched entrance, it's huge. Wow! Deb, this is even weirder than the Carrmire gate, it's so, *so*... What a strange thing to do,' I said, nodding in bewilderment.

'Now look more carefully at that entrance as we approach. What do you see on the other side?' Deb nodded ahead with a grin and big brown smiling eyes. Something was silhouetted in the distance just beyond the gate. I looked hard as the car rose and then dipped on a rolling switchback, leading us towards the gateway.

'No shit! There's a bloody great obelisk on the other side. Must be enormous. It's perfectly in line with the road. It's moving up and down into the exact centre of the entrance arch. Just like…' words failed me as I watched a giant phallus entering and withdrawing from the gaping arch of the gate – 'bloody hell!'

'Early 18th Century erotica on a grand scale,' Deb announced triumphantly to my very slack jaw.

We circumnavigated the obelisk's 30-metre tall shaft and turned east towards the car park. It was still early and only a few of the hundreds of daily visitors had arrived. We stopped and sat in silence, absorbed by the bold images we had just experienced. I opened the window and let out a slow, quiet sigh, breathing-in the scent of the rural June air.

'What a bloody entrance, when did you say all this was built?

'Oh, it all went up between about 1700 and 1730. It was mostly Hawksmoor's work. He was Wren's pupil in the 1680s. He did those spectacular churches in London that we're always going to visit on school trips. Vanbrugh supposedly did the fiddly bits on the main house, but he was no architect, more a visionary and playwright. That's when he wasn't in prison of course...' Her smile lit up the car; she was in her element.

'I've never seen so much esoteric stuff in one place. Who *is* this Hawksmoor character?' I wondered. 'He, the owners, or someone, was obviously trying to make some sort of statement here. Unless obelisks, domes and flaming urns were the trendy 18th Century equivalent of garden gnomes?'

'Thought you'd like it. Come on, there's more to see…'

I was smitten.

We liberated a very eager Norton from the back seat and collected a small rucksack containing lunch from the boot. The plan was that we'd visit the grounds first, saving the interior of the house for later, if we had time. Ahead was a wide, grey, gravel path that passed across the long south face of the house before gently curving to the south-east. The path ended in a temple-like lodge about half a mile on. I ogled the extravagant decoration. Acres of fine Georgian glass and blonde stone illuminated Castle Howard like a beacon of confidence. This was a palace in East Yorkshire.

'Actually, the owners were not really top-drawer aristocrats. It was Charles Howard, the third Earl of Carlisle, who built this.' Deb waved her hand across to the statues that loitered in the formal gardens surrounding the large ornamental fountain. 'His ancestors owned a fortified castle near Hadrian's Wall and came from the border country between Scotland and

England. They were certainly rich though, but not *that* rich. Charles Howard took a lifetime lease from his grandmother for the land. It's not a vast track, but it's enough to say to the world that you have at least – *arrived!'*

'You can say that again,' I gasped.

'...and here we have the Temple of the Four Winds.'

The building had a small dome sitting on a square base with four arched porches as entrances, mounted on a raised stone platform. It looked like a folly. We climbed a dozen steps and peered through ornate windows into the temple's single room and admired its intricate geometric tiling.

'What's down there?' I pointed towards some ruins that lay along a boundary wall.

'That's what remains of the Temple of Venus. It was demolished in the 1940s,' Deb read from her small note book.

'Let's walk down and back through – what is it called?' I unfolded the map. 'Raywood, that's it, towards the north face of the house. We can check out the lake and then walk back out past the car park and back down towards the Pyramid Gate.'

She stopped and looked about her in panic.

'Where's Norton?'

'He's already halfway down the track - see. He seems to be enjoying himself, tail up nose down, let's just hope there aren't any rabbits around.'

After a cursory look at the neglected remains of the temple, we turned towards the house and walked through the wood. Twenty minutes later we were considering the half-filled bowl of a 35-metre-wide reservoir; its central pedestal unadorned. Perhaps Neptune once stood on this podium, grasping a menacing three-pronged trident.

As we walked past the north face, our attention was caught by a children's play area, all primary colours and jumbled slides. This obvious recent addition jarred uncomfortably with the elegance of the manicured landscape.

'This is the vantage point they always filmed Brideshead Revisited from isn't it?' I ventured.

'So, you did at least some research before our trip.' Deb flicked her eyes in mock sarcasm.

'Yes, well, I watched Brideshead again. Well most of it anyway. I've been busy with Colston and the Bristol stuff.'

'Oh yes?' Deb replied, her voice rising slightly in interest.

'Trying to understand what this connection between Colston and Draper is all about. I told you, didn't I?'

'What?' Deb wrinkled her forehead.

'Those three biographies I found in your Dad's box, that escaped being put into the fire: one on Colston, one on Draper and another about Brunel. I can't for the life of me see a connection between the first two and Brunel, other than maybe Bristol itself. There was an old VHS tape as well, but I chucked it and can't remember what was on it...' I paused and feeling a twist of anguish, turned to face her.

'I'm so sorry that I burnt your Dad's stuff, Deb, I am really, really sorry, I feel foolish now for getting so paranoid. If I still had those maps and books I would have been so much further down the road in understanding all of this.' I gesticulated wildly in frustration. 'What an idiot I've been!'

Deb replied with a shrug, before flicking a mischievous smile. She clearly was not *that* attached to her Dad's memorabilia.

'I can see why they filmed Brideshead from the north face, it's not nearly so disturbing, is it? I said quickly changing subject. 'No occult monuments or other fiddly eccentricities to confuse the viewing public.'

Deb read from her little note book: 'George Howard had three daughters, a son and a wife who eventually left him. Apparently, his son was both boring *and* self-obsessed. The eldest daughter gambled away a fortune after marrying against his wishes and the middle daughter married a serial adulterer. Charles ended up living alone for the last decade of his life. But he did quite well for a while when he was younger, especially when William III was around. For a short time, he was the First Lord of the Treasury. The most important political post in the realm. He was a liberal, a Wigg and a member of the very exclusive Kit-Cat Club.'

'Colston wouldn't have liked him. He didn't care for liberals and from the complete lack of Christian icons around here, I would say he wasn't much of a God-botherer either. Well, not in an organised religious way.'

'There's a small family chapel attached to the house though,' Deb replied.

'Yes, well you would have had to display some sort of Christian reference just for the sake of form. But all these obelisks, pyramids and even Atlas holding up the zodiac in the middle of the fountain, it all speaks to me of something far more exotic.'

'Come on, let's walk down to the front part of the Estate; there's a massive mausoleum and another pyramid to be found. We can stop and have a picnic by it.'

The Mausoleum loomed-up from the expanse of a smooth close-cropped hay field. Large and shaped like a child's drum, it was topped by a shallow dome supported by a ring of 15 columns 15 metres high. It was precise, powerful and looked like it belonged somewhere else – perhaps on an Athenian hill. I scanned around and noticed to the south, in the half distance, a pyramid several metres tall. Like the Mausoleum, it was isolated by fields of yellow hay. Here was another fragment of ancient Egypt; a squat testament to the fact that something quite strange had been superimposed on this rural Yorkshire valley 300 hundred years ago.

'I expect you could see the pyramid from the house. It's big enough!' I said, quickening my pace, eager to explore the next item in this 18th Century Disney World of the esoteric. 'So, what's this pyramid all about then?' I enquired, trying to keep the lid on my excitement.

'It says that it's got a room inside. Must be that door.' Deb pointed to the base of the pyramid's streaky black stone. 'It contains a bust of Charles's grandfather.' Deb looked puzzled, 'What an odd thing to do, build this thing and stick a bust inside it?

'Time for a tipple?' I said, unpacking the wine from the rucksack.

'Only a little. I am driving after all.' She smiled. Her cheeks had caught the morning sun. We lay down and inhaled the sights, sounds and smells of mid-summer. To my right, another castellated wall extended to a round, arrow slotted watchtower. In the hazy heat I began to fantasise that we were refugees from the film set of a creaky Errol Flynn epic: 'The Knights of the Crusaders' or some such. It was not the only thing I imagined. Deb stretched out beside me on the blanket, looking up to the wide, open sky, reminded me of times long gone. If only they could be recovered, I mused wistfully.

Enough of that. I tore my thoughts back and distracted myself by counting stones.

'Did you know, there are 33 courses of masonry in this pyramid, if you include the missing capstone,' I said brightly.

'Are there really?' She rolled onto her side and studied me through half closed eyes.

I recounted the stones then busied myself assembling the remains of the picnic, struggling to keep my fantasies at bay.

'All this was built around the time that the first accurate survey of the Giza pyramid was undertaken. That must have led to some raised eyebrows when they discovered all that sacred geometry built into the design. They must have wondered which culture was the more advanced.'

'You've certainly been doing your homework, Sam.'

I smiled, flattered by her interest.

We fell silent as we watched a couple and their dog approach from a wood to the south-east.

'Norton's not on his lead. I should really ... with another dog approaching,' Deb said.

'I wouldn't bother. He looks too knackered to trouble another dog.'

The elderly couple stopped, passing the time of day as their own ancient labrador took a cursory interest in Norton, before joining him in the shade of the pyramid.

'We retired here a few years ago, just down the hill, near the village. It's lovely but the walk through the wood is getting a little too much for Poppy.'

'We thought of going through the wood on the way to the Mausoleum, there'll be more shade, I suppose.' Deb nodded towards the slumbering dogs.

'It's quite a long walk,' replied the man, slapping a walking stick to his stout boots, summoning the recumbent Poppy.

'Take this path.' The woman held a frail arm to the east. 'When you get to the funny statue thing, turn left and go on past the other pyramid. It's not far from there to the Mausoleum, though you can't get in there anymore, can you Gerald?'

Funny statue? Pyramid? What else was there to discover?

As they moved on, I hustled a reluctant Norton into life while Deb packed the rucksack.

More curious monuments? I felt the thrill of exploration return as we set off towards the woods.

'Oh look, here we are.' She pointed along the path to a little junction.

Fifteen minutes later we found ourselves in front of a heavy stone pedestal, moss-covered with age and neglect. It was topped by four sweetly grinning cherub faces surrounded by foliage. The combination was somehow reminiscent of the moment of birth. Thrusting its way through them was a small stout obelisk sprouting more foliage around its tip. The whole monument seemed to throb with earthy fecundity.

'Goodness, I wasn't expecting this,' Deb said in a higher voice, 'It's all rather erotic, isn't it?'

'Oh yeahhh.' I grinned. 'It's very *thrusty*. It looks like it's about to spring forth prodigy – maybe a wood elf or something.'

'I think you mean progeny,' she smirked. 'I wonder what the Temple of the Four Faces actually means?' She was circling the monument, studying the map while keeping a close eye on its the pointy summit.

'Doesn't your notebook tell you?' I replied.

'Nope. Nothing about this or the next one.'

'Come on, this way.' As she motioned me to take a new path leading deeper into the woods, I noticed Norton was no longer bounding along but plodding behind, his arthritic right hip obviously complaining.

After about 300 metres heading north-east, we came to a small clearing to find the second promised monument.

'Weird-looking pyramid.' I was confused.

'Looks half-done somehow, like the blocks have no mortar course.' She brushed her hand over the smooth dark stone. 'It's like the baby of the other one. How tall do you think it is?'

'Five, maybe six metres,' I replied.

'No inscription. No nothing. Not even a word about it in the guide book.'

'Strange that it's buried away in the wood like this. Why would you want to do that?' I shrugged.

'Let's move on to the Mausoleum, come on. Once we've seen that, it'll be nearly tea time.' She made it sound like an incentive to coax a reluctant pupil.

Even so, we didn't make it as far as the Mausoleum. Norton's hip was giving him too much grief. We took the straightest route we could across the rolling hills, to the house and its promise of shade and refreshment. Although we didn't see it close-up, the Mausoleum is so large that even from several hundred metres away, Hawksmoor managed to convey his pre-eminence as designer of houses for the dead. We sat in the shade and enjoyed our well-earned Yorkshire tea as we surveyed the extraordinary landscape. There was so much to take in. Too much, in fact, for one day's visit. We agreed to postpone a tour of the house. The prospect of a return to Castle Howard with Deb was loaded with significance and allowed me the smallest glimmer of hope. Could she really be contemplating a future for us?

'Like over-ripe camembert.'

'Oh, Jesus, Sam, that sounds terrible.' Simon furrowed his brow as if trying to manifest the odour.

'It's worse. That's just his breath. You can't begin to imagine what emerges from the other end...' I glanced to the floor, despondency etched on my face.

'Didn't Debbie say anything?' Simon asked between thoughtful sips of cider.

'Well, yes and, er, no. I didn't actually ask her specifically, if you know what I mean. I had slept with him before in the same room. I must have been too drunk to work out who was responsible then. It can be eye-wateringly bad.'

'Can't you have him put down?'

'Oh sure, that would go down *really* well. Sorry Deb, I had your Dad's dog put down on account of his appalling breath. No - I'm just going to have to get used to it. He's a dear old thing, very affectionate and pretty smart, too.' I recovered my sense of humour, nodding towards Simon: 'Anyway, where's Nick tonight?'

'Oh, I forget to mention. He'll be along later with Billy.'

'Yeah? Oh, great.'

'He's been teaching him squash. I think he's been going even more regularly since the heart attack. Secretly, I think he likes it. Billy's a novice, so he's got a chance of beating him,' Simon said with a flick of a sly grin.

I hadn't seen Billy since before the trip to Castle Howard two weeks earlier. I'd been busy adapting to having an old dog in my life by spending more evenings at home. My little stacks of unread books grew daily. For each one I read, two more would be bought. Finding pieces of the Bristol jigsaw and pursuing the enigma of Colston was demanding increasing amounts of my time.

'Hi Nick. Hey Billy. How's it going?' I studied each in turn.

'He's good – a quick learner.' Nick looked flush, with pearls of sweat or shower water glistening on his temples.

'Oh, I'm taught by a master. Nick's a clever player.' Billy was looking smart and cool as usual, effortlessly arranging a stool on the other side of the table.

'It was a good workout, I enjoyed it,' Nick said, smiling at a coy Billy.

With Rangi's recent arrival, our Friday night group was now complete. Old Tom, sitting next to me, nursed a tankard and muttered to me about shelves. He casually mentioned that he'd seen Billy in the pub several times prior to Nick's heart attack.

'Why would he want to come across town to drink in this pub?' I pondered.

'He's a funny looking fella all right. I reckon he was looking out for someone...' Old Tom was adding to the mystery.

'Maybe he had some sort of premonition about Nick's heart attack.' I was contemplating this when Rangi leant forward.

'How'd you get on at Castle Howard, Sam?'

'Great. We got on well, had a few good laughs. Saw some amazing stuff. You should go Rangi, you and Nick. It's very beautiful. There's a lot to see.'

'...And how was it with Debbie?' Rangi raised an inquiring eyebrow.

'Deb? She likes to be called Deb these days. Anyway, well it was nice, spending so much time together. Gave us a chance to relax. But we did *not* sleep together, if that's what you're getting at,' I replied meeting her gaze.

I'd enjoyed my evening with Rangi and felt relieved that there was a kindred spirit so close by. Her Maori stories had inspired me to press on. It was good to know that other cultures and races had similar esoteric ideas and traditions. I talked about the obelisks and pyramids and my idea that there are alignments and patterns hidden away in the landscape. She soon switched seats with Old Tom. Billy sat opposite, looking conspicuous in a close-fitting black T-shirt and black track suit bottoms. He never seemed to wear anything with a logo or name on it. No shouty labels for Billy.

'What about Colston? What more have you dug up about him?' Her black corkscrew hair tickled my bare arm as she turned.

'Colston?' Put it this way ... if it's been written, I've probably read it – *twice!*'

I recapped what I knew of his life, including a further sliver of detail that had cropped up in an obscure legal document.

'Just before he died, Colston and his grand-nephew bought the River Avon, from the source to the River Severn. Locks, stocks and floating barrels. Quite a sound investment, I would have thought.'

'Gosh, who would own it now?' Rangi asked.

'Haven't a clue, to be honest. I've become really intrigued with Colston though. But I've no idea where it will all end. I know there is more to uncover about him and Bristol. I just wish I hadn't destroyed that bloody box.' I ended with a long guilty sigh.

'*What* box?' Rangi frowned and leant closer.

'I didn't tell you, did I?' I sat back and gritted my teeth, offering Rangi a thin smile.

'It was an old toolbox I found in the loft at Deb's dad's place. It was up there on its own, nothing else, just stashed away in the corner. Deb didn't want it, so I took it home. It was full of documents, maps and books and one old VHS tape. I burnt it all in my wood burner after a session with him.' I nodded towards a drowsy Old Tom.

Rangi drew back, her mouth twitched in contemplation.

'So, what about the contents? Did you take any notes? What can you remember?'

'Not a lot. I read it through the night I opened it. Just thought it was a random load of weird junk. I didn't understand much of it anyway. Gordon probably just stashed it in the loft to get it out of the way.' A note of defensiveness was creeping into my voice.

'Oh dear, Sam,' Rangi paused, grinning but with a look of concern. 'You do know, don't you? That box was meant for you to find...'

My stomach dropped, as my glass clanked down-hard on the table.

'I know. I've been in denial since my trip with Deb. I might have destroyed an amazing stash of knowledge.' I looked to my feet in despair.

'Don't get me wrong, Sam, but didn't you think it a little funny that you were the only one of Debbie's old friends to be invited to her dad's funeral? It had been ten years, Sam. Did you not think it all a little peculiar?' Rangi's warm eyes focused accusingly on mine.

'This just makes it worse. The more I learn the more I realise what I lost in that mad, drunken, stupid – *thing* I did!' I shivered in recall. 'I haven't been really drunk since.' I let out a long shaking sigh hoping none of the others would notice.

It was all so obvious. Gordon painstakingly selected the books, maps and documents along with other clues. What was on that tape? I bet every bloody little thing was important. I tried to recall the maps, remembering the names; Cabot Circus and Temple Circus. Why call these maps after a shopping centre and a traffic island that didn't even exist yet?

'You were distracted by Debbie, weren't you?' Rangi interrupted my thoughts, offering a sympathetic smile.

'Yes, I know. Oh, bloody hell!' I sat back into the chair emptying my glass. 'But why me? Why choose me? I'm just a builder who happens to be his daughter's ex-boyfriend...'

'Don't put yourself down, Sam. You've done that way too much over the years. Gordon chose you very carefully, that's why he left you that telescope in his will. That was the bait to get you to attend his funeral and meet Debbie again. He knew you would offer to help clear the house and eventually find the box. He knew you still cared for Debbie and would help. It was all set up. You played your role perfectly, exactly as Gordon, bless the man, had planned.'

'You mean apart from the bit where I incinerate it all. - Oh *fuck...!*' I clenched both hands, digging fingernails into my palms.

'He obviously wanted this information to become public after his death and left you the clues that would allow you to work out what he, and maybe other people, had been up to. A bit of a treasure chest really. *I think he wanted the world to know what he had known in secret...'*

I slumped further.

'There were three books that didn't get burnt. I took them out when I first opened the chest. I stashed them in my book cupboard, so I missed them when I burnt everything. But no, the thing is, they were just regular books that you can buy anywhere. That's why I took them out.'

'What were they?' Rangi inquired.

'Biographies, all three of them: 'Colston – His Life and Times', Sir William Draper and one on Brunel. Colston and Draper were both born in Bristol, but Brunel wasn't. Though he did spend a lot of time here, he said it was his favourite city. I'm thinking that the three of them were Masons and that was the reason the books were in the box. But I have found a connection between Draper and Colston, with that obelisk, dome and urn alignment on Clifton Down. Oh - and that strange business with the painting at the Museum.'

'Yes. You told me. Anything else? Who was this Draper fella?' Rangi asked.

'Who was Draper? If you like cricket you may have heard of him, but otherwise...' I shrugged. 'He was involved in setting out the rules of the game. His dad was a Customs man in Bristol, so a modest start. He must have been very bright and determined because he won a scholarship to Eton which basically set him up. He passed through Cambridge University while signing-on in the Army, ending up as a Lieutenant General. He famously held the city of Manila to ransom for a million in gold from the Spanish; hence Manila Road in Clifton. It's where the dome I told you about is.'

'Nothing else?' Rangi said.

'Well, only that Colston died the same year that Draper was born, but that's just a funny coincidence.'

'When exactly was Draper born, was it *after* Colston's death?' Rangi sipped her cider and studied me closely.

'I don't know. His biography just says 1721. I've checked him out on the net and there's even less written about him than Colston. I don't remember anyone giving an actual date of birth.'

'I suggest you check that out, Sam.' Rangi spoke slowly and deliberately. 'He was born in Bristol, wasn't he? There will be something *somewhere*. They tend to hang on to baptism records.'

Rangi paused before continuing in a different tone.

'I think you should get off your arse and do some real research. It's obvious to me that there's a lot more to this.'

'I'm doing research. Doing it all the time.' I sat up and frowned in defence. 'In fact, I'm planning on a trip to London soon, to check out where Colston lived. I've only got so much time, you know. I do have to earn my living.'

'Get-on-with-it-Sam.' Rangi dropped the words out.

'I'm thinking of going to Mortlake, actually. That's not so far from Wandsworth.'

Rangi's mood changed as she grinned '...and Debbie no doubt.'

'Mortlake? Did I overhear? You might be going to Mortlake?' Billy swivelled to face Rangi and me.

'Oh, yes Billy. Probably the Saturday after next.'

'I would love to come up with you, if you're going in your van. I've friends in Putney I can stay with, we could see Mortlake together.' Billy's eyes shone.

'Yes, of course it would be great. You'll get a chance to meet Deb. You'd like her. I'm not planning on staying though. Have to get back for the dog.'

I supped my cider as I reflected on Deb and Billy finally meeting. I wondered what she would make of him.

The next morning, I set off for Glastonbury with Norton soon asleep in the foot-well of the van. I was eager to escape the confines of the city and promised him a cool, wooded walk. Crumbly's offered a sanctuary from a world I was beginning to feel at odds with. The small group at the café accepted me and appeared genuinely interested in my research. No one jeered or laughed as I struggled to explain new ideas. It was a retreat, an aid to inspiration, a group of eccentrics, and they were happy to help. I had privately christened them 'the Ponytailed-ones', though hardly any of them had long hair. I always left Glastonbury with an armful of books and a head spinning with new perspectives. Today's visit was to prove no different.

'What a lovely old dog – is he yours?' Sophie gently inquired, smoothing Norton's black coat.

'Yes, I suppose he is. He's a lovely old boy; he belonged to the dad of an old girlfriend. The owner passed away and...' I smiled at Norton's handsome but now slobbering face, 'I've ended up with this old boy, haven't I?'

'He must be hot. Shall I get him some water?' Sophie offered.

'No, not to worry, it's on its way. Colin and John are at the counter.'

I was surrounded by a gaggle of dog lovers. It was another warm day and the courtyard in front of Crumbly's was lively with chattering tourists and sedate locals. To the uninitiated, Glasto' comes as a bit of a shock. At some point the small former market town spawned a hypermarket for the mind, body and soul. The main street is devoid of the usual symbols of corporate mass production, and instead encapsulates the knowledge of the ages. Wicca, Druid, Hippy... all beliefs catered for in an almost seamless sweep of esoteric shops and vegetarian cafes.

'More cake, anyone?' John said, as he stood and checked over our small gathering. His faded orange singlet stretched across his belly like a drum skin.

'I'll pass thanks,' I said, patting my flat stomach.

He sauntered to the till, his brown cowboy hat adding to his jaunty demeanour. By the time he returned, two tables had been slid together to accommodate further arrivals.

'John Michell's, *The New View Over Atlantis* was a seminal book. He connected a lot of dots about what our ancestors understood. Though fragments of this once-universal knowledge can still be found around the globe; Aboriginals, Hopi Indians - the Chinese,' said John.

'...and Maori,' I interjected.

'Yes indeed. There are complex sacred sites on widely different continents, that appear connected by measure and geometry. As Michell said: *'A great scientific instrument lies sprawled over the entire surface of the Globe,'* John replied.

'The Chinese have Fung Shui universities thousands of years old,' Colin added above the murmured agreement of the audience.

Tall John continued.

'Oh yes. The whole country was considered a garden that was tended and moulded to conform to a science hundreds of generations old. Now we're supposed to believe it was all just junk, a *pseudoscience.* As if the Chinese would breed complete dolts for generations. They would *literally* move mountains to improve the flow of an invisible force that western science says does not exist. Nonsense. When the British started to build the railways in the 19th Century, the Chinese argued that you cannot build a railway with a completely straight path. It would adversely affect the *lung-mei* or dragon paths. This may have been self-evident in the past. Who's to say that our ancient ancestors didn't directly experience these energies? There's no doubt that the science of geomancy was both advanced and universal. Druids, Pythagoreans and the Gnostics all understood. They shared the same *gnosis.*'

'This knowledge, it all eventually went underground in the West, didn't it? I asked.

'Yes, the Masons hoarded a lot of the secrets for themselves but there were other groups. A lot of mystery schools. Some still existing, that go back thousands of years. Membership is often strictly by birth, from father to son for generations. All very exclusive and discreet. Restricted to just the elite, the same close-knit families...'

'Like the Howards of Castle Howard, you mean?' I said.

'Yes Sam, I think you're onto something. I reckon there really *is* something hidden in plain sight. Laid out across the landscape. Erected in our towns and cities. There, right in front of us muggles. But most people are too blinkered, too comfortable with their ignorance to look for it,' John added.

'Like what, though?' I asked.

'Well, take obelisks. What do they mean to you, Sam?'

'Pointy concrete pillars? War memorials? Phallic symbols?'

'Ah yes, well for starters, they're not usually made of concrete. They're made from materials containing a lot of crystal. And that's because crystal is an excellent conductor of electromagnetic energy.'

'And what's the point of that?'

Colin jumped in. 'Have you ever wondered why graveyards are so full of obelisks? Wealthy Victorians, especially the Masons, believed that after death, the soul continued to resonate. By plonking an obelisk over the body they'd be radiating their soul and maybe even fast-tracking its journey up to the heavens.'

'Oh right. OK. But what about those huge obelisks dominating the big city squares all over the world?'

'Well of course, they're very important beacons of power,' John said. 'They radiate earth energies on a grand scale. Like phone masts – we can't see radio waves, but they're being transmitted all the time.'

'Wasn't there some story years ago, about a plan to cap 100 of the most prominent obelisks all around the world - with gold?' asked Colin.

'Ha – yes!' said John. 'Gold, obviously, is a tremendous conductor, so they'd be super-charged. In fact, it only happened in a handful of places. The cost would have been astronomical. It's an interesting thought, though: the global landscape one great big electromagnetic network, with all these spikes amplifying energies or intentions emanating from the seats of government. Washington DC, London, Paris, The Vatican...'

After our discoveries at Castle Howard, the fact that obelisks could have a function beyond being purely decorative didn't seem quite as outlandish as it might have done to the average tourist.

'And there are plenty of larger examples of ingenious architectural manipulation,' added John. 'Three thousand years ago man lived in harmony with nature. The food source didn't come from a factory to start with. They lived comfortably enough to invest huge resources into structures that had no obvious production or defensive purpose. All over the world these sacred sites may have been built for a specific and, until now, hidden purpose. What if their primary function was enlightenment of some kind? Something we can only dimly perceive? Built for the very transcendence of consciousness...'

Tall John studied his audience as he theatrically opened his arms, waiting for a response.

'The churches have often hijacked the sacred sites for their own purposes; building directly over ancient stone circles,' Sophie added.

'I think they were harking back to a time when there was no religion that placed itself between you and your experience of God. You held God within you,' John replied.

'You perceived the world in its *entirety*. All was an expression of a benign divinity. No separation between man and nature.' John dabbed at the remnants of his cake, before continuing. 'I think the Templars were onto something. They did come across knowledge that was not the same as the distorted vision of the Vatican Church. A much older, more accurate source of worldly wisdom. Including knowing all about the earth 'grids'- those patterns formed by the many frequencies of energy that invisibly flow around us. It seems that our distant ancestors used crystals to enhance and transmit the effect. A kind of low-tech circuit board. Locating them on nodes of energy lines and often perfectly aligned to solar and lunar movements. The funny thing is that they left very little else around. Few palaces, docks, houses; just the remains of a bunch of consciousness-empowering temples that we would struggle to build today.'

'What was it that they were after?' I asked John directly.

'Immortality, conscious immortality – *maybe*...' John shrugged before continuing his impromptu discourse. 'Otherwise, what else were they built for?' He scanned his captive audience.

'It's not that we've found much in the way of artefacts, you know, tangible, physical things at these sites. What else would drive man to these extraordinary lengths, if not for the chance of immortality? What else is there? I mean once you've got a roof over your head and a meal on the table and no threat of anyone taking it away from you, what's next? Any sacrifice is worth a chance at immortality - isn't it? The Druids taught that not only do we reincarnate, but we can retain the memory of our previous lives. All those experiences carried forward. You can also consciously guide the process to target where, when and how you reincarnate. This is what they were up to and that's why they often borrowed money from fellow Druids for repayment in the next life. There's plenty of evidence that the light from the sun and the moon influences all of nature. They were amplifying those effects using these consciousness machines.'

Colin broke the thoughtful silence.

'Maybe it all worked really well, and these enlightened souls all buggered off to somewhere nicer; another planet altogether. Leaving us poor saps behind. No wonder this place is in such a mess, if all the really smart guys left...' Colin shrugged despondently, coming to terms with his status as abandoned reject.

I collected Billy from his aunt and uncle's house and we made our way through the early morning traffic towards London. I was excited at the thought of a whole day chasing Colston and having a chance to spend more time with Billy.

Colston's only confirmed home outside of Bristol was Mortlake, in what is now a suburb of south west London. He lived there from 1689 until his death in 1721. I was nurturing the hope that maybe something of that era had survived and might provide another clue for my jigsaw.

The plan had been to meet Deb mid-morning at a café in East Sheen, the village adjoining Mortlake. She had recently visited the local history group in Richmond and had armed herself with maps and other bits and pieces, but as it turned out, our meeting plans were aborted. Martin had had another serious malfunction involving a business conference that conflicted with Josh's sports day, leaving her no choice but to stay with Josh. It would be just Billy and me after all; exploring until mid-afternoon, when he would leave to meet his friend Lamin, in Putney.

The van was noisy at motorway speeds. The drone of the old diesel punctuated by thuds from the back as another tool or useful piece of timber found a new home. We kept our conversation to a minimum during the two-hour journey, as my thoughts dwelt on being so close to Deb and yet not being able to see her. I consoled myself with fantasies about discovering further esoteric treasure in Mortlake.

We parked in East Sheen, a mile or so away from Mortlake. First stop was to check out a 'Colston Road' that ran along the back of the busy Upper Richmond Road.

'What you got in dat rucksack *t'ing* Sam?' Billy inquired in his customary lilt.

'Apart from lunch, an old map of Mortlake. Debbie printed it out, so we can find the spot where Colston lived. The house may have long gone, but with street names, this map, and a picture of his home, we might uncover something.'

'Why don't you dowse the map to find the location. Let the universe tell da t'ing?' Billy asked.

'*Ah* - good point. I've experimented with a pendulum and map dowsing but haven't been comfortable with it. Denis the dowser suggested I practise. He says it saves his feet when he's out exploring. I don't trust my judgement, I suppose. With rods, I can understand you clearly pick up an invisible stream of something, and the rods react to it. But with a pendulum it's a different matter.'

Billy slowed-up and stopped, deep in thought. I noticed how smart he looked in a cream-coloured linen jacket. It fitted him as if it had been tailored.

'It's all energy, man. Everything but *everything.* It's all buzzing energy. Everything around us. Nothing is solid, nothing is quite what it seems to our eyes; it's just an illusion t'ing, this solid world. A map is just a portal in an endless field of energy. A glimpse into another place, another time. It's like opening a little door. We are all entwined, all joined together.' Billy curled his hands together as he spoke. 'Nothing is separate, nothing is alone. It can all be understood...'

'How do you mean?'

'When you open a map, you're opening a portal to somewhere else. The early maps were called portals. A port is an entrance t'ing and everywhere else is connected to everywhere else.' Billy paused in thought for a moment. 'Do you remember the film Monsters Inc. Mr Sam? You remember it, don't you?'

'Well yes. Bit of fun.'

'Do you remember the chase with all those doors opening and closing?'

I tried to recall the scene.

'Yes, of course, that part when he's jumping about opening all those doors on the conveyor belt?' Billy nodded, smiling in encouragement.

'Yes man, a map can be seen in many ways and one of them is as a door*way* – an energy doorway.'

'Like the Matrix film, all that stuff about interconnection,' I said

'Yes, dat's right, Mr Sam. When you use a pendulum 't'ing on a map you're remotely sensing the energies that exist in the place it represents. Try thinking like...' Billy paused in thought, '...higher dimensionally about the world, not three dimensions but *multiple* dimensions. Reach out with your mind and it will come to you.'

'In that case then, photographs and paintings of people will emit the subject's energy - like a kind of extension of their essence,' I said with caution.

'Oh yes. Of course. One of the first t'ings I remember from ma school was the mega portrait of the Queen behind the teacher. It wa very big. We all had a sense that the Her Majesty wa' with us, even when I knew she lived a long way away. You see everything, even lines on a plain paper page, emits streams of energy that you can find with a swinging pendulum. Try it sometime. It's cool man, you'll learn a lot of t'ings. Use the pendulum on a blank piece, let it swing a little bit and then ask your question. Start with saying; show me a *No* and then show me a *Yes.* It'll go one way or the other for you, but never the same way. Question it man, ask it to show you the energy coming from the paper.'

We continued our slow walk along the High Street as I listened intently.

'Now, if the t'ing works well, you should get no reaction with a blank sheet. There has been no focused conscious intent. The pendulum will just hang all limp. Draw a circle and you will get a response. It will spin in one direction or the other. Sometimes though it just rocks side to side. It can really, really spin if your *intent* is strong. It spins because your intent is imprinted on the paper.' Billy tapped the side of his head in emphasis. 'Try it for yourself Sam.'

'I will.' I looked sheepishly to the ground before looking up at Billy. He seemed so earnest and impassioned, I felt my heart expand with affection for him. He looked embarrassed, as if he could read my thoughts.

'Ah, here we are - Colston Road.' I studied the map that Deb had posted. At the end of the 17th Century, Colston had built a row of alms-houses close by, but they had since been demolished with the widening of the High Street. We walked slowly along what is now a service route on the lookout for signs. As we emerged at the Sheen Lane end, we were confronted with a familiar object.

'Oh yes, of course, I should have guessed. An obelisk, and quite a big one too,' I said, hands jauntily placed on my hips.

Billy dashed across the road.

'It's a memorial to the Dead of the First and Second World Wars,' he called out enthusiastically as I approached.

It was about five metres tall with a steep pitch to the tip - reminiscent of the famous and much larger, Washington Monument. Like so many obelisks, it stood in full view but might as well have been invisible; passed and ignored by shoppers and vehicles day-in day-out, presumably only coming into service for the town's annual wreath-laying ceremony. I took a couple of pictures before we set off north along Sheen Lane towards Mortlake village, my heart buzzing with anticipation.

We had a lot to get through. I needed to return to Bristol by early-evening to walk Norton.

'Oh look, isn't that a dome on that corner building?' Billy said pointing along Sheen Lane.

'If that's a dome, then I wonder were the flaming urns are? They'll be around here somewhere. But where?' I looked up and around, studying the rooftops. 'Yes. There, over there!' I pointed to the parapet of a curved red brick building just opposite the obelisk. 'Two of them on top. Do you see?'

'Is that a set then, Mr Sam - obelisk, dome *and* flaming urns?'

'Oh, yes,' I replied, feeling smug. We continued to stride purposefully towards Mortlake village.

'Keep your eyes open, Billy. According to the map, Colston's home was just beyond the old brewery site. The grounds stretched out to the river and west, probably covering all of what is now Mortlake Cemetery.' I stopped and studied the map under the welcome shade of a large London Plane tree. 'Quite a large plot of land even in the 18th Century. He was a keen gardener and had some interesting trees that he would have brought back from his travels. There were several statues and maybe a garden temple or two. They might still be around.' I caught my breath, intoxicated by the anticipation of discovery.

My pace quickened as we crossed the road and headed towards a collection of large, blank-looking industrial buildings. It was the brewery, still standing on the same site marked on my 19th Century map. Beyond that was an expansive sports field. As my stride increased, I narrowed my eyes, peering towards something weirdly familiar on the far corner of the field. Whatever it was, it was certainly at odds with the new housing development.

'Good *God!* Is that what I think it is on the other side of the field? Up into the corner, look, can you see it Billy?'

Still standing after 300 years, were the original posts and gates that once belonged to Cromwell House: Colston's home for 30 years.

'Ha, ha!' Billy laughed, and, for a moment, an enigmatic look flickered across his face. My forehead creased in reply.

'Where's that photo of the house?' I asked, as we approached a pair of four-metre high stone gate pillars. I could see through the ornate ironwork gates that the ground beyond was choked with brambles. 'Nothing else is left but the gate...' I said as my shoulders dropped.

After a brief sigh, I continued my search through the rucksack.

'Billy, Billy! Come over and look. The picture from Colston's biography. It's an exact *bloody* match!'

Billy looked down at the photo as an inscrutable smile drew across his tanned face.

'That looks like mean bush to me man. Could be big problem to get through,' he said, guessing correctly that I was contemplating an enthusiastic clamber over the gate.

'I guess you're right, silly idea really. But it is amazing, isn't it? How have these gates managed to survive all this time, especially when they lead to nothing and nowhere?' I stepped back absorbing the scene. Another quiver of excitement ran through my chest.

'Yes, man. Looks like some brothers wanted them to survive.' Billy nodded, pursing his mouth, deep in contemplation.

'Well some group or other. You would have to be organised and in a position of authority to make sure they remained after all this time. It's not as if they have any function anymore,' I said, my hand absently stroking one of the pillars.

'There's no sign, no plaque t'ing, no writing - anywhere.' Billy was purposefully striding down the small lane that led to the river. I peered wistfully through the gates, imagining the ornately-attired Colston as a ghost drifting through the undergrowth.

'Look at this,' he called out, pointing to a billboard a few metres down the lane 'They're going to redevelop the site soon. And guess what? It's going to be called the *Trinity* Centre.' He chuckled to himself, clearly relishing our discoveries.

'I love this stuff. It's like some kind of a game - you could call it *'Hidden in Plain Sight'*. It's all here. I mean, around us, another world exists unnoticed by all but those with the curiosity to stop and look.' I let out a long sigh before turning to Billy. 'I feel quite high; could do with finding somewhere to sit down. Maybe we should stop for some lunch now. I've brought some sandwiches, thought we could carry on down this lane to the waterfront, sit by the river? I said.

'No pub t'ing?' Billy inquired with a knowing grin.

'No, not today. I've got plenty of driving to do later, and I really do want to keep a clear head for this afternoon when we visit St Mary's. I've a hunch there may be even more stuff at the church.'

St Mary the Virgin lay partially hidden from Mortlake High Road by a screen of mature trees. A well-used footpath passed to the west, taking the walker from the comparatively peaceful village to the urban bustle of East Sheen. I stood across the road and studied the peculiar-looking church tower.

It was square and formidable. Built in four stages and topped by a cupola, the shape of which I recognised from pictures of the Dome of the Spirits on the Temple Mount in Jerusalem. But this one was made of wood, painted white with an elaborate wind vane at its summit. We walked along the public path before entering through the base of the tower into a large nave over 30 metres long. A vaulted roof with massive chocolate brown beams spanned impressively across the room. We parted and drifted around taking in the monuments and ornaments of the well-used church.

'Oh, now, this is interesting,' I called to Billy. 'Here's a plaque to Dr John Dee and it says he was an eminent astronomer, mathematician and astrologer and he is likely buried here, under the alter.' I turned grinning across the pews at Billy. 'How very interesting! What a coincidence. Dee and Colston frequenting the same church.'

'Dee?' Billy asked with eyebrows raised, prompting me to explain.

'He was very influential during the 16th and early 17th Centuries. He was a mathematician and astronomer – also an alchemist - who lived 100 years before Colston. Regularly consulted by Elizabeth I amongst many others. As a result, he became wealthy and amassed a large collection of books and manuscripts. It was one of the largest in Europe, bigger than many of the universities. Much of the library would be considered very esoteric these days. He was so well-read that if you wanted the inside track on what was going on, you came here to Mortlake, and took tea with Dee,' I said theatrically.

'Hey man. Over there, look it's a Templar cross. Do you see?' Billy had one arm pointing, the other calling me to his side. 'There, that corner, by the alter t'ing?'

'Yes. That's a classic Templar cross. They certainly like to leave their mark...' I bent down and examined the plinth. 'There might be somewhere, a lamb holding a flag. They like that one too.'

I stood up and turned to Billy, now on the other side of the aisle.

'I was thinking...that cupula up on the roof, you know, the big domed thing? It's very reminiscent of All Saints Church in Bristol. The Templars were big on the Dome of the Spirits, believing it to be the very spot of the high alter of Solomon's Temple. That's the centre of the world to a Templar and Colston happened to be the churchwarden responsible for a very unusual tower - *for 30 years.'*

'Isn't that just a caretaker kinda job? What's so important about that?' Billy asked.

'The churchwarden was the very centre of the parish. He was responsible for its physical fabric while the vicar looked after the spiritual. Vicars were quite transitory in those days and would move on to other parishes regularly. The churchwarden on the other hand, held a much more powerful, pivotal position. He would have been very much in control of how this church worked.'

I scanned the busy interior.

'You know Billy, other than that, the rest of the church doesn't inspire me at all. There's nothing very spiritual about the place - the children's play areas, Twitter signs, and community drop-in zones have put pay to all that.'

Outside, the afternoon was warming up. We had walked along roads busy with cars in the July heat. This and the excitement of discovery was making me tired and light-headed.

'I'm going to go and check-out the graveyard, maybe sit down and have a drink,' I said, as I studied the back of Billy's preoccupied figure.

'Yeah man, I'll join you shortly.' He was busy using his phone. 'I'll be with ya, I just need to check out t'ing, you know. Be with ya real soon.'

I left the nave and walked out from the tower into the bright sunlight, turning left to join the public footpath. An ornate iron gate led to the southern section of the cemetery and as I passed through it, I was confronted by a large, clearly ancient, three-metre high stone arch. It seemed out of place, surrounded by the tombs and headstones of the compact graveyard. It looked as if it should originally have surrounded the entrance to the church tower, but subsequently got repositioned for some reason.

I found a sheltered spot over a tomb, sat down on the cool stone slab and slipped out of my sticky sandals. Placing my bare feet against the marble sides, I settled comfortably with my back against the trunk of a small tree. I could almost feel a trickle of energy begin to flow from my fatigued feet into the earth. I looked up and studied the arch with a slow, indolent eye, and smiled, gently amused by its blatant incongruity. An involuntary sigh was followed by a deep intake of breath that drew-in the seductive scent of summer. The hum of busy insects provided the perfect soundtrack. Tufts of tall grass and fragrant flowers grew haphazardly between the ancient headstones and wafted gently in the barely-moving air. The cemetery seemed to shimmer in the afternoon heat.

A frail, elderly woman appeared, pulling an old shopping cart. The persistent squeak of its damaged wheel cut through the peace. I closed my eyes, letting my shoulders slowly drop as I relaxed against the smooth bark. As the trolley and its owner passed into the distance, I became aware of someone else following the same path. I opened my eyes, squinting in the glare and saw a much younger woman, pushing a colourful buggy. It was decorated with a multi-coloured jumble of baby paraphernalia. She was talking to the baby in a calm, loving voice. As I gazed in at them, the outline of the mother gradually dissolved until just a sparkly image remained. My pulse quickened as I observed bubbles of light floating around her like golden halos. Small, wispy streams of pink twisted as they flowed from her bosom towards her child. Maybe this was love becoming manifest, I mused, in awe at what I was witnessing.

My heart swelled with compassion for this stranger and her baby.

They continued along the tree-lined path, with little trails of light still dancing around them like tiny fairies. The space along the lane glittered and flowed, and there, surrounded by gravestones, I had the sensation that I was absorbing the cumulative energy of all those who had previously passed. I caught my breath. The world of *matter* that I had known for 44 years seemed to be dissolving and then reforming into all its discrete elements. I felt an incredible wave of love reaching out and turning back towards me. Waves of scintillating, dancing light passed effortlessly through and around me. Now I understood. All that is invisible to the eye can become visible through the heart. I perceived a new world that only the movement of the rods had previously indicated. I was enthralled as two oceans of multi-hued light washed through me and then under the stone arch. The energy moved apart and drew together as if it was a pulse. At the centre, under the apex, I could see a narrow band of stillness; like the centre of the wake from a speeding boat. Now everything made sense. Understanding without thought. It was all just *so*. A sense of compassion and wonder began to spread from my heart to the very tips of my shaking fingers.

'Sam... Sam?' Billy's familiar voice called me back. He approached with a misty yellow aura surrounding him. He came close, bending and looked directly into my eyes. I sensed the presence of something very special, very loving in Billy. Had Nick been right in christening him an angel?

'*Sam*? Are-you-OK?'

He shuffled closer and shook me gently. His long brown fingers curled over the knuckle of my hand. It felt calm and reassuring.

'Got something to show you Sam. Some good t'ing.'

'Yes. Sure – *sorry* Billy. I feel a bit out of it. I think I may have fallen asleep.' I pushed a hand through my tangled hair and sat up. My tee shirt clung stubbornly to my back.

'You look like you've been somewhere else.' Billy laughed. 'Here *look*. This place we are at. It's very, very special place man – 'tis the *place of balance.*'

'Balance? The balance of *what*?' I felt confused, stifling an involuntary yawn.

'The point, Mr Sam, of balance. Between da spiritual and da physical. Between the energies of matter and spirit. It's here, at this very place...'

'What are you talking about?'

'I've drawn it out.' He produced a leaflet from the church marked with biro on the back. 'You remember the two latitudes? Those latitudes that were on that map - *yes*? He pointed to an outline of southern England that he'd drawn, showing two lines passing like a band from London to Bristol. He'd marked them 'physical' 51.51 and 'spiritual' at 51.428571 degrees latitude.

'That's where Avebury is, isn't it? 51.4 and something.'

He sat down next to me in the shade. Even in this heat, he was still wearing his linen jacket.

'If you take 51.428571 away from 51.51 you get this result.' Billy underlined the number with his pen for added effect. 'Now if you divide that result by two and add the result to the lower number you get 51.4692855 decimal degrees latitude. And that is the point of balance on the Earth's surface between the two *separate* fields of energy. The spiritual and the physical.' He grinned at me expectantly.

'And... *so*?' I replied.

'The tomb we are now sitting on Sam, this one *here,* is at exactly that latitude – *to the metre!*'

I stared at him, then looked up at the arch in front of us, suddenly understanding its amazing significance. 'Holy shit, Billy ... it's the bridge between two worlds. Dee's Union of Opposites.'

'*This is the line of mystical harmony...*' he sang out the words with a smile a mile wide.

We sat together in contemplative silence. I felt drained.

'Are you OK to get home, Mr Sam? You look pale.'

'Yes. I'm fine, but I could do with a coffee. It must be time for you to leave?'

Billy nodded and I got to my feet. 'Then I'll walk with you to the station. It's on my way back to the van, anyway.'

Something profound had happened to me during that brief hazy interlude in the graveyard. Something I couldn't quite get my head around and didn't feel I could share with anyone else, not even Billy. When we got to the station we hugged for a moment at the entrance and I stayed watching as he walked to the top of the ramp. He turned and waved, beaming his immense smile.

Heading back to Bristol, I trundled along the slow lane, content to follow in the wake of the lumbering trucks. My mind kept straying back to those moments of vivid images and delightful emotions and I couldn't keep the grin from my face. I was treasuring the knowledge that I'd been given a fleeting glimpse into another dimension.

How very curious life had become.

'*Eh* - what?'

I turned slowly, confronted by the dark pools of Norton's eyes. He was huffing in that way dogs do when their needs become urgent.

'Oh Norton! I'm so sorry, you must be bursting.' He was at my bedside, a great enthusiasm shook his body, his tail reinforcing the pleading look on his broad black face. I sat up, noticing the edge underneath my hand was sticky. Clear, viscous fluid oozed from my fingers. I let out a deep sigh, studying his purple gums. They bubbled like bath water.

'OK. OK. We're going soon – *two* minutes. I've got to get dressed first, then we'll go straight out. What time is it? Oh, shit! It's after three!' I looked straight back at the poor animal. 'How on earth did you manage?'

I paused.

'Oh... Please no, Norton - you haven't, have you?' I pleaded, as my thoughts turned to the surprises that could be laying in wait for my bare feet.

It turned out that Norton had been on his very best behaviour while I slumbered through 15 hours of oblivion. I couldn't understand why I didn't feel incredibly rested and energetic. Instead, listlessness had consumed me. We left the house, Norton pulling heavily on his lead, and made our way to a small abandoned patch of green. This had become his fossicking heaven. Returning for breakfast, I struggled to recollect yesterday's dramatic experience in Mortlake. My overworked brain went around in circles, distracted by the very images I was trying to understand. But - I did *feel* something. Something that was at once powerful but also subtle and so, so sublime.

After feeding the famished hound, I retired to the front room and slumped onto the sofa. Norton joined me, huffing that I'd taken his favourite spot. Even so, he quickly fell asleep in his old arm chair.

Who really *was* Billy? How come he had all this knowledge? It's not like he'd studied it. You'd think he had a Ph.D. in metaphysics. He seemed to have an innate awareness.

And why his interest with Colston? He'd really enjoyed the Mortlake thing. I didn't understand why he should be so interested, a young bloke from a small Caribbean island and a *steam train* enthusiast to boot. That surely is a bit weird. Cricket fanatic yes, but steam trains?

Who is he kidding?

Should I confront him about all this?

And Deb? What was I to do about her...?

I missed her.

On impulse, I picked up the phone. She sounded excited to hear about our discoveries; echoing my enthusiasm for the surviving gate, the arched monument and its pivotal location.

'Does that *exact* latitude go through Colston's house as well as the arch?' Deb asked.

'Well, no...' I hesitated. 'Studying Google Earth, it does look as if it goes through the grounds and quite close to the house. I read he had a little domed monument somewhere in the grounds. Now long-gone. My bet is that the latitude went through that...'

'So, his grounds would be what is now Mortlake cemetery. Is that right?'

'Yes. There could be some remains or indications in the layout.'

'What larks, Pip.' She said playfully.

'Other stuff happened as well, some of it rather strange. Sort of spooky.' I said cautiously.

'That sounds intriguing. You'd better leave that until we're together.'

'Yes, we should meet up soon. Maybe a Saturday? Just for the day. Somewhere mid-way along the M4. I'll bring Norton of course. I'm sure Josh would enjoy walking him,' I replied.

'Great idea.' Deb paused. 'Poor old Norton. How is he getting on?'

'Slow and arthritic, otherwise tail-waggingly happy.'

'Look, Sam. You know you said that Norton had difficulty getting up into your van? Would he find it easier if it was a car he got into?'

'Yes. A car would make it easier. Why? What do you have in mind?'

'Well, I've been thinking about you.' My heart lurched. 'Dad's old car. It's not really very useful in Wandsworth. I've decided to keep the Micra after all. Can't sell it for what it's worth, anyway. So, I was wondering if you might like it. Not to buy, of course. I don't suppose a car like that is worth much these days.' She sounded hesitant.

'The Volvosaurus?' I joked.

'Yes. Would you like it?'

'Maybe? It's funny, I've been thinking that the van doesn't get the use it used to have. Especially as I have to remove all my valuable tools every night, to stop it being broken into. At least if they can see what's in there, they might not bother, and it'll save my door locks being repeatedly damaged. That Volvo is as solid a car as you could find. It's in great nick.'

'Yes. Oh, it's perfect. Everything works, and it goes really well.'

'I know. I've been in the passenger seat.'

We agreed to meet in Marlborough the following Saturday. I would come by bus with Norton, while Deb and Josh brought Gordon's car from London.

By mid-morning I had started to recover and was glad to be brought back to earth for a few days' good work. A few hours later I had a call from James, my big extension customer, asking me to call by his house early the next morning.

'Settlement cracks in the render. Not too much to worry about. We should leave it for a few months to sort itself out. I'll come back then, hack-out and re-render,' I said, looking near the roof line.

'Well if you think so. But won't the damp get in?' said James.

'No. Not really. It'll be fine,' I replied in my most reassuring voice.

I was getting busy again with work and did need to give the building a chance to settle, otherwise I could end up doing the job twice. James was a bit of a worrier. In fact, anxiety was his default position.

By Saturday I was keen to escape the clamour of the City. Leaving early, I set off for the Mendip Hills, a few miles south of Bristol, for a long walk with Norton. If all went well I would reward us both with a trip to Glastonbury for tea and cake at Crumbly's.

Sure enough, by lunchtime we were ensconced with the Ponytailed-ones. This time though, I found I was no longer the centre of attention. The talk instead was about the intrigue between two local authors. It seemed their respective partners had run off to the States together, to live in bliss in Sedona with a guru. Quite a leap from the hedgerows of Avalon.

I was feeling relaxed, enjoying the gentle banter, when Tall John gestured me in the direction of a man sitting close by, introducing him as Howard.

'It's Sam – isn't it?' A large, grey bushy beard inclined towards me confirming his suspicions. 'It's Howard. You might not remember? Howard Wills, the architect!'

'Bloody hell!' Through the mess of salt and pepper growth I could just make out his once-familiar face.

Howard-the-architect! Well, well. He had been a contractor I'd regularly worked with. A useful man to know when you needed to take a wall or two apart.

'I know. I look a little different - hah! It was all suits and ties in those days.'

Howard stood up straight as if in salute and announced. 'I've still got one, though. Hangs in the wardrobe of my barge.' His eyes twinkled.

'You look as if you've been living in the outback for the last decade,' I said, astonished.

'Well... it *has* been about a decade, hasn't it? You were buying a house, last time I saw you. Did you take it in the end?'

'Oh yes. Still live there. Funnily enough, I'm now seeing that same girlfriend, again – Debbie.'

'Not the really pretty one who wanted to settle down? So, did you settle down with her?'

'No.' I reflected. 'Someone else slipped in while I was dithering.'

'You know, this is kinda of spooky us meeting like this? Do you remember when you gave me a DVD with those drawings of your new house on it?'

I nodded thoughtfully.

'Well, I also opened one of the other files on the disk. The one with the film...'

'What film?

'Yes. *Oh* yes!' Howard drew himself closer as if conspiring, put his hand firmly on my arm and jiggled it. 'Changed my life. It really did, you know – changed everything.' He let go and flopped back into his seat with tired, heavy eyes. I felt a stab of alarm. What on earth had I done to bring about such a seismic change in this man?

I remembered having a swift half with him. That was probably the last time I had seen him. Presumably, that's when I handed him the disk? He liked to talk about his daughter and 'the missus' of course. Quite sweet really. A straight bloke. I recalled that after several 'halves', he had confided in a whisper that at uni he'd once been handed a joint. It had made him feel giddy and then ravenously hungry; his first and last walk on the wild side.

'So, what was on that disk, then?' I asked intrigued.

'The film. *The Film!* The one you put on for me?' He sat up as if I should understand. I continued to look blankly at his hairy, crumpled face.

'No. Can't help you there. I only remembered putting on a couple of drawings and some other stuff. Definitely no film.'

'Well, *'Crop Circles – Crossovers from Another Dimension'* was on it. It blew me away.' Howard brought his arms dramatically together and threw them apart as if an explosion had really occurred.

'That doesn't sound like any doco that I would have watched. Now, maybe, but not then. I was strictly meat and potatoes in those days. No room for funny stuff.'

Where had it come from? I had a vague recollection of trading DVDs with the regulars at the pub. Could it have been one of them?

'But what happened? What happened to you?' I urged.

'Bloody crop circles, that's what. *Croppies!*' Howard paused, catching his breath. 'Well you know the story? The one about all the croppies being hoaxes perpetrated by the nefarious, but amazingly talented duo, *'Doug and Dave'*. Our men with the planks and string.'

I nodded in agreement. I had never considered myself a sceptic; I understood there was something odd about the whole crop circle mythology, but like most people, I'd never really given it much thought.

Howard continued.

'Well, that's a load of rubbish of course,' he spat, his hollow eyes opened wide. He had the features of someone that had encountered resistance.

'They're far, far too complex to be made by people in the middle of the night.' Howard struck the table with his balled fist, jolting me upright. 'Some of them are enormous. Hundreds of feet across. No one has ever been filmed making any of the serious glyphs – *yes*, some of the simpler ones, but not the big stuff. And they're perfect. Every one of them, perfect geometry, no wrong angles, no wobbly lines – no mistakes. It's as if they had been executed on a drawing board. Never, *ever*, any mistakes. That's what started it all. It's the question architects and engineers would ask themselves. Why were there no mistakes?'

Howard studied me intently before adding.

'There's a great secret about them that I've discovered.'

I smiled benignly and cleared my throat. 'Well, *I've* been on the trail of secrets too; but without your apparent success.'

At that point we were interrupted by a young waitress who efficiently cleared the tables. She smelt of baking and left with an order for two more coffees. I noticed that the group had melted away as our conversation became more intense. How odd it was that he should place such importance on something that I couldn't even remember. Even so, I warmed to his 'born again' enthusiasm.

Howard explained how, after watching the film, he'd persuaded 'the missus' to go out with him and see if they could track one down.. They never found any but ended up in a small cafe almost entirely populated by crop circle enthusiasts (it was mid-summer). This was a bit of a culture a shock to his wife, who hadn't had the benefit of seeing the film, and completely freaked out. During the ensuing, protracted argument, it emerged that he had been regularly cuckolded by his neighbour – a night worker. The incident sparked the fire that ended his marriage. Within months he had left the family home. After a few adventures, he'd ended up living on a narrowboat on the Kennet Canal and since then, had devoted his energies to solving a remarkable enigma.

'Look Sam, this is not the place to chat. But I know all about Avebury. I know why it was built. From what you've just told me, your knowledge slots right in. You'll be amazed when I tell you. Come over and stay if you want - on the canal. You'll love it, it's right in the middle of nowhere.'

'Can I bring my dog?'

Howard beamed.

He might look as if he had been living in a ditch, but there was no denying his energy and his passion. His enthusiasm was infectious.

I was intrigued to find out more about his discoveries on the rolling chalk downs.

'I'm worried about poor Norton.' Deb studied me with a look of growing concern.

We had met up in Marlborough to exchange Gordon's old, but immaculately-maintained car.

'So am I. The poor old boy is really getting on, and all this moving about seems to have affected him.' I had grown embarrassingly fond of the smelly, dribbling canine, despite his personal hygiene problems.

'Yes, I know, but what I meant was that Josh is going to put him back in the car after their walk. Only it's warming up out there and he could over-heat.' Deb nodded towards the window and the glare of the High Street.

'The trees around the park should keep the shade on the car. Or... maybe we should head back after our cake and bring him with us to the Mound,' I ventured.

'I wanted to talk to you about that.' Deb's face dropped, becoming serious.

We were sitting in the bay window of one Britain's finest cake emporia - all linen and icing sugar. It was busy. Full of obese tourists celebrating their good fortune at landing in this story-book location. Each table displayed its own little temple of layered chrome and china bearing a staggering array of sticky confections.

'Could we pop into a couple of shops first? There's some bits and pieces I need. I've got to get some things for Josh. He's on a camping and hiking thing with the Scouts next week. You don't mind, do you?' Deb cocked her head pleadingly.

'No, no, of course not,' I replied, rather too quickly.

It was always going to be a short day together. Deb had to get back 'at a reasonable hour' and I was due at Howard's narrowboat for dinner. But I was keen to visit Marlborough College's mysterious 20-metre-high tree-covered 'Mound'.

'We can all go over to the Mound later, together, the three of us and Norton,' Dcb bargained.

Replete with cake, we set off along the high street. It was midday and already hot.

'I need to get Josh a new rucksack and a couple of shirts. Do you know the town? I'm afraid the rucksack must be a very specific brand - *Blue Sky.* It's got to be the right label.'

Fortunately, most of the shops had air conditioning. I made the most of the cool breeze as I watched her forage professionally amongst the racks.

'So how was it with Billy at Mortlake?'

'Ah yes, it was great to see him, he's very easy to be with.' I reflected before continuing: 'He's like – well easy. Not in your face; kinda knows what's what.'

'You must be getting to know him quite well?' Deb gently probed.

'I'll be honest; I find him a bit of an enigma. He's great company, but I get the feeling that there's an awful lot more to him than he'll ever let on.'

'I'd ask him a few questions - *if* I ever get to meet him.' She observed me carefully.

'Yes, yes you must. Come down again. I'll organise it.' A weekend together - what could be better, and with Billy as an added incentive...

Deb turned and smiled, as she replaced a rejected rucksack.

'Can we just pop to another shop? This one doesn't stock Blue Sky.' I followed her out. 'So, tell me all about Mortlake. What's this about John Dee?'

'He's probably buried under the alter of the church where Colston was warden for 30 years.' I followed her into another outdoor pursuits shop. 'He had an enormous library and most of it disappeared about 100 years before Colston arrived. I'm wondering if Colston might have rediscovered it, or at least part of it. I'm sure that's why he lived in Mortlake. To be on that special location that John Dee would have known about. It's been described as a place of '*mystical harmony*.' I'm not sure of course, but I've been wondering if maybe Colston could have discovered some secret about reincarnation. He seems to have been pursuing something or other and the way I see it, if you have already met all your material needs, and he was certainly rich enough to buy whatever he wanted, then what's next? Hasn't immortality been the pursuit of rich, powerful people throughout the centuries. What about the Egyptians?'

Deb stopped and turned.

'That's a coincidence. A couple of weeks ago, we went on a school trip to see an opera about Dee. How funny,' she reflected. 'It was great. I remember the tenor was especially good, the one that played Walsingham. What was his name?' She paused in contemplation for a moment. 'So, Sam, are you saying what I'm thinking? That Colston had discovered some secret about being reborn, maybe even with a memory of your past life? Like those Druid people you told me about? Do you think he could even have been reborn as Draper within months of his death? Could that be what the alignment on Clifton Down is all about - some special secret confirmation?'

'Well it's an interesting idea, isn't it? There seems to be a pretty strong link between them – as if they were in the same club. It could give a whole new layer of significance to that painting we saw at the M Shed - '*Some who have made Bristol Famous*'.

'Have you checked Draper's actual *birth* date yet?'

I admitted that I hadn't. I didn't expect to find anything. And anyway, Draper was almost certainly born before Colston's death in 1721. It was mid-October. That's a lot of months into the year. I would have to spend ages pouring through reams of dusty old books, just to prove my own theory wrong.

'Ask Simon. He's a historian. He'll know,' Deb said firmly.

It wasn't long before we were back out in the hot August sun inspecting shop windows. I checked my watch. Time was moving on, but just as I was about to raise the point, Deb dived into another shop.

I followed her in, ruminating on just how exclusive this rucksack of Josh's could be.

'It's nice and cool here, isn't it?' I commented, as Deb inspected another array of fancy-looking kit.

'Castle Howard was lovely. Don't you think Sam?' She smiled coyly.

'Yes, it was.' I placed myself next to a large chrome fan. 'I've got a map that I had laminated and drew on. Found some interesting stuff.'

'Oh yes,' she murmured distractedly, as she held a bag aloft, peering for the elusive logo.

'Yes. Interesting, very interesting indeed. The Stray points south directly towards the village of Buttercrambe about seven miles away. This may have been where King Edwin was crowned King in 625AD and might just be where King Athelstan held the first convention of stonemasons in about 935AD. Forming them into a Guild for the first time and...' I held a finger up in emphasis, '...considered by some scholars to be the true birth of Freemasonry in England.'

'Now that's interesting,' Deb said emphatically.

'...and not only that, the Stray and the position of the house hold further secrets.'

'Go on.' I could see she was still listening when we found ourselves back outside and heading for the next outlet. I followed a step behind her as the pace quickened.

'Ah yes. If you take the total length of the Stray and mark out the positions of the gates and monuments along it, the pyramid gate appears at the position of the Golden Section, the sacred ratio,' I called through a shop door. 'The house is set out to the Golden Section on the path between the obelisk and the round reservoir. It runs alongside of it. The line of the Golden Section runs to the north through that little monument by the lake and out across to the war memorial in the village. The Obelisk is also exactly half a nautical mile from the reservoir.'

'So tell me about the dowsing. How are you getting on with it?' Deb asked as I followed her back across the busy high street.

'Fine. I've been using the pendulum on my map of Bristol. It shows that Brandon Hill is a hot spot. It pulled like mad and spun-up. It's made from something called Brandon cyst, which is full of crystal. It's the same type of stone as the Sarsen stones at Stonehenge. Looks like Brandon Hill is one huge piece of crystal. Now I'm starting to wonder why the south face has never been built on. That's the solar gain side. The sun would heat the bare ground increasing the vibration of the crystal.' I paused, embarrassed at my theory. 'It's just an idea. Probably wrong about that last bit.'

'One more shop and that's it.' Deb turned and flashed a smile.

I loitered outside, trying to suppress my mounting irritability in the oppressive heat, as I speculated on how many other *'bits and pieces'* were still on her list.

After several minutes she emerged, triumphantly swinging a large paper bag.

'All done. We'd better hurry back to the park. I'm worried about what Josh might be getting up to. He can quickly get bored during the holidays...' She glanced at me as we crossed the busy road.

'You alright?' Deb enquired.

'Yes. Of course,' I said abruptly.

We found Josh dawdling some way along the river from the park. It was obvious that both he and Norton had joined several others and gone into the water. His blond locks now looked dark and limp. Deb was irritated with him.

I accepted despondently that the visit to the Mound was off the schedule. We hardly spoke as we returned to the car, although I did offer to take them directly to Swindon to catch the train, calculating that a dripping-wet child might not have been so welcome on the local bus.

As we pulled into the station, Deb leant over and kissed me firmly on the cheek.

'Sorry we didn't get to your hill. Maybe another time?'

'Yes. No problem. I'll call you soon about Billy. Would you still like to meet him?'

She nodded, 'Absolutely. *Of course,* Sam.'

Drawing away from the kerb, I watched in the mirror as she struggled to comb Josh's tangled hair. I was feeling increasingly attached to them both, and yet still very much the outsider. They had their own life, I reflected.

'Fuck! Where *is* Howard's bloody boat?'

The canal meandered on and on. I'd stopped under the shelter of a large beech tree with Norton panting heavily beside me. It was beginning to look like we had been led on a merry chase. Had I pissed Howard off so much in the past that only now was he extracting his revenge? It was nearly six o'clock. The long, hot day had not been helped by an uncomfortably early start.

I could smell myself.

My notes from our conversation at Crumbly's said 'Park up at the Barge Inn, then head west (left from your side) and walk along the tow path until you find 'Dorothy'. It's not far.'

The canal, the Kennet and Avon, is part of a network of rivers and canals that, with a suitable type of craft, allow you to travel the Thames from the centre of London to the River Avon at Bristol, 120 miles west. Howard lived in the most remote part. The Vale of Pewsey is a stretch of narrow canal that saunters its way along the southerly edge of the Wiltshire Downs. The wheat coloured rolling hills were clearly visible from where I was standing.

I'd passed about eight or nine narrow boats, before coming up to one festooned with solar panels and plants. As I approached, its owner emerged. I returned his generous smile and inquired if he knew the whereabouts of 'Dorothy.'

'Howie's, you mean?' His late middle-aged bronze face looked relaxed in faded blue shorts and white T-shirt.

'Yes, that's right. Do you know him?' I replied, eager for a clue.

'We all know each other – it's difficult not to.' My new acquaintance smiled, pointing along the bank. 'He's two more along, just around the bend. Beyond the little footbridge. He likes to be out on the edge of town, if you know what I mean.'

As he spoke, a bundle of black and white fur bounced up from the galley and leapt onto the footpath. We exchanged greetings, though Norton appeared less enthusiastic, as the owner urged the young collie to join him.

'Have a nice evening,' he called, as he set off along the path towards the pub; a small branch snatched-up and thrown, much to the delight of the barking 'Sweep.'

Howard spotted me as I walked under the footbridge. Dressed in shorts and a T-shirt with 'Generation X' bannered across it, he was still difficult to recognise. His appearance had changed so much - from straight-laced business suit to bushy bohemian with belly.

'Great to see you Sam – *Dorothy* welcomes you!' Howard gestured me extravagantly on board.

I walked the little plank and stepped down into another world. The floating capsule was tidier than I had expected and smelt encouragingly of fragrant cooking.

'That's the Pulao - *Kabuli Pulao*. Hope you don't mind, it's a vegetarian supper. Needs to 'brew' for an hour or so in a warm oven.' I was guided through into the saloon.

'Smells lovely. I've brought some wine.' I released my small rucksack. 'I'm sure Norton would like a drink, it's been a hot day for him.' I looked back, feeling concern as Norton cautiously negotiated the narrow steep steps from the entrance about mid-way along the narrowboat.

'It used to belong to an architect I knew in Bristol - John James. JJ. Do you remember him?'

I shrugged my shoulders in ignorance and made myself comfortable at the table.

'Silly bugger started speculating with property all over town. Came a bit of a cropper over it. This was one of the assets he had to get rid of quickly. I could just afford to pay for it out of the settlement with Helen. She got the house.' Howard grimaced briefly. 'In fact, she ended up with most of the stuff. I bought this outright. Fitted it out a bit and moved in. One decent job a year pays all my fixed costs.' Howard patted the seat next to him looking very satisfied with his new-found life.

I nodded as I scanned the wood cabin and experienced my first twinges of jealousy. The ash-faced interior was lined with numerous little shelves and pockets, all filled with useful stuff. A small black wood burner squatted in the corner near the galley door. It was all so 'worked-out', with no small space wasted. I sank back into the soft cushions. Sparkles of canal light danced across the ceiling. On the opposite bank the hay field rolled down to the water's edge. Beyond that lay more fields. Lots and lots of fields, with not a house in sight. I sighed and inhaled the sweet rural air.

'Have a shower and change. You'll feel a lot better. There are clean towels in the bathroom. I've got a full water tank so help yourself. Meanwhile, I'll organise the wine.' Howard spoke while slicing and dicing in the miniature kitchen.

He was right about the shower. The day's stress washed well and truly into *Dorothy's* waste water tank. I returned to the comfortable saloon wearing a generously donated clean T-shirt.

'I was trying to remember how we met,' I said.

'Oh, that's easy. I'll never forget that bloody job. Don't you remember? In Cambridge Row? That four-storey Georgian terrace.'

'Oh, *yes!*' My stomach shifted as I recalled the bad dream that was Cambridge Row. 'Number 12 - what a nightmare!' I slumped further into the cushions.

Howard chortled to himself while he filled tumblers with ice-cold white wine.

'Do you remember that first site visit, when you took me around the back, through the basement door? I was speechless,' said Howard, his bushy eyebrows drawn apart in mock surprise.

'Anyone would have been,' I said.

'You could see the rafters in the roof, 12 metres up – *from the basement!*' Howard returned to the saloon drying his hands before easing into the wood and leather of a well-worn captain's chair.

'More like 15 metres. He'd taken nearly all the timber in the building and turned it into welsh dressers or tables. Floorboards, joists, beams, even the architraves around the doors. He didn't care. He flogged what he'd made in the street when there were no floors left.'

Howard interrupted my reminiscing.

'What an idiot, there was nothing preventing that whole lot from coming down. He could easily have killed someone.' He shook his head in despair. 'I could have been in serious trouble over that you know. If that had happened these days, Health and Safety would have been all over it - *all over it!* You could never have got away with simply putting the timber back. Wasn't the landlord a friend's dad or something?'

I nodded.

'What was his name? The bloke who did all the damage.'

'Tim Murphy, a real charmer. Worked his way around Bristol before disappearing with the tax man in hot pursuit. That was the late Nineties, I reckon.' I replied.

'Yes – it's coming back to me now, you used to call him *Termite Tim.*'

Howard, who obviously had a soft spot for dogs, judiciously stroked Norton's head while feeding him small treats. Norton slobbered in gratitude. 'I think you told me later that he'd been doing this all over town, stripping out the insides of derelict houses and shops?'

'Or just renting the whole building and doing it anyway,' I replied.

We laughed and toasted ourselves.

'Now Sam, I'm interested in what you've discovered about Avebury that you seem to find so interesting.' Howard leant forward, looking earnest.

'It's Avebury's location that I find intriguing. How did they manage to locate the stone circle with so much precision? It's *exactly* 51.428571 degrees latitude. That strange number being what you get when you divide 360 degrees by seven. Why do you think it was so important to be on that spot?'

'Yes. After you told me at Crumbly's, I checked it out on Google Earth. You're quite right. It's very odd. 51 degrees etcetera runs right through the middle of the circle.'

Howard topped up my tumbler as I returned to my story.

'I'm still puzzled about the 33-degree stuff and Giza. If you add the numbers 51428571 together, you get 33, the distance in degrees longitude from the Giza pyramid. That's some coincidence?' I shrugged.

'Ah Sam... Giza! The mainstream media is keen to debate about *how* the pyramids were built but rarely anything more. They act as if that's the only mystery about them.'

Howard turned to examine several neat shelves of books. As he did, I glanced outside to catch three swans gliding silently past, their forms perfectly reflected in the twilight water.

'Here, look, I have another numerical coincidence for you.' Drawings and loose bits of paper were spread across the table. 'Did you know that the latitude, in decimal degrees, of the Giza pyramid is the same number, all to a decimal place or three, as the value of the speed of light in metres per second? It runs right through the middle of the King's Chamber in the Pyramid of Cheops. Just below the pinnacle. I mean, how is that even *possible*?'

Howard's eyes widened as he amplified his question with splayed hands.

'But Avebury,' he dramatically lifted a forefinger. 'Now that is very interesting. It gets side-lined by nearby Stonehenge, of course. I sometimes wonder if that's not deliberate. You see, its function, as a device, is much more obvious than Stonehenge. When you take the trouble to *really* look.'

He sat back and unconsciously resumed fondling Norton's soft ear. 'It was solving the purpose of Avebury that led me into understanding the why of crop circles, you see.' Howard leant forward conspiratorially. 'I believe Avebury was deliberately built as a sophisticated - *water treatment plant...*'

'Water treatment? Really? That's a lot of effort to supply a few local farmers with irrigation. And four thousand years ago?'

'Ah! No.' He waved a finger towards me. 'It's not water for the local farmers and villagers. No, not at all. It's water for the people and plants of the London basin – and even beyond.'

Howard studied my face.

'Look Sam, I'll draw a plan and section of Avebury for you.'

His experienced, fluid fingers glided over the paper.

'Avebury was built as a 1000-metre-wide circular trough for the collection of rain water. The spoil from the ditch was used as a catchment bank. It was...'

Howard paused, 'a reservoir. Yes, that's it, a very special kind you see; it was all dug out of chalk. Possibly the largest chalk field in the world. The porous sides were then lined with clay to stop the water from soaking away. At specific times, such as after the *midsummer sunrise,* the 'plug' would be pulled, and the water would soak into the very porous chalk of the Wiltshire Downs. Just like emptying a bath really.'

'But to what purpose, Howard?' It's a lot of effort just to make the ground underneath wet.' I was puzzled.

'The water of course. It would have been treated before it was released into the water table. By collecting rain water, you would have started off with distilled water. No minerals and shit, just clean neutral water – OK? Now, you must have heard about Professor Emoto and his experiments with the qualities of water?'

I raised my eyebrows vacantly.

Howard lent back and turned to his bookshelves. Grabbing a volume, he flicked through pages containing images that looked like ice crystals.

'Look at this, Sam. Emoto has been working for years demonstrating that water responds to its environment. Not only that, it appears to respond to consciousness: our thoughts, emotions and feelings. Water is the ultimate chameleon. It will change its molecular crystalline structure in response to a stimulus. But you need to activate it the correct way. Do you see what he's done in these photos?'

'So, people were manipulating the quality of their water with their *thoughts*? You mean the Druids or whoever?' I tried to disguise my confusion.

'Yes. Yes! But using other energies as well. Like making a big bowl of soup – energetic soup. Lots of different ingredients. The small inner stone circles of Avebury could act like calendars with each signalling the position of the sun and or the moon. The crystal monoliths that surrounded the ditch and those in the middle were used like amplifiers and modulators of these different frequencies. So, at different times of the year they would collect different energies from different sources. Now there are two famous ley lines: the Michael and its companion, the Mary. They flow across England from St Michael's Mount in Cornwall and cross at key points such as Glastonbury, and of course, Avebury. The ultimate direction of flow is aligned to the summer solstice. They both end up disappearing into the North Sea at Norfolk. All this, plus the heptagonal energy of the magical 7th Latitude that you discovered.' Howard grinned.

'So, people would charge up the water before releasing it all to soak into the ground?' I said.

Howard studied me thoughtfully.

'Now, water has all sorts of interesting qualities and homeopathic medicine exploits these qualities in its treatments. In homeopathy, it's the unique vibration of the plant that you are seeking to impart. Not the substance itself. So, what you are doing in effect is encoding the water. Every species has its own unique frequency... Take lavender, for example. If you want the benefits that come from that plant, you place its extract into a vessel of distilled water and by using a variety of techniques, impart that frequency into the coding of the water. This will change the crystalline quality; how the molecules themselves bond together. Emoto and many others have clearly demonstrated this. You don't need the plant itself, you just need its energetic signature. Even if that plant is a potential poison.'

Howard's enthusiasm was evident. He spoke between excited sips from his tumbler.

'When you ingest this specially-energised water, the cohesive structure alters the less-structured water that we, in turn, are made from. Remember, Sam, every cell of our bodies contains water molecules. It affects our health and, many believe, our consciousness directly. We are, in effect, large bags of water and the quality of that water influences our wellbeing. We can benefit from a more balanced state of health. Mental, physical and spiritual.'

'But it still seems like a big operation for a pretty localised community. How could it possibly have been worth it? I still don't get it,' I said.

'Did you know that Avebury sits above one of the largest and highest aquifers in southern England? And from deep underground, the water bubbles to the surface and is exposed to the effects of sunlight for the first time at, or very, *very* close to, the circle. That same aquifer turns out to be the source of the River Kennet, which becomes the Kennet and Avon Canal. The *very* one we're floating on. From here if flows due east into the Thames and London.'

Howard topped-up my glass.

'As the water flows from its source, it will alter the quality of the water that it flows into. Especially if it's 'charged up' and geometric. It will override the more chaotic structure of what it flows into.'

We sat in silence as I reflected.

'How did you work all that out?

'It all started with a visit to Stourhead Estate, just south of here, with Denis-the-Dowser from Crumbly's. We were having a mooch around the lake when we decided to explore further up the valley. We soon came upon an unusual and curiously-isolated monument right at the head of the valley.'

Howard produced a photo.

'What on earth is it?'

'It's St Peter's Pump. It originally came from the very centre of medieval Bristol. It once sat at the junction of Dolphin and St Peter's Street, now part of Castle Park. It covered the primary aquifer, the main source of fresh water in the middle ages. It was moved to Stourhead by Act of Parliament in 1766. In other words, the Hoare family, the lot you told me who ended up with Colston's money, bought it off the city and placed it over the prime aquifer of the Three Wells Valley. This is the source of the River Stour that flows into the English Channel at Christchurch, Dorset, 60 miles away.'

'Amazing - but what does Denis say about all this?

'He reckons it's all about the energy that's contained in the monument; its unique signature, he says.' Howard swung about and found another pink folder before producing several more photos.

'That's an obelisk on top,' I noted with surprise.

'It is indeed. Denis found a really strong vortex there. The crystal stone of the monument is a very powerful radiator. The weight of it alone would have had a piezoelectric effect.' He responded to my quizzical look. 'You know, when you put crystal under pressure you get a current. The same thing powers the watch you're wearing. This single monument represented the energetic heart of the old city.'

'So, there's some truth in the old belief that the source of a river is very significant?' I said.

'Yes, of course, of course. A small amount of water can have an enormous cascading effect. It's the same at Avebury and all over the chalk downs of southern England. Chalk has special qualities.'

Howard lent across the small table.

'Do you know that chalk can be 50% saturated with water before it dissolves? It just soaks it up like a sponge.'

He raised himself up and started to pace the saloon.

'Chalk is full of micro fossils. It is, in fact, the product of trillions upon trillions of skeletons, from millions of years ago. So much former life. A matrix of disintegrated and recrystallised fossils. It's a huge reservoir that someone, or some group, also understood. They used that knowledge to re-programme vast amounts of water. Chalk has neutral ph. It's completely inert. It's the perfect medium for the job.'

He paused and took another sip.

'When the 'mix' was ready, they would pull the plug. The water would flow through the porous chalk, re-programming the water table as it flowed east towards London and the North Sea.'

He studied my face intently. I responded with wide glassy eyes.

'Oh, shit, Howard - this is heady stuff! I could do with a break, just to digest it all.'

'Oh, err, yes.' He paused, swaying in the twilight, deep in thought.

'Actually Sam, do you mind if I invite a fellow bargee over to eat with us?' I'm sure you'll like her – she's fun.'

I grinned in response, content to allow the wine to take its full effect.

Howard shifted piles of photos and paper looking for his mobile.

A large, bubbly and posh-looking sixty-something women appeared, brandishing two bottles of red wine. She introduced herself, with a confident handshake, as Sue. It wasn't long before she was asking how I'd become interested in 'Howie's' research. I summarised and asked about her own journey.

'Well Sam, Daddy was in the RAF back in the Sixties. He was mostly stationed just up the road, so I grew up in Wiltshire and never left, apart from University. Anyway, before he died, while I was caring for him, he told me he had seen something *unbelievable* while he was a pilot. But tantalisingly, he wouldn't tell me the details, even as he was dying, for goodness sake. But there was a big hint, that what he witnessed jolly well changed his mind about what's really going on around us. This of course made me even more curious.' Sue raised her eyebrows in emphasis, before continuing. 'Has Howie talked about the Pleidean's yet?'

'Er no, he hasn't,' I replied, a little apprehensively.

'Sue thinks it's the Pleidean's leaving messages, you know, information in the patterns of the crop circles.' Howard nodded towards our new guest sitting at the head of the small rectangular table. She was clearly comfortable and very at home in the surroundings.

'We both came up with the idea together really…' Sue preened, '…You see, Sam,' she waved her now empty glass around for effect, 'it's like this. A couple of hundred thousand years ago, these Pleidean's, arrived and fiddled with our DNA and made us into some sort of hybrid human. They've been keeping an eye on us ever since. Croppies are one way of influencing us lot, you know, the collective consciousness.'

'Without breaking the universal law of free will,' Howard interjected nodding to Sue, before turning to face me.

'They programmed the water table using sacred geometric knowledge. It's all there if you decipher the language they use. You see, Sam, the patterns are very symbolic in themselves, but they're also energy fields. Patterns, that recode the water lying directly beneath them by changing its molecular bonding. The chalk downs are a vast, saturated sponge. The vibration from the crop glyphs encodes the crystalline structure of the water, well before it comes out of your kitchen tap. It's like that thing they do with sand on a vibrating plate – cymatics. That's it. I'm sure it's called that?'

'Right, OK - *but* what percentage of crop circles appear on chalk then?' I challenged.

'About 95 per cent.'

How was this so? I reflected. I couldn't help being intrigued, but clung on to rational objectivity for as long as I could.

Howard turned, picking up a small tube that had been standing upright against the bookcase. It was marked: Bedrock Geology UK South. He unrolled it expertly. My eyes tried to take in the colourful, almost psychedelic patterned map. He pointed out the immense fluorescent green sweep that is the chalk field of South East England. I looked up at his beaming face as he produced a transparent overlay marking the locations of known crop circles since the 1960s.

I straightened-up and took half a step back. It took a moment to focus, as my tired and now inebriated brain struggled to process the information. Like one of those computer-generated patterns, a picture suddenly jumped out, causing me to catch my breath.

'Oh *shit!* That's pretty, bloody obvious – *isn't* it?' I paused. Howard and Sue looked expectant as they silently studied my reaction. 'Oh, shit guys. That's a *clear* pattern...'

And there it was. The obvious focus of hundreds of crop circles - Avebury.

'You see, it's all about water and our minds, which also happen to be full of it.' Howard tapped the side of his head in emphasis and his eyes twinkled in the candle-lit saloon.

I exhaled. I'd finished my wine far too quickly but was still thirsty. '*Fuck,* Howard!'

He was grinning for Cheshire.

'What's it all bloody about then? I mean - *what's going on?'* I glared from one to the other.

'Don't ask Howie dear, it's *all* just a figment of his exaggeration,' Sue trilled. The two of them collapsed in laughter.

'I'll tell you what...' she placed a warm hand on mine, '...anyone who wants to *really* know about the croppies, should start with Chilbolton and the face with a disk.'

'What about it? What's so special about that one?'

'Well, apart from the fact that the glyph is huge, complex and precisely accurate, it's the location, *and* that it's clearly linked with one that appeared the previous year. But what makes it really special is what's been found encoded into its design.'

'Was that the one with the humanoid face and CD disk – back in '02?' Howard asked. 'I remember the message in the binary code.'

'A message? What sort of message – what? From the *Plyerdee-ans?* I said, head spinning.

Sue reached over the table and pulled a blank envelope towards her. A pen was produced from a voluminous handbag. She wrote slowly and deliberately as Howard looked on, nodding his approval. Then she rotated the message so I could read it. For the first time that evening, she looked serious.

It read:

'Beware the bearers of false gifts and their broken promises. Much pain, but still time. There is good out there. We oppose deception. Conduit closing.'

'How did you get on with Howard?' Big John said, his full, red lips smeared with icing sugar.

I had returned to Crumbly's the following weekend, eager for further spiritual and intellectual stimulus.

'Fine, it was great. He's in a beautiful spot, isn't he? What a thing to do, to transform your life so much, especially at his age. He made the right move. What an adventure.' My heart had warmed towards Howard.

'I do like his theories about the croppies,' Sophie interjected.

Big John took the podium.

'Interesting theory. Joins a lot of dots for me. It's laughable when the newspapers try to mock the whole crop circle thing with their – 'This is how it's done' stuff. On what evidence, eh? We get what? We get a couple of dozen big ones most years and some are obviously man-made, you can tell by the errors in symmetry. But most of them, especially the complex ones, are perfect. Absolutely, geometrically perfect in their execution; no errors. None, *at all* – how could any group achieve that, in a few hours and, in the dark? And - *then* not want any public credit or even recognition! Even bloody Banksy has a name. The subject matter and information encoded doesn't get commented on much either, does it? No mention of high-level physics, complex geometries with novel solutions and spiritual insight.' Tall John was in his element.

'And don't forget, they leave no muddy feet marks.' Colin waved a finger at Tall John and grinned.

'Maybe they use sky hooks to get into position,' I quipped.

'Perhaps they rehearse, you know, in some giant redundant aircraft hangar before they go out for the night,' Colin added.

'They'd need a lot of bloody chalk,' Sophie responded.

We all laughed at Colin's improbable scenario. An assemblage of white coated, elderly Oxbridge professors running around with string and bundles of chalk, orchestrated by some Busby Berkeley type with a step ladder, whistle and an enormous loud hailer.

'The professors with the tesseracts; can you straighten-up the fourth dimensional overlay – hurry up please, do remember we only have five hours before sunrise.'

As the laughter died down, Colin leant towards me. 'How's your Bristol stuff coming along Sam?'

'Not bad, not too bad. Why do you ask?' I replied.

'Well, it's just that I've recently finished a workshop about the Green Man and the Druids, and it's given me a few ideas about Bristol.'

'Oh yes?' I shuffled closer.

'I was thinking about Queen Square in Bristol, and the way that when it's looked at from above, you can see that the paths may have been laid out as a representation of the Sun Cross or St George's flag. You know, like St Peter's at the Vatican and the 13th Century Temple of the Templars in Paris. It looks to me like a ritual location. The Druids and others are keen to use locations like that to celebrate with ceremonies at special times.'

'You mean like the solstices and equinoxes,' I interrupted.

'Oh yes. They had loads: eight feasts for the spirit and four for the material world every year.'

'That sounds like a lot of partying,' I replied.

'Of all the ritual days, there's one that I think you might be interested in. Samhein. It was the end of the year when Mother Earth could give no more and a purifying fire was used, just before dawn. Animal and even human sacrifices were offered to ensure the successful rebirth of the seasons.'

Colin studied me.

'The fire was about cleansing the earth and the blood spilling, fertility. These events happened on sacred sites and other carefully-selected places that resonated with the right energy, usually a vortex point.'

'Like that thing...' I clicked my fingers in recollection, '...moxabustion. That's it, I think? What acupuncturists sometimes do.'

'That's right, same idea, but bigger and a little more terminal,' Colin said flatly.

'Maybe Cabot Tower is some sort of Templar obelisk. Well it's obviously a very masculine symbol. It would be the male pole of an electric circuit. That makes Queen Square a good candidate for the female or positive pole. Giving us two poles... a dipole, that could be the foundation of an electromagnetic circuit in the very heart of Bristol. That would make Queen Square quite interesting. Especially, as it's surrounded on three sides by water which flows through the gorge to the curiously named River *Severn*...' Colin drew the figure seven with his finger on the tea-soaked table. '...and out into the Atlantic Ocean.'

Colin paused before frowning conspiratorially.

'Do you remember the riot of 1831?'

'Not particularly. Just one of many, knowing Bristol,' I said lightly.

'Well, the one in 1831 was a bad one - a very bad one. No one knows how many were killed and injured, probably hundreds. Many burned alive in torched buildings and cut down by the Dragoons' swords. After three days it came to a bloody climax at dawn on 31st October. This happened to be the same date for the traditional Druid fire ritual: Samhein.' Colin shuffled closer.

'What are you saying?' I said.

'That the riot of 1831 might have had something to do with the Druids - or some other group - and their taste for ritual sacrifice,' Colin said emphatically.

I pulled back and studied his fifty-year-old face. Solid conviction gave a firmness to its lined complexion. Although I'd only known Colin six months, he had impressed me with his insights, particularly about Bristol. The city was only 20 miles north, but others in our little group hailed from much further away. We shared an allegiance to Bristol and I felt I could trust his theories because of this.

'Are you serious, Colin? I thought the Druids were gentle tree-loving folk? I mean if this did happen as you say, wouldn't somebody have got onto it by now? Written a book or something exposing it all? It really doesn't seem very likely that anyone could conveniently arrange a huge riot and get people slaughtered at a place and time of their choosing.'

'I know, Sam, but my intuition tells me there was more to the 1831 riot than meets the eye.'

I shrugged.

'Well you should have a look. Books, some written at the time of the event, throw light on the funny stuff that went on. Read up on it but keep an open mind. Some of the reports from the time are quite strange. Something else went on over those three days. *Something* that had been strategically planned.'

'OK. But I'm quite busy already. There's a stack of books next to my bed, mostly unread. I'm sure there might be something to it, but...'

'I really believe it's got something to do with the stuff you found in that box. Check it out - it might just turn out to be another piece of your puzzle,' Colin urged.

'Got that date for you, Sam,' Simon announced, with a hint of intrigue in his voice, as we settled into our familiar seats at the King's Head.

'Oh great...' I said, as my chest gave a nervous heave.

He produced a glossy A4 image from his overused brown briefcase.

'This is a photocopy of Draper's baptism record from St Augustine's. Now at that time, baptism was held as soon as possible after the birth. So, although this is a record of his baptism, not his birth, the gap between them wouldn't have been very large. Do you see Draper's entry?'

I scanned the image, impressed by the neatness and uniformity of the entries – until I reached Draper's.

I checked the date.

'March 25th. Oh, *no*...' This was long before Colston's death on 11th October. My heart sank at this road block to my reincarnation theory.

'Check the year, Sam. You might find *that* quite interesting.' Simon grinned as he repeatedly tapped the image with the end of his ubiquitous biro.

'1723.'

'But I don't understand, his monument and biographies all say 1721...'

Simon raised his eyebrows, nodding slowly and conferring more about the quality of historical research than I could possibly understand.

I stared at the entry; it said: *'William Inglby Draper, the son of Mr & Mrs Draper, baptised March 25st 1723.'*

'Is this right? There couldn't be another Draper?' I asked, momentarily confused.

'Unlikely. He's in the right place and his middle name is correct. It was his mother's maiden name. We are lucky that St Augustine's Parish was so respectable and included residences up Park Street and into Clifton. They have good records and although St Augustine's was demolished, a copy of the records ended up with the Corporation early on. You can find them yourself, they're still on the microfiche.'

As I supped my cider and reflected on Rangi's insistence about investigating Draper, it occurred to me that now might be a good time for a dinner party. I could invite Billy, Deb, Nick, Rangi and Simon. Not only had Deb not met Billy, but she had not seen the others for over a decade. How nice it would be to get everyone together again after all these years. And of course, this would give me an opportunity to update Deb. And what better reason for her to stay over until Sunday?

Deb's voice was gratifyingly enthusiastic.

'Yes Sam, I'd love to. But not until the weekend after next, I'm Josh-free then.'

Josh-free? I'd grown to like young Josh and increasingly looked forward to seeing him, but on the other hand, a child-free weekend together sounded even more appealing.

'So, what else are you up to with this jigsaw puzzle of yours?' she asked.

'Well, do you remember Colin, one of the *Ponytailed-ones* down at Crumbly's? You remember, I talked about him a little while back? Well he gave me some sort of lead. Not sure what to make of it yet, though.'

'Oh yes?' Her voice lingered across the *yes*.

'If you remember, Colin's originally from Bristol and studies local history. He's particularly clued-up on one event. The 1831 riot in Queen Square.'

'Ah ... right ... We did that one at school. It was about the Reform Act, wasn't it? Getting rid of the rotten boroughs and such like. Colin likes a nice riot, does he?' she joked.

'He thinks there's more to it, that it was a put-up job,' I said hesitantly.

'Put-up job? By whom...?' Deb's voice raised in sudden interest.

'He thinks that several curious events happened over the three days of the riot and that it was deliberately scheduled to take place on that particular date,' I said.

'He's not on about it happening on Halloween, is he? Sam, you mustn't fall for all that stuff, you're smarter than that,' Deb said firmly.

'I'm going to consider it. There *might* be something. Something new that can be added.'

'I expect there's nothing new. You'll be wasting your time.' My heart dropped. I decided to let this go and changed the subject to Norton and his recent adventures.

But her sceptical response and my obstinacy energised me to delve further. I was intrigued by Colin's theory and decided another visit to the library was warranted. That opportunity arrived a few days later when lousy weather delayed a day's work.

The riot of 1831 was the largest and bloodiest in Bristol's already-violent history. It's not known how many died, as no official record was gathered. The cause is understood to have been the threat to the passage of the Reform Bill in Parliament, which would become a major step in the consolidation of democracy in Britain. Sir Charles Wetherell, the Recorder of Bristol, had a direct interest in the bill's failure. He had been elected in the very rotten borough of Borough Bridge, in Yorkshire, a constituency that returned no fewer than two MPs for its 48 franchised voters. Just days before his scheduled visit, an audience of over three thousand had gathered in Queen Square to listen to impassioned speeches in support of the bill.

Sir Charles Wetherell's carriage arrived in Bristol on the grey autumnal morning of 29th October. By the time he reached the Court House his flamboyant presence had attracted a large, angry crowd. Within an hour the Court was abandoned, with Sir Charles only just escaping. He beat a speedy retreat to a pre-arranged appointment - a banquet at the Mansion House on Queen Square.

Meanwhile, Colonel Brereton, Bristol's most senior military officer, was nervously assembling a small troop of Dragoons on College Green. Brereton was deeply concerned by the mood of the crowd and by the very limited resources he had been allocated. Cavalry were effective in open spaces like Queen Square, but vulnerable in the alleyways of the city. As Bristol's Recruitment Officer he understood that hundreds of troops were stationed within a day's ride, but none were available in Bristol. His problems were compounded by his inability to find a magistrate or Corporation member. Without their explicit sanction he had no authority to act.

In the early hours of the morning of the 30th, a small group surged forward and attacked the Mansion House, with Sir Charles still inside. The dignitaries hastily retreated upstairs, increasingly fearful for their lives. By now, the vast stock of wine in the Mansion cellars had been liberated, fuelling the mood of the crowd. Brereton and his Troop, frustrated by the lack of orders, withdrew from the Square. Sir Charles eventually made his escape, turning up several hours later in the significantly quieter streets of Cardiff.

Bristol had just elected a new Mayor – Charles Pinney. A wealthy but modest family man, he was considered an outsider by many in the Corporation, having spent much of his life on his plantation in the Caribbean.

During the rest of the night and the following day, a large crowd appeared to move purposefully from one prison to the next. Press reports commented about the presence of *'well-dressed men'* who appeared to be directing proceedings. Hundreds of prisoners were sprung by the mob, to the cheers of the exuberant and increasingly-drunken crowd.

Meanwhile, Brereton quickly discovered that many key decision-makers were out of town. Mayor Pinney searched in vain for missing magistrates, vital to validate his instructions. He was floundering and unable, or unwilling, to act without consultation.

Bristol was in chaos. The north and west sides of Queen Square engulfed in 30-metre-high flames cast a deep red glow seen as far away as Cardiff. The lack of direction caused frustration for other members of Brereton's small command. Captain Warrington exclaimed that there must be a *'great screw loose somewhere,'* as he surveyed the apocalyptic blaze. By 2 am on the morning of the 31st, the hopelessly outnumbered dragoons withdrew from Queen Square and returned to their temporary barracks on the edge of College Green.

Even Brunel had become involved, returning from London by overnight mail-coach, volunteering as a Constable. His experiences left him in deep shock and unable to publicly discuss or complete his meticulously-kept journal.

The scene was set for a bloody climax as dawn approached.

At 3 am, Pinney reappeared and acted with uncharacteristic decisiveness in instructing Colonel Brereton:

'...to take the most vigorous, effective and decisive means in his power to quell the riot and prevent further destruction of property.'

Embers cascaded out of the night sky, illuminating a manic scene of drunkenness, plunder and arson. Military reinforcements were finally arriving, and the scene appeared to be set for violent confrontation. Near dawn, action was taken when Brereton led 21 dragoons along Prince Street and across into Queen Square at a canter. Their lethal swords had remained in their sheaths. What happened next turned events around decisively. As Brereton tried to hold his dragoons on station, a Major Mackworth suddenly appeared from behind him, sword drawn and at full gallop charged past, shouting for the men to follow *'...in the name of the King!'*

Long, very sharp sabres are designed for the swift removal of limbs. The crowd panicked, fleeing in terror, as a vicious flesh-chopping machine charged. It was not easy to escape as the Square had narrow exits. The assault lasted several hours and by 10 am survivors had all but dispersed. The dragoons, having done what they had been trained to do, returned to their temporary barracks on College Green.

As Brereton collapsed onto his cot, Mayor Pinney and several of the previously-missing magistrates, sent an urgent dispatch to the Commander in Chief of the British Army. It placed the entire blame for the failure to stop the riot and the carnage that followed on Brereton's exhausted shoulders.

As the rioters dispersed, orders were posted that anyone seeking medical attention would be scrutinised and those with wounds would be arrested. This discouraged many from seeking help and unknown numbers died from their festering wounds.

After a very public trial, four rioters were hanged from the gates of the New Gaol. The remains of the gates are still evident, having survived the destruction of the rest of the building; a macabre and forgotten legacy. Another memorial, in the form of a life-sized statue to Sir Charles Wetherell, lies partially hidden in the garden of the famous 15th century Red House on Park Row.

In late January 1832, after attending Court and hearing the prosecution's case against him, Colonel Brereton committed suicide, orphaning his two young daughters.

33 Dinner parting

By Wednesday morning it had dawned on me that I'd invited *two* vegetarians to Saturday's dinner. What on earth was I going to feed them? Cooking was an elusive art and I normally kept to a limited and predictable menu. For Billy and Simon, this would exclude anything they might like. But my drowsy call to the Universe was promptly answered by the garrulous Kate, bellowing out in her Irish vowels from the back door.

'*Sammy* - you decent?'

'Kate! My ally. Come in. I'm on the sofa.'

'What's this then. Recipe books? And what was all that vacuuming last night? What are you planning?'

She filled the door frame, one hand firmly placed on her broad hip, the other balancing an old tartan cake tin.

'I'm in a fix, Kate. Can you help?'

'You're an idle lump. You and that smelly dog. Your only exercise is wrestling with *'His Flatulence'* on who has first dibs on that enormous sofa.'

I could see Norton was listening, eyes closed, ears pricked.

'You've got to help me, *please*, it's important. I need your expertise. I've invited two vegetarians to dinner.'

'I could have guessed. You need a menu, don't you? For Saturday?'

'Yes, and...'

'Six is it? I can see you've brought down those extra chairs. Anyway, not that you deserve it, I've got this for you…' She smiled as she presented the cake tin. 'I've ended up with too much. It's chocolate fudge, with fresh cream in it, so keep it in the fridge. Anyway, you had better be in on Friday night. You'll have a lot of work to do. And don't you dare let that smelly beast eat my cake.' She glared at the prostrate Norton.

I busied myself preparing for the dinner and Deb's arrival. Kate had it all organised, even producing a dessert. A note attached said: *'Men are incapable of making anything that doesn't involve custard. So I made this for your friends to enjoy instead.'*

I'd just returned from my final shopping trip on Saturday morning, when the phone rang.

'I'm sorry Sam, Josh has a raging temperature. He's supposed to be with his dad this morning, but I just can't let him go like this. Martin honestly hasn't a clue when it comes to sick kids.'

'Oh no.' My heart dropped. 'That's awful. Poor old Josh. I'm so sorry. We'll all miss you.'

'I know. I was so looking forward to it. It would have been lovely to catch up with everyone.' Deb paused. 'Look, how about next weekend? I want to come down and say a last goodbye to the old house before the completion goes through. Friday would be good. I finish early, and Josh is staying at his friend's. I'll catch the train.'

'Yeah, that would be great. Stay over and go back on Sunday. Norton will be pleased to see you.'

'Yes, I rather miss the dear old thing,' Deb said wistfully. 'I'll have to be back in time for Josh's return in the afternoon, though.'

'I'll invite Billy. It shouldn't be a problem for him. He doesn't seem to go out much. When he's not working, he seems to stay in studying, as far as I can make out. Just the three of us then.'

Billy arrived on the dot of seven and presented a large, brown unlabelled bottle.

'It's Joseph's special spiced rum. It's a long time old. He no longer drinks it. My aunt, she says *no* - so he has a lot going spare. He wishes you the best.'

I cursed the fact that Deb couldn't greet him. That big grin of his would have won her over. Norton made the effort; wobbling along the hall into the kitchen, wagging his thick tail with abundant enthusiasm. Billy bent down fussing him as we caught up with the news. I filled a couple of glasses from a keg of 'Pip and Core Slightly Sparkling'. It was nice to see him, but I sensed something wasn't quite right. Perhaps he was nervous about the dinner party? Maybe. An hour later, Nick, Rangi and Simon arrived; their rowdy banter suggesting a warm-up at the King's Head. Everyone settled themselves around the heavily-laden dining table as I explained Debbie's absence.

'I was looking forward to seeing her,' Nick announced, as he brandished two wine bottles from his rucksack. He was soon reminiscing with a story about a party he'd been at with Debbie, a long time back. I retreated to the kitchen, anxious to follow Kate's comprehensive instructions to the letter, if not the minute.

The cider hit the spot before we moved on to the wine and by the end of the meal we were all quite pissed; except for Rangi, who 'liked a tipple' but never actually drank very much of it. Billy produced his uncle's rum. Its spicy aroma reminded me of toffee.

The conversation had meandered around during dinner, but a note of tension crept into the atmosphere as Simon moaned about another *'bloody audit'* at the University and Nick fretted about the politics at the Council House. *'Bastards,'* he muttered.

Rangi inquired how my research in Bristol was going. I wanted to share my discoveries but felt embarrassed with Simon sitting next to me.

'Simon. Now didn't *you* do something about that 1831 riot?' I asked.

He blinked, his face now flushed.

'Yeah. Yeah, I remember. Turned out to be a lot of bloody work. Should have done the earlier bridge riot instead.'

'Can you remember what you made of what happened?' I said.

'Why, Sam? Have you been reading books again? You'll get a headache,' Nick quipped sarcastically.

'I did it for the money. Some history group or other. It was supposed to be an easy hundred.' Simon held his glassy gaze on me.

'Do you remember who was responsible for it? I mean, could it have been prevented?' I asked hesitantly.

Nick interrupted.

'Why do you want to know this Sam? How come you're interested in something that was over…' Nick looked up glaring at me in hostility, '...over a …170 years ago. It just isn't important anymore.'

'Just curious. I was wondering what Simon's take is on it. That's all,' I replied, cautiously side-stepping antagonism.

Nick continued to glare at me. We were all drunk; Nick and Simon having had a head start. But the rum, which was delicious and very smooth, was rapidly levelling the score.

'Well it was Wetherell, wasn't it? Bloody Wetherell and his pompous bloody attitude and that rich twat – *Pinney*. He was another coward who wouldn't make any damn decisions. And then Brereton, he was the fall guy. Got completely stitched-up. Poor bastard…'

'Do you think there was anything, you know, a bit dodgy about it?' I asked encouragingly.

'There's always something a bit dodgy going on in Bristol. Especially if the Corporation has anything to do with it.' Simon paused, leaning closer. I could smell the Caribbean on his breath.

'You're not harping on about that Halloween *crap,* are you?' Nick spat the words, shaking his head in mock despair.

'No Nick. No, no, not at all.' I leant back, waving my palms in defence. 'Just, you know, hoping to get an idea on what Simon thought about it all. He is the expert after all.'

Rangi got up and diplomatically cleared away the plates, excusing herself to '*potter about*' in the kitchen. I could hear the windows drumming to the sound of heavy rain, the first wild weather for months.

'It was quite obviously a complete cock-up all round and could either have been prevented from happening or at least been contained to a skirmish or two,' Simon paused, 'if there had been sufficient troops, or any at all, and I mean troops, not cavalry. The dragoons would have been pretty useless and vulnerable in the tight streets and narrow lanes.'

'That's just my point. Why no troops - just cavalry? You need quite a bit of space for cavalry to have any chance of operating.' I paused. 'It seems it was Lord *whatsit's* decision, when he ordered that the cavalry be kept out of sight before nightfall. Why? What advantage would that have, unless you were planning on pouncing on the mob in a space big enough for cavalry to do its job?' I paused for a moment adding, 'The more I read and the more I think about it...'

'*Bollocks* Sam,' Nick shouted. 'You seem to see conspiracies in every fuckin' thing. Can't you just accept, *occasionally*, that nearly everything bad that happens is because someone, somewhere fucked-up?' Nick struck the table, and a splash of spittle hit the top of his hand.

'Sam. You know, plenty of highly-qualified experts have researched the riots before you,' said Simon.

'Yeah. You seem to think you're always bloody right with all these stupid damn theories of yours.' Nick glared directly at me, his cheeks reddened in anger.

'Well, I think this bloke Colin may be onto something. It's not just the date, but the place as well.' I was emboldened by my own research. 'I think Queen Square is a portal or sacred site. There's something special about that place.'

Nick looked away towards Simon as if seeking confirmation. Billy was sitting quietly as he had done for most of the night. I studied his face as he looked directly at Nick.

'You have turned into a fucking idiot, Sam. You had some brains once, I thought, but not now. All this bullshit.' Nick shook his head in an evident display of frustration.

'Is this the kind of spaceport that Branson might be interested in leasing?' Simon quipped. The formerly tight knot of his tie now dangled languorously an inch or more below his neck.

I didn't want the evening to end badly. Not like this. We all drew back as Rangi reappeared, wiping her hands. Then Billy suddenly intervened.

'The *Duppy men* – 'tis the Duppy men and their bad *t'ing.*' He stared, as if in a trance, across the dining table.

'*Duppy* men, what on earth are you talking about, Billy?' Nick shifted his gaze and grinned open-mouthed at him.

'Who are the Duppy men, Billy?' Rangi inquired gently.

'The Duppy men did it, they planned it all along. I tried to stop it all. It was a terrible bad t'ing. The Duppy men, no good, I tried to stop them. I knew but could not stop them - *the Duppy men*. It waz bad, very bad. I could never write about it. Everyone drunk – no good.' Billy turned to me, his face full of emotion. 'You must understand, I could not write my journal. It *ailed* me badly. But I did my best t'ing'...' Billy turned back and looked at Nick and Simon in turn. 'Sam he be right. It was the most terrible t'ing...'

'Jeez Billy, you alright? That bloody rum of your uncle's. It's got to you too,' Nick said.

'You must know it first. All magic must be fore*warned*. They must always tell you what they're going to do.' Billy studied us in turn. His familiar face now filled with anguish.

'What Billy? What was said?' I stared at him intently. Was he in a trance? Why was he speaking like an eye witness?'

'The Duppy men. They tell you first. It *ware* a man – Matthew. Matthew Bridges. He spoke at a big meeting. Many months before, everybody hear him say:

'Death is preparing his phantom dart, soon it will strike. I see a dark veil drawn, I see a throne dashed to earth, I see a mighty blaze as of a city flaming to the heavens.'

Billy stopped, turning to look directly at me, his eyes ablaze.

'Thus, will Raphael read the sky...'

'Fuck me!' Nick spat. 'I've had a *fukin'nuff* of this nonsense.' He threw himself back, folding his arms in protest.

Simon reached into his coat pocket and produced a much-thumbed note book.

'What are you writing for *fuck's sake*?' Nick called as he sat back up, swaying menacingly towards him.

'What he just said?' Simon responded, throwing a thumb towards Billy.

Simon showed it to Billy, who quietly nodded agreement.

'...you ready Rangi? Time, we went back to sanesville,' Nick called out to the kitchen as he stood up unsteadily, scraping the chair legs across the floor. 'You coming, Simon?'

'I'm sad you're goin' so soon, Nick, you're a good man me t'ink...' Billy offered to shake his hand. Nick took it, but I saw his wrist was limp. He quickly let go, before turning and mumbling about his coat.

'You know Nick, it's not the truth you're interested in. You're frightened to look beyond what you already - *believe* is the truth.' I spoke in anger and immediately regretted it. Nick, ignoring my remark, hurriedly pulled on his coat. He shouted at Rangi to 'hurry up' before heading for the front door.

The evening was not ending well.

Nick slammed the door as Simon gathered his raincoat and umbrella and quickly, though more quietly, followed Nick. He looked sheepish and offered me a half smile as he passed me in the hallway. Rangi came close, reaching up and pulling me towards her. We hugged in silence. I let out a long slow sigh. She turned and hugged Billy before reaching for her umbrella and coat. I held the door as she stepped into the rain.

Turning to go back to the dining room I found Billy standing right behind me, his coat already on. He looked tired. His normally sparkling silver-grey eyes were full of water.

'You going as well? Bloody hell...' I said with a loud sigh.

'I must go. You're a good man Sam, a very good man. You will find your heart if you seek it. You will find the knowledge. The *gnosis*. The truth will come to you...' His luminous eyes were framed in red.

'Thanks for coming Billy. I'm so sorry about Nick. He can be such a prat.' I snorted away a tear and closed the door, slowly turning the mortise key.

My heavy legs got me as far as the dining table. For a long time I sat motionless, gazing into an empty glass.

'Oh dear...' I sighed long and low.

The sweet scent of Joseph's spiced rum hung over the room like a shroud.

'Sammy?' Kate announced her arrival at the back door. 'You look as if the tax man has caught up with you.' She tried to smile, but her forehead revealed otherwise.

'Oh yeah. Hung over from last night. Come in. Come in, sit down, I'll put the kettle on. I've got some lovely cake.'

'I heard some raised voices. Sounds like there was a falling out. You, and that tall, flashy feller. Nick is it?'

'Oh God, Kate.' I sighed. 'Yes. And it was probably my fault.'

'Now, that doesn't surprise me. Another one of your theories - *was it*?'

'Yeah...' I let the cake tin drop onto the table. Feeling hopeless as I sank into my favourite chair.

Kate leant across, one hand cupped to her mouth, the other pointing upwards to the bedroom.

'So – *umm* Deb, then. How did that go?'

'Oh no. She couldn't make it. Her kid, you know...' I looked directly at Kate. 'But she's coming next weekend.' I shrugged my shoulders and smiled weakly. 'Look, I must thank you for all your help. The food was great. At least that worked!'

'This cake is burnt,' declared Kate, forensically examining the contents of the tin.

'No, it's lovely.' I blew a kiss in affection.

'Left it in a bit too long,' she announced out-loud, to no one.

'No complaints here.' I smiled as my mood eased. 'I shall cook the same for Deb as I did last night. That part really worked at least,' I muttered.

'You're a toad Sam. Can't you be more inventive?'

'Not with Deb at stake. She'll be impressed by the veggie cooking, won't she?'

'I'd be careful with that one, Sam. Don't make too many assumptions about what she wants.' Kate gave me her stern look.

'I know, I know. But she's definitely keen, otherwise she wouldn't be making the trouble to come over,' I explained.

Kate looked sceptical and offered a weak smile.

For the next few days I was busy with work; a knock-on effect of taking so much time off the previous week to prepare the dinner party. It was not until Wednesday evening that I got around to inviting Billy. He'd been able to come the previous Saturday, so I was assuming Friday wouldn't be a problem for him. As I sauntered up to his house, I reflected on how familiar my life with him had become and how he unfailingly raised my spirits.

'Billy's not here. Did he not tell you?' Patricia stood in the doorway, hands busy with a tea towel.

'No.' I paused in thought, confused. 'Well I don't know. What was he supposed to tell me?' My stomach started to knot.

'He's left. Left on Monday with Lamin. For the *Gambia...*' Patricia's voice shot through me like a dart.

'The Gambia? What's that all about?'

'Did he not tell you? That was not good, he should have said. He's gone off to do voluntary work. Somewhere up-river.' Patricia paused as she recollected. 'He told me he wanted to be near where our ancestors came from. Near our cousins.'

'No, I, er...I had no idea about any of this. I, I...'

'I don't know when he'll be coming back. He's finished his course and passed his exams. He should have told you about this...' Patricia looked annoyed, and, by the tone of her voice, wasn't expecting him to return any time soon. Unconsciously I stepped back towards the kerb.

I made my excuses and handed her a torn slip from my notebook. 'If he should write or anything, this is my home address...' I felt embarrassed. Excluded. But then, what kind of relationship did we have anyway, other than steam trains?

Returning home, bruised and confused, I couldn't get Patricia's face out of my mind. There was a closed-down look. As if my turning up unannounced was some kind of insult.

Norton was letting me know that it was now walkies time. I considered his soulful, dark eyes. 'What a bloody thing to do,' I said, as another flush of anger passed through me. The thought that Billy had just flown away without even a goodbye. I stewed about it until Norton's persistent huffing urged me into activity.

'Come on then. Yes, it's time for your walk,' I said struggling to my feet. He responded with two happy woofs and continued to wag for England.

'Well at least I've got you – eh, old chap.' He didn't look up. Intent as he was on checking out the malodorous cocktail at the base of the local post box. As he cocked his leg for the umpteenth time, I reflected on whether this spot was the doggie equivalent to a FaceBook page. A sort of wee mail. What had he just posted? I let him do his thing and returned home to the refuge of my sofa.

As my thoughts drifted around Billy and his sudden departure, my mind went back to his strange trance-like comments at the dinner table.

'You must understand, I could not write my journal.' What on earth had he been talking about? Was Billy writing a book? And why did he talk about the riot as if he'd actually been there?

And now he was gone. He must have known he was leaving all the time he was sitting at my table, yet he said nothing.

The kernel of anger grew.

Had he told Nick of his planned departure? Was I the last to know?

I decided I wasn't going to tell Deb about his disappearance until she arrived. At least I had Debbie, my lovely Debbie, to look forward to.

Damn Billy.

With Billy obviously out of the picture, I abandoned plans to cook dinner for Deb at home; opting instead for one of our old haunts, for a more romantic and, hopefully, intimate experience. The Avon Gorge Hotel is one of Bristol's most prominent venues. Several stories of Victorian splendour sit on the very edge of a dramatic hundred-metre-deep gorge and offer dramatic views that stretch out to Dundry in the east and the River Avon and Brunel's Clifton Suspension Bridge in the west.

My building work had suffered. My thoughts were either with Deb or interspersed with painful reflections on Billy. He had some fascinating and enigmatic ideas and I regretted not having written more of them down. But at the time it had felt a bit too insulting to do that. Billy was no guru. He might have been mature for his age, but he was also a vulnerable human being like the rest of us. I chuckled to myself, recalling how his immaculate appearance became more dishevelled as he necked half pints of cider at the King's Head.

The phone buzzed in my pocket. The text read: *'Sorry: Stuck at Reading Station. Some sort of hold-up. Might be another hour before we can get going again...x'*

So much for a relaxed drink on the Terrace Bar. It was all going to be a push now. We might have to go straight into dinner. What a shame.

The train finally arrived two hours late. Deb was obviously frustrated by the delay, as she recounted the irritations of the other passengers' behaviour.

'Where are we going?' She looked confused as we left the station.

'Oh, sorry, I didn't tell you. Billy can't make it, so it's just the two of us tonight.' I turned and smiled. 'I thought we could have dinner together at the Gorge, like we used to. One up from my dusty house,' I said cheerfully.

Deb sat back and studied my face.

'So, what happened to Billy?' Her voice betrayed just a hint of scepticism.

'He's gone. *Well.* What I mean is, it seems he's left Bristol and gone to the Gambia. As a volunteer or something. He could be gone for quite a while. I don't actually know,' I faltered.

'Didn't he tell you he was going then?'

'No, he didn't. I found out from his Aunt Patricia when I went to invite him for this evening.' This felt distinctly awkward.

Deb didn't reply, but the set of her mouth looked mildly disapproving. Disbelieving even.

We arrived at the hotel and went straight into the restaurant in silence.

'So, I'm not going to meet this mysterious Billy, am I...?' She frowned.

'No – well maybe he'll come back. He did, after all, say this is where his heart was. Here in Bristol.' I forced a thin smile.

Deb looked away, scanning the other diners.

'This has become a real tourist spot, hasn't it?' she whispered, leaning towards me.

'Yes, I guess,' I replied, a little taken aback by her sudden change of subject.

'Anyway...' She paused, shuffling slightly before looking directly at me.

'What went on at Mortlake? You said something strange happened?'

I told her about the Cromwell House gate posts and the curious arch in the graveyard.

'You've already told me, and very interesting it is too. Like a good mystery novel – *almost*. But you alluded to something more when we spoke on the phone. I forgot to ask you when we were in Marlborough.' Deb looked serious.

I cautiously opened-up about the heightened senses that had awoken within me. Producing ever subtler scents and sounds, and Billy's bright aura. She listened attentively and pursed her lips in thought.

'That's quite a weird experience you had Sam. You sure you didn't just fall asleep in the sun? You must have been pretty tired by then.'

'No, I've gone over it again and again in my mind, but it was far too lucid. It felt more like a trance. I could perceive so much. I could think things and see them happen. It was a bit scary. It was *so* powerful, it took me a couple of weeks before I started to get back to normal. Something strange and rather wonderful happened to me that afternoon.' I felt relief at finely telling her.

She looked confused.

'You hadn't by any chance, been smoking that pot of yours?'

'No, no. Please understand. It was a very special moment. I don't really know what it was. It might never happen again, but it *did* happen,' I stressed.

'Was Billy there? What did he think about it then?' Deb demanded.

'I didn't tell him. I was too all over the place to discuss it. I needed space to think about what had happened,' I replied.

Her eyes narrowed. 'Claire says you've gone all New Age; a bit of a hippy.' She spoke just as the waiter arrived. His gaunt, sixty-year-old face flickered briefly in amusement.

We ate, mostly in silence, occasionally commenting on the quality of the meal. I decided to try and rescue the evening by telling her about my experience with Howard.

'Did I tell you about what happened after I left you at Swindon?' I said cautiously.

'No, you didn't. How did you get on with him? I don't remember meeting Howard but think I remember you talking about him years ago. How is he?' Deb smiled, prompting me to reply.

I recounted the evening as best as I could recollect. We laughed together about Termite Tim and his house recycling activities.

'They'd call it up-cycling these days,' she said with an ironic smile.

My pulse calmed as she visibly relaxed.

'More wine?' Deb looked indecisive. 'Don't worry, I thought we'd get a taxi back...'

We talked about life on a narrowboat and whether it would be any good.

'The view is lovely, isn't it?' Deb gazed thoughtfully out of the panoramic window. 'What's all this about the crop circles then? Surely they're all done by hoaxers?'

'Well, not according to Sue and Howard's theories,' I replied.

She looked incredulous.

'So, who is supposed to be leaving this 'encoded' information, then, Sam?'

'...Ah well some group or other,' I stammered under her gaze. 'Not sure really... They haven't exactly left an address.'

'Hmm...' she looked unconvinced and changed the subject.

'What about the Bristol thing? How are you getting on with Colston?'

'Well I've been reading up on Bristol's history again. Colin, you know, one of the Ponytailed-ones at Glastonbury?' Deb nodded. 'Anyway, he's quite knowledgeable about Bristol history and thinks that something suspicious happened in 1831, around the time of the riot.'

'What was that then?' she spaced her words carefully.

'Oh, well. He thinks the riot was deliberate; planned months beforehand by some group or other. It was like a Druid sacrifice or something.' I mumbled as I realised I had just dug even deeper, into my hole.

'Isn't Simon an expert on Bristol? What does he think about this theory of yours - sorry Sam, of Colin's?'

'Er, not very much really. We talked about it at the dinner. He wasn't very accommodating about the idea.'

'Well I'm sure he's more of an expert than this Colin,' Deb replied.

'OK, yes. But Colin has a different perspective.'

'You're sure right about that, Sam.' Deb interrupted. 'Is that the one that happened at Halloween or something? Yes, it is, isn't it? You do seem to be tipping over the edge a bit. All these theories of yours. Some of them are rather strange, you know. I bet you fell out with Simon over this – didn't you?

I sensed something was up.' She paused as I shrunk into the seat. 'Frankly Sam, you really are getting into way too much nonsense these days. I don't mind all that mystery stuff, it's a bit like a badly-written Dan Brown novel, but you're really starting to lose your grip on reality with all this.' She leant towards me with a very serious look. 'You're not doing yourself any favours, you know.'

'Colin is very knowledgeable. He's done his research and he's found some interesting stuff. I've checked it out, and it seems to add up. And so, has Howard, actually.' I could hear myself becoming more defensive. 'I've known him a long time and I respect his research, he's put a lot of time into it. So has Colin. You know they don't just dream these ideas up. It's taken a lot of study and - and thinking. Looking at things from other perspectives. The problem is, when people start condemning things without even bothering to investigate them. Some people would say that was the height of ignorance.' My heart beat hard.

'Are you saying that I'm ignorant because I don't agree with all this weird stuff?' Deb said.

'Look, no – of course not I'm...'

'Sam, I think you'd better call the taxi. I'm not in the mood for any more of this. And as for Mortlake? I think you just fell asleep in the sun and dreamt it all.'

'No, it wasn't like that, not at all,' I interrupted.

She ignored my halting attempts to explain.

'And this thing with Bristol. Seems to me you've been led up the garden path. I bet Colin, whoever he is, is having a good old laugh about it right now.'

My hands gripped the table, my face flushed. She continued her assault.

'But this crop circle nonsense is seriously worrying me. You're a dreamer, Sam. You need to watch some proper television. There are excellent documentaries that show exactly how those things are made. They've filmed them doing it. I'm much more inclined to believe some well-researched and informative programme on television than the likes of someone living on a barge...'

'Narrow boat, actually,' I interrupted.

'I don't care. I really am not *that* interested...' She looked at me with scorn. 'I think you should turn your attention elsewhere, Sam.' She paused for a few moments. Her tight lips said it all. 'I'd like you to order the taxi now, please. I have to be up and gone early tomorrow.'

I sat dazed and shocked, contemplating the rubble of what had been a carefully-planned evening. It was clear that back-peddling, subject-changing or even an outright apology would be futile. Silence was now my only option.

Deb left early, before breakfast. She fondled a happy Norton and gave me a chilly embrace at the front door before putting on her rucksack and setting off to her childhood home for one last visit.

After closing the door, I slumped onto the sofa and distractedly watched Norton as he struggled to clamber into his armchair. Even he seemed dejected and withdrawn. I glanced up at the clock. It was just after nine. I sighed. How could it all had gone so wrong? Perhaps Deb had been upset about her impending final visit to her old home. I stared at the fireplace for an hour, hoping she might call. Thoughts drifted past, suddenly an involuntary shiver ran the length of my spine. It made me sit up. I looked across to Norton.

'Thank God I didn't tell her about the bloody *Pleidean's...*'

The next morning, I lay in bed until my bladder forced me to the bathroom. Returning, I called to Norton that we'd be off for his walk *real* soon. The dear old chap is so patient, I thought. After dressing, I made my way downstairs for the start of my morning routine, putting on my work boots and grabbing the lead from the back of the door.

I called out to the absent Norton. 'Come on boy, time to get out of that chair. Come on Norton come on old boy – *walkies!*' I turned into the front room. 'Come on, you lazy hound, you still asleep?'

He lay in his chair like an old black bear.

'Come on then boy, get up...'

I stood near the door staring at his motionless form. My stomach caved in.

'Norton! – Norton, *oh Norton*...'

I held my breath. 'Oh no.'

His enormous purple tongue hung like a rag from the side of his greying jaw. His last mouthful of saliva had run down the chair and collected on the carpet. I instinctively stretched out and stroked his inanimate head, tasting the salt from my tears.

'Oh Norton, you, silly old dog. Why'd you have to go?'

I kneeled, placing my right arm around his shoulders and buried my face into his neck. He was already cold. Lifeless. I cupped his sweet, black face in my hands, no longer caring as my fingers slipped through the last of his frothy saliva. His eyes shut in permanent slumber.

I slumped to the floor. Holding his droopy paw, I sat motionless with my devoted companion until we were disturbed by the clatter of the letter box. More bills and shit, I thought dully. They can stay with the rest of the festering pile.

I'd had enough of the world anyway. It could just - *fuck right off.*

We stayed there together for an hour, the silence only interrupted by my deep shivering sighs. The emptiness of the room became palpable as I mourned the loss of my dear old friend.

'What a lot of shit is going on, eh Norton?' I whispered plaintively.

'Deb...? No, I'm not going to call her, I'll wait 'til she rings me. She laid into me, she can damn well be the one to apologise.'

My breaths shortened.

I felt my face flush as I shifted to a more comfortable position. Fucking Nick – and bloody Simon; he hadn't exactly defended me either. What a great pair of mates they were.

And even Billy! How could he have buggered off without a word?

'Bloody woman. She can sodding well call *me* if she wants to know about Norton. Fuck her.'

I undid his collar and placed it on the mantelpiece, promising him I'd polish the tag and oil the leather. I made my way to the kitchen and decided to wait awhile before calling on Kate. She'd know what to do. But my eyes were red, and I didn't want to let her see just how vulnerable I had become. I stared at the floor, motionless.

And then the phone rang.

'Oh, hi James, how are you? I said politely. It was my big extension customer.

'Hello Sam. Could you come over? We need to have a chat about the job.' He sounded a bit curt. Formal even.

'Yes, of course. Later this week?' I replied.

'Um, the sooner the better. Could you make it tomorrow morning? There'll be someone here I'd like you to meet.'

'Yes, sure, tomorrow would be OK,' I replied, puzzled.

He definitely sounded tense. Was this about their friend's kitchen that Jean had mentioned? More work then; can't be bad. I cheered up momentarily.

Or could it be about those settlement cracks – *could it?* I thought we'd already agreed to wait before sorting that out. I felt a spasm of trepidation.

I stood up and shuffled back to the front room, staring at Norton's purple tongue.

'Oh shit, what am I going to do with you?'

Kate shouted from the other side of her back door. 'OK, OK ... stop your knocking, I'm coming right now.'

I started to speak, then sighed deeply, catching my breath. Tears ran down my cheeks, ruining my plan. Kate reached out grasping my arms.

'Sammy, what is it? What's happened?'

'It's Norton – he's died, died in his sleep. What am I to do? What am I going to do with him Kate?'

'Oh, the poor old boy.' She hugged me to her before placing a protective arm around my shoulders as we made our way back through the gardens to my kitchen.

'Well, Sam, you can call the vets and they can look after all the arrangements for you. They'll charge of course, but they would come and collect him. Would you like that?'

I stood upright, my back against the living room wall and studied Norton's familiar face.

'Oh no, I'm not having that. He deserves something better than being dumped in a black bin liner, for Christ's sake.'

Kate smoothed Norton's coat as she offered me a tentative smile.

'Where I grew up, we would bury our animals in the garden; we had our very own pets' cemetery.'

I'd never had pets when I was young and felt shocked at just how bereft I was feeling. I'd only had him a few months. Jeez, some people have dogs and cats for years; how do they cope when the time comes?

I thought for a moment, rocking gently on the balls of my feet.

'The garden's very small.'

Kate gave a shrug.

'There is that patch by the back fence. Do you think that would do?' I said.

'Well, it will be the first bit of gardening you've done in a year or two,' she smiled.

I sat heavily on the sofa and studied Norton.

'Do you think I should tell Deb?'

'That's up to you, Sam. Expect she'll find out eventually whatever you do.'

'Yeah. When she calls to apologise, I'll tell her then.'

Kate stood up to face me.

'Don't count on her calling *you* Sam,' she warned, waving a finger towards me.

'Oh, she will. She will...'

Digging Norton's grave helped. The day had been overcast and cold, and as I dug, I felt a few showery drops on my face and hands. The back garden looked sombre, reflecting my mood. The poor animal deserved some dignity, I thought. The idea of him being taken away in the back of some van or other, to be disposed of without due respect upset me. No, not that for old Norton. He was surprisingly heavy. I felt awkward, not wanting to grip too tightly in case I hurt him. We laid him onto his favourite army blanket. Originally white, it had long since taken up a salt-and-pepper appearance. Norton had been a prolific shedder of hair and mud.

'Of course, if he'd been a Viking dog they'd have buried him with his old armchair.' Kate said, prompting me.

I stopped mid-shovel, turning to her and grinned for the first time that day.

'No. That would have been the Egyptians. The Vikings would have set light to his armchair and cast him adrift. I can see it now,' I held my right arm aloft, 'floating into the sunset under the Suspension Bridge.'

Kate had the most magical way of improving my outlook. There was something about the *Irishness* of her. We grinned briefly at one another, as we lowered him carefully into the metre-deep hole.'

'Would you say that's deep enough?' Kate inquired.

'Oh, yes. He's not going, anywhere is he?'

Bless him, I thought. The most innocent, trusting creature I've ever had the privilege to know. I covered him with the damp topsoil, offering the spade to Kate. We both took turns to pat the soil down.

'I should plant a rose or something,' I said, leaning thoughtfully on the shovel.

'I'd say a lamp post would be more appropriate,' she replied with a wily grin.

'What the *fuck!...*'

I stepped back in shock.

'This is Mr Harris, he's from the *Council.*' James, standing next to me, opened his arm towards a man in his mid-fifties. He was dressed in ironed jeans and an enormous fluorescent jacket. A canary with a clipboard.

Mr Harris nodded from the far side of a three-metre-wide hole in the garden of James and Jean's house. A large crack above the bathroom window and other signs of substantial building movement had appeared, scarring the formerly pristine white wall. But the biggest shock was the sight of the Italian flagstones I had so meticulously laid, lying jumbled-up like playing cards, a full metre below my feet.

'Mr Samuel Cartwright?' His voiced landed like a lead weight. A fleeting memory surfaced of that terrible day at school with the broken window in the headmaster's room. I nodded in reply, looking up briefly in acknowledgement, before returning my gaze to the ground – *or the lack of it,* around me. 'It appears we have a very large hole, Mr Cartwright.' He paused, examining me intently. 'I understand you were the builder of this extension and that you submitted appropriate planning consents for this structure?'

'Er, yes. Yes of course. I did it all properly. I did all the paper work...'

'Would you have your Site Investigation Reports to hand?' Mr Harris asked with formality.

'Er, - *no?*' I creased my forehead. 'What do you mean *Site Investigation Reports*?' I could feel the heat from James's eyes as they bored into the side of my face.

His Luminescence spoke as my knees buckled.

'You were required under Section 42, Clauses 7 and 8 to ascertain by means of 'correct investigation,' the structural integrity of the proposed building area as per drawing number 7.'

My bowels dissolved.

'I... I *hand*-dug the footings myself. All to the right depth,' I pleaded, scanning James's stern face for support. 'There weren't any holes then. I mean, how was I to know what was underneath? I... I can't *believe* this.'

My finger nails dug into my sweaty palms.

'I suggest you contact your insurance brokers, Mr Cartwright.'

Mr Harris's glowing presence had just sucked the life out of me.

'Mines,' I mumbled, as I nursed my third pint. '*Fucking* mines.'

'Look Sam, we've all done it, built extensions around here. Everyone knows there's a risk. But a site investigation at the back of those terraced houses, you gotta be joking, it's just not practical.'

It was Friday and my old builder mates were holding court in the front bar of the King's Head. 'You'd have to crane the drilling rig over the bloody roof. And then there'd be no room to rig it up. Never heard of it done around here, it's ridiculous.' A small group of dusty middle-aged men nodded in gloomy agreement.

I left them conferring with worried looks. East Bristol was riddled with undocumented and unregulated coal mines, some of them lying close to the surface. Building around here was a lottery, and it appeared that I was holding the wrong ticket. I made myself as comfortable as I could at our usual Friday spot. Other than yesterday's shock, I was apprehensive about my first meeting with the gang since the disastrous dinner. When Nick and Simon arrived together, they stood for a while at the bar talking. I watched in interest as Simon offered to buy the first round. A carefully-calculated gambit of his; it would be the shortest of the evening.

'Sorry to hear about Norton, Sam. Old Tom told me last night.' Nick held out his hand in a gesture of friendship. 'And sorry about the other night. I was seriously pissed-up.' He held on with a tight grip. 'Rangi gave me a right bollocking for it all. Sorry mate.' He offered a tentative smile.

I sighed in relief.

Simon gave me a large grin as he sauntered from the bar. For the first time in months I felt the need for the companionship of old and dear friends. After the shock at James and Jean's, I'd returned home feeling dejected and spent a long, restless night brooding over my growing list of worries. Nick sat next to me as we began our ritual round of news stories. I soon realised that he didn't know about Billy's departure.

'What?' he barked abruptly.

'Where's he gone?' Simon asked, displaying more eager curiosity than concern.

'The Gambia, it seems, with his friend Lamin,' I replied.

Nick scowled in annoyance; Simon wore a deeply puzzled frown. The silence was eventually broken by Nick, as he sat back in his chair. 'Funny bloke though, a bit peculiar I always thought.'

'Had some strange ideas. Seemed to think he knew a lot more about the world than the rest of us,' Simon added as he looked to us for approval.

'And what was all that 'Duppy Men' business at your place? What was he going on about?' I could see Nick was hurt by the news and doing his best to distance himself from his original reverence.

'Yes – I checked-out Duppy Men,' said Simon. 'Apparently, it's Caribbean for malevolent spirits. Well it was all pretty weird. His mind seemed to flip into some sort of *altered* state. Duppy men? Caribbean ghosts...? I wonder what that has to do with a Bristol riot?' As he speculated between licks of a torn crisp packet, a familiar female voice broke in:

'Death is preparing his phantom dart, soon it will strike. I see a dark veil drawn, I see a throne dashed to earth, I see a mighty blaze as of a city flaming to the heavens.'

We all turned to Rangi as she arrived from the bar and pulled up a stool. She smiled at us in turn, unwinding her latest combination of multi-coloured scarves.

'That was well remembered,' I said.

'Not really. Simon copied it down, didn't you?' Simon nodded before raising his arm and a theatrical forefinger and adding:

'Thus, will Raphael read the sky.'

'Where was that quote from? Do you know, Simon?' I tentatively asked.

'I do, yes. I found it in a curious little book: '*The Bristol Riots: Their Causes, Progress and Consequences*.' By 'A Citizen.' It quotes a Matthew Bridges from some big gathering months before the riot and Raphael was the title of a popular astrological ephemeris at the time. Weird that Billy should have known this stuff...' Simon reflected.

'I'm convinced there was a lot more to him than he ever let on,' I replied.

I felt abandoned by Billy, and I was not alone. Rangi sensing my all-encompassing feeling of loss, leant over the messy table and squeezed my knee in affection.

'I'm so sorry about Norton, Sam'. I studied her face. Rangi's compassionate eyes said all I needed to know.

'Yeah, bummer. You didn't get to enjoy him for very long. Sorry to hear it mate,' Simon added.

'Thanks guys. At least *he* was dependable,' I said. My companions recoiled.

'No, not you guys. Deb. She went off in a huff and hasn't even bothered to call me to apologise. Or even thank me for dinner,' I said indignantly.

Rangi looked at me carefully then asked what had happened. I gave her the abridged version.

'Sounds to me like you were talking bollocks again,' Nick said, before realising Rangi had changed her focus and was now glaring intently at him.

'Yes, um, sorry mate.' Nick patted my arm with a look of rueful self-consciousness.

'That's OK,' I said, staring into the distance with a forced smile.

After several pints, I returned home, sober and preoccupied with the potential consequences of the previous day's awful meeting. I knew the insurance company would pay out for a rebuild and probably re-home Jean and James while it went on, but it could still have very serious financial consequences for me.

God knows where all this could end up.

For most of the weekend I was overwhelmed with anxiety, as my mind tumbled from collapsing buildings to Deb's evident indifference. By Monday I was spent. Common sense should have told me to take time off, but I didn't. I stomped around at my new customer's house in an increasingly frustrated mood, sensing that the day was already somehow jinxed.

The job involved replacing an old lead water supply pipe with a healthy new blue plastic one. To feed the pipe through the length of the house to the stop tap, I would normally have removed several floorboards along the hall, carefully de-nailing and stacking aside as I worked. This day though, I decided to cut a few corners in my attempt to finish the job early and retreat to the pub. In my haste, I broke a cardinal rule. I crowbarred a board up and tossed it aside without first de-nailing it, then watched with indifference as it fell between two joists into the dark, shallow basement. Half an hour later I jumped down, unaware of the three inches of rusty cut clasp nail that lay in wait. Unaware, that is, until it pierced the worn sole of my left boot and passed into my foot.

I was alone in the house and in too much pain to think about driving to A&E. Luckily my mobile summoned a rather alarmed taxi driver to the front door. After some negotiation: 'You'll have to pay a cleaning surcharge if you bleed on the floor, mate', we arrived at the busy casualty department with my bloody foot swathed in a bath towel. I left several hours later, bandaged and drugged, with two crutches dispensed as a parting gift.

Exhausted, I collapsed onto the sofa, wrapping myself in a blanket and staring dumbly at Norton's old, and now very poignant armchair, until the drugs took their soporific effect. At some point during the night I stumbled and hopped my way to the downstairs toilet and, unable to negotiate the stairs, returned to my cushion-padded refuge. Circumstances appeared to have brought my shuddering world to a complete halt. The nail had penetrated right through the foot, causing more damage than I'd initially realised. *'Expect to be hobbling about for a month – maybe more.'* This meant that it could be a couple of months before I'd be fit enough to deal with the rigours of a typical building job.

After a few days, and thanks to the wonderful support of Kate (*'lazy beggar!'*) I started to resurface, even answering the door to a drunken Old Tom. His continued insistence that I sort out his bloody shelves had begun to piss me off and I made short work of our doorstep meeting. I waved my crutch in the direction of his home and suggested he might try and find someone else. Offended, he dropped his gaze before shuffling slowly away.

I returned to my sofa and groaned in despair.

'What do I do now?' I plaintively asked my empty home.

I had my rainy-day stash and the profit from James and Jean's job was still sitting, mostly untouched, in the bank. The state of my foot limited my options, but with no Norton to look after, I could at least get away somewhere. I needed to escape, to regroup, but had to be close enough to Bristol for bandage changes and check-ups. The Mendip Hills, just south of the city, came to mind. It had been a long time since I'd taken a break for anything more than a long weekend. In the days of 'Dunrubblin', my old campervan - I would regularly make trips out of town, sometimes just for the night. I smiled to myself as I recalled some of those wonderful mornings. All dew and bird song.

Though I no longer owned a camper, I did have an automatic car. And somewhere, an old tent and sundry camping gear. I remembered Gordon's legacy – the telescope, lying upstairs still unused in its chest. It wasn't too heavy to handle, and just might provide a bit of a distraction.

There was another good reason to leave this comfy sanctum sanctorum, though. It was becoming obvious that consuming increasing amounts of cider was not helping my state of health. Kate was making louder and ruder remarks about the load she was being asked to carry back from the corner shop - *'my cat's wee smells better than that stuff...'*

She could have a point, bless her.

It took nearly a week of painful tottering, but I finally filled the cavernous Estate with what I hoped was adequate gear and headed for the hills - literally.

But the first night turned out to be a disaster. Although I'd left in brilliant early September sunshine, by the time I reached the campsite, an hour's drive and 300 metres higher, it was drizzling persistently. The campsite was not much more than a farmer's field, with woods on three sides and a view down the hill to the west and the broad silver path of the River Severn.

I hopped around; my bandaged foot shrouded in a black bin liner. Setting-up was slow and occasionally painful. I was alone, except for a zipped-up, expensive looking bell tent in the corner of the field. Despite its fancy appearance, it was surrounded by drifts of discarded tins and bits of paper. Messy buggers, I tutted.

My plastic sock caused me to slip several times. Chunks of dungy-smelling mud glued itself to my anorak as I struggled with the bright red *'bugger to put up'* nylon tent. Increasingly dispirited, I took a break and gave serious consideration to packing-up and retreating home.

When the tent was finally erected, I discovered I'd forgotten to buy the little gas canisters for the stove. There was still one left inside though; probably enough to boil a single kettle. But I watched with increasing despair as the remaining gas sputtered away.

'Just my luck,' I growled, screwing my face up at the taste of the tepid brown water.

And no dinner either.

Exhaustion and the lack of anything else to do, induced a deep, drugged sleep. But within three hours I was awake and shivering. The sleeping bag had been more than adequate in the insulated campervan, but at this elevation, on an exposed hillside and a centimetre from damp grass it was a different story. 'Shit - *this is not fun!*' I shouted, tossing from side to side. I speculated about how long it might be until sunrise, so I could pack it all up and head home. Eventually, I succumbed and dozed miserably towards the morning.

39 Meeting Doug

'Hello, *Hello?* Mate. Are you awake?'

The disembodied words were repeated, or maybe just echoed in my head as consciousness returned.

'Sorry – what?' I replied.

'Oh, sorry mate. Didn't mean to wake you, but - would you like a mug of tea, like? I've brought sugar if you want it.'

I opened the tent flap and peered up to see a scrawny face with a big smile revealing several pointed stubs and a lot of gaps. He was thin, much too thin. The skin sagged from his lined face like doll's house drapes.

'I got here after you and overheard you in the tent, like. You seem to be havin' a hassle. Thought you might like a mug of tea, bro?'

Thus began my fortuitous association with 'Doug', a sometime poet and itinerant with a wicked grin and wild blue eyes.

He looked easily ten years older than his stated age of 42. It quickly became evident that he was rootless – physically, spiritually and morally. He had obviously spent a lot of time outdoors; his weather-beaten face and hands were the colour of cooked lobster.

I thanked him for the proffered steaming mug and huddled up my knees. The tent had started to catch the morning sunlight, warming the air inside. I shuffled in comfort as I sipped the fragrant tea. Funny, I mused, how someone dressed in stained, torn jeans and sockless trainers, could drink exquisitely-flavoured loose-leaf Earl Grey.

I watched, intrigued, through the tent flaps, as my new neighbour set up a large canvas pagoda. A stainless-steel flue attached to the side of the tent, puffed little balls of smoke that drifted slowly into the dark wood nearby. It looked idyllic.

Doug spotted my interest and waved me over. As I slithered out of the tent, I hesitated, reflecting on last night's bitter cold. What if I just pulled the tent up instead, threw it all in the back of the car and headed for home? And the promise of a nice, hot, one-legged bath.

He watched my progress with a friendly smile as I made my way slowly towards him. Standing under the completed pagoda, I cast my eye over its shiny contents. His gaunt appearance, threadbare clothes and lack of serviceable teeth contrasted weirdly with the impressive collection of high-end camping equipment surrounding him.

'All free!' he announced, grinning madly and waving a bare arm at the bell tent's multi-coloured prayer-flagged entrance. I peered inside at what appeared to be a temple to the god of opulence; complete with chandelier and large Hopi dream catcher. Doug beamed, his arms spread in pride as I gawped in wonder. The canvas pagoda swept like a tan sail over the course grass. He poured more tea and offered me a choice of several elaborate camping chairs. Next came a large, tartan rug bearing the Harrods label, with matching cushions.

After introducing myself I asked how Doug had ended up living in luxury on a hill in the Mendips.

'*Hee, hee,* it was so funny – so *fuckin'* funny.' As he waved his arms around I caught a glimpse of several angry scars slicing along the inside of his thin forearms.

'I sneaked into Glasto, you know - the festi...? I got in before they put up that fuckin' big fence, like. Hid out for a day or two. Then got lucky and found an empty crew tent and, well... moved in. I even urn't some cash doing odd jobs from the lads and girlies like. Good lads they were.'

He looked pleased with his luck.

'Anyway like, on the Sunday night, when it's all full-on, I get caught with no wrist band and thrown out by Security. I lost me kit and everythin'. Bastards wouldn't let me collect any of it.' As he spoke he expertly ran his tongue across a couple of cigarette papers, before adding a trail of pungent weed from a large bud.

I declined his offer of the first toke.

'Well, I don't know what I'm doin'. I'd bin' on the piss and pills all day. So, I'm stumbling about in the dark down by Orchard Gate, trying to find some way back in, when I come across this, like, private campsite. There's no security to be seen and the only people around were a couple having a fuck-off shouting match. She's in this big Range Rover yelling at this bloke, like. He's in hippie crap. You know, right wanker outfit, tie-dye shirt and funny trousers. He was covered in mud and well out of it; dazed like a zombie man, I mean, he looked well-fucked. Ha, ha, *ha!*'

Doug caught his breath then started to choke, knocking his tea flying onto the adjoining sheepskin-covered chair. The still morning air was now filled with the sweet odour of skunk weed. Ignoring the spill and with a deepening red face, he continued his story.

'So, the bloke spots me standing at the gate and asks, like, if I would strip all this gear and *'tidy it all away'* for him. Posh bastard. There was, like, these two big bell tents and loads of shit.

Doug's rasping cough interrupted the story, again.

'He gave me a hundred quid to pack it all up and stick it in this box trailer. But after about ten minutes - it was now getting light - I could clearly see that his missus, '*Amanda dahling*' had not had a good Glasto. She was goin' on and on and shouting and screaming, chewing his balls off, saying she wasn't going to stay a minute longer *'in this frightful mud and those 'orfool pooh smells...'* So, he turns to me and asks if I want any of their stuff. Next thing, he gets into the Range Rover, and after lots of skidding and shit, she hammers it through the gate and up the lane - full fuckin' throttle like.'

Doug inhaled deeply.

'Anyways... no one was about, so I decided to crash in one of the tents and see who might turn up. But no one did. After a few more days, Security came around and told me I had to move it all. I told them I didn't have no vehicle. Well..., next thing they're callin' up some volunteers or Christian charity shit. They soon turn up all eager like and offer to pack it all into this trailer.' Doug grinned manically. 'Fuckin' funny, so fuckin' funny – fuckin' what!'

His chest heaved as he caught another wheezing cough.

'So, this lot pack all this stuff into the trailer. This lot of *do-gooders.* They had a brand-new Landy and all. Towed it down to my mate's garage in Shepton - for free. Couldn't believe my fuckin' luck.'

'Amanda dahling.' Doug sashayed in his chair, hand on hip mimicking the couple.

'Weekend hippies!' I chortled.

Doug stopped in mid cough and studied me very carefully.

'Rich *fuckers,'* he spat in a hard, broken voice.

I liked Doug.

He may well have been a borderline psychotic with a sporadic smack habit, but he was funny and quite disarming. I wasn't at all surprised to learn that he had three different mothers to his five children. He seemed to live life in a manic orgy of drugs and *'piss'.*

I spent the rest of that day and the next at his mercy, watching him brew up copious amounts of tea from a kettle heated by his amazing little wood burner. This not only kept the tent warm with just a few twigs, but he produced, much to my surprise, a decent stew. We were mostly left alone in the field. It was school term-time, and this had always been an unofficial site, blessed with one smelly toilet and a cold shower. Listening to Doug, he was not someone who overly encouraged discourse; it was like being washed away and dissolved in a stream of '*deals, meet-ups and doss pads.*' Few of his dreams seemed to have come to fruition.

By the end of the second day I'd bought the bell tent and its contents from him for a wad of cash. It had occurred to me that with the right kit you could live under canvas in some comfort. It was no luxury campervan in the South of France, but a more convenient and alternative on the West Mendips. Doug introduced me to the farmer, Marby, who promised to keep an eye on it - for a modest weekly consideration. He gave me the impression of someone who didn't want for much in life, not even finding a good enough reason to visit the sinfulness of *'Brizzle.'*

Leaving the tent up and taking a risk on it still being there on my return, meant I could turn up and use it without messing about. A nightmare for someone obliged to hop everywhere. I drove Doug to the bank to get the cash, and then on to Shepton to retrieve the other tent. Lack of a key for the garage door was dealt with by breaking the lock with a bar, and when that didn't work, twisting up the side of the door with the same bar. Like some sort of demented parrot, Doug laid a trail of destruction as he skidded from one situation to the next. He left a few days later with his new tent and a 'borrowed' Transit van in which he was driving to Cornwall 'for the fuckin' cold months.'

After he'd gone, I busied myself cleaning up and examining exactly what I had acquired. There was a two-burner gas cooker with grill, a cute-looking purple enamel stove with a hot plate and obligatory shiny copper kettle. The big double bed was made from an air mattress with two firm camping mats on top. I spent another couple of nights in increasingly organised comfort before deciding I needed to make a trip home. I was planning for a longer stay.

The front door moved painfully through a heap of post. I sorted through it, expectantly looking for Deb's familiar writing, but found nothing. I piled it all up, leaving it unopened, before easing myself onto the stairs. For the first time in several days, the sharp pain of lost love returned. Time to face facts, Sam, I reflected. The flame of hope that had flickered back into my life was now well and truly extinguished.

And she still didn't know about Norton. I didn't have her address, so writing wasn't an option. The longer this went on the more awkward I felt. I hesitated. Should I call her one last time and break the news?

My heart hardened.

I was not in an apologetic frame of mind and certainly didn't want to face more recriminations from her. No, I would return to my retreat in the hills, unwilling and unable to deal with the emotional carnage at home.

It made sense to have no stairs and everything in one open space. It was easier to live in the tent than the house. I shivered. The house was damp, even after the drying summer sun. It was a sure sign that my neighbour's neglected roof was, once again, leaking and finding its way onto my side – bastards! I sighed heavily, knowing we would end up in court again before he'd do anything about it. As I hobbled around, the urge to escape the familiar walls intensified. I gave the rooms a critical appraisal. The house was full of half-completed *'home improvements'* that lay scattered about like dusty sores.

After filling the kettle, I sat at the kitchen table and studied the idle collection of trains along the shelf. Maybe I should finish my rail terminus project? But I'd lost interest after Billy's sudden departure. It wasn't the same anymore, its modelled innocence seemed tarnished after all the recent events.

41 New intentions

By the third night in my new canvas home, I was in agony. The painkillers handed out by A&E had run out. I hadn't realised how effective they were and therefore had not rationed their use. I'd also binged on the cider and now that was gone. As I sobered up, I rediscovered a world of unremitting pain. I struggled, turning slowly over and over in bed for what seemed like hours, eventually succumbing, but not waking until the warm sun arrived in the early afternoon. I used a small bucket to pee in and drank my way through what remained of Doug's inherited Gunpowder tea. Cup after cup, until I'd filled the little bucket and hobbled off into the woods to dispose of its contents. On my return, I stopped, momentarily studying the early evening sky. Bright dots were just peeking through the blue veil. It was going to be a good night and my best chance yet to assemble and use the telescope. I needed something to distract me. Maybe a trip to the stars would help.

My luck was in. A crescent moon was just beginning to set. Astronomers can't view a full moon with the naked eye because it's too bright, but the silver slice offered a manageable degree of glare, allowing more detail to be seen. I was keen to use this big bright object to line up the small spotting telescope on the back of the tube. This would be vital if I was to find anything else of interest. As I fumbled in the twilight, my excitement grew at the prospect of my first close-up view of the Moon. Simon had told me, from his *'astronomical days'* at school, that it was quite something, but it was setting quickly as I tried to track it and focus in. *'Come on, come on,'* I urged in frustration, as more branches obscured the view. Suddenly, and with pin-sharp clarity, the surface burst spectacularly into my eye.

'Wow...!'

My cry of surprise echoed across the dark damp field as Marby's dog offered a soft 'woof! woof!' in response.

I had never *ever* seen anything quite like it. My eyes feasted on this previously unknown topography. But then it was gone, leaving just a blur of black branches; nothing but black. I sat still on the ground, dazed, as I replayed the fleeting image.

'Thank you, Gordon,' I called out into the damp October air.

After that high point, I spent an hour trying to find a planet - or in fact anything really. Lots of blurred stuff, a fantastic number of stars, but without names they just looked like a lot of sparkles. It dawned on me that I was handling a scientific instrument rather than a sophisticated toy. At the very least I would need a star atlas.

The pain had kept my mind off a lot of things. My mobile was long dead of course. Not that there would have been a signal here. I was enjoying my isolation and spent the next few days relaxing into it, as I quietly studied the neighbourhood from the comfort of my 'designer' camping chair. I looked out onto the empty fields and realised how Doug had chosen the location very carefully. Though sheltered by deep woods on two and half sides, it offered stunning, expansive views to the west and up to the north, then along a shallow valley chequered with tumble-down walls. One afternoon, covered in my comfortable Harrods blanket, I watched as Marby and his bonkers collie rounded up several hundred sheep. They ushered them through a gate and into a little lane, all to the soundtrack of baleful bleating.

By the fifth day the pain had subsided. The lack of cider had sharpened my senses and I was finally beginning to feel in control. My filthy bandages needed changing. This would involve a trip back to Bristol. I decided to visit the Ponytailed-ones in Glastonbury first.

I hobbled into Crumbly's to be met with a cluster of sympathetic helpers.

'Sounds like you're having a bit of a time of it, eh?' Tall John smiled as he organised a second seat to rest my tender foot.

'Sometimes the Universe just has it in for you,' Sophie added, resplendent in a green velvet dress, flecked with clusters of spangly beads. A curious Druidic fascinator of a hat was perched precariously on her head. 'Ay, the best place to be I'd say, up on those hills, near a nice beck.' She nodded out of the windows towards the Mendip escarpment that loomed over the Levels.

'I think you've landed on your feet up there. Make the most of it, Sam, before the winter sets in,' Tall John added enthusiastically.

'What are you going to do though, between your bouts of star gazing?' asked Colin.

'Well, I've not really thought about it. The foot is still painful, so I find it difficult to stay with one thought for too long,' I replied, ticking off a silent mental list.

'Why not do your Bristol thing? I really thought you were onto something a couple of months ago. You should do it,' Colin urged.

'Yeah, well, I got into all sorts of trouble with – *that* stuff. I don't know if I want any more hassles right now. Who's going to believe me anyway? Except you lot. Nobody I know in Bristol is remotely interested in any of my discoveries.'

'Do it for yourself, bro. For yourself. Don't worry about anyone else. If it's truth you seek, you'll find the answers. Look, didn't you tell me that some bloke in Bristol had left you some sort of treasure chest, the one you had the map from?' Colin inquired.

'You mean Deb's dad's stuff? It was a toolbox, actually, and that's exactly what got me into all this mess in the first place,' I replied, with a stab of guilt.

'And it's what will get you out of it as well. He's bloody given you all the clues, Sam. Just get organised. Get curious again, don't let this chance slip by,' Colin urged.

Inspired, I left Crumbly's and decided to have another go at unravelling Gordon's secrets. I owed it to him to discover what it was that he had so calculatingly left me as his legacy.

Thankfully, I didn't need to go back to the hell of A&E; it was just a case of seeing a district nurse at my local walk-in centre. I enjoyed the physical attention. My foot was healing though it was still swollen, blue and very tender. I stayed the night at the house but didn't sleep well, my thoughts returning as if spring-loaded, to more perturbing ideas. I rose early and by nine, I was out of the door, carrying maps of Bristol and Castle Howard under my arm.

I'd had the maps laminated so I'd be able to use wipe-clean felt pens. This made it easier to experiment. I found a useful piece of ply to serve as a mounting board and then dragged a surprisingly heavy box of reference books to the car. My last job was to make a simple pair of compasses, large enough to draw big circles over the city. My self-confidence was returning. I was excited at the prospect of discovering *what* exactly Gordon's mysterious maps had shown. The pile of unopened post got bundled up into a convenient black bin liner and dropped into the back of the car. I promised myself I'd sort through it all during an idle moment.

A familiar call interrupted my thoughts.

'Sam! *Sammy...*'

Kate was striding towards me from her front door.

'Oh, hello Kate. Sorry I've not been around much recently,' I said sheepishly.

'You're a hopeless case, Sammy. No wonder your life's in such a mess if you're never around to pick up the pieces.' She came to a halt at the front door and folded her arms. She was breathing heavily.

'Sorry, I've been camping. It's good...' I paused adding, 'I've been keeping off the cat's wee you'll be pleased to hear.'

'Good. Time, you pulled your socks up,' she said, as if berating an entire platoon.

'I'm only wearing one,' I quipped.

She ignored my witticism. 'A man's been knocking on your door. Did you get any messages he might have left?'

'No, but they'll be in this bag with the rest of the post. What did he look like?'

'Tallish and smart with neat hair. So not likely to be any of your loutish clan.'

'Sounds like James, my customer with the hole in the garden. I can't be dealing with his fussing right now. If it's important he'll call me. He's got my number,' I said with finality.

'You're a useless inebriate, Sam. Why I bother, I've no idea...' Kate paused, before turning back with a coy smile. 'Look, I've got most of a Coffee and Walnut left. You might as well have it. I'll never finish it. Don't expect you're eating well.' She quickly disappeared through her front door, returning with a large colourful tin. As she pulled at the lid the unmistakeable aroma filled my nostrils. I peered inside and examined what can only be described as God's Comfort Food.

By midday I was back at the campsite, stopping at the gate to chat with Marby. He was busy doing something mechanical to the oldest and shabbiest Land Rover in Somerset. I quickly accepted his offer to give me a hand shifting the books and equipment into the bell tent. The weather was on the turn - a storm was brewing.

It took longer to set up the table than to find the two intersecting circles of the Vesica Piscis. I had rigged up a couple of bright candle lanterns in the centre of the tent and placed the board across two folding plastic trestles. It was dark and windy outside, but the canvas palace was warm and getting comfortable.

I thought of Billy's words at Mortlake and decided to try the pendulum method of dowsing, rather than the trial and error of drawing innumerable circles over the map. I leant over the makeshift table whispering, *'Show me the greatest energy here.'* As I swung the glass bob across the city, it started to 'tug' and pulled towards the centre of first one, then another secondary focus. The first had a clockwise swing of the bob, the second, anti-clockwise. Were these the two centres of Gordon's Vesica Piscis? I checked several more times, the pendulum spinning impressively over each centre, gaining momentum in my sweaty hand until almost horizontal.

I started to fidget – feeling like someone in the grip of a strong caffeine rush.

Using the home-made compass with a blue-tipped pen taped to the end. I positioned the point on the *male* pole, the obelisk shaped Cabot Tower on the peak of Brandon Hill. Then I set the nib into the centre of the *female* pole, Queen Square. With one hand holding the compass upright and the second moving the pen north towards the heart of old Bristol, I watched as the pen passed through one significant building or monument after another. Colston's Circle.

My chest heaved with excitement as I completed the first circle. Then I reversed the compass, placing the point on the statue of King William III at the centre of Queen Square and drawing the second intersecting circle. This I labelled Queen Circle.

Standing upright to admire my achievement and contemplate the significance of what lay before me, I remembered the morning's shopping. Celebratory brandy had been included.

My wobbling hand poured a small tumbler-full.

So, there it was. Finally revealed – Gordon's Vesica Piscis!

I raised the glass and saluted the city I had called home for 44 years.

On Gordon's charts were circles overlaying a plain-hand drawn map of the city. It had been devoid of landmarks, but instead, contained sets of numbers that made no sense to me. It was as if the authors wanted to disguise its route. I leant awkwardly on my crutch and studied the pattern on the map. Getting to the bottom of the intent and history of the Vesica was going to open up a whole new avenue of exploration. Was this what Colston had found, or planned himself in an act of supreme focused intent? Could this be what lay behind the enduring power of his name?

What appeared to be unmasked by the geometry of the Vesica was the very strategic placement of significant buildings, including most of the bridges in the city centre. For at least two hundred years, if not more, perhaps since Colston's time, perhaps longer, these buildings have been bathed by an invisible stream of energy of some kind. Its apparent electromagnetic qualities exploited by several different structures in fascinating ways. So many questions sprung from this discovery. Was this part of the original Templar knowledge? Did they dowse and detect these invisible currents? Did Colston, with the help of Dr Dee's esoteric library, create the blueprint for the Vesica Piscis here in Bristol? Are there other energy networks like this in other cities, waiting to be discovered?

I sipped the smooth brandy deep in thought, smiling as I reflected on my journey from ignorance last winter to the obsession that now gripped me, here in a small field, high above the city.

Nearly all the paintings I'd seen of Colston showed the same gesture of his finger pointing downwards. In other symbolic works of art subjects are depicted with a finger pointing up, suggesting knowledge of the 'Creator' and a possible allegiance to Saint John the Baptist. This symbolism has sometimes been attributed to the Templars and can occasionally be found on obelisks in cemeteries. But Colston was always depicted pointing *down*. Maybe this was a clue, for those curious enough to look, to his secret legacy.

My thoughts turned to an old drawing I'd seen on the internet, of the Knights Templar district in Paris. The patterns it had revealed gave an important clue about Bristol. As I understood more, I had begun to recognise Templar motifs dotted all over the city. Brunel's original Crusaders theme at Temple Meads Station, later superseded by the Paris Temple-style new entrance, now lacking the pyramid roof but still displaying its four watch towers. I could see by the path of the circle, that closing the station's original terminus now made more sense. It sat right in the path of the eastern circle of the Vesica Piscis. Did they find that the steel railway lines interfered with the flow? Like the Chinese and their outrage in the 19th Century at the British Empire's insistence on straight railways and the havoc they caused to the flow of *lung mei*? The current path of the railway snugly follows the southernmost edge of the Vesica, but never crosses it.

Night was closing in as I stumbled out of the tent and across the field, seeking a signal for my newly-charged phone so I could call Rangi. I was enthusiastic to the point of incoherence as I explained my discoveries. She eagerly accepted my offer of a day out in Bristol the following Saturday. Returning to the tent, I did a little one-legged dance. And then returned to the table, unable to take my eyes off the laminated puzzle. I continued to make new discoveries until the bird's early morning song interrupted me. By dawn I couldn't wait until Saturday. I was excited but curiously nervous. Maybe I was fabricating these patterns from my own blinkered perspective? Joining up the dots to fit my preconceived theories. I urgently needed another opinion. The Ponytailed-ones were my obvious sounding board. They would recognise the significance; they'd be able to perceive what I was so clearly seeing.

Having left the campsite at a time when only the farmers were up and about, I was the first of our little group to arrive at Crumbly's. I hobbled up to the large corner table, feeling excited but light-headed from lack of sleep, carefully placing the taped-up tube containing the map behind the bench seat. I intended to do a bit of a Nick; unfurling what had kept me up most of the previous night with a flourish, before an astonished audience. After an hour, several coffees and a slice or two of breakfast ginger cake, I was becoming increasingly frustrated at their non-appearance.

Colin finally arrived, limping badly and using an old goose-headed stick to steady himself. It was strange that I hadn't noticed his limping before, but I guess I had rarely seen him out of his chair. He grinned broadly and joined the end of a small queue at the counter. I declined his offer of yet another coffee.

'Where is everyone?' I asked, as he approached.

'Oh Sam, I guess you weren't here last weekend – were you?' Colin settled into his familiar chair, his thin face unshaven. He slid his walking stick under the chair as if to conceal its use.

'Ah well, Sam, it's all change here…' He shrugged, opening his arms wide, 'More room at the table, at least.'

'Where's Tall John? He's always here!' I said, leaning forward in anticipation.

'He's gone,' Colin replied succinctly.

'Gone where? Where's he gone?'

'Sedona.' He paused, before adding: 'He's gone to paint a mansion...'

'Paint a mansion?' I looked incredulously at Colin, who smirked in reply.

'Yup. Just packed a bag and left. Locked up that little house of his and headed for the sun. For a thousand dollars a week, full-board. Oh, and the chance to meditate with a couple of hundred others. Mostly women, I gather.'

'Has he gone off with that guru fella who came over a few months back? The one that went back with those two women?' I asked.

'You mean Jenny and Ann – yup, spot on.' Colin couldn't contain his mirth producing a big grin between bouts of giggling.

'He's a sly one. Did he tell anyone?' I inquired.

'Oh no. He just went. I mean, a thousand bucks a week – *cash!* Can't be sniffed at, you know.'

'Yeah, but ... wasn't he writing a book? And giving talks and stuff, and all that metaphysical thing he was going on about. I, I don't understand...' I stuttered in shock.

'Don't be daft, Sam. Give up a thousand a week and all those free-loving followers?'

'But he was *'Tall John,'* an institution around here. I mean he *knew* stuff, lots and lots of stuff,' I pleaded.

'That's not all.' Colin paused, leaning towards me.

'Sophie's gone as well. Back oop-north like,' he mimicked. 'She's gone; moved, given up her lease, everything. Off to stay with her very pregnant daughter. She left on Saturday, just before John's departure.'

'Bloody hell. That was quick, I only saw her the other week.' I was feeling deflated, having by now abandoned all plans for a theatrical 'reveal' with the map. Tall John *and* Sophie, I missed them already.

'I liked Sophie,' I said weakly.

'And that's still not all.' Colin paused, studying me with a sly grin from across the cluttered table.

'Denis the dowser has gone as well.'

'Denis...? What, back to Oz?' I replied, holding my breath in shock.

'No. He's at Durham University.' He raised his bushy eyebrows and nodded gently as if Denis had passed straight by Durham and had ended up on Mars instead.

'He's at a University? You're shittin' me.' I sat upright catching the ball of my left foot on the bottom of the table leg. I yelped and grimaced in pain. 'A *student* at his age?'

'He isn't a student.' Colin sat back and continued his broad grin.

'Well, what's he studying then?' I asked, puzzled.

'He isn't studying – *oh no!*' Colin flayed his arms erratically as he spoke.

'What then?' The last bite of cake remained untouched as I registered the awful reality of 'Ponytail World's' dissolution.

'He's a Senior Research Fellow at the Department of Geo Biology. The bastard's going to get a pension - and everything!' Colin beamed.

'But... That's like a proper University. It's not one of those places with a post box in Puerto Rico – is it?' I leant forward, straining to make sense of this latest development.

'Straight-up Sam. I'm not messing with you. He told me that some old bloke who attached himself to one of his tours at Avebury, not only ended up dowsing like a good'n but liked what he'd heard from Denis. Apparently, he asked loads of questions before buying him lunch in the pub, leaving a card and disappearing off with Denis's email address. A couple of weeks later he gets contacted by this department at the University saying there's this position available as Senior Research Fellow in Earth Sciences. They want to know all about Ley Energies and stuff. They're really *serious* about it.'

'Their having him on. I mean, *aren't* they?' I said incredulously.

'Not at all. It seems he shares a lot of Howard's theories. Well, not the Croppies stuff...,' Colin challenged my expression, '...but the megalithic business. They've recently found enormous amounts just under the surface. Possible temples, circles, geometric patterns. Shedloads. They're scanning the ground using radar and lasers and it's most impressive. I tell ya Sam, from what Denis was saying, they've got a lot of kit and some very bright people using it. It turns out that his idea about our ancestors treating the chalk downs of Southern England like a giant sponge with an electric circuit, is being given serious attention.'

Colin beamed.

'I remember Howard saying that, you know, electrically-charged water might influence the organisation of thought,' I said.

'Yes Sam, our ancestors understood water in ways that we haven't even thought of - yet.'

'*Shit...*' I said, falling back into the seat. 'Good old Denis. He's worked so hard these years. How wonderful that he's going to get some sort of recognition and security. Let us raise our cups to him. *God bless Denis!*'

We fell into silence, reflecting on the recent turn of events.

Finally, I spoke up.

'You wouldn't fancy a day out exploring Bristol this Saturday, would you? With lunch on me. I might have another big surprise for you.'

I dropped the maps and appended notes on the passenger seat and urged the car into life. Condensation clung to the glass as I made my way out of the camping field and headed to the central bus station in Bristol to collect Colin. I found him waiting patiently just outside, coffee beakers in each hand. We headed across town to Rangi's and the starting point for a whole day's exploration. I was feeling edgy as my imagination danced in anticipation about what we might discover. The path of the circles of the Vesica Piscis had passed through so many significant sites in the city.

We arrived at ten and, after introductions and a few pleasantries, I unrolled the map.

'So this, my friends,' I said, pointing to the diagrams, 'is what I've come to believe is Colston's biggest legacy – the *Vesica Piscis!* Do you see Colin? Cabot Tower as the upright 'male' pole,' I nodded in expectation of his input. '...and the female pole, Queen Square.'

'Oh yes. It's pretty bloody obvious isn't it? When you see it...' Colin passed a thin finger through his unruly hair as he leant over the table.

'That looks impressive. There's a big chunk of the city within these circles.' Rangi turned to look directly at me. 'You've calculated the distance between the poles?'

'Yes, it's...,' I leant over the map to read my own writing. 'It's 3,040 feet give or take a foot or two.' I wobbled my right hand in emphasis.

'Do you *know* what 3,040 ft is?' Colin beamed at us both, before cocking his head towards me.

'What? You mean, what's it in metres – in *yards?*' I replied.

'No, mate. 3,040 feet is exactly half a nautical mile. This means that these circles are each one nautical mile wide. Exactly one Admiralty Mile.'

'How's that different from the regular mile then, Colin?' Rangi asked as she topped-up our coffee mugs.

'A nautical mile is the distance travelled by the sun in one minute across the Earth's surface. It's one minute of longitude. In other words, an exact fraction of the Earth's surface rather than the familiar terrestrial mile.' he replied, adding. 'Have you checked the solar alignment of the *Vesica?*'

'Yes,' I said, casting my eyes from one to the other as they sipped their coffees thoughtfully. 'It's an azimuth of about 114 degrees. In other words, the path that the first rays of sun take at dawn on the Druidic New Year - 1st November. Straight across the Square and up the hill to Cabot Tower.'

'That is interesting; Samhein,' Colin replied, returning to study the map.

'Or... it could be sunrise on 31st October. Remember 31st October 1831!' Rangi covered her mouth in shock.

'Oh shit,' I said, pulling away from the map. 'I hadn't thought of that.' I leant back, resting my full weight on my remaining crutch.

'I'd love to see the astrological chart for that night.' Rangi added with a tight grin.

'Sam, this is amazing stuff. You must be pleased to have been able to uncover so much even after the accident with the wood burner,' said Colin with a sly smile.

'Oh – *that.*' My heart dropped at the mention of my cider-fuelled paranoia. 'That was an insane thing to do. But...but I just didn't understand then,' I looked pleadingly across the table to Rangi's tanned face. 'I just didn't understand that it had been left for *me.*'

'It's amazing though, looking at it. What a project.' Colin glanced up at me. 'I'm assuming you're thinking that these energy flows have been deliberately channelled and positioned. By human intent, rather than simply existing or evolving, you know, in nature?

I looked at his face expectantly. I hoped he would answer his own question.

'God knows. I don't know. There's so many questions...' I replied, wistfully staring at the map. After a moment's reflection. 'I'm not sure what to think. I expect the answers were in one of those books I set fire to. There was no shortage of diagrams to study.'

'I wonder what would have inspired Colston to do this?' Colin said. I searched his face for any hint of enlightenment.

After a moment's silence he replied to his own question, his voice low and deliberate.

'Unless he found the *original* Vesica Piscis.'

'*Original* Vesica?' I said, head pitching back in surprise.

'You mean there's *two* sets of circles in Bristol?' Rangi said.

'Could be. What if the Knights Templar got in there first – back in the 12th Century? It's well-known that they bought back all sorts of knowledge from the Crusades. Including very sophisticated architectural know-how. The Islamic masons were streets ahead of us at the end of the 11th Century.'

I don't think we have time today to do any more exploring. One Vesica Pisces at a time is more than enough for me.' I replied.

'Yeah, another time. I'd check it out though.

I paused in thought.

'If what your saying is correct, I wonder if there's any physical evidence - buildings and the like.' I said, my curiosity triggered.

'Well there's no shortage of odd buildings dotted around the city.' Rangi said, peering over the map.

'Well, Temple Church would be an obvious centre for one of the circles,' said Colin.

'I know you guys might find this hard to believe, but I took a language degree.' he added.

He must have noticed my look of surprise.

'Well the word 'circus' means circle in Latin,' Colin explained.

'What are you getting at?' I replied.

'In the last decade or so the Council have created two new districts in Bristol – Cabot's Circus and Temple Circus.'

'Hang on – I remember now, on Gordon's charts - the names Cabot's and Temple Circus. Now that *does* make sense.' I nodded, grinning with excitement.

Colin stepped back, standing upright against his cane.

'That's it then. Colston learns how to dowse, and maybe, just maybe, he gets hold of the remains of Dr Dee's library. He uses that knowledge to find the original Templar circles dating back to the 12th or 13th Century. Or maybe another dowser tells Colston about them, who knows, but...' Colin looked to Rangi and then me for confirmation, '...he comes up with a plan to supersede or at least to complement the Templars' original Vesica Piscis.'

I interrupted: 'Or complete an existing plan, by building Queen Square to mimic the square at the Paris Temple, making sure it's surrounded on three sides with water. A job the Templars may have started back in the 13th Century, when St Augustine's Reach was dug.'

'Exactly,' Colin replied waving a finger at the map.

'Well, he had the money, the opportunity and the timings *are* spot-on,' Rangi added.

'Took them a little longer to place Cabot Tower. But it would have been part of a long-term plan. A plan implemented in secret, generations ago and slowly developed, so as not to reveal the truth to the muggles - us lot,' Colin said pointing at himself.

'And look at the positioning of the Council House in front of College Green. Right through the centre of the axis of Colston's Circle,' I said.

'So, there you are Sam. You've got two circuses now. Cabot Circus, Colston's original you found and just maybe Temple Circus, Colin's earlier one.' Rangi beamed.

'A four-ringed circus!' I exclaimed.

'Sam, you've opened a new door on the city with this research of yours. They'll probably want to erect a monument in your name.' Colin prodded me gently with his stick.

'Um, not sure I'd want that,' I replied grinning sheepishly.

'What? Even if it's an obelisk?' Rangi replied, her eyes twinkling.

45 The tuning fork

After parking the car, we walked east along Corn Street towards St Nicholas Market Hall and its landmark four bronze pillars. These were the famous Bristol Nails positioned across the front of the building.

'The city seems a lot busier these days. More people about,' Colin said, his voice edged with anxiety.

'Not to worry; we won't stay long. Our next stops are going to be a lot quieter,' I said, as I gathered the pair around me. We huddled in the doorway of the former home of the 18th Century Bank of England, opposite the Hall and directly on the path of Colston's circle. The heavily-decorated stonework had several depictions of the pagan Green Man carved into its embellished lintels.

'If you hold the map and find our position, I'll dowse along Corn Street and see if I can pick up the energy flowing in Colston's Vesica Piscis. Check to see if it correlates with the map.' Armed with my coat hanger rods, I walked up to the crossroads of Wine Street and Corn Street. This was the point at which the Bristol Cross, now relocated to Stourhead, once stood.

I strode purposefully back, west down Corn Street, jostling with eager shoppers, holding the two rods in front of me like an outlaw in a cowboy western. I was curious to see if the energy flow passed through All Saints Church, but the rods didn't move until I got to the first, eastern-most Nail standing in line with the side of St Nicholas Market. This was consistent with my map, which showed the path of Cabot Circle passing through the Statue of King William III in Queen Square. Then north through the ornate Customs House, crossing Baldwin Street, through the former Fish Market, before running the length of St Nicholas Market and passing across the Four Nails.

The rods remained in their open position until I passed the fourth most westerly Nail on the other side of the Market. Even though I was feeling desensitized by the crowd, I could pick up the tug of Colston's Circle through the rods. I turned, grinning madly, as Rangi leapt onto her toes and waved across a sea of people. Colin grinned and nodded in satisfaction.

'That was clever,' he said on my return; nudging my leg with his walking stick.

'Yeah, thanks. I thought for a moment I was going to impale that teenager,' I said breathless.

Rangi snuggled further into the rainbow plume of her scarves and giggled, kissing me lightly on the cheek. 'How's your foot without the crutch?

'Not too bad. Just don't want to spend too much time on it, though,' I replied.

'So, what's so special about these 'Nails' then, Sam? You and Colin seemed keen to start here first. Why?'

'Because they were repositioned in a straight line directly in front of the market a couple of hundred years ago. The merchants of Bristol used them to for doing deals. Placing money and promissory notes down on these metre-wide bronze tops. It's claimed that this is where the phrase *'to pay on the nail,'* came from,' I replied.

'Out here in the open? In the rain? In the middle of the busiest street in Bristol? Wasn't that why the market was built in the first place?' Rangi creased her forehead.

'Yeah. I've always thought that sounded a bit odd too,' Colin remarked quietly.

'I did a check-up and found that there were places in Europe with similar customs, but they were nearly all in cities that are warmer and drier. To me, it looks likely that the Nails were repositioned to serve another function entirely - as large earthing rods!' I said, turning to Rangi.

'Earthing rods?' she look puzzled.

'Yes. Electricians sometimes hammer bars of copper into the ground when they're rewiring a house. Then attach an earth cable from the main fuse box. It's a safety thing. These four 'Bristol Nails' could be functioning as super-size earthing rods. They're all made from highly conductive bronze. The merchants would stand at the 'Nails' unwittingly bathed in the conducted current. Like it was part of an electrical circuit.'

Rangi and Colin nodded thoughtfully.

'Come on, let's get back to the car and out of this crowd,' I added, noticing Colin had already turned, tapping the edge of the pavement with his ornate walking stick.

As we set off into the traffic, Rangi quizzed me.

'Where were the pillars before they were moved? Where did they come from?'

'They were in a small passage called St Stephens' Alley at the back of All Saints Church. Just a few feet from Colston's tomb as a matter of fact.' I said.

'That Church is amazing,' Colin said wistfully. 'While you were doing your stuff with those rods of yours, I was checking out Colston's All Saints next door.' He paused for reflection. 'I don't think I have ever seen anything close to the weirdness of that spire above his tomb and I have never, ever, seen so many flaming urns in one place.'

'There are rather a lot aren't there? Twelve to be precise,' I said adding, 'The whole dome thing appears to be a copy of the Temple of Spirits on Temple Mount. Very similar to what I found at Mortlake a few months ago.'

'There's 13,' Rangi said quietly from the front seat.

'No, I'm sure there's only 12. Four marking the corners and eight around the octagonal base of the dome,' I replied.

'Sorry – there's 13,' Rangi said with finality.

'Where's the 13th...?' Colin interjected.

'On the wall outside that nice Italian restaurant. It's in a direct line going west from the Nails and Colston's dome.' Rangi paused as Colin and I tried to Recall it. 'It's been there forever. Nick took me there on my first night in Bristol. I'll never forget that evening...' Rangi smiled mischievously before continuing. 'I remember seeing it lit up.'

By now, we had escaped the narrow roads at the heart of the old city and had turned onto the busy one-way system of Rupert Street.

'Where next, tour guide?' Rangi's warm smile acknowledged that she had forgotten her original reservations about wasting a whole day with a couple of obsessives.

'Bristol Royal Infirmary. The good old *BRI.* I've got something to show you both, something I'm sure you haven't noticed before. It's a funny little dome that's attached to the front of the hospital. Look,' I said pointing with a nod of my head.

I pulled the car to a halt just beyond the entrance to the Eye Hospital. We couldn't hang about for long. There were serious traffic issues, not least ambulances flying past every few minutes. 'Look up to the end of the street, across the road by the pedestrian crossing.'

Colin pushed between the two front seats to get a better look, and a whiff of body odour passed through the car.

'Oh yes, do you mean that little dome on that square-looking building?' Rangi pointed towards the windscreen.

'That's it. A little dome that's made from Portland Stone, which happens to have a very high crystal content. What we're looking at is a crystal dome right in front of Bristol's main hospital,' I said.

Colin unrolled the map and shared it across the front seats. The large laminate spread under my chin, like a bib.

'That's the exact northern meeting point of the two circles of Colston's Circle. They cross just on that spot were the dome is. Never noticed that building before. God, talk about hidden in plain sight.' Colin excitedly pointed to the map as Rangi studied the geometry.

'If the eye of the Vesica is that part were the two circles overlap, the birth canal of the trinity,' Rangi said pointing, 'Is that then the *clitoris* of Colston's Circle...?'

'Umm, never thought of it like *that*,' I replied, contemplating possibilities. 'It's certainly the northern crossing point of the two flows.'

'That makes the southern crossing point, somewhere in north Bedminster; so that would be its arse then,' Colin said, grinning at us in turn. His scruffy demeanour and questionable personal hygiene reminded me of Doug. 'Fuckin' great stuff!' he barked, as we set off along Upper Maudlin Street, taking a right turn into St Michael's Hill.

As we slowly passed Colston's Alms Houses on the right, Rangi read aloud from the display board, 'It's such a bloody shame that Colston was such a ruthless slaver,' she said.

'Well - *no one's perfect,*' I trilled.

'No, Sam, we have to recognise what he did. He made an inconceivably vast fortune out of the suffering of others. An unscrupulous trader who swapped cheap beads for human beings, before exploiting them on his own plantations.'

'Before poisoning everyone in Britain with refined sugar that would prove to be as addictive as opium,' Colin added quickly.

We gloomily reflected on the enigma that was Edward Colston.

'The good, the bad; the black, the white. It's about duality. We can't abandon our research just because the social norm of 300 years ago is no longer acceptable,' I said defensively.

'He did more than most, and most of what he did was in secret,' Rangi said, quoting Colston's mysterious memorial.

'Why've we stopped?' Colin inquired.

'We're here. The next revelation. Let's cross the road; you'll be able to see better.'

'This sounds intriguing, Sam,' Rangi grasped my arm as we dodged the late morning traffic.

'Aha - the Bristol Homeopathic Hospital!' Colin announced.

'Yes, and notice the roof,' I said, pointing up into the clear autumn sky.

'More bloody obelisks,' he shouted.

'one, two, three, four, five ... six of them, across the gable end,' said Rangi.

'And smack in the middle of Circle flow, do you see?' I proffered the map.

'Now that's interesting.' She pointed at the map. 'Do you see how the Hospital outbuildings follow the curve of the circle along Cotham Hill? It looks deliberate.' She ran her finger repeatedly along the axis.

'That makes sense when you think that homeopathic treatment is ultimately about finding the right resonance. The current flows through the building, conducted and reflected by the obelisks on the roof and at the same time, absorbed into the medical treatments.'

'Well, Sam, this trip of yours just gets more fascinating. The idea that there is some elite group that's able, over generations, to plan and plot the positions of these hospitals along energy pathways. It's really mind-blowing.' Colin spoke with a faint crack in his voice, checking Rangi's face for approval.

'Well, you'll both love what's next then,' I said, as we returned to the ancient Swedish tank.

I drove towards Henbury Road and Colin let out a cry.

'Bloody knew it!' He grinned, grabbing my shoulder excitedly as he craned forward to get a better look. 'Clifton *bloody* Catholic Cathedral! He let go, sinking back into the black leather. I checked the mirror. He had a triumphant look on his face.

'That's a weird looking Cathedral. What a crazy shape,' Rangi said from the front seat. Why *is* that?

I looked at Colin, and back at Rangi, before announcing:

'It's a device, Rangi, a very large device.' I raised my eyebrows and checked her face as we turned into Worcester Road.

The ultra-modern design of the Catholic Cathedral had shocked people at the time of its unveiling. Triangular roof pitches intersect each other in a bold display of the geometry of six. Its design was not for the faint-hearted, being almost entirely devoid of traditional religious symbolism.

We parked up close, and as Rangi and I gathered our belongings, Colin was already on the steps approaching the north-west entrance. He came to a halt, gazing up to study the dramatic roof.

As we caught up, he started to narrate.

'Built at the beginning of the 1970s when the Vatican decided that the original Cathedral was in the wrong place. The architects admitted that the design was 'controversial',' Colin held his hands up mimicking the quote, 'but were guided by detailed specifications from Rome...' He stopped in thoughtful reflection, a look of surprised relief on his face as he continued. 'I had digs over there; do you see that top right-hand window? That was my bedroom, it looked right out to these fantastic spires. Every time I glanced up from my studies there they were, sorta taunting me. Those three giant slabs of concrete poking out of a pyramid for a roof. Puzzled me for years. Until now.' Colin's eyes glazed, and his beatific smile lingered.

'Well it needn't anymore. Colston's Vesica not only goes directly through the three spires, but they're also orientated to the Circle as well. It's spot-on Colin,' I said waving the laminated map in front of him.

'Makes sense though,' he added. 'The roof's covered in conductive material, walls covered in crystal and three massive concrete spires that vibrate. *Yes,* they actually vibrate - like tuning forks.'

'*Tuning forks?*' Rangi asked, confused.

'Yes, it's obvious what they're here to do. The concrete fingers collect energy from Colston's Vesica, and transmit it through vibration, into the building. Come on, let's go inside. You'll be amazed.' Colin beckoned us, tapping purposefully. I hobbled along, my foot aching.

Rangi followed us through the swing doors. She had not known of the Cathedral's existence and was astounded to discover it in the affluent neighbourhood of protestant Clifton.

'What a place to put a Cathedral, so far away from the city centre!' she exclaimed, and then stopped abruptly at the sight in front of her.

The three of us stood together just inside the entrance. We were alone.

Deep blue-green light from abstract stained-glass panels cast a glow across the floor and shimmered in the low autumn light. The crystal stone altar, several metres in front, stood in isolation as the vast space soared above us.

'The hexagon shape is used everywhere,' Rangi announced as she drifted between the rows of pews. 'Doesn't feel like much of a sanctuary though, does it?' she added with a conspiratorial softness.

'Notice the massive amount of sound-deadening material lining the ceiling with all those conical baffles,' Colin said, pointing upwards.

'This lot looks more like the set of a 1960s Bond movie than a place of worship,' Said Rangi.

'Depends on what you're worshipping,' I said in a loud whisper, chasing my dowsing rods out through the south west exit of the Cathedral, picking up the flow and following it out into the road. Colin and Rangi watched, fascinated by the rods' movements.

'You know it looks very much like this building was placed here to take full advantage of the circular energy,' Colin said.

'That's two hospitals and a cathedral so far Sam. Whatever next?' Rangi cocked her head like a curious robin.

'Next, it's coffee and cake time. We can sample the delights of Clifton Village,' I said, as we clambered back into Gordon's faithful old car.

I parked close to Christ Church and walked towards the village before stopping to unfurl the map, pointing out the obelisk that had started the whole business back in May.

'That's it? Looks kinda of lost, here doesn't it?' Colin reflected.

'Well it's definitely, most definitely *not* lost. Do you see the cenotaph with the flaming urn sitting on top?' Rangi and Colin nodded. 'Well cast your eyes across the road to the house with the lead covered dome on top.' I looked at Rangi and Colin in turn. 'That's the alignment that points straight to Colston's Church,' I said, smiling broadly.

'You mean Colston's Circle goes right across Manila Avenue and through that dome?' Colin looked amazed. 'Hang on, is that the line you told me goes through the doors of 33 Colston?' I nodded.

'There's Draper's monument. The house he lived in for decades was very close to this spot,' I said.

'Sam, you must have been so, so, bloody...' Rangi paused searching for the right word. 'Bloody, *bloody* amazed when you first drew this out.'

I replied with a smile but Rangi's words passed through me. Amongst all this excitement, a sense of loneliness had been welling up. I missed Deb and her support. She'd have been thrilled to see a very large piece of the puzzle fall into place. There were times, over the last few months, that I had felt very isolated. I'd been mocked and had exposed myself to playful and sometimes aggressive ridicule. Colin and Rangi were my vindication. This was as real to them as it was to me. Not just the swinging rods confirming the flow, but the whole thing. The whole 'stuff' as Colin would say. It had all evolved beyond a mere set of coincidences, into a persuasive package of evidence, that pointed to the presence of a hidden knowledge. A concealed science. These buildings were massive great signposts testifying to that truth.

We hurried on to a café but at the last minute decided not to stop after all. Time was precious and there was much more to see.

'So, we can walk from here. There's one thing of interest in the village and that's the circle passing through that restaurant facing us at the end of the Mall. Can you see it? Quite an ornate building?'

Rangi and Colin nodded as we walked towards it.

'Well, I don't know if you still remember, Colin, from your student days, that...' I pointed, '...was a branch of Tyndall's private bank.'

He stopped and tapped his stick, deep in thought.

'Was that the one with the flunky in a morning suit who opened the doors?'

'Yup, spot on. The circle would have gone right through the wood-panelled foyer.'

'Bankers have always been interested in this stuff, you know - *fung shui* and that,' he added.

We turned right and headed for Cornwallis Crescent, a few minutes' walk away.

'Of course, Clifton's almost entirely owned by the Merchant Venturers; they could do what they liked up here,' Colin explained as we turned into Royal York Crescent. 'You look at their website today and you'll see smiley children and care homes, but there's also a delicately-worded reference to the Slave Trade – which, needless to say, they bank-rolled. Mind you, they weren't all bad; it was their collective money box that helped pay for the construction of the Suspension Bridge and the Great Western Railway. You could say they were behind, or certainly influenced, a lot of Bristol's major building projects. For a long time they've owned a huge amount of land hereabouts – not least the site where the Catholic Cathedral is built. 'The funding of the Cathedral was very touch and go you know, until a secret benefactor turned up and wrote a very large cheque...'

'Oh Sam, this is all so exciting.' Rangi hugged me briefly as we reached Cornwallis Crescent.

'The Crescent is named after General Cornwallis. He lost the battle that would lead to the end of the American colonies. Rather surprising then to name one of the longest and most magnificent crescents in Europe after him,' I said, with a smirk.

'Well, he was fighting a brother Mason at the time,' Colin responded.

'That's true,' I said. We reached the halfway point along the four-story curving Georgian crescent. The front doors were on the north face, and to the south were magnificent communal gardens.

'Here we are then,' I said unfolding the map. 'This is Polygon Lane.

'Polygon Lane? That's an odd name for a footpath...' Colin said.

'Well, it leads to Polygon Crescent just below us. The Circle passes directly through the gap. Like how the railway snakes along the outside of the Vesica Piscis. It's as if they didn't want the flow to be unnecessarily affected,' I replied adding, 'I suppose you've noticed the similarities between the arc of Colston's Vesica and that of Cornwallis Crescent.' I pointed to the map. 'Further evidence that Bristol has been strategically planned-out.'

'Yes, Washington DC was as well, with a similar system of geometric shapes, said Colin. 'And did you know that even *Milton Keynes* has an alignment right down one of its main avenues – the aptly-named Midsummer Boulevard.'

'Well, it's certainly beginning to look like there was a controlling mind, or minds, behind Bristol's city planning. Can you see the social housing development in front of the Crescent and right under the circle? They all have copper roofs. An expensive, but highly conductive solution for keeping the rain out,' I said.

I looked at my companions. Colin was starting to look fatigued and my foot was increasingly painful. It seemed like a good time for lunch.

The suggestion was well-received, so we returned to the car and headed down Clifton Hill and over to the Cumberland Basin.

Colin studied the map laid out on the back seat. 'Have you noticed how many of the bridges in Bristol have the Circle passing over them, especially crossing where the bridge meets the bank?'

'Yeah, I noticed that. Could be some sort of magnetic attraction. You know, to pull the energy across the river,' I said cautiously.

'Sorta earthing thing again – like the Nails,' Colin added.

'Why not? What we're dealing with here is some kind of giant, city-wide electromagnetic circuit.'

'I still find this hard to believe. How have they managed to keep this a secret for so long?' said Rangi as we pulled to a halt, close to the busy restaurant.

'But nobody has hidden anything, have they?' I replied. 'It was always there if anyone took the trouble to look.'

We settled down to a late lunch. I pushed the boat out and bought a bottle of decent wine to toast our day's exploring.

'Is the other part of Colston's Vesica - the Queen Square one - is that like this? I mean there seem to be all sorts of interesting places on that circle as well?' Rangi said between mouthfuls.

'Well we haven't the time to go around that one today. Maybe some other time. Colin, you've got to catch the bus back to Glastonbury, haven't you? We'll run out of time to check it out.'

'Yes, but what's on that line, Sam?' Rangi asked.

'Wills Tower at the top of Park Street. Those expensive new flats at the bottom of Jacob Wells Road – Capricorn Buildings.'

'Capricorn, did you say?' Rangi interrupted. 'That fits.'

I continued: 'The circle goes through the gap right in the middle of them before crossing the docks and passing over the deck of Brunel's SS Great Britain. Then through the suburbs of Bedminster, before passing the prominent green *dome* of the old Wills tobacco factory.'

Colin interrupted: 'On East Street? Yes, I know that one. At the end of East Street before the pedestrian area. I worked out of the Council offices nearby. Oh yes, I can see it now, great green bell-shaped dome, sits on all that lovely red brick.'

I continued with my list: 'Then it's through Barts' spice factory, over the Bath Road Bridge and between the twin domes of the Midland Railway building.' Colin and Rangi looked dazed. 'We can check that out on the way back, but it goes past the entrance of Brunel's Temple Meads.'

'So, it connects Brunel's SS Great Britain with the Great Western Railway. That is clever,' Rangi noted.

'Yup, and there's more. It crosses the Avon behind the railway station, passing through the Common Grounds event area by the Knights Templar pub.' I paused for a moment, casting a glance across the messy table at my astonished companions. 'Then flows alongside a new 13-storey building called 'The Eye'. Which happens to be the exact almond shape at the center of the Vesica. Unmistakable proportions,' I explained with confidence.

'What was it that Tall John would say?' Colin asked. 'They practise their magic in front of us - and we never notice,' he quoted.

'Wow, Sam,' Rangi looked dazed, if not a little tipsy. 'The whole city's been planned out in circles.'

'And after that...?' Colin urged me on.

'Oh. The Tower in Broadmead. You know it Rangi, roof looks like it's a giant ski jump. Orientated to the circle as well.'

'Oh yes, yes, I know.' Rangi nodded quickly.

'My brain's fried, Sam. I've got go to get back to the sanity of Glastonbury. It's been one hell of a day and a brilliant lunch. But, well, I'm a bit speechless. There's so much to this – *and* the implications.' Colin shook his head in wonder.

We collected our coats and stepped into the dim autumn twilight and chatted about nothing, exhausted by our discoveries. I set off for the bus station and soon arrived at the St James Barton roundabout. The low rumble of the engine gave a background beat to our individual ruminations.

'Sam, what latitude are we on?' Colin asked tentatively.

'Fifty-one degrees and some, why?' I replied.

'It's not fifty-one degrees and *two* minutes, is it?'

'Oh no. That would be at the latitude of deepest Somerset, miles to the south of here. *Why?*'

'Well, you remember the Avon Council House across the road? Now look, they've changed its name,' Colin said pointing out over the dashboard.

'Ah yes, it's now called '51° 02'' I replied, noticing the illuminated sign high up near the roof.

'But, if we're not anywhere near the 51° 02' latitude, why on earth would they have used those numbers for this building?' Colin asked.

'Unless the number two is a reference to the two latitudes marked on Gordon's map. What Billy said - the Spirit and the Material?' I murmured thoughtfully.

'The lights have changed, Sam. Come on, let's go and check out those round glass panels in the archways, where the road runs underneath. See if they're still there – they've always puzzled me. I've got time before the bus leaves. We can park up around the back and I'll walk to the bus station.' Colin spoke in short excited breaths.

We found a parking spot and walked down Cheltenham Road to the back of the former Avon House, now rechristened *'51° 02'*.

The 1970s multi-storey building is supported across the busy Cheltenham Road by two heavy concrete arches. In the centre of each is a three-metre hole covered by a glass sheet with depictions of the Earth clearly etched on their surface. Arching bands like hoops cross the faces, each one showing a slightly different latitude. We were looking at Gordon's map, made large and very, very public.

'Another piece for your puzzle, Sam...' Rangi turned and grinned. My shocked face couldn't form itself into a response.

'It's my unhappy duty to inform you, Mr Cartwright, that you are in a state of financial distress following the withdrawal of services by the Global Finance and Risk Corporation on behalf of the Better Builders Insurance Group.' Gerald Soames settled his corpulent frame into a large executive chair.

'And how far does this *'financial distress'*, actually go?' I replied, sweaty palms rubbing against my thighs.

My solicitor's office was as joyless as its inhabitant.

'Your current state of liquidity, or *illiquidity* – to be precise,' he paused for a small smirk, 'prevents you from being able to fulfil your financial obligations. Your capital and current assets having been eliminated by your outstanding liabilities.' Soames looked as if he had just heard that lunch had been cancelled.

'You mean I'm *broke?*', I croaked.

'In a word Mr Cartwright - yes.'

I sat up, pushing against the wood and leather of his enormous desk.

'It appears that you failed to respond to three letters. One of which was a recorded delivery item from your brokers: 'Kingston Black' of Knowle. As you are now aware, a claim has been made against your assets by a Mr James Lockie, of Easton, Bristol. This action was forced upon him by the withdrawal of coverage by...' he squinted. 'the Global Finance and Risk Corporation following the non-payment of your annual premium.'

I sat back and looked out of the window. It was another busy day down there for Poundland.

'What are my options?' I asked meekly.

'Our advice would be to borrow capital by offering security on the equity of your property.' He looked up to check that I had understood.

I nodded like a robot.

'Or you can sell your property and use the proceeds to settle your liability. Soames growled as he homed-in for the kill.

'Or you could claim bankruptcy. But that would be of little purpose as you have sufficient assets to settle this claim.' He settled back and clasped his hands in satisfaction over his tight, shiny waistcoat.

'I'll have to think about it,' I replied.

The solicitor rose slowly from his chair and with surprising agility, proffered a pale clammy hand.

'Thank you, Mr Cartwright, I'm glad that Langhorne, Bridger and Lloyd could be of service today.' He squeezed his lips into a tight smile adding, 'And under the circumstances, could you arrange immediate payment with my secretary, Miss Lambton as you leave? We would be most grateful.'

'You're an indolent toad, Sam! Kate's eyes flashed alarmingly.

After our exciting day of discovery in Bristol, I had returned to the house. There I rediscovered the miracle of central heating. This might prove to be at least *slightly* dryer than a Mendip field in early November. I reflected on the letters that had brought about my financial crash. The post had followed me around, the black plastic bag languishing in the boot of the car for weeks. At some point, Marby had organised a drop of wood for me at the field gate. I'd cleared out the boot to load the logs, leaving the bag at the gate to collect later. Marby had mistakenly collected it as rubbish. Roughly two months' mail had ended up in the Cheddar Community Recycling Centre, and I was none the wiser as to its contents.

'I'm not going to make you any more cake, Sam. It must be doing something to that small brain of yours.' I had never seen Kate so upset. You would have thought it was her house I'd lost.

'I'm sorry Kate, I really am...' She stood over me, proffering a mug of tea.

'Drink this. Proper Irish Tea. It'll cheer you up,'

We were in her kitchen rather than mine, which was unusual. She liked to be in control and preferred to make random visits to me rather than my visiting *'at inconvenient times, with those dirty boots of yours.'* But this was different. For the first time, I had begun to accept the imminent loss of my home. Since the knock on the door shortly after my return and the opening of the writ, I knew I was in serious trouble. If I had thought about it at all, I'd have assumed that the insurance renewal was automatic, needing no agreement from me.

For the next few weeks, my initial dumb horror gave way to frenzied activity as I tried to unravel the situation. The writ for the expected rebuilding cost was not far off the equity I had in the house. They would only accept a '*Specialist Contractor*' to do the restoration work. That excluded me and any of my builder mates, so I couldn't even undertake the repairs at a cheaper rate. I decided that borrowing the money over 10 years, the longest period I could get, was not an option either. It would have meant paying the equivalent of two mortgages a month. If I gave up food and drink entirely I might just be able to do it. So, the decision to let the house go, was really my only acceptable option. Loveless, jobless, dogless and about to become homeless.

I retreated to the house and the temporary sanctuary of my sofa.

Once I'd started to let go of the house emotionally, the next hurdle was - what to do next? I fantasized about adventures abroad. I had bought the house not with any money-making plan, but because 'I'd be daft not to'. On the rebound from Debbie, I'd thought I'd be kept occupied fixing it up. But my initial enthusiasm had slowly evaporated. It had ended up as a large storage shed with a model railway that had been designed to keep me out of the pub.

Come to think of it, the railway was the only thing I had put much energy into. Recent discoveries had taken away my child-like commitment and replaced it with indifference. And I no longer wanted to be in the garden - my eyes and thoughts drawn to dear, smelly old Norton.

I pondered about my changing circumstances. The discovery of the Vesica in Bristol had caused a lot of excitement. My interests were changing; perhaps I was becoming more introspective. It increased my sense of isolation, though. Rangi and Colin had been supportive, but I missed Deb's thoughtfulness and intimacy. I thought about Josh. I'd never had such an affinity with a kid. I mostly found other people's children a nuisance, if not a complete pain. But Josh was different. I felt relaxed with him, not sensing the need to prove anything.

The weeks passed. I was occasionally using my crutch, though the pain had eased. I'd been keeping my head down. Living on what cash I had while I waited for the house to be sold. Although I'd lost the counsel of both Tall John, with his extensive knowledge of the Templars, and Denis, whose dowsing support would have been welcome, I'd gained an ally in Colin after our exciting Bristol tour. We met regularly at Crumbly's, and over several further visits I made a few more acquaintances.

Colin had mapped out lots of curious alignments, including extending Colston's Vesica Piscis axis from Queen Square north west through Cabot Tower and out towards the River Severn. The line passed through Clifton, over the Gorge and through the doors of Leigh Court. Discovering that it was on the exact latitude *to the foot*, as Colston's church in Mortlake. The line kissed the circle of energy next to Leigh Court that Billy had described all those months ago. It continued as far as the M5 Avon Motorway bridge just as it touched the southern bank of the river. Always bridges and banks, I reflected.

The house business had left me deeply embarrassed. For the sake of a £96.03 insurance premium I could have saved my home. Nick and Simon were sympathetic up to a point, but underneath, my credibility had suffered, and everyone was feeling awkward. My builder mates in the pub visibly shrank as I approached; nervous that my bad luck would rub off. Behind those thin smiles I could see fear. Or maybe it was just my own fear reflected.

I stayed home and toyed with plans for a new future.

And then one day, out of the blue, the phone rang.

'It's Deb – *Debbie,*' came the low, hesitant voice.

'Oh, hello Deb,' I replied, as indifferently as I could. 'How are you?' My chest heaved.

'Er, oh well – as well as could be expected.'

'Good,' I said flatly.

The line went quiet; I could hear her breathing.

'Sam. I - I need to apologise to you for my behaviour.' Then quickly: 'I'm so sorry Sam, I must have hurt you with all my unkindness, I didn't mean it.'

'Yes ... well I'm sorry too. It was a very difficult time.'

'I've heard the news about your house. Claire called me. I'm not sure how she found out. I guess you're not a confidante of hers, are you?'

'No one's a confidante of Claire's, Deb.'

I was sitting upright on the sofa staring at the redundant television through a corridor of books and rolled-up maps. The house had become a mess as I got underway with the task of sorting. As we spoke, I surreptitiously moved the empty flagons into a line on the hidden side of the sofa.

'Yeah, I know what you mean...' Deb hesitated.

I broke the silence.

'Norton's died,' I blurted.

'Oh my God, no! How terrible,' she replied, clearly shaken. 'Josh will be so upset, he's been asking how I thought he was getting on.'

I felt a jab in my chest. Poor kid, how could I have hurt him like this by not calling? That was selfish of me.

'We buried him in the back garden. I think he's quite peaceful. I planted a rose on top.'

'Oh, that's lovely, Sam. Thank you so much for what you did, I feel indebted. If you ever want another dog, I'll pay...'

'Thanks for the offer, but right now is not a good time for a pet.'

'Sam, although I'm sorry to hear about you losing the house, there is another reason for me calling. Something else I need to apologise for.'

I took a short breath in anticipation.

'There's a teacher at school, Jilly, who has become a good friend. We get together sometimes over a bottle or two of Prosecco. The other week she told me that she's an *esoteric* astrologer, whatever that is. An experienced one anyway. She's been practising for years. To be honest, I thought astrology was a load of rubbish; a twelfth of the population being told when they could expect to be lucky in love. I had no idea that planetary alignments have been studied for thousands of years to plot auspicious dates. Dr Dee was even asked to plot the date for the coronation of Elizabeth I in 1559. And even William of Orange's arrival at Brixham was on an astrologically-important day. There's an obelisk there with the date inscribed on it. Jilly calls it 'Elective Astrology'.'

'Oh yes?'

'Anyway, I was telling her about your Bristol thing, the 1831 business.'

'I'm flattered'.

'Yes, well, anyway. What I was saying was that 31st October 1831 was a special day of the year and the riot might have been staged to happen on that date.'

'Yes, go on,' I said, too intrigued to conceal my interest.

'Jilly cast a chart for that date and got really excited with the results. I couldn't quite follow what she was saying, but that date turns out to be very special, and not just because it's Halloween. There was a very significant astronomical *and* astrological event at dawn on that day, and not just then either, but other related dates in the weeks and months before and after. Like there was a timetable supporting all the things that happened.'

'Really?' I said, eyes widening.

'I'm not Jilly; I can't do the astrology thing, but I downloaded a star viewing programme. Have a look and see how many planets, along with the moon, are in alignment on October 31st 1831. Switch on the charts for the western zodiac – it's very telling.'

'Yes. OK, I will. Let me have the name of the programme. I'll check it straight out. Lots of thanks for this.' My heart thumped in response to her interest.

We went on to update each other on recent developments and I told her about finding Gordon's circles and the link to our original Draper alignment. As she began to relax it was just like talking to the old Deb again. She was becoming excited by the significance of it all and her enthusiasm was infectious.

I missed her.

'It would be nice to meet up again, Sam. Josh would love to see you. He thinks your funny.'

'I bet.'

'I'm going to have to go before my paint dries.'

'Decorating?'

'No! Picture painting. I've started up again after all these years, using the old paints you rescued from Dad's. It's wonderful, I'm really enjoying it, I'd forgotten how nice and satisfying being creative is. I'm now competing with Josh to see who can fill the flat up with stuff the quickest.'

Using the star-mapping programme, I dialled back down the centuries to the early morning of 31st October 1831. With the star lore option switched to Western, I scrolled slowly forward, minute by minute, keeping focus on the horizon where the sun would rise in a few hours. Regulus, the Regal star soon appeared, nestled in its home between the front paws of Leo the Lion. Then, at 2 am, Saturn, the 'harvester of souls' appeared, perfectly placed between the two rear paws of Leo. It was now 3 am, the moment when, after three days of dithering, Pinney, The Mayor of Bristol, gave the order to an exhausted Colonel Brereton:

'To take the most vigorous, effective and decisive means in his power to quell the riot.'

Ten minutes later, the moon appeared, positioned equidistantly between the royal Leo and Virgo the *'Mother of the Harvest'.* At 4.30 am, Venus rose fractionally to the right of the Virgin's hand, bearing her symbolic harvest of corn. At 6 am it was Mars' turn, considered by many to be the vehicle for sacrifice. Then, just 15 minutes later, Mercury. As the sky unfolded its message, chaos reigned in Queen Square, with the north and west sides engulfed in massive flames. The Dragoons, led by Major Mackworth, swords drawn, sliced their way through the panicked crowds. The sun then rose *precisely* along the axis of the Vesica Piscis, throwing its light across the Square, over College Green and up Brandon Hill to the future site of Cabot Tower - exactly half a nautical mile away.

Was this what Billy had meant when he quoted Matthew Bridges?

'Thus, will Raphael read the sky.'

'OK, OK, I thought. This sort of star and planetary alignment thing was impressive, but presumably must be happening all the time? I scrolled backwards then forwards several days. It was clear that this amazing configuration moved in and out of alignment with the 31st as the absolute focus. I skipped a year forward, then back, without any interesting skies. Before long, I had travelled a hundred years forward and a hundred back without finding any conjunctions to equal that fateful morning in the autumn of 1831. Given Saturn's 29-year orbit of the Sun, there would be few opportunities for a similar configuration.

This new astrological tool clearly had all sorts of potential. Castle Howard was an obvious choice, but before that I wanted to check the alignment that had kicked off the whole story. The Draper obelisk pointing to Colston's tomb in All Saints Church. This had become even more interesting after discovering that Colston's Circle passed precisely through the dome, after bisecting the spires of Clifton Cathedral. I was not disappointed. The straight line that continues through the centre of the building known only as 'Colston 33', is aligned to sunrise on 3rd October. I watched astonished as the Sun rose smack in the centre of the lower forearm of Virgo grasping her corn.

The hand that gathered souls.

I let out a huge shaking sigh and whispered a thank you to Deb and her friend for their insight. The last pieces of Gordon's extraordinary puzzle were falling into place.

The hours slipped by in frantic activity.

I soon discovered that the sun rose in London in the *palm* of the hand of the goddess Virgo, on the very day of Colston's death, 11th October 1721. Had he really arranged his own demise? Could this have been part of the secret to conscious immortality. To stage the time of your death to coincide with major astrological events?

It was very late when I finally turned my attention to Castle Howard. I was so astonished by the speed and the implications of what I found, that I paced the room, constantly returning to the screen, to reassure myself I wasn't dreaming, chuckling to myself until dawn.

By a stroke of good luck, it was half term the following weekend, which meant that both Deb and Josh were able to stay. She was very intrigued and had made me promise to reveal the great secret hidden in the Howardian Hills of North Yorkshire. The timing was great. I'd recently made some important decisions and it would be nice to share these in front of everyone at Friday night's pub session.

But before that, I needed to mend the broken fence between me and Old Tom. Those weeks holed up under canvas had given me time for self-reflection. I'd gained a few insights listening as the rain softly pattered on the canvas. Even so, I couldn't quite dispel the kernel of anger I felt towards Old Tom; still blaming him for making me so paranoid that I'd burnt Gordon's treasure chest.

'Samuel?' his grey stubble seemed to bristle in surprise.

'Hello Tom; I hope this isn't too inconvenient?' I enquired cautiously.

'Oh no, Sam. Door's always open for you, my lad. Come in, you've arrived at just the right time. I've just opened a gallon of Whitworth's 'Death by Acid' – it's a good drop.'

Tom ushered me in, as I stepped through the door into an unfamiliarly dazzling hallway.

'What the *hell!*' I took a step back in surprise, momentarily struck by the change in décor. 'Your old lady must be spinning in her grave, Tom,' I said with a broad grin.

'She's been dead 20 years, so I don't suppose she cares all that much,' he replied without emotion.

'But it's, it's a sort of, well - puce,' I said with genuine astonishment.

'Marr – *gental* Paradise.' Old Tom's accent curled around the vowels.

Worse was to come. The formerly-orange kitchen was now a lurid lime green. As he filled a couple of ancient tumblers my thoughts returned, with a shiver, to my previous visit.

'I have a meetin' with the supervisor – next Tuesday.' Old Tom raised his eyebrows, waiting for a response.

I stared blankly at him.

'The girls – the girls! You're going to get those girls back. You sly old fox! You're a filthy pervert Tom.'

'They like my cider,' he whispered conspiratorially.

'Well it's great the Council considers you to be a man in need. Funny how the colour changes everything. Your house always looked old-fashioned when it was that purply-brown colour.'

'Ah, well the Missus' grandfather painted that,' he said with pride.

'Anyway Tom, I'm sorry about being rude to you last month. It really wasn't necessary, and I've come to ask if you still want me to do those shelves. I've got the car outside with the roof rack on and a boot full of tools and if it's con...'

The old man beamed.

One trip to the timber yard and a few hours later we had an alcove full of shelves.

'Sam, that's lovely. These films will look right proper up there.'

'Can I give you a hand to put the tapes up? I'd like to see it all finished,' I asked.

'Of course. Go and fill these up while I start to unpack.' He proffered an empty tumbler.

I'd no idea how knowledgeable Tom was, until now. We worked together, sorting his collection of mostly 1930s, '40s and '50s movies. He could talk about the directors and writers as knowingly as he would the actors.

'Do you have a favourite actor then?'

'Oh yes – Archie Leach,' he responded quickly, before adding, 'My grandfather was in the same Lodge as his dad.'

'Archie Leach?'

'Yes. Don't you know who he is? You've lived in *Brizzle* long enough.'

'Ah yes, of course – *Cary Grant*. He was quite a charmer, wasn't he?' I could picture the film star looking relaxed in a great-looking suit and a deep tan.

Tom talked with enthusiasm about each of Grant's films, as one by one we placed them in chronological order on the shelf. He talked about the actor's early life. I wondered how he must have felt when he discovered, after 20 years, that his 'long dead' mother was in fact alive and in an asylum in Bristol.

Suddenly my grip tightened around a tape.

'Fuck, Tom – that's the bloody film I threw away!' I exclaimed.

'What – *'Bachelor Knight'*?' he wrinkled his forehead.

'Yes!' I leant towards him, excitedly tapping the cover. 'That's the bloody film I threw away. The same bloody film! I recognise the label. It's the one that came out of Gordon's tool box...'

Old Tom steadied himself and slowly, painfully, sat down. His spindly legs splayed out like dry twigs.

'That's the film, eh?' He rubbed an old scar on the back of his hand. 'That makes sense.' He raised an arm in emphasis. 'Cary Grant was a Templar, you know.

The *Knights Templar*? I said feeling shocked.

'Had the knowledge and all that.'

'Really? How do you know he was? Did he tell people he was?' I asked, trying to conceal my scepticism.

'He wasn't allowed to. Being a Templar is a big secret. You can't just go around telling everyone you meet. Don't be daft, Sam.'

'But what was he doing in Gordon's box?' I reflected for a moment. 'Yes. Now I understand. *Jeez*. What a thing. It all seems to make some strange sense.'

'What does Sam? What are you *talking* about?'

'Oh, nothing. Well, not yet. I'll have to think this all through. Got to check a few dates first. Promise to tell you soon, though.'

'This film,' Tom tapped the cover with a gnarled finger, 'is one from the late 40's. He appears several times dressed as a knight in shining armour to the fantasy-obsessed 15-year-old Shirley Temple. Her sister is a judge; the very much older Myrna Loy.' He grinned knowingly.

'That's not a lot to go on, Tom,' I replied.

'Old Cary had a lot to say over what went on his movies, an' he used to drop in little clues to his being a Templar. That's what makes watching him so much fun. He was right clever.'

'Like what? What makes you think he was a Templar?'

'It's a bit like, well, you just build a picture from the clues. You might like to know that Cary Grant made a total of 72 movies in 33 years.' Tom waved a finger at me.

'Did he really?' I asked with an involuntary jerk.

'Did you also know that Cary Grant and Randolph Scott at one time lived together in Malibu? I've got a photograph somewhere showing the pair of them wearing pinnies. You know aprons like my masonic apron. I know this Sam, because I've still got mine upstairs.'

Old Tom paused, his grey face showing signs of a flush as he caught a thin breath.

'Look Sam my lad, I watched Cary a lot. These clues would crop up all over the place. *'To Catch a Thief'*. One of his best. His abrupt answer to the Insurance Agent's question of 72 as the number of Nazi's he had killed.' Tom shrugged his angular frame. 'At the climax there is a chase over a roof. It's covered in those obelisks and flaming urns you're so interested in.'

'Dear Tom - this is a whole new piece for my puzzle! I'm amazed. To think, I came here to put up shelves and you give me a whole new insight in return.'

'And watch the very last scene when he's in the arms of Grace Kelly. He turns slowly to reveal just one eye directly at the camera. The one, the *All-Seeing Eye.*' Tom held his hands together forming an eye shape. 'And Sam, go and check out that statue of him, down by the docks. He's carrying a script. I'll let you guess which film.'

49 The heart revealed

I woke early, after a restless night that proved the accuracy of the label 'Death by Acid'. It was Friday and in a few hours Deb and Josh would arrive to a tidy kitchen and clean sheets. Getting the house ready had been a poignant experience, knowing that they would be my last guests. I was excited by their imminent arrival, but a knot of anxiety persisted. I couldn't get Josh out of my thoughts and needed resolution to that question that had been floating around, like an old sea mine, for ten years. Was he my son? Had *he* been the reason for Deb's sudden departure? Had I missed something? I'd felt drawn to this gangly kid when we first met at Gordon's funeral. The need for an answer was even more urgent now that contact with Deb had resumed. Maybe today I could summon the courage to ask her directly. I plotted ways of keeping Josh distracted while I confronted Deb.

As I tried to imagine what it would be like to be his father, my thoughts kept returning to Martin and what *he* would feel. To discover that you had been so deceived for so long. How difficult that must be to suddenly have to share your child's affections, dreams and aspirations with another man. This could be messy, especially for poor Josh. Perhaps, I reflected, it would be best that he remained in the dark about his parentage until he was older.

Several loud thumps from the front door brought me back to the here and now.

'Hiya,' I called out from the front step, as Deb and Josh unpacked her Micra. 'Did you have a good trip?'

'Oh, yes fine, though we did have to stop twice to relieve our fellow passenger.'

Josh appeared from the far side of the car, pulled along by a very excited small black dog.

'Who's this?' I asked him as his furry friend jumped up to greet me.

'He's called Snowy, Sam – *Snowy!*' Josh gathered up the lead as I followed them both towards the kitchen.

'I'll get him some water. I'm sure I still have some biscuits left.' I looked at Josh's broad grin. It felt good to have both Josh *and* a dog in the house again. Then my heart contracted at the realisation that this would be the last time.

Deb entered the kitchen, dropping a couple of small rucksacks to the floor. She leant over and surprised me with a soft kiss on the lips.

'How do you like him?' she asked, as I embraced the black lamb-sized bundle of fur.

'He's lovely, when did you get him?'

'A couple of days ago. He's a rescue dog. One of the retired teachers from the school is very ill and can't look after him anymore.'

'Does he like going for long walks?' I said to Josh as we both smoothed Snowy's coat.

'Oh yes, he's got masses of energy,' he smiled, kneeling closer.

'Bizarre choice of name isn't it?'

'That's the name he came with. It's the only name he responds to when you call him,' Deb explained.

'You know, Josh, I've still got Norton's collar and tag. It's on the mantel piece. Would you like it as a keepsake?'

'Oh yes please. It might fit Snowy when he gets bigger.' At that, Josh bounded into the front room. He returned moments later with a very puzzled expression.

'What's the matter, darling?' Deb inquired.

'It's the tag. Norton's name wasn't Norton.'

'What do you mean, Josh?' I replied as I filled the kettle.

'It says – No-et-on.'

'Let's have a look ... '

'Huh, that is so weird. Look Deb, Josh is right. This tag reads Noeton, not Norton. It seemed we all misheard Gordon, or rather heard what sounded the most probable.'

'What a strange name, I wonder what it might...' Deb was interrupted by Josh, pulling eagerly at her arm.

'It means: To awaken and become conscious,' he carefully read from his phone's screen.

'Goodness! Well done.' Deb rubbed Josh's bushy head.

'Hmm...' I replied, 'though possibly a bit confusing for poor old Norton.' I chuckled as I remembered Gordon's sly smile. He'd put considerable thought into every aspect of his life.

'But very apt, don't you think?' Deb grinned. 'Can I ask - where's he buried?'

'I'll show you both,' I replied.

The three of us stood in the small yard and held a spontaneous vigil for the poor old boy. I broke the respectful pause with news for Josh.

'I've got a present for you. Would you like to see it?'

'Yes, yes. What is it?' He bounded up and down, exciting Snowy to feverish tail wagging.

'It's upstairs. Come on I'll show you.'

'Oh wow – a train set! Wicked!' He looked entranced as he studied the trains and buildings around the dining table-sized layout. I handed him the controller.

'It's not finished yet. The train will move, but only along that bit of track,' I said, pointing.

'Oh, Sam that's a wonderful gift. But I hope there's room for it in Josh's bedroom?' Deb looked apprehensive.

'Not to worry, I've thought that through. I've designed it so it can tip up out of the way when it's not in use.' I mimed the process to reassure her.

'But it must have cost...?'

I interrupted her. 'It's OK. It really is. I couldn't take the shelf railway with me, so I've cannibalised it. It's better than sitting in a crate, getting damp in storage somewhere.'

'You're not moving straight into a rental house, then?' she asked.

'No, not yet. I've made other plans. But let's talk about that later,' I replied.

We left a distracted Josh and retreated downstairs to sit around my chaotic dining table. Deb scooped-up a handful of photographs and print-outs. 'Looks like you've been busy since I was last here?'

'Not much else to do, with this still bandaged.' I lifted my leg to demonstrate. 'It's been good that way.' I left a discreet pause before continuing: 'I wondered if maybe Josh could play with the trains while we had a swift drink at the pub?'

'Hmm.... I don't know. He's not familiar with your house. And anyway, I'm not sure about leaving Snowy.' She looked torn.

'Isn't Josh old enough to look after Snowy himself? I'm sure he won't mind. I've even bought some treats.' I smiled as I waved a bag of 'artisan' crisps.

'Maybe. Let me think about it,' Deb said distractedly. I returned to shifting and sorting maps around the table.

'So, what have you got to show me that got you so excited?' She cocked her head slightly and smiled.

'I used that star programme you told me about and checked out lots of alignments. Found all sorts of *very* interesting things.'

'So, come on tell all. What's all this about Castle Howard?'

'Ah yes. Castle Howard,' I said raising a finger. 'Remember the obelisk?'

'The big one on the main drive? Yes, of course Sam. Who could forget that phallic trick with the pyramid over the gate?' She blushed.

I uncovered the map of Castle Howard and pointed to a series of different coloured lines drawn in felt tip and projecting like rays from the obelisk on the Stray. They flowed in one direction; eastwards toward the sunrise.

'Going clockwise and starting at the north end, this top line points to the Temple of Venus. This is the point on the horizon where Venus, the Masonic Morning Star, rises at dawn on 1st May. Which happens to be Beltane, the time of union, fertility and harvest. We still celebrate the day'.

I opened the laptop and clicked the star chart programme into life. It blinked its location as Castle Howard. Deb absently ran a finger across the map along the axis of the obelisk to the temple on the far side of Ray Wood.

'What's that mean though?' She asked.

'Er, well I'm not entirely sure. Not yet anyway. I've only had a few days to get my head around it all.'

'Maybe it's symbolising love. As the path of Venus across the sky draws the shape of a heart. Do you remember it was in that little book you leant me?'

'Yes, that could be it. Good point. Wasn't there something else about the orbit of Venus and Mercury representing the Trinity?' I paused in thought, reflecting on her observation. 'From the obelisk to the reservoir, is the prime axis of Castle Howard. The house is built at a tangent from it. It also happens to be *the same* distance as between Cabot Tower and Queen Square. Half a nautical mile!'

She raised her eyebrows in interest.

'That could mean that a Vesica Piscis the same size as the one in Bristol was used in its layout,' I said.

I caught her eye and smiled before continuing.

'Now, along with the Stray, this line between obelisk and reservoir is the foundation stone, so to speak, of the whole layout. Do you see the obelisk is at the left, or westerly corner? That's the anchor of the scheme. Now, at sunrise on 3rd September when...'

'Wouldn't the sun also rise there in April sometime as well?' Deb interrupted.

'Yes, it would. But it doesn't seem to rise anywhere significant in the sky in April. Although Pisces is interesting now I think about it, with its connection to the fish's bladder, the Vesica Piscis. But, no, I think September is the month because of this...'

I brought the laptop back to life. Across the screen flowed the familiar pattern of the Zodiac. I scrolled the screen star chart programme forward until 3rd September. Then rolled the minutes away to dawn. The sun appeared on the horizon directly on the line from obelisk to reservoir, rising precisely in the centre of the Lion's paw in Leo.

'And ...?' Deb smoothed her chin, rocking her head.

'A few months ago, I came across an article about secret Masonic handshakes. And this one,' I pointed to the scan from the article, 'is the grip of the *Master* Mason. It's known as the 'Lion's Paw' or the 'Ma-Ha-Bone'. It's the strongest pass grip used by the Freemasons.'

'That *is* interesting.' Deb nodded approval.

'OK, well the next line from the obelisk is through the Temple of the Four Winds. This is sunrise on the equinox: 21st March and 22nd September. The four winds, the four quarters, the four seasons that are ruled by the sun's movement. A marker thrown up to the skies. But, it's at the next alignment when Castle Howard gets *extra* interesting. Do you see how I've drawn the line from the obelisk, then diagonally through the centre of the Mausoleum? It marks the path of the sunrise on 2nd October.'

I paused to allow Deb to catch on. Memories of our trip together in the summer shimmered in my thoughts.

'This is the true day of Colston's death in the Julian Calendar, *before* an extra ten days were added in the mid-18th Century. That's when we moved to the Gregorian calendar. Do you see? It's smack-on,' I announced, opening my palms.

Deb studied the map forensically, deep in thought.

'But wasn't Castle Howard built in the early 1700s, years before his death?'

'The house? Yes. But the first mention of the Mausoleum wasn't until June 1722, some months *after* his death. Now this is where it gets even more curious. The next two lines each pass through those two monuments we discovered hidden away in the woods. They're tricky to spot on Google Earth, but this really old six-inch...' I produced a map from under a pile of notes, 'shows them up clearly. This is the line from the obelisk to the pyramid we found. Remember? This marks sunrise on Samhein, the Druid new year on 31st October, and the same alignment as Colston's Vesica. Interesting eh?'

Deb flicked between the laptop and the large map several times.

I continued, 'This last one takes it to another level. Do you remember the Temple of Four Faces? The one with the little obelisk and all those cherubs?'

'Yes, I remember, that's the one you said was overflowing with fecundity...' she replied with a coy grin.

'Yes, yes good. Well, this line marks sunrise on Colston's birthday...' I tapped the map repeatedly.

'Does it *really*? She paused in shock before turning to me. 'What's it all mean, though?'

'Good question. What *does* it all mean? My guess is that Colston was part of the money that was backing William of Orange, the first masonic King, and that Castle Howard has been used, at least in part, as a memorial to *him*. A very large and esoteric memorial.'

'But why in Yorkshire?'

'As you can see by the state of the table, I've been busy with background research and discovered that the first ever congress of Stone Masons in England was held very close to Castle Howard. The Stray may not be just pointing at Regulus, the royal star, as it crosses the Meridian, but quite possibly to the place where the congress of 935 AD was held. It's also *exactly* half-way between the Scottish Rite lot in Edinburgh and the London York Rite Masons. It's relatively safe and quick to sail along the coast, rather than going over land. You could sail to the Humber and get within a short carriage ride of the Estate for a convenient meet-up with the Bretherin.'

'So, you think Castle Howard was built by Freemasons as one of their major meeting places?'

'Yes, and Colston might have helped out by writing a few very large cheques. Remember the Bank of England and the Hoare Bank were both formed just before Castle Howard was built and George Howard was the Chancellor of the Exchequer for a period.'

'Where's all this going, Sam?'

'Well, the Druids believed that you could guide your soul through reincarnation to be reborn at a time and parentage of your choosing. Now we've established that Colston was an incredibly shrewd and powerful figure. Possibly a power behind the throne and heavily tied-in with the early Masons. We also know he was hungry for knowledge – his role at John Dee's church in Mortlake demonstrates that. So, what if he was successful in discovering the means to achieve conscious immortality? Imagine for a moment that he was able to select or even design the blueprint for his next incarnation. Where would he pitch-up? What about this Draper bloke – there are countless 'clues' linking the two men, and Draper was born after Colston's death. Reincarnated as Draper, Colston's soul could have travelled the world – literally experiencing life on a global scale. Draper's life was about conquest, the challenge. Even though he failed to gain the full glory he craved.'

Deb's eyes widened.

'Oh my God! Yes, I see. And after Draper… Brunel!'

'Yes – it all makes sense. As Brunel, he could have left his mark all over the city he loved – not just creating engineering masterpieces, but influencing their very location, at the critical points on the map. Brunel's name is *everywhere* – the station, the Suspension Bridge, the SS Great Britain. Every child in the country is taught about his achievements.'

I studied Deb's elfin face and offered a grin.

'And there's one more incarnation to add – *Cary Grant*!'

'Oh, come on Sam - you can't be serious! Cary Grant? How on earth can you make that jump?' Just because he came from Bristol … '

‘Remember there were three biographies that didn’t get burnt from Gordon’s treasure? Colston, Draper and Brunel. But there was also a VHS tape that I threw away. It wasn’t until I was doing a little job for one of the pub regulars, that I recognised the film from the cover. It was the same as Gordon’s. Cary Grant was born here in Bristol and maintained a strong connection with the city. He came back here frequently, even after his mother’s death.’

‘But why…?’

‘Imagine Colston’s immortal soul. After you had incarnated into the lives of Draper and then Brunel, what would you be looking for next? Fame and adulation on a global scale. Don’t you see?’

‘But - Cary Grant?

‘Yes. Why not? Who wouldn’t want a life like his? Wealth and adoration. He was probably idolised by more people than any other film star in the 20th Century.’

Deb sucked her breath as she considered my theory.

I continued: ‘We’re talking about a period from the early Thirties until his death in 1986. His films where shown all over the world in countless cinemas to adoring women. And not just that; men loved him too and wanted to emulate him. He was a legend. One of the biggest. Colston’s ego and service-to-self, writ large. What’s intriguing me now, is, who would Colston choose to be after that? Even during Cary Grant’s lifetime, he might have continued evolving – Grant experimented with LSD before it was made illegal and he was a long-term member of a magic club in Los Angles. And by all accounts had a vast esoteric library, maybe even echoing Dr Dee’s collection. So, he wasn’t just a playboy; he was a highly-intelligent man, clearly interested in pushing the boundaries of human experience.’

‘And then what? Where do you go once you’ve had it all?’ Deb pursed her lips in thought.

We studied each other in reflective silence.

‘This is a lot to take in, Sam. Colston reminds me of Woody Allen, and that character he played - Zelig. The mysterious enigma at the centre of all that international fame.’

‘Well he was certainly in the right place at the right time and had the money to make things happen.’

We were interrupted by Josh bouncing down the stairs and demanding snacks.

‘I’ve got some treats for you,’ I said, looking at Deb, ‘that your mum will approve of.’

As he demolished a packet of organic potato chips, Deb and I sat down together at the dining table. After a moment's reflection, I decided to bring up something Billy had frequently hinted at.

'You see Deb, Billy kept talking about finding the 'Heart of Bristol'. *Not* finding your heart in Bristol. He was quite specific. He said, 'finding the Heart *of* Bristol'. What did he mean? At first, I thought he meant, you know, the centre, like the old mediaeval centre where Colston is buried. But that seemed too obvious. Then I started looking for something that physically resemble a heart – but I couldn't find anything.'

'Is that why you've got all those medical pictures everywhere?'

'Yes,' I replied, holding up a Wikipedia diagram of the human heart. 'I kept it here while I was looking at the different roads and lanes in these old maps. Can't get a match anywhere though. Thing is, Billy was rather keen on me finding it, so I keep looking. He said that there really was a heart in the city, that if I found it, I would have found my own heart.'

'Have you looked for a cartoon heart shape, Sam? You know, a symbolic heart. Like the shape of a rose petal or the one that Venus draws in the sky. The Templars loved their symbols.'

'Well, it doesn't seem very likely, somehow. I can't see the Templars as early graffiti artists.'

'What about the Temple Rose, the rose petal that looks like the Venus heart?' Deb paused allowing me a moment to reflect before continuing, 'Did you not know that the street close to the original Knights Templar church is called Temple *Rose* Street?

'Er, no...?'

'Can I look, can I look - can I?' Josh interrupted.

'One of these...' Deb drew a classic pointy love-heart. He nodded and took the pen and started to doodle his own heart shapes.

'I'll look for it, I like puzzles.' He smiled, looking up for approval. I'd noticed he'd got taller and thinner since his last visit.

'Thanks, but my reckoning is that if there *is* a heart in Bristol, it's not going to look like something off a Valentine's Day card, but like an anatomical heart.' I produced a couple more medical images, complete with valves and tubes and drew out a simplified outline on a piece of A4 note paper.

'Do you think it might be some sort of road network or junction of roads? Maybe a housing estate like Knowle West's hexagon?' Deb inquired, anxious to quell Josh's new-found enthusiasm. 'Josh! Don't cover the maps with your sticky fingers. Listen to me. Would you be OK to stay here while Sam and I go to meet some old friends?' Her smile betrayed a motherly concern.

'You want to go to the pub, Mummy?' Josh replied as he held up and slowly rotated a 14th Century map of Bristol.

'Well ... yes, but we'll only be around the corner.' Deb smoothed his head as she spoke.

'That's alright, Mummy. Daddy goes to the pub all the time and lets me play.'

'Is that right...?' she glared.

I speculated on Martin's forthcoming interrogation.

'It's here, it's here!' Josh repeatedly tugged at my jumper. 'On this map. Look Mummy, Sam, it's here!'

'Where Josh?' I asked, indulgently. He started to draw on the lamination.

I followed the red line and watched as the enormous shape of a cartoon heart appeared across 14th Century Bristol. One part followed the bank of river Avon as it flowed from the old city wall downstream to Redcliffe Bridge. The other side mirrored by the original course of the moat as it flowed to meet Redcliffe Bridge. There appeared an almost perfect symmetry between the two sides of the shape. It exclusively used water as its boundary.

'That does look like a heart Sam, don't you think?' Deb studied the map closely.

'You see – you see! I found the heart!' Josh's excitement started Snowy barking at full volume.

I held the map up for closer inspection.

'Oh, *fuck*...Oops, sorry Deb,' I cupped my mouth and looked apologetic. Josh smirked approvingly. 'You see how the Templar church is dead centre? Width-wise and along the axis from the water.'

Her face lit up with curiosity.

'Well,' I paused, thinking quickly. 'It looks to me that this heart shape, from the pointy bottom of it and up through the footprint of the original Templar church, is aligned to sunrise on the Solstice. The summer Solstice, the feast of St John – Jeez, well done Josh, I think you may have found something I have been looking very hard for, for a long time.' I proffered my hand towards him. He momentarily looked confused, then tried to shake my arm from its socket.

'That's just amazing. Hidden in plain sight.' Deb looked up as we beamed at each other.

I sat down, shocked by the discovery of the heart. Having successfully solved the enigma, Josh bounded back upstairs, chased by Snowy. He was soon making train whistle noises. I shook my head slowly and wondered.

'I've spent so long on this heart business. I've been so puzzled by it. And along comes Josh and, almost as an afterthought, homes right in on it! And I can see how the Templars did it – they even paid for part of it!' I paused, lost in thought. *'That's* why they built their church smack in the middle of the Avon's muddy, high risk, flood plain.'

'Come on then, maybe it's time to go to the pub. What do you think?' I said. Deb's dark eyes flashed a smile as she checked her watch.

'Well, we mustn't stay long; or at least I can't, not with Josh on his own, he's too young. Snowy will need a walk as well.' She'd returned to mother mode.

'Yes, of course, we can be quick,' I replied, still distracted by the map.

When Deb returned from instructing Josh *'not to leave the house'* we gathered our coats off the pegs in the hall. As we passed the living room she glanced in. Her attention was immediately caught by a collection of photographs on the mantel piece. They'd been left there by Billy months ago.

'Is that Billy?' She enquired as she picked up the top one.

'Yes, it is. He's standing in front of his uncle's steam train. He used to get paid to polish the brass. It's an early Kerr Stuart 0-4-2 class. Can't be many of them left...'

She looked up and blinked, deep in thought, before returning her gaze to the image, evidently fascinated by the impressive little train.

'Did you say Rangi had some footage of Billy, she'd taken?'

'Yes, I'll expect she'll be at the pub with Nick. Why?'

'Never you mind for the moment. But you may be in for another big surprise this evening....'

We set off towards the pub in silence. It was three days before Christmas and the misted-up windows added to the festive atmosphere. Our breaths produced trails of white in the cold damp air.

'You're quiet, Sam.'

'Yes. Sorry Deb; lots on my mind, I guess.'

'That heart thing is important to you, isn't it?'

'Well – *yes.*' I stopped. A cone of light from a street lamp highlighted her beautiful hair. My heart was a tangle of emotions as I turned. 'He's very clever, isn't he?'

'Who ... Josh? When he's paying attention, he is.'

'He spotted the heart almost straight away. I've been struggling with it for months.' I paused, then turned and took hold of Deb's slender arms, scrutinizing her eyes. 'Is Josh mine, Deb? Is he my son? I need to know.'

'Yours?' she replied with a look of confusion, her eyes widening as she tipped her head back. She replied with a smile. 'Don't be so silly.'

'But you suddenly ran off, as if, as if...I wasn't *good enough* to be his dad.' I flushed in recollection. Letting go of her arms, I turned away, my heart beating against my ribs.

'Sam. Listen to me.' Her voice hardened. 'He's not your son. He's Martin's. Let me say it again...' She leant forward in emphasis. '*He's* not your son.'

'But... How can you be so certain? He *might* be, chronologically?'

'No. He's not, because, as a matter of fact, Martin insisted on a test. He argued with me over it. God, he humiliated me. It was never the same between us after that.'

I pulled her to a halt and examined her expression, reflecting on how little I knew of her life. Was that why she'd separated from him? I wondered.

'Martin turned out to be a poor choice of life partner.' It was Deb's turn to catch my arm as we studied each other. Her chest heaved. 'He cared more about himself and his money than he ever did about Josh *or me.*'

I was lost for words as we resumed our slow walk towards the King's Head, my bare head now cold and damp. I pulled my lapels closer and shivered.

Finally, Deb spoke.

'Josh might not be your son, but I can tell you who is...'

I stopped and turned, briefly touching her forearm. Her expression had changed, she looked amused and flashed her even white teeth.

'*What?*' I replied, as I steadied myself.

She placed her hand on her hip and her head on one side as she confronted me.

'It's Billy, stupid! Billy what's it? Billy ... Wells. *He's* your son.'

'What? No, that's not right. He's from the Caribbean. I've been nowhere near there. No, he can't be. He's too old.'

'Don't you remember? I do. It was one of your irritating habits, talking about your exes as if somehow *I* would be interested.' Deb glared, and I slumped with inadequacy. 'Mary, *black* Mary. Before you went to Australia. When you were still at Uni. You told me she was a bit potty and disappeared on you.' She paused in recollection. 'You said she had a funny relationship with her parents who were mega-religious. Didn't you say that?'

'Well, yeah.' I shrugged, shaking my head in confusion.

'She's Billy's mother, the sister of his Aunt, Patricia.'

'But Deb, how can you be so sure?'

'The photos, *silly!* The way he's standing. That's you. You all over.' She mimicked the pose and swaggered for several feet.

'But I...' my empty stomach flipped in recognition.

'That's you. I've studied enough old photos of you to spot that pose of yours - straight out!'

'You can't base my paternity potential on a *swagger*...'

'You bet I can. He's even got one shoulder slightly lower, just like yours. You just wait. If Rangi's still got that bit of film. The one with Billy you told me about, I'll know.' Deb beamed in triumph.

'Hello Debbie. How are you?' Nick rose from his seat before kissing her lightly on the cheek and turning to introduce Rangi.

'Thanks Nick, it's nice to see you again – and Rangi. We're old friends, aren't we?' They embraced across the littered table. Simon stood in turn, and stiffly proffered a hand. Deb surprised him by leaning forward and planting a kiss on his pale cheek.

'Hello Debbie; nice to meet you again.' Simon grinned nervously.

'Even Old Tom is here.' I turned, holding Deb's hand as she offered a handshake with the other, to a surprised Tom. 'Now you stay here, while I get drinks. I'll manage. Sit over there by Rangi. I'll grab another chair when I get back.'

On my return from the bar, Deb and Rangi were deep in conference, huddled over a shared phone. They looked up and grinned as I approached. Judging by their looks, I was now a confirmed father.

I wondered what that must feel like and then the penny dropped. It was *me.* I was the father that Billy had come to Bristol to see. That was how he'd known my name, even before we met, so dramatically, in this very pub.

Deb held out the screen for me to inspect. It was Billy and Nick leaving a football stadium. Billy looked uncomfortable in a colourful scarf as he smiled nervously at the camera. Nick grinned at his side. By the look on his face the home team had won.

I studied the screen as Billy walked towards the camera.

My thoughts were disturbed by a jumble of excited voices as the profound and shocking revelation became public.

Nick leant over and glanced at the screen, declaring with a sceptical lilt, 'Yeah - in another life he is!'

Simon took his turn, muttering, 'All odd, all this is very odd, very, very odd indeed...'

Old Tom came over and after watching, offered me the conspiratorial grin of an ancient impotent getting their first erection.

I leant back against the frame of the chair and listened in dazed silence to the excited banter. This was all way too much to take in, I reflected, as Nick lurched towards me on the bench.

'Enough of all this Billy nonsense.' He waved a slack hand. 'So, mate. What are you going to do now the house is going? You going to rent?'

A small attentive audience gathered. I spied Deb's concerned face as Rangi, hand cupping her mouth, scrutinised me.

'Well,' I paused, gathering my thoughts. 'I've decided to go on a bit of a trip. One that I've been promising myself for a long time. I'm going back south. But this time I'm heading all the way, straight to New Zealand – Aotearoa!' I raised my voice to a cheer and glanced smiling at Rangi.

'From sofa to so *far*,' she cried in delight. I turned and raised my glass towards her, smiling in acknowledgment.

'Why?' Deb pulled at my sleeve, prompting me with a look of astonishment.

'Well - I got thinking. I'd always wanted to go there since my days in the Outback. I often wondered what it would be like to be some place where it's only the mozzies that bite.' I forced a grin.

'There's more to it than that, though, Sam – *isn't* there?'

'Err, yes. You're right, there is a little bit more to it, Rangi,' I replied quietly.

'Well, what is it?' She leaned forward, her round face alight with interest.

'It's in Auckland. I've been busy with Google Earth and I think I've discovered something odd at the bottom of some place called 'One Tree Hill'. It's got me curious to see what else there is to be discovered.'

'Waste of time, mate. You should stay put and write a book about all this rubbish you've already claimed to have found.' Nick leaned forward, hands on thighs, as he checked faces for confirmation.

'I thought about it, especially after the Castle Howard discoveries. But then, someone at Crumbly's Cafe said I'd be lucky to sell a couple of hundred, and most of those would be at remaindered prices.'

'Write a novel instead,' Rangi said encouragingly.

'Like anyone would believe all that bollocks anyway,' Nick replied with a generous grin.

'Na – he's right,' I replied to Rangi. 'I can't write. I've been a builder all my life.'

'Actually Nick, I don't think what Sam has been researching is all bollocks.' Deb leaned over Rangi, tapping Nick's arm.

'I agree with you Deb. Don't be too hasty to condemn.' Rangi waved a finger.

'Nick,' I replied, 'Bristol's full of curiosities.'

'Like what?' He taunted me with a knowing smile. He was enjoying this.

'How about the Bristol Council House you spend so much of your time asleep in? Walk through the front door and what's the first thing you are confronted with? A massive three-metre-wide Zodiac clock. Did you never ask yourself what that is doing in a secular government building?'

Nick shrugged.

'Or what about the two massive gold unicorns standing on either end of the building? Or the pitch of the roofs they're sitting on? They may just be identical to the Giza pyramid.'

'Oh yes, those,' Deb said with a distant look.

'Yes. What about that?' Simon said sitting up.

Nick replied with a shrug, '...it's just a Bristol thing, unicorns.'

'To some people, the magical unicorn's horn represents the energy of the vortex. The same vortex produced by Colston's Circles -the Vesica Piscis.'

Simon leant forwards. 'Are you saying those unicorns are somehow pointing to those invisible energies of yours?'

'Might be. Might well be.' I shrugged. Simon sat back and offered a frown.

'You're barking mad,' Nick beamed, creasing his hollow cheek.

'Not completely. Mad enough to believe that one of only four known portraits of Edward Colston hangs on the ground floor of that same building. It's in the chamber next to the main entrance. Smack on the Cabot Queen Square alignment. From the back wall, he looks across College Green to Trinity Lane and the center of the Vesica. I think he was deliberately positioned be...'

'Does he really?' Deb interrupted, her voice lilting in surprise.

'Sam.' Simon looked earnest 'Do you really believe the whole city has been laid out with these alignments - like Washington DC was?'

'No, of course not. Not the whole city, just important parts of it. Washington DC was designed all at once, by one man. Bristol, like most other cities, has evolved over time. If it had been rebuilt, it would have been obvious. But has been done in a piece-meal way over centuries. It's slowly been developed. And it's still going on now. I'm convinced we're surrounded by symbolism in buildings and monuments, and that maybe they also have a function as indicators of a hidden knowledge. It's there right in front of us. But we need to make the effort. We need to become curious.'

'Mate, you live in a proper dream world.' Nick rolled his eyes.

'Maybe, Nick. Maybe I'm imagining it all...'

'Those that have eyes that can truly see,' Rangi announced. 'My grandfather taught me that when I was a little girl. You know, learning to see.'

'Or...' Deb interjected studying Nicks face. *'He who does not understand, should learn or be silent.'* To quote Dr John Dee, eh Sam?'

'Well, we'll all miss you, mate. Good luck with that trip, you might talk nonsense these days but, we'll miss you anyway.' Nick turned, glancing at Simon, who stood offering his hand.

'Yes, good luck Sam. Sorry about the house thing. I know you'll get another sometime. Come back soon, won't you.' Simon looked serious as Nick stared at his pint.

'Erm, I've got a bit of news too...' interrupted Deb. 'Josh and I are moving back to Bristol.'

'You are?' I leant towards her feeling my heart contract.

'Yup. Dad's money has come through, and I want something bigger and more peaceful than a poky flat on a busy road.'

'How lovely!' Rangi clasped her hands in pleasure before hugging a surprised Deb.

'Yes. It's the right time to move as Josh is going to big school next year. I need to do it now, if I am going to do it. Anyway, the flat's too small with all his stuff and my canvases everywhere. To think I nearly gave all my art away. Now I'm looking to buy somewhere with a nice studio room.' Deb turned, blowing a little kiss.

'Reckon your boy would like Sam's place with its trains.' Old Tom raised his glass and grinned.

God. I'm going to really miss her.

'I've certainly got a lot to think about on this trip, haven't I?' I turned to Deb but by the wide-eyed look on her face, she was evidently not listening.

'Billy...!' Deb called out catching everyone's attention.

'What about him?' I replied, looking around.

'Billy! Now I *understand*.'

'Understand what? Come on Deb – what is it?'

'He wanted you to understand *before* he went away. Something so important to him. So important that he had to leave to make sure you'd understand.'

'What are you on about?'

'Billy Wells is the reincarnated soul of Colston,' She poked me with an outstretched finger. 'Don't you see? After so many lives devoted to the acquisition of wealth, power and fame, he realised what was missing. He needed to experience life in service to others. To help other people, not keep pursuing his own selfish needs. So maybe the soul of Cary Grant *did* evolve after his extraordinary life. Only this time he chose to be a modest nurse – giving rather than taking. Sort of coming full circle. Don't you see? The philosophers say that the greatest source of happiness comes not from indulging yourself - but from helping others.'

I was starting to feel overwhelmed as I studied her soft brown eyes. The past year was galloping through my mind as the jigsaw pieces slotted into place. And there was Billy Wells, right at the centre of it all. The heart.

I eased up onto my good foot. My hand gripped the side of the table. The chatter died to a hush, as I surveyed my attentive audience.

'I just want to say…' I paused for dramatic effect.

'That it's, it's...'

I raised my glass in salute.

'It's - *my* round.'

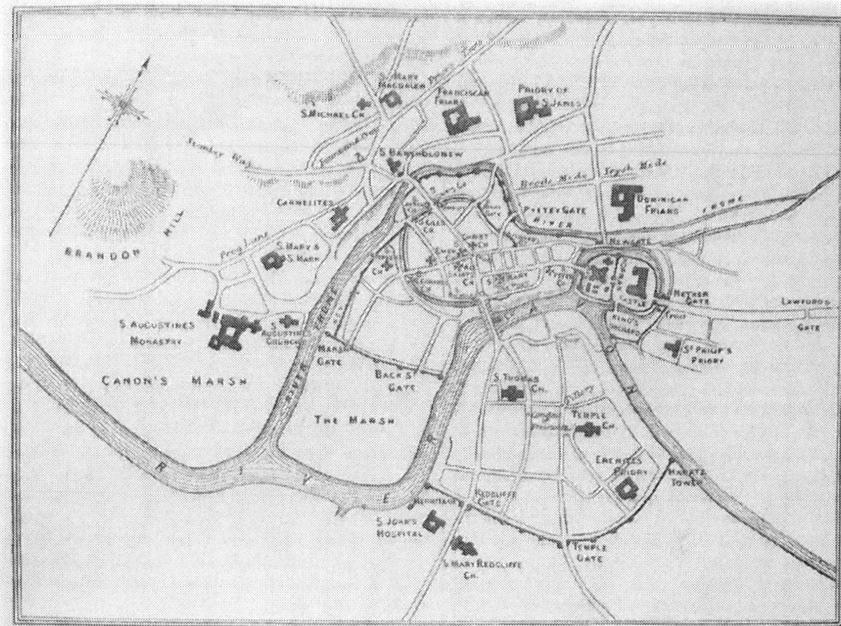

Map of Bristol in the 13th Century, showing the whole of the Walls and the sites of the ancient Churches and Religious Houses.

Afterword

At the time of writing, nearly all the buildings, monuments and locations mentioned in this book exist, exactly as described by Sam. All the measurements are accurate and can be easily verified. The characters, however, are entirely fictitious.

About the Author

Pete Wheldon was born and educated in Surrey. He lived in Europe, South Africa and New Zealand before settling in Bristol.

Having been a teenage student of astronomer Patrick Moore, he became fascinated by the cosmos, as interpreted through geophysics, geometry, spirituality and mysticism. Over many years, he researched the links between these subjects and secretive organisations such as the Freemasons and the Knights Templar.

His first novel, *Colston 33*, sets out to reveal some of the esoteric knowledge he discovered.

34612691R00141

Printed in Poland
by Amazon Fulfillment
Poland Sp. z o.o., Wrocław